Trapped

Suddenly, a voice nearby whispered urgently, "Missie, don't turn round, stay has you are. You an' Pikkle 'ave got ter get away from 'ere sharpish. It's a trap!"

Startled, Mara opened her eyes and leaned around the rock. "Sergeant Sapwood, what are you doing here?"

Goffa sprang up. He came dashing over, spear at the ready. "Wot's goin' on 'ere? Who are you talki—"

Sapwood leaped out in front of him, poised for action. With a yell the ferret thrust the spear forward. Sapwood neatly sidestepped, kicking the spear adrift with his long hind legs. Goffa tried to make a grab for it but he was confronted by the champion boxing hare of Salamandastron. In swift succession two neat left pawhooks thudded to the side of his head, followed by a powerful straight right paw, smack dab on his chin. Goffa crumpled to the ground, senseless.

Pikkle came dashing over, puzzlement and concern on his face. "I say, steady on, Sappers ol' boy . . ."

Sergeant Sapwood seized him by the ear. "Liddle block'eads, there's a whole harmy of vermin jus' over yon 'ill. Yore in a trap. Run for yore lives!"

∞

THE REDWALL BOOKS

Redwall
Mossflower
Mattimeo
Mariel of Redwall
Salamandastron
Martin the Warrior
The Bellmaker
The Outcast of Redwall
The Pearls of Lutra
The Long Patrol
Marlfox
The Legend of Luke
Lord Brocktree
Taggerung
Triss
Loamhedge

The Great Redwall Feast (picture book)
A Redwall Winter's Tale (picture book)

OTHER BOOKS BY BRIAN JACQUES

Seven Strange and Ghostly Tales
Castaways of the Flying Dutchman
The Angel's Command

The Tale of Urso Brunov (picture book)

Salamandastron

BRIAN JACQUES

Illustrations by Gary Chalk

FIREBIRD

AN IMPRINT OF PENGUIN GROUP (USA) INC.

FIREBIRD
Published by Penguin Group
Penguin Group (USA) Inc., 345 Hudson Street, New York, New York 10014, U.S.A.
Penguin Books Ltd, 80 Strand, London WC2R ORL, England
Penguin Books Australia Ltd, 250 Camberwell Road,
Camberwell, Victoria 3124, Australia
Penguin Books Canada Ltd, 10 Alcorn Avenue, Toronto, Ontario, Canada M4V 3B2
Penguin Books (N.Z.) Ltd, 182-190 Wairau Road, Auckland 10, New Zealand

Originally published in Great Britain by Hutchinson Children's Books, London
First published in the United States of America by Philomel Books,
a division of The Putnam & Grosset Group, 1993
Published by Firebird, an imprint of Penguin Group (USA) Inc., 2003

3 5 7 9 10 8 6 4

THE LIBRARY OF CONGRESS HAS CATALOGED THE PHILOMEL EDITION AS FOLLOWS:

Jacques, Brian.
Salamandastron / by Brian Jacques.
p. cm.
Summary: Urthstripe the Strong, a wise old badger, leads the animals
of the great fortress of Salamandastron and Redwall Abbey against
the weasel Ferhago the Assassin and his corps of vermin.
ISBN 0-399-21992-7 (hc)
[1. Animals—Fiction. 2. Fantasy.] I. Title.
PZ7.J15317Sal 1993 [Fic]—dc 20 91-46423 CIP AC

ISBN 0-14-250152-2

Printed in the United States of America

Salamandastron
and
surrounding
country

N
W
S

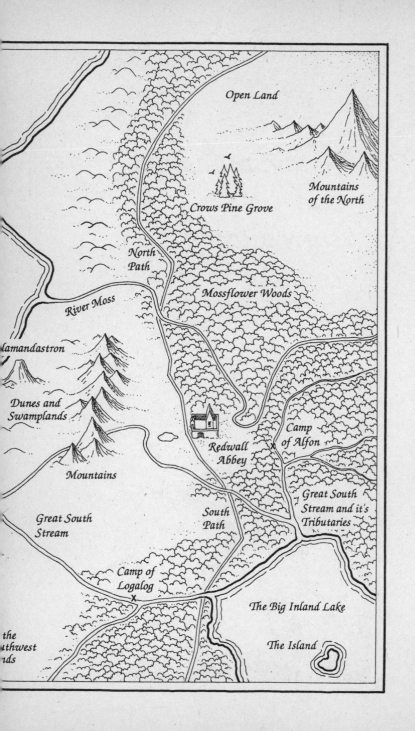

The dormouse was a jolly plump old fellow, clad in a rust-colored jerkin, his white beard curled and trimmed neatly. An infant mole, who could not sleep because of the onset of spring, sat beside him on a mossy beechlog in the orchard. Together they shared an early breakfast of oatcakes, hot from the kitchens, and two of last autumn's russet apples. Dawn was touching the earth with its rosy paws, promising sunny spring days as a compensation for the long winter Redwall Abbey had endured. Soft white clouds with golden underbellies hung on the still air, dewdrops glistened on new green grass, budding narcissus and snowdrop awaited the coming of the sun-warmed day.

The dormouse nodded sagely. "Soon be pickin' a Nameday for this good season, aye, soon."

The small mole chewed slowly at his oatcake, wrinkling a black button snout as he gazed up at the elder.

"You'm said you'm tell oi a story, zurr."

The dormouse polished an apple on his jerkin. "D'you like my stories, Burrem?"

The little fellow smiled. "Burr aye, oi serpintly do, zurr!"

1

His friend settled down comfortably on the grass, propping his back against the log.

"Right then, it's a good long one. We'll have to break off for lunch and tea, supper, too, maybe. Ah well, here goes. Once upon a time . . ."

Colder than the winter wind howling its dirge through the Southwest Forest.

Colder than the snow blanketing tree, rock and earth in its silent shroud.

Colder than ice that lay on water and hung in shards from branches and bushes.

Colder than these was the smile of Ferahgo the Assassin! Ferahgo was still young, but as the seasons passed his evil and infamy would grow, and everybeast would come to fear the name of the blue-eyed weasel.

His band searched the wrecked badgers' den, scavenging and snarling over winter food and the few pitiful possessions strewn among the debris. Smiling pitilessly, Ferahgo stepped over the bodies of the slain badger Urthound and his wife Urthrun, the last two brave creatures to stand against him. Stealth and deceit, reinforced by a crew of backstabbers, were the Assassin's trademark. He had tricked the badgers into thinking this would be a peace conference. Fools!

Migroo the stoat pulled aside a heap of dried moss. "Chief, look!"

Two badger babes lay huddled together, mewling

and shivering as they stuck their heads up, lips pursed in a plea for mother's milk.

Migroo laughed. "That one looks like his father, but this other one, Chief, it's white. I thought all badgers had stripes."

Ferahgo tickled their nose tips with his knifepoint. "They're both males. One is a proper badger, the other is an albino. They might not be orphans today if their parents had not resisted me."

Migroo watched the point of Ferahgo's knife. "What're yeh goin' t' do with 'em?"

The Assassin shrugged and sheathed his blade. "Nothing. The winter will take care of Urthound's whelps."

Fondling the round gold medallion he had taken from the neck of Urthound, Ferahgo gave one last glance around.

"Now nobeast in the Southwest is left to oppose me. Come on, my Corpsemakers!"

The weasel swept out into the wintering forestlands with his band, a smile still fixed in his beautiful light blue eyes.

Behind him in the ruins of the den the two badger babes, one striped, the other pure white, snuggled against the cold body of their mother. They made pitiful little noises, waiting for her to wake and comfort them. Outside the snowflakes blew gustily between tree and bush, chased by the soughing wind.

It was cold.

But not as cold as the smile on the face of Ferahgo the Assassin.

BOOK ONE

Questors and Runaways

1

Many and many a long season had come and gone since that fateful midwinter day in the Southwest Lands.

The only sound disturbing the stillness of a high summer noontide was that of seabirds plaintively calling as they wheeled and circled overhead. The vastness of the sea lay becalmed, without blemish of wave or white-crested roller, still as a millpond, mirroring the faded blue of a cloudless sky. Obscured in its own heat haze, the sun blushed forth a radiant golden wash, tinting sand and rock with a soft amber glow.

Above the tideline stood the great citadel of Salamandastron, the mountainous shell that had once been a volcano when the world was young. Through countless ages it had been ruled by the mysterious badger Lords and their friends the hares of the Long Patrol. The entire rock was a towering fortress, riven through with caves, passages and halls, standing guard to protect the shores and all the sprawling country of West Mossflower.

From Salamandastron's main entrance a solitary set of pawprints led through the sand to a limpet-crusted outcrop by the sea. Perched on the stone, chin in paw, Lord Urthstripe the Strong gazed seaward, clad in his stout forge apron, devoid of armor or sword. At one with earth, sea and sky, the badger Lord sat alone with his thoughts. Mara had not been home for two nights, and he was worried. Had he done the right thing, adopting a young female badger? She was one of the few badger maids ever to live at the mountain; traditionally it was the preserve of single male badgers. Five seasons ago his hares had found her among the dunes, a tiny whimpering babe, lost and alone. Urthstripe was overjoyed when they had brought her to him. He cherished her as the daughter he had never had. But that was when she was an infant. He was a badger Lord, with many things to attend to, and as she grew up, so they had drifted apart.

Life presented various obstacles to Mara. She had come to resent the strict ways and regimented existence at Salamandastron. Urthstripe became awkward and severe in his dealings with her, and Mara in her turn was rebellious of his heavy-pawed authority. Against Urthstripe's wishes she had gone off two days ago, with her close friend Pikkle Ffolger, a young hare.

The badger Lord scowled. Pikkle was far too wild and erratic; Mara would never grow up to be a proper badger Lady running about with the like of that mischief-maker. But that was the way of things between them now—if he lectured her or threatened penalties he felt like an ogre. So they avoided each other, she going her own way, and he unhappily having to go his.

Sergeant Sapwood loped slowly across to the rock. He bobbed about, shadow-boxing until Urthstripe noticed him. Sidestepping, the strong lanky hare tucked in his chin and hooked out a left paw.

"Haint much t' do out 'ere, sir. You a-comin' in for summat to eat? There's wild oatcakes, bilberry tart an' cold cider. You haint touched vittles since yesterday morn."

Urthstripe climbed slowly down from the rock and

growled anxiously at the hare, "Any sign of Mara yet, Sergeant?"

"Nah, not so far. But don't you fret y'self, sir. She'll come trottin' back wi' young Pikkle, soon as they're hungered enough. D'you want me to send the missie t' you when she does arrive back?"

"No, but let me know the moment she's back home. See she gets a good meal, and then . . . then send her to me!"

Sapwood ducked and feinted as they made their way across the shore, swaying lightly on his paws as he circled Urthstripe.

"C'mon, sir. Let's see you try t' put one on me button!"

The badger Lord tried to ignore his pugnacious friend, but Sapwood persisted.

"Go on, sir, try the old one-two, eh?"

Urthstripe halted, blinking as the hare bobbed and dodged under his nose.

"Really, Sapwood, I'm in no mood for sport."

The Sergeant dabbed a swift paw at Urthstripe's jaw. "Oh, 'ave a go, sir. Try yer luck!"

For all his great bulk the badger was surprisingly swift. He spun sideways, clipping Sapwood under the chin with what he judged to be a light tap. The Sergeant was bowled over, knocked flat on his back. Instantly the badger Lord was at his friend's side, his huge striped face showing concern.

"Sap, are you all right? I didn't hurt you, did I?"

Sapwood sat up. Uncrossing his eyes and rubbing his chin, he chuckled ruefully. "Bless your 'eart, sir, I'm as right as rain, never saw that'n comin', though. Good job you never punched your weight, or you'd 'ave knocked me block clean off!"

With their paws about each other the two friends entered Salamandastron, chatting and chuckling about old fights and bygone battles.

Before he entered the mountain, Urthstripe could not resist casting a final longing glance to the open country. Disappointed that he could not see Mara arriving home he heaved a lonely sigh and followed Sapwood inside.

A massive ridge of mountains created a high spine down the land east of Salamandastron. In the foothills to the south they gave way to swamplands, which in their turn led to the dunes sweeping in from the west. The early noon sun was causing grasshoppers to chirrup and rustle in the rock-strewn foothills.

Ferahgo the Assassin sighted his skinning knife at one insect which was about to leap. He flicked the knife expertly. His aim was good: the keen-edged blade sliced the grasshopper in two. The knifepoint was still quivering in the ground as Ferahgo pulled it free and wiped it clean on the grass.

"That's one grasshopper won't jump any more," he chuckled. "Am I not right, Migroo?"

The stoat nodded vigorously. "Aye, Chief, 'twas a grand throw!"

Ferahgo sheathed the weapon in the crossbelts he wore diagonally across his chest. Two other knives were encased there, each as sharp and deadly as the one he had thrown. Smiling, he rested his paws on the broad belt supporting his short kilt of skins. He had grown taller and more sinewy than other weasels. The seasons seemed to lend an extra sparkle to his eyes, which were light brilliant blue like a fresh spring sky; beautiful almond-shaped eyes, with deep laughter creases etching their corners. Many a stranger had met death through the deceit and vicious cruelty which lay behind those innocently smiling eyes. Every weasel, stoat, rat, ferret or fox in his army of Corpsemakers knew that the more Ferahgo the Assassin smiled, the more evil and brutal he became. His reign of terror had spread and flourished in the Southwest Lands until the whole country trembled with fear at his name. Ferahgo!

This summer he had decided to push further north. None of his army dared question the odd decision, though they speculated in secret as to his reason for such a long trek. The horde lounged in the dunes and the foothills—some stretched on the sun-scorched sand and grass, others seeking the shade of rocks—apparently idle, but ever vigilant for their leader's commands. Disobedience to Ferahgo meant death.

The Assassin stretched luxuriously upon the dry curling grass and closed his eyes, enjoying the still warmth of summer. One eye suddenly snapped open as he called to a weasel stationed in the rocks higher up.

"Feadle, keep your eyes peeled for my son and Goffa. Don't go to sleep up there."

Feadle made a show of scouring the terrain north and west before shouting back down, "I'll let you know as soon as Klitch and Goffa show up, Master. Don't you worry!"

Ferahgo's reply gave the lookout good reason to stay awake. "Oh, I'm not worried, Feadle—but you should be, because if you miss them I'll skin you alive with my knives. Keep those eyes open now, there's a good weasel."

It was a plain-spoken, matter-of-fact statement, but everybeast within hearing knew that the Assassin was not joking. Ferahgo seldom joked, even though he did smile a lot.

Dethbrush the fox and his six tracker rats loped in from the south. He heard Feadle announce their sighting from his high perch: "Dethbrush an' the trackers coming in, Master!"

The fox stood by as Ferahgo, still lying down with his eyes closed, questioned him.

"You have not brought Dingeye and Thura back with you?"

Dethbrush was weary, but he did not dare sit or relax. "No, Master. We tracked them for two moons. They have gone east, into the flatlands on the other side of these mountains."

Ferahgo's paw strayed to the handle of his favorite knife. "It does not please me when my orders are not carried out."

Dethbrush tried hard to stop his limbs trembling; he swallowed hard, licking at dry lips.

"Master, we searched night and day without rest. They must have found a way to cross the south stream—that is where I lost their tracks. I thought it would be better to report back to you, rather than get lost in strange country."

Ferahgo opened his eyes. He was not smiling. "You did right, Dethbrush. Rest and eat until tomorrow. Then you will go tracking again with your rats. But remember, I want Dingeye and Thura, or their heads, brought back here to me. It is bad for the morale of my Corpsemakers if they realize that deserters can escape my punishment and roam free. Do you understand?"

Dethbrush gave a sigh of relief and nodded. "I understand, Ferahgo. This time I won't fail you."

Ferahgo closed his eyes. "Make sure you don't, my friend." He smiled slightly and waved a paw in dismissal.

Dethbrush went to look for water, his mouth dry with fear.

2

Redwall Abbey slumbered peacefully under the noon-tide sun. A songthrush trilled sweetly from the surrounding greenery of Mossflower Woods, its melodious tune echoing from the dusty red sandstone walls of the main building to the outer ramparts. Somewhere in the Abbey pool a trout half leaped at a passing gnat, missed it and flopped back lazily into the water. Two moles lugging a trolley laden with vegetables for the kitchen turned at the sound, commenting in their quaint mole-speech.

"Ee be a gurt noisy trowt that un, eh, Burrley."

Burrley, the smaller of the two, wrinkled his button nose. "Hurr, you'm doant say. Oi'd be gurt 'n' lazy iffen oi dwelled inna pond wi' nothen t' do. Ho urr!"

They trundled into the Abbey, speculating on the easy life-style of trouts who lived in ponds.

Mrs. Faith Spinney was picking fruit in the orchard. The good hedgehog lady muttered quietly to herself as she checked the contents of her basket.

"Early plums, gooseberries, small pears . . . dearie me, they are liddle uns too. No mind, they'll make tasty cordial. Damsons aren't near ready yet—pity, I do like a good damson pudden. Now let me see, what have I forgotten?"

The sight of a tree jogged her memory.

"Apples, of course! Those big green uns be just right for bakin' pies."

Standing on tip-paw, she reached for a large green apple hanging from a low bough.

Zzzzip! Splott!

An arrow sped by, a hairsbreadth from Mrs. Spinney's paw. It pierced the juicy apple, sending it spinning from the bough onto the grass. The hedgehog dropped her basket and dashed off, ducking low and shielding her head with both paws as she whooped out in terror. "Ooowhoo, help, murder! We're bein' attacked by scallawagians!"

Help appeared swiftly in the form of a brawny male otter.

"Sink me! What's all the to-do about, marm?"

Faith Spinney was hiding behind a gooseberry bush with her apron over her head. She peeped out at the otter. "Hoohoo! Do 'urry an' sound the alarm bell, Mr. Thrugg. Just lookit that apple lyin' in yonder grass!"

Striding boldly over, Thrugg retrieved the apple. Pulling the arrow from it he looked about, nodding grimly. "There there now, marm. Don't get yore prickles in an uproar. Everything's shipshape. I didn't clap eyes on the villain who shot that arrer, but I'll stake me rudder I know who it is that did!"

Thrugg filled the basket with the fruit that had spilled out, adding the apple. Placing a paw gingerly about Mrs. Spinney's bristling shoulders, he led her off toward the Abbey, carrying the basket for her.

Afternoon summer tea at Redwall was always very good. The mice who formed the Brother and Sisterhood sat among other creatures in Great Hall. There was never any distinction to class or species; all were

14

Redwallers and friends, and they mingled freely, sharing the delicious repast. Hot scones, hazelnut bread, apple jelly, meadowcream, redcurrant tart, mint tea and strawberry cordial were consumed in great quantities.

Abbess Vale, successor to old Abbot Saxtus, sat dwarfed in the big badger chair at the head of the long table. Redwall Abbey had not seen a female badger guardian in many a long season, old Mother Mellus having gone to her well-earned rest quite some time ago. Beside the Abbess sat Bremmun, a venerable squirrel. He leaned across to speak to her, raising his voice over the hubbub and jollity of Redwallers at tea.

"You heard what Thrugg had to say about Samkim?"

Vale put aside her beaker. "Yes, I heard all about it."

Bremmun chose a slice of the latticed redcurrant tart and ladled it thickly with meadowcream. "Shall I leave it for you to deal with as Mother Abbess, or do you wish me to do it?"

The Abbess turned the beaker slowly in her paws. "You are both squirrels. I think it would be better if it were to come from you, my friend. Samkim can be very naughty at times, but I've always liked the little fellow. I really don't have the heart to scold him. I'll leave it to you if I may, Bremmun."

Those on serving duty were beginning to clear away the dishes, and one or two diners were rising to leave. Bremmun rapped the tabletop sharply with a wooden ladle.

"One moment, friends. Your attention, please!"

The hubbub of conversation stopped immediately. Those about to leave respectfully kept their seats. Reaching beneath the linen table runner, Bremmun produced the arrow Thrugg had given him. He held it up for all to see.

"This shaft was loosed in the orchard this afternoon. Would the creature who fired it please stand forward!"

Amid a scraping of wooden benches everybeast

15

turned to watch two small figures emerge from the table nearest the door. Many a knowing nod was passed. Samkim and Arula again!

The young squirrel Samkim was a strongly built fellow, wearing a beret sporting a wren feather at a jaunty angle. Straightening his soft greencloth tunic, he strode up to the long table, unable to extinguish the roguish twinkle in his hazel eyes. Arula the young mole padded alongside him. She, too, was clad in beret and tunic, though her small round eyes were downcast. Samkim's head was barely visible over the tabletop as he denounced himself to Bremmun.

"The arrow is mine. I shot it! Arula had no part in it."

The mole shook her velvety head. "Ho no, zurr, 'twas oi who axed Sankin to shoot 'ee arpel, hurr aye. 'Tis moi fault, zurr Brumm'n."

The squirrel's voice was loud and stern. "Silence, missie! Samkim, this is not the first time. A short while ago an arrow was found lodged in the kitchen door, then one of the gatehouse windows was broken by an arrow. Later it was Brother Hal who was the victim of another arrow. He has a permanent furrow through his headfur—a fraction lower and he would not be with us today. Now it is poor Mrs. Spinney's turn. The good lady was half frightened to death by your archery. What have you got to say for yourself, young squirrel?"

Samkim shrugged apologetically. "Sorry, I never meant to hurt anyone."

Bremmun hurried around the table to face the culprit. "You never meant to hurt anyone? A bow and arrow is a weapon, not a toy! But you do not seem to realize that. Oh no, off you go, willy nilly, firing arrows carelessly without a thought for anybeast . . ."

Arula interrupted, pointing to herself. "Et wurr moi fault, zurr. 'Twas oi oo tol' Sankin t' do et!"

"Quite so, quite so, Arula." Bremmun waved her aside distractedly. "Now, as for you, Samkim, you young wretch, you make me ashamed to call myself a squirrel! Mother Abbess was far too upset by your disgraceful behavior to speak to you; therefore it is my painful duty to do this. Both of you, Samkim and Arula, are confined to the Infirmary until further notice! I am sure Brother Hollyberry can find lots of tasks—scrubbing, bedmaking and washing floors—for both of you. Your meals will be delivered to you up there, you will sleep in the Infirmary and under no circumstances must either of you leave, until the Mother Abbess and I have decided that you are fit to join ordinary decent Redwallers again. Furthermore, Samkim, if I ever hear that you have been within paw's length of a bow or arrows again, you will be in very deep and serious trouble. Do I make myself clear?"

Two young heads nodded miserably.

"Yes, sir."

"Hurr, clearer'n broit summer morn, thankee, zurr."

Silence fell over Great Hall as the two miscreants were led off to their fate by Brother Hal. Punishments and penalties were an absolute rarity in the friendly Abbey.

Bremmun returned to his seat. Leaning across, he whispered to Abbess Vale. "Thank goodness that's over with. Do you think I was too hard on them, Vale?"

She folded her paws in her lap. "Yes, Bremmun, I do. Oh, I know that Samkim and Arula are always in trouble, but they are young. Restricting their freedom to the Infirmary is very severe, I think."

Bremmun looked uncomfortable and shrugged apologetically. "Not to worry, I won't keep them confined there for long. They'll soon learn their lesson. Did you notice little Arula? I had to try hard to stop myself smiling—there she was, standing up bold as a stone, taking all the blame herself."

The Abbess pursed her lips to hide her own smile. "Bless her, she was very brave. Those two are true friends, even if they are a pair of scamps. Young ones like them are the very backbone of our Abbey; they do not lack courage or honesty. We need creatures like that. They will take the reins and show an example to all in the seasons to come."

Samkim and Arula sat on a bed facing Brother Holly-berry. The ancient healer and Keeper of the Infirmary leaned back in his armchair, chuckling dryly.

"Thank your lucky stars there wasn't a badger sitting in the chair today. By the fur! You two would have really found out what punishment was like. Those badgers were very, very strict!"

"Boi ecky, lucky fer us'ns, Bruther. Oi 'spect 'ee bad-ger'd choppen our tails off an' fling uz in 'ee pond!"

Hollyberry adopted a mock serious expression. "Aye, that's just the sort of thing badgers would have done in the old days. Righto, you two, no more trying to flannel me. There's the walls, doors, cupboards and shelves to be washed, windows to be cleaned, sheets to be coun-ted and folded, lots of torn nightshirts to be sewn, pillowslips to be scrubbed . . ."

He watched their faces going from glumness to despair at the mention of each new chore. Chuckling aloud, Hollyberry rose and patted their heads. "But we'll start all that tomorrow. You can have the rest of the day off. Sorry you're not allowed out, young uns. Maybe if you look in the big cupboard you'll find a game of pebbles and acorns. Oh, and some candied chestnuts in my little locker here. That should keep you amused until bedtime or thereabouts."

Samkim rubbed his paws delightedly. "Thanks, Brother Hollyberry, you're a real matey. Er, were you ever naughty when you were young?"

The old mouse looked secretively to and fro as he whispered, "Naughty? Let me tell you, young un, I was known as Hollyberry the Horrible when I was a little mouse. Old Abbot Saxtus said that I was the reason he was gray and bent double. Listen now, I've got to go and tend my herbs in the garden. Do you think you can behave yourself while I'm gone?"

Arula draped a clean sheet over her head. "Gudd zurr, lookit oi, hurr hurr, a snow-whoit choild oi be."

3

Pikkle Ffolger searched the corners of his knapsack and came up with a single wild oatscone, which he wagged in Mara's face.

"The last bally scrap of tuck between two stout 'n' starvin' travelers, would y' believe it, old chum!"

The sturdy young badger maid plucked the scone from his paws. "There were four oatscones in that bag before I went to sleep last night. You flop-eared glutton, you've scoffed 'em!"

Pikkle placed a paw over his heart, his face a picture of injured innocence. "Scoffed? Did I hear you use the expression scoffed, O boon companion and playmate of my younger days? Nibbled daintily, picked idly at, maybe even mouthed a morsel or so. But scoffed, never!"

Mara broke the scone in two and tossed half to him. "Listen here, Ffolger me old Pikkle, don't try baffling me with flowery phrases. You're a scoffer and you always have been, so there!"

Grinning from ear to ear, Pikkle scoffed his half. "Oh well, truth will out, old gel, wot? I say, it's goin' to take us until late night to get back to jolly old Salamawotsit. I bet we're both in for some pretty stiff words when old Urthstripe catches up with us."

Mara slumped moodily in the hollow of two dunes, her appetite suddenly gone at the thought of returning to face the badger Lord.

"Huh, Salamandastron—I wish I never had to go back to that dreary mountain, Pikkle. Day and night, dawn to dusk, it's watch your manners, learn your badger lore, keep your room tidy, sit up straight, don't slouch, do this, do that, don't do this, don't do that. I'm sick to the stripes of it all! Isn't there somewhere young ones can do what they want, have fun all day, without elders and grownbeasts making you do silly boring things . . . ?"

"Then come with us—we do as we please!"

Mara and Pikkle looked around in surprise. A pair of young creatures, a weasel and a ferret, appeared around the dune.

The garrulous Pikkle winked and grinned cheekily at them. "What ho, chaps. Who are you?"

The weasel smiled back. He was a handsome-looking beast, with the brightest blue eyes Mara had ever seen. "Hello there! I'm Klitch and he's Goffa. We've come up from the Southwest Lands."

Mara sized the pair up. The ferret was a shifty-looking creature, dressed in a long tunic that had obviously been cut down to fit him. He carried a spear and wore a dagger in the piece of rope that served him as a belt. The young weasel was a different matter altogether. His clothing fitted perfectly. He wore a smart yellow tunic, and on his woven belt hung a short sword, complete with case. He also sported a pair of thick white bone bracelets. All in all he appeared quite dashing. Mara felt self-conscious; both she and Pikkle were clad in the homely sand-colored smocks worn by those who lived at Salamandastron.

"My name is Mara, and this is my friend Pikkle Ffolger. We come from the mountain fortress of Salamandastron, almost a day's march north of here."

Klitch smiled oddly. "But you don't want to go back, right?"

Mara stood up, dusting sand from herself. "Oh, we moan and groan a bit, but we always return there. It's our home, you see. Tell me, did you and Goffa come all the way up from the Southwest by yourselves?"

A quick smile passed between Klitch and Goffa, then the weasel shrugged carelessly.

"Oh, more or less. We do exactly what we want and go just where we please. Isn't that right, Goffa?"

The ferret leaned on his spear and nodded. "Right!"

"But you two are only young ones, like us," Pikkle interrupted. "I say, who allows you to carry weapons like that?"

Klitch's blue eyes twinkled merrily. "Nobeast allows us to do anything—we feel like having weapons, so we carry 'em and don't give a hoot for anyone!"

The more Mara heard from Klitch the more she admired him.

He drew his sword and swung it, neatly clipping the heads from two dandelions growing amid the reedgrass. "So you're from Salamandastron, hellsteeth! That's a right old mouthful of a name. Tell you what, me and Goffa here will walk along with you. I'd like to see this place. You can tell me all about it as we go."

Without further preamble the four young ones set out for the mountain, chatting and laughing. Klitch was an amusing talker with lots of interesting tales to tell. He was also a good listener and paid rapt attention to anything Mara or Pikkle had to say about their home—so much so, that eventually they were doing all the talking and he was doing all the listening. Goffa rarely spoke.

The journey did not seem half so arduous with friends to share it. Still, it was night when they came within hailing distance of the great mountain.

Windpaw, a fully grown female hare, met them as

22

they crossed the shore. She nodded at the two new-comers and shook a cautionary paw at Mara and Pikkle.

"We were about to send search parties out looking for you. Mara, you are untidy. Where in the name of seashells have you been?"

Pikkle waved a paw airily. "Oh, here an' there, y'know. Thither an' yon, as they say . . ."

Windpaw silenced him with a frosty glare. "You can tell that to Lord Urthstripe, young Ffolger. First you'd both better come with me. Have you eaten today?"

Mara indicated the ferret and the weasel. "Meet our friends Klitch and Goffa. They'll need food too."

Windpaw shook her head doubtfully at the thought of a ferret and a weasel entering the fortress. She looked them up and down, then snorted. "Hmm, they look young and hungry enough, I suppose. Follow me."

Klitch bowed gracefully, putting on a smile that would have charmed a bird from its nest. "Thank you kindly, beautiful lady."

Windpaw sniffed. She led them through a concealed entrance. "The dining room is down that passage. There's a bowl of water and towel as you go in. Make sure you wash your paws before sitting down to eat."

Klitch winked at his companion. "We wouldn't dream of eating with dirty paws, would we, friend Goffa?"

The ferret winced as Klitch kicked his paw. "Ouch! What, er, oh no, of course not!"

There was good hot mushroom soup, vegetable pasties, a flagon of mountain pear cordial, salad, and a beechnut cake preserved in honey. They ate with full and hearty appetite, Pikkle Ffolger putting away twice as much as the others.

Lord Urthstripe and Sergeant Sapwood entered the dining room just as the meal finished. The badger's jaw tightened at the sight of his two visitors. Sapwood crossed his paws behind him and held his breath. Both Pikkle and Mara fiddled about needlessly with their empty bowls, keeping their eyes fixed firmly on the tabletop to avoid the badger Lord's fearsome gaze.

Showing flawless good manners, Klitch rose, nudging Goffa to do likewise. The weasel's blue eyes shone with sincerity as he spoke.

"Lord Urthstripe, I believe. I hope I find you well, sir. I am Klitch and this is my friend Goffa, and we both wish to thank you for your good food and kind hospitality."

For a long time there was silence. Urthstripe was staring at the weasel strangely, as if trying to remember something. Pikkle dropped his spoon, and the clatter of wood on stone seemed to restore the badger Lord to the present. He bowed his head in curt acknowledgment of the weasel's compliment, though the distaste in his voice was plain.

"This is my mountain, Master Klitch. While you are here I must treat you both as guests. If you have finished eating, my Sergeant will show you to a room where you will spend the night. After breakfast tomorrow you must both leave Salamandastron. You will be given food for your travels. Now I bid you both a good night. Sergeant!"

Sapwood came smartly to attention. Grim-faced, he led Klitch and Goffa off to their bedchamber.

When they were gone the badger Lord folded his paws across his broad chest and faced Mara. "Young maid, have you nothing to say for yourself? Missing, without a word to anybeast for two whole nights. Now you return, bringing a ferret and a weasel here!"

Mara shook her head in bewilderment. "How could you be so rude to those two young creatures? They are my friends . . ."

Urthstripe's paw crashed loud against the tabletop.

"Friends? A ferret and a weasel, they are not friends, they are vermin! Have you no sense, Mara? Ferrets, weasels, stoats, rats and foxes have caused murder and warfare in Mossflower since before the days of my ancestors. Who are they with? Where is the rest of their band?"

Screwing up his courage, Pikkle chipped in. "I say, sir, steady on! Those two chaps were all alone when we met 'em. They traveled up from the Southwest. Actually, they're rather jolly—"

Urthstripe's roar cut him short. "Silence, Ffolger! When I want your opinion I shall ask for it. Go to your room, this instant! It's time you learned to grow up and show some hare responsibility."

Pikkle vacated the dining room in haste, knowing it was useless to argue with a badger Lord of Urthstripe's temper. Huge tears welled from Mara's eyes to drip on to the table.

The badger Lord gave a deep sigh of helplessness and shook his great striped head. "Mara, little one, please don't cry. I'm sorry I lost my temper, but I thought you knew about our enemies."

The badger maid rubbed paws into her eyes, sniffing. "They're not all enemies, but you don't seem to care. You don't even want me having Pikkle as a friend. Sometimes I wish I was dead instead of being stuck inside this miserable old mountain!"

Urthstripe pulled a spotted kerchief from his forge apron and gently wiped her eyes, sadness and concern showing on his heavy features.

"Please don't say that, Mara. You are all I have, and someday when I am gone the duty may fall upon you to rule this mountain. I know it is a lonely and demanding life, but it is our solemn duty as badgers to protect Mossflower and its shores. Only then can good honest creatures, not as strong as we, live in peace and happiness. You must believe me, Browneye."

25

The sound of the pet name he had called her as an infant brought a flood of fresh tears. Mara dashed from the room, calling as she ran to her bedchamber. "I don't know what to believe anymore. I just want to be somewhere where I can be happy!"

Urthstripe sat at the dining table. Shutting his eyes tight, he gripped the table edge until his blunt claws scored deep gouges into the oak. When he looked up again, Sergeant Sapwood was standing there. Quickly composing himself, Urthstripe asked in a gruff voice, "Are those vermin securely locked in their room for the night?"

The hare sat down beside him. "Aye, sir. I turned the key meself."

The badger Lord's eyes narrowed in a hard line. "Good! I'd hate to think that a ferret and a weasel were skulking about our mountain during the night."

Sapwood tapped a paw alongside his nose. "Haint much fear o' that, sir. I posted two sentries near their door—Catkin an' Big Oxeye. If'n they ever did manage to sneak out o' that room, those two would really find theirselves wi' problems. Big Oxeye don't like vermin, no sir!"

Urthstripe could not resist a small chuckle. "Almost makes you wish they'd try something, doesn't it? It's been a few seasons since I saw Oxeye chastise an enemy."

The Sergeant nodded wholehearted agreement. "Hoho, 'e can chastise all right. I never did see anybeast return for a second 'elpin' off Big Oxeye!"

Soft summer night cast its shades over the mountain stronghold. The two friends sat up into the small hours, discussing and reliving old days of past seasons. Outside, the full moon beamed down upon the deserted shore, tipping countless small wavetips with a thread of pale silver light.

Perched high in the rocks of the lookout post, Feadle strove to keep awake. He spat on his paws, rubbing them hard into red-rimmed eyes. Blinking intently he peered among the moon-shadowed dunes, fearful lest he miss Klitch's return.

Ferahgo sat apart from the rest of his band, pawing thoughtfully at the gold badger medal about his neck and stirring the flames of a guttering fire. Keeping his voice low, the Assassin spoke to a small stringy water rat seated close by him.

"Tell me again, Sickear, how did you find out about the mountain?"

"I was a searat, and I saw the place a few times, Master, though only from a distance. They call it Salamandastron."

Ferahgo stroked the badger medal, repeating the name slowly as if it were a magic charm. "Salamandastron. I like the sound of it. Salamandastron. But tell me the rest, you know, the part I like to hear."

Sickear repeated the tale, as he had done many times in secret to Ferahgo since joining his band last winter.

"The searat Captains said there was great treasure hidden inside the mountain—their old legends are full of it. The fortress is guarded by tough fighting hares and ruled by a badger Lord—always has been, since anybeast could remember. The present ruler is called Urthstripe the Strong, a great and fearsome warrior."

Ferahgo moved closer to the speaker, his eyes shining blue in the firelight, aglitter with greed. "The treasure— tell me about the treasure!"

Sickear swallowed hard as the Assassin's claws closed on his shoulder. He repeated what Ferahgo wanted to hear.

"It is said the great badgers never lacked riches. As each one lived out his seasons, or died in battle, so his possessions were added to the pile, hidden somewhere inside the mountain. Pearls from the sea, many-colored

27

precious stones, armor wrought from silver, gold and copper, spears and other great weapons, all made by the badgers at their forge. Bright war axes that can cut through stone, shields that are wonderful to look upon, swords with blades that can slice armor like butter, red and green stones set into their handles, sheathed in cases of the finest . . . aaaarrghh!''

Ferahgo's claws had pierced the rat's shoulder. Sickear whimpered in pain, tears rolling down his narrow face. The weasel Chieftain freed his claws from the matted fur and flesh with a quick wrench. Slumping to one side, Sickear moaned piteously, trying to lick his injured shoulder. Ferahgo grinned, his strange blue eyes twinkling in the firelight like a happy infant.

"Oh, I'm sorry, friend. I must have got carried away. Never mind, it's only a scratch. The best thing for you is fresh air and something to take your mind off it. Listen now, you shin up those lookout rocks and keep Feadle company the rest of the night. It'll do you good. Stop weeping and groaning now. Come on, up you go!''

The Assassin's eyes smiled wide and innocent as he watched the injured Sickear hauling himself painfully up among the rocks. With a note of deceptive concern he called softly up to the weary lookout, "Not sleepy yet, Feadle?''

The lookout stared down into the treacherous blue eyes smiling up at him. Straightening his back against the rock, he sang out in an alert manner. "No sign of your son or Goffa yet, Master. I'm wide awake!''

Feadle's heart sank at the cheerful reply.

"Good work! Stop up there and keep Sickear company. Keep your eyes open now, both of you. There's a fresh edge on my skinning knife that I haven't used yet.''

Feadle stretched down. Grasping Sickear's paw, he helped him up to the lookout post. Below them Ferahgo lay flat on his back, watching through half-closed eyes.

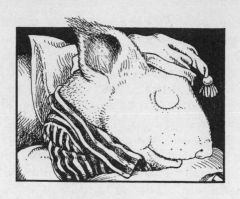

4

Rosy dawn light caressed the Abbey walls as Bremmun the squirrel climbed the stairs to the Infirmary. Knocking softly on the door, he entered. Brother Hollyberry never slept in a bed; he sat propped up by cushions in his armchair, watching the birth of another summer day rise over the windowsill. Arula and Samkim lay asleep in their beds. Bremmun nodded toward them, keeping his voice low.

"Good morning, Brother. How are they today?"

Hollyberry yawned and stretched in his chair. "Morning, Bremmun. See for yourself. I worked the tails off them both until late last night, washing nightgowns, stitching pillowcases. They're two very sorry young uns—cried themselves to sleep after all those chores."

Bremmun's face softened, and he stared guiltily at the two young sleepers, Arula sucking her paw, Samkim with his bushy tail curled under the pillow.

"By the fur 'n' whiskers, Brother, you must have driven them hard. They look completely tuckered out."

Hollyberry raised his eyebrows. "I was only carrying out your instructions. You set the penalty."

"Do you think they've had enough?"

Hollyberry snorted. "Hmph! What do you think!"

"Yes of course, they have been punished sufficiently. When they wake you can tell them they are free to leave. D'you know, I feel quite awful about the whole thing. I just hope those young uns have learned their lesson."

Hollyberry breathed on his spectacles, polished and rebalanced them on his nosetip, and stared earnestly at Bremmun. "Oh, I'm sure they have. Hmm, quite sure!"

A rather shamefaced Bremmun tip-pawed out, closing the door carefully behind him.

Samkim opened one eye and stifled a snigger. Brother Hollyberry wagged a paw at him.

"You squirrelly little wag, you were listening!"

"Hurrhurrhurr! Oi wurr a-listenin' too, zurr Berr'olly."

The old mouse shook his head ruefully. "It's not good for young ones to hear their elders tell lies."

Samkim sprang grinning from the bed. "But you weren't telling lies, Brother. You just forgot what sort of jobs you gave us. Eating candied chestnuts is very hard work—my jaws are still aching!"

Arula tumbled to the floor, clinging to her pillow. "Aye, zurr, an' playen yon game. Boohurr, those pebbles 'n' acorns be fearful 'eavy. 'Spec' moi young mussles be infected fer loif, hurr!"

A smile hovered about Hollyberry's face. It was soon replaced by a grin as his chuckles turned into rib-quaking laughter. Arula and Samkim rolled about the floor in merriment.

"Ahahahahoohoo! Old Bremmun had a face on him like ahahaha! Like a frog suckin' a rock. Heeheehee!"

An infant dormouse pursued Abbess Vale across the front lawn from the Abbey to the gatehouse. "Muvva Vale, Muvva Vale, when's a Nameday?"

The old mouse turned her eyes skyward in despair.

"Dumble, will you please stop pestering me! I haven't had breakfast yet and I can't think right if I'm hungry. Now be off with you this instant!"

The little dormouse carried on tugging Vale's habit and pleading. "Owww! Stoppa momint, Muvva Vale, an' say when's a Nameday, or Dumble turn all purkle an' cry!"

The Abbess halted and wagged a severe paw. "You'll turn purple and cry, eh? Are you threatening me?"

The infant smiled and nodded. "Mmm yeh, Dumble go all purkle an' cryancryancry lots!"

Mr. Tudd Spinney limped out of the gatehouse, shaking his walking stick aloft. "Whoa now, who's a-doin' all the cryin' 'ereabouts? Spike me if it ain't young Dumble. What'sa matter with ye, liddle laddo?"

The Abbess struggled to unfasten Dumble from her habit. "Would you believe it, Mr. Spinney, this rogue says that if I don't choose a Nameday he's going to cry and cry."

The hedgehog threw his ash stick in the air and caught it. "Dumble, you liddle pudden, what a good idea. Come on, marm, pick a Nameday or I'll join 'im. You ain't heard me cry—I'm a champion wailer, an' I c'n turn purple too!"

"Shame on you, Mr. Spinney. I can't even think up a proper name for the season yet."

Dumble fastened himself to the habit skirt again. "Owwww, 'urry up an fink of one, Muvva Vale!"

She set about detaching him once more. "The Summer of the Annoying Baby Dormouse—that's about all I can think of at the moment!"

Mrs. Faith Spinney came bustling out of the gatehouse. "Summer of the Villainous Archer, more like it. Ooh, that dreadful young Samkim!"

Thrugg and his sister Thrugann trudged up to join them. Between them the two otters bore a fine netful of fresh water shrimp. Thrugg held them up proudly.

31

"Caught at dawn in our own Abbey pond, marm. They'll make a tasty soup with plenty o' pepper an' bulrush tips. Stow me gaff, I've never seen so many shrimp in that pond as there be this season. I reckon that ol' trout ain't eatin' 'em—he's got too fat 'n' lazy. Lookit, there he goes now!"

The ancient trout flopped noisily on the surface. As they walked in the direction of the pond, Tudd wagged his cane. "That there fish be older'n me. I recall he was near full growed when I was only a liddle 'og, y'know. Great walloper!"

They stood at the pond's edge. From just beneath the surface the trout watched them, its mouth opening and closing slowly. Thrugg shook the dripping net at it.

"Look 'ere, matey, we pinched all yore shrimps!"

The big fish performed a moody half-leap, splashing them with water as it fell back into the pond.

Dumble stuck out his tongue and pawed his nose at it. "Lazy ol' trout!"

Mrs. Spinney produced a dried plum from her apron pocket, and triumphantly she stuffed it in the infant's mouth. "That's it, the Summer of the Lazy Trout!"

The Abbess pulled a wry face. "Oh dear, I'm not sure I like that. Seasons are usually named after trees or flowers. Summer of the Lazy Trout, hmm, a bit irregular, but in the absence of a better name I suppose it'll have to do. When do you want it held?"

A concerted shout went up. "Tomorrow!"

Abbess Vale looked to her friend. "Very short notice for a Nameday. Could you cope, Faith?"

Mrs. Spinney straightened her apron and mobcap in a businesslike manner. "Ready an' willin' to try, Vale!"

At this they all gave a rousing cheer. Tudd Spinney tripped on his stick and fell, and little Dumble got overexcited and leaped over Tudd, straight into the pond. Thrugan waded swiftly in and hauled the dripping infant out.

After breakfast the word was all over the Abbey. Over at the south wallsteps young creatures whooped and jumped with delight, Samkim and Arula among them.

"It's tomorrow! Hooray! The Nameday's tomorrow!"

"There's going to be a party! We're going to have a party!"

Clad in a clean dry smock, Dumble led them, marching up the steps and along the ramparts, chanting the traditional rhyme which young ones recited in anticipation of the feast.

"Food to eat and games to play.
Tell me why, tell me why.
Serve it out and eat it up.
Have a try, have a try.
Nameday, Nameday, fun and game day,
Come, Brother, Sister, join our play.
This season has a name!"

The great Joseph Bell pealed out happily over the sunny morn, and birds twittered in excitement over the joyous din. Old Abbeydwellers who were not busy in the kitchens gathered on the lawn to watch the young ones and remember long-ago Namedays they had enjoyed taking part in.

Other creatures outside Redwall heard the sounds of celebration that morning—Dingeye and Thura, the two stoats who had deserted Ferahgo's army some weeks earlier. They lay in the ditch on the opposite side of the path which skirted the west wall. Days and nights of roaming the west flatlands, scavenging, begging and thieving to eke out their mean existence showed on their gaunt faces. Dingeye was sleeping in the warmth of the morning sun, dreaming of roast meat and red wine, when Thura shook him.

"Lissen, can yer 'ear that mucker?"

Dingeye sat up. He rubbed his face with a ragged sleeve and waggled a paw in his ear to clear it, cocking his head on one side. Gradually his ugly face split into a crooked grin, and he waved his paw in time with the chanting.

"Yersss, yersss indeedy! Sounds like a good ol'-fashioned whoopdedoo. Wot d'you make of it, mucker?"

Thura was chewing a blade of grass. His stomach growled loudly, and he pulled a face and spat out the grass. "Erm erm, I'd say it soun's the same ter me as it do ter you. Somebeast ringin' billyo out of a bell, a load of young uns settin' up a racket. All soun's very nice, though. 'Ere, wot d'you reckon that place is, mucker?"

"It's an abbey."

"A nabby? Wot's a nabby?"

Dingeye shoved Thura sideways, and he rolled down into the slime. "An abbey, weedbrain, *abbey*. That must be the one called Redfall, or summat. I 'eard of it one time off of a fox."

Thura stood up, wringing damp and ooze from his dirty shirt. "Huh, you don't know any foxes, slobber-chops. An' if yer did they prob'ly wouldn't wanna know you. Redfall Nabby, chah!"

Dingeye leapt on him and clamped a paw over his mouth. "Shurrup, somebeast's a-comin' this ways."

Several moles came trundling along the path in the wake of their leader, a Foremole. The stoats watched from the ditch as the Foremole hailed the walltop.

"Yurr, gudd morn to 'ee, Sankin, an' 'ee, young 'Rula. Be guddbeasts naow an' oppen 'ee gate fer uz."

The young ones skipped down the west wall steps to open the big main gate of Redwall. As the moles filed in, Dingeye nudged Thura.

"Come on, mucker. 'Ere we go. Imagine yer a mole, and we'll latch on to the line an' march in with 'em!"

Scurrying across the path, they joined the file behind

34

the back mole, crouching double and making moleish sounds. "Hoo arr, mucker, ho urrmucker, hur hurr!"

Walking with heads down, they marched slapbang into Thrugg. The brawny otter grabbed both stoats by their scruffs. "Back oars, mateys. Where d'you think yer off to?"

Dingeye fell on all fours. Grasping Thrugg's left leg, he began wailing outrageously. "Ho, woe is us, sir. Kindness'll foller yer all yer days if'n yer shows pity on a pair of gentlebeasts fallen on 'ard times!"

Thura joined his companion, clasping Thrugg's other leg. "Wahaah! Yer a luvverly creature, sir. We 'ad a mother once, just like yerself. Don't turn me an' me mucker away yet Lordship. Show charity ter two starvin' wretches. Whahahaah!"

Thrugg folded his paws across his chest, unable to move one way or the other. He called out to Samkim above the wailing, "Cut along an' fetch Abbess Vale, young'n. Sharpish now!"

By the time the Abbess arrived the two stoats were facedown on the Abbey lawn, kicking their limbs and blubbering unmercifully. She held up both paws. "Silence, please. Stop all this caterwauling. You're not injured!"

Dingeye appeared inconsolable, strewing grass on his head, pounding the earth with all paws and sobbing brokenly. "Not injured! Aaaaaooowwww! Kind lady, if only you knew the 'arf of it. If yer calls starvin', ill fortune an' limpin' round the land till yer paws are wore down t' the bone not injured, then so be it. But say nothin' of the days of 'eartache, an' the freezin' cold rainy nights, an' not a pudden rag atwixt me an' my mucker 'ere t' keep us warm an' dry from the thunder an' lightnin'. Not injured, yer say? Wahahahaah!"

Samkim and Arula could not help giggling at the tragicomic display put on by the two stoats. Abbess

Vale silenced the young ones with a stern glance. Turning, she addressed the stoats in a no-nonsense manner.

"Tut-tut! If you wish to stay at our Abbey you must cease this disgraceful exhibition immediately. Do you hear me?"

Instantly Dingeye and Thura stopped howling and sat up.

"Do yer mean we c'n stay?"

"An' we can come to yer whoopdedoo an' scoff . . . I mean 'ave summat to eat?"

The Abbess nodded. "Redwall Abbey is a place of peace and plenty, but while you are here you must observe our rules: to live in harmony with the creatures about you, and help the sick, the aged and the very young. Also you must never raise a paw in anger against any creature. We are a peaceful order, we tend the land and prosper from its bounteous way of life. If you are willing to abide by our laws then you may stay here gladly."

The Abbess's words set them both off afresh.

"Whaahaah! Forgive me fer cryin' luvverly lady, but you reminds me of me ol' mother—she looked just like yew!"

"Whaaaaw! Lackaday, I never knew my mother, but I'm sure she woulda looked just like yer too. Bless yer, mum, with yore kind eyes an' gentle voice an'—"

Thrugg and the Foremole hauled the stoats upright.

Tudd Spinney looked doubtfully toward the Abbess. "What d'you think, marm? Pers'nally, I don't much care for the look o' these two."

Foremole seconded Tudd's opinion. "Burr, nor do oi. They'm looken loik a roight ol' pair o' gullywashers!"

The Abbess stroked her chin thoughtfully. "Hmmm, I can see what you mean. What do you think, Bremmun?"

Recalling his harsh judgment of Samkim and Arula, the old squirrel shrugged uneasily. "Well, they do look rather pitiful, Mother Abbess, but I think the decision is finally yours."

Dingeye's voice quivered with emotion, and he went limp in the Foremole's strong grasp, shaking his paws in despair.

"The decision is yores. 'E's right, lady. Turn us out, back inter the crool world. We should never 'ave darkened yer doorstep, two misfortunate wretches such as us!"

Despite his size, Thrugg was softhearted, and he sniffed aloud. "Stow that kind o' talk, matey. Our Abbess ain't got an 'eart made o' stone!"

Thrugg's words seemed to make up the Abbess's mind, and she nodded decisively. "All right, you can stay. But remember this: whilst you are guests at Redwall you must behave, mind your manners and keep your paws to yourselves. Is that clear?"

Dingeye and Thura broke away from their keepers. Falling on all fours, they began kissing the hem of the Abbess's robe.

Trying not to grimace with distaste, she shook them off. "Here, Samkim and Arula, I've a job for you. These two creatures are your responsibility while they are with us. If you need any help, ask Thrugg or Foremole. Dear me, how I wish Redwall had a badger Mother again. Right, back to work, Redwallers. There is much to be done if we want a good Nameday tomorrow!"

The Abbeydwellers were dispersing as the squirrel and the mole introduced themselves.

"I'm Samkim and this is Arula."

"Pleased ter make yer acquaintance, young'n's. I'm Dingeye, this is me mucker Thura. Righto, where do we eat an' sleep?"

The odor of unwashed stoats made Arula wrinkle her nose. "Nay nay, zurrs. 'Ee'll be worken awhoil afore it be toim to eat an' sleepen. Us'ns be agoin' to 'elp in 'ee kitchens, a-cooken an' a-baken."

Thura brightened at the mention of food. "Cookin 'n' bakin', that sounds all right ter me, mucker!"

Samkim blanched. He, too, had caught the unsavory whiff from the ragged pair. He grabbed both by their paws. "Not so fast, friends. First you must take a bath and get clean smocks!"

Dingeye and Thura recoiled in horror.

"Bath? Not me, mucker. It ain't 'ealthy!"

"Dingeye's right, young un, bathin'd be the death of us!"

Samkim gave a broad wink to Thrugg and Foremole. "Perhaps you would like to take our friends for a stroll by the Abbey pond? It's lovely in the summer."

A short time later two clean smocks lay on the grass at the pond's edge. Foremole stood menacing the stoats with a long window pole, Thrugg was in the water with a block of soap and a scrubbing brush. Dingeye and Thura clung to each other in panic as Foremole prodded them pondward with the pole.

"Coom on, durtybeasts. Washen woant kill 'ee, hurr hurr."

"Mercy, yer Honor. That stuff's water—it's all wet!"

"Aye, an' there's a fish monster in there. I can see it!"

Playfully Thrugg splashed water at them. "Bless yer filthy 'earts, mateys, he don't mind if you don't. Get yer paws wet now. Come on, this is the best lilac an' heather soap. Sink me if you don't come out smellin' like two pretty flowers!"

There was a final shriek of terror as Foremole pushed them in with the window pole, and stood menacing them with it. "Naow do 'ee be still whoil Maister Thrugg scrubs you'm mucky ol' necks."

The otter went to it with a will, ducking and scouring.

"Owoch oo oo! Soap's in me eye, sir. I'm blinded. 'Elp, 'elp!"

"Waaa! Water's gone up me nose. Please, sir, no m— Glubbublub!"

5

Friar Bellows was as wide as he was high. The tubby mouse looked up from trimming pie crust and winked at Samkim and Arula. "Hoho, what can I do for you two liddle rips today?"

Arula tied on an apron. "Hurr, zurr Bellers, 'ee were agoin' t' show us'ns 'ow to make a Gurtall cake, doant 'ee amember?"

The Friar gave them each a honeyed damson from a big jar. "So I did, so I did. Hmm, you must have clean paws to make a Great Hall cake. Let me see them."

He inspected the two pair of freshly scrubbed paws. "Very good, very good! Hmm, righto, climb up on these stools and check the ingredients with me. Here's the list."

"Arrowroot and pollen flour."

"Chopped chesknutters an' 'unneyed damsens."

"Very good, very good. Sugared violets and raspberries."

"Flaked beechnuts, dried plums and rosehip syrup."

"Woild buttercup cream, hurr, an' blackb'rry cream, zurr."

"Very good, very good. Almond paste, greensap milk

and young crystallized maple leaves. That seems to be the lot!"

As they mixed the ingredients, Friar Bellows kept an eye on them, while at the same time overseeing other kitchen helpers. Bellows seldom missed a detail of any kind.

"Brother Hal, watch that dandelion custard, it's coming to the boil. Very good, very good. Rub the arrowroot and the pollen flour together, dribbling greensap milk in slowly like thus. Very good, very good. Dumble! You're supposed to be chopping those candied chestnuts up, not gobbling them. I'll whack your tail off with a frying pan, my laddo! Now, add the flaked beechnuts, saving a few to scatter on the almond paste, and put a few more dried plums in. Arula, line the bottom of the baking dish with a dusting of pollen flour. Right. Place the honeyed damsons and raspberries so, one damson, one raspberry, in nice neat rows. Very good, very good! How's the leek and cheese flan coming along, Sister Nasturtium . . . ? Dumble! What have I told you?"

When the Great Hall cake was mixed and set in its dish the two companions slid it far into the oven with long wooden paddles. Magnificent aromas of bilberry scones, hazelnut muffins and oatrose turnovers assailed their nostrils from the top shelves of the four-tiered oven. They washed cake mixture from their paws as Friar Bellows explained the next step.

"Very good, very good, you two! The cake will be baked and taken out to cool. Once it is firm enough, here is what you do: slice it longways three times, bottom layer spread with rosehip syrup and sugared violets, place next layer lightly on top—this one will be spread with blackberry cream sprinkled with crystallized maple leaves. Next layer lightly on top—that's the secret, lightly—spread with almond paste scattered with flaked beechnuts. Very good, very good. Pay attention now. Top layer, spread thick with wild buttercup cream, dash on some chopped chestnuts, then a light coat of rosehip syrup to give it that lovely faint pinkish color, and presto! There we will have a Great Hall cake. Very good, very good!"

As the kitchens were very hot and crowded, Mrs. Faith Spinney had prepared a light lunch of summer salad and mintcream wafers near the gatehouse wall. The workers ate gratefully, some lounging in the sun upon the grass, others sitting on the wallstairs in the shade.

Samkim and Arula sat on the grass with Dingeye and Thura, chuckling gleefully as the stoats recited the catalog of atrocities perpetrated upon them since their arrival.

"On me oath, muckers, I don't know which was the worstest, starvin' an' trampin' outside or gettin' dragged in ter this Redhall place. It's a crool life, I tell yer!"

"Yer right there, Dingeye. Call that 'ospitality, gettin' near drownded by a fierce waterdog, nearly et by a monster fish, an' 'avin' flowery soap stuffed up yer nose. Hah! An' that's besides bein' bopped on the bonnet by a mole with a pole."

"Yer right, mucker. If I'm not dead with flooenzer from gettin' a bath by nightfall, me name ain't stoat!"

Thura shuddered violently and plucked at the sleeves of a clean but much darned smock Foremole had made him put on.

Dingeye waggled a paw in his ear to remove surplus soap. "Phoo! That's some kind o' welcome fer two pore stoats, mucker—an' they burned our good clothes too. Makes yer wonder wot these woodlands is comin' to. I tell yer, that's the first bath I've took in me life, an' the last one, too, thank yer kindly!"

Samkim and Arula could hardly eat for laughing, and

little Dumble was doubled up with an attack of the giggles.

Samkim poured cider for all. "Hahahaha! What—hahaha—happened then?"

Dingeye quaffed his drink indignantly. "Well may yer ask, mucker. That there longtailed bully of a hotter an' that savage liddle molefeller dragged us along to the kitchens to 'elp."

Thura's mouth was watering. "Aye, the whole place was full of scones, an' cakes an' trifles an' flans an' puddens an' custids an' . . ."

Dingeye took another drink to wash the taste of soap away as he complained bitterly. "But did we get to work among the goodies? Not a frog's chance, mucker! That fat ol' Friarmouse took one look at us an' sniffed. Aye, sniffed, 'e did! Then 'e tells that hotter an' his pal the Fivemole to put us to scrubbin' greasy pans clean. Up to our noses in more water—it was 'orrible, awful, I tell yer. Two noble stoats like us, togged up in smocks like a pair o' dog's dinners, wipin' an' a-scrubbin' at black pots an' crusty ol' bowls. Good job they let us come out 'ere in the fresh air. I was about to throw meself in the sink an' drown all mizzuble like in that there greasy dishwater!"

Arula was drinking from her beaker as he issued this statement. Unable to laugh and drink at the same time, she fell forward, sputtering out a spray of cider. "Burrhurrhurrhurr! You'm pore beasts 'ad a drefful toim of et all, tho' I do say it moiself. Hurrhurrhurr!"

Thrugg strode cheerily up and grabbed the unhappy stoats. "Righto, mates, vittles is finished. Back to the galley now, me lucky layabouts!"

Thura gave a heartfelt moan of despair. "I've gone all limp, mucker. That dishwater's gone ter me brains an' it's affectin' me paws. No more pots 'n' pans, please!"

Dingeye wriggled feebly in Thrugg's grip. "If I dies,

43

mucker, promise you'll put a pot an' a pan on me grave, ter show wot caused it all!''

Samkim interceded with the otter on their behalf. ''Let them stay here awhile, Thrugg. They look more worn out than two of last season's apple cores. Oh look, Sister Nasturtium is here!''

The Sister was a plump mouse, very pretty and jolly, and she had always been very popular with the young ones. They pushed about, making room for her.

''Yurr, marm, cum an' set along wi' us'ns.''

She sat with them, helping herself to food. Samkim began coaxing her into singing; Nasturtium was famed throughout Redwall for her fine voice.

''Sister, these two poor stoats have never heard you sing. Could you do a little something for them, please?''

She gave a good-natured laugh. ''It's not them, it's you who wants me to sing, Samkim.''

The young squirrel flushed. ''Oh please, Sister, we all want to hear you.''

Nasturtium put aside her food and took a sip of cider to clear her throat. Other Redwallers gathered closer to listen to her melodious voice.

''In days of old a warrior bold,
All pawsore, tired and lame,
Came marching through the winters cold,
And Martin was his name.
Martin, Martin, the Warrior of Redwall,
With courage and his trusty sword, he came to save
    us all.
Now in those high and far-off days,
The country was oppressed
By vermin cruel, whose tyrant ways
Would let no creature rest.
But truth and brav'ry won the day,
For through all Mossflow'r wide,
Good honest creatures made their way

To stand by Martin's side. . . . And they cried:
Martin, Martin the Warrior of Redwall,
With courage and his trusty sword, he came to save
    us all.
The evil ones he put to flight
And justice he restored.
His heart was strong, his cause was right,
And mighty was his sword.
He helped to build our Abbey here,
The land rings with his fame.
Now peace lives here, we know no fear,
For Martin was his name.
Martin, Martin the Warrior of Redwall,
With courage and his trusty sword,
He came to save us all!"

Every creature joined in the last rousing chorus and set up a loud cheer. The echoes bounced off the homely red walls and soared to the blue summer skies above. Dingeye and Thura cheered as loud as anybeast, then they looked at each other in slight bewilderment.

"Wot're we cheerin' for? We don't even know who Martin is."

"Well, whoever 'e is, I bet 'e don't 'ave ter wash pots 'n' pans. Oh aye, I shouldn't think they'd be a-sayin', ''Ey you, with the mighty sword, get those greasy ol' pots scrubbed.' "

Samkim explained about Martin to the stoats. "Martin the Warrior is the symbol of our Abbey. He lived many many years ago."

Dingeye waved a careless paw. "Oh, y'mean 'e's dead. No wonder they never make 'im wash pots, heeheehee! Yowch!"

Thrugg had clipped Dingeye neatly over the ear. "Show some respect, matey. Martin is our Abbey Warrior."

Ruefully rubbing his stinging ear, the stoat complained, "Well, 'ow was I ter know? Besides, if a creature's dead, then 'e's finished, an' that's all there is to it."

Sister Nasturtium patted the stoat's back. "You don't understand. Martin may have died a long time ago, but his spirit lives on in the very stones of Redwall and its creatures. Maybe he has not been seen or felt because this is a time of peace, though in troubled times he has visited certain ones and inspired them to great deeds."

Thura scratched his head. "Have you ever seen Martin?"

A silence fell over the company as they watched Nasturtium. She looked as if she were dreaming. With her eyes wide open fixed on the red stone walls in front of her, she started slowly to recite words they had never heard before.

"I am but an orchard shadow in the sunny tide of
    noon,
The dust of olden seasons on a stone.
My paw is light and silent as a waning autumn
    moon;
I walk the halls of memory, alone.
You may hear me as a whisper that the wind has left
    behind,
Or see me as the pale calm light of dawn,
Feel me take the toll of care, from off your sleeping
    mind,
In times of deep despair and hope forlorn.
Then I will be beside you in the corridors of dream.
A warrior's strength I'll give to you, my friend,
Like the waters of a storm that swell a tiny mountain
    stream,
A mightiness your loved ones to defend.
Injustice and evil will flee from your law,
As all about you will say,
'There walks one touched, by the Warrior's paw.'

So wait, I will find you one day."

In the eerie hush that followed, little Dumble's voice piped up. "Aaaahhh silly! I no no worra's all about, Sista."

Nasturtium blinked and shuddered. "That makes two of us, Dumble. I don't know what made me say those lines, I've never heard them before. It was . . . it was as if someone else were speaking and not me!"

Brother Hal, who was sitting nearby, stood up quickly. "Can you remember the poem again, Sister? Wait there, I'll go and get quill and parchment. It is my duty as Recorder to write it all down."

Nasturtium shook her head. "Strange, I can't remember a single word. I'm afraid the whole thing has gone clear out of my head. How odd! It's as if some other creature was in charge of my tongue, and my mind too!"

Friar Bellows came panting up. He was waving a ladle. "Come on, you lot. Nameday tomorrow. The food isn't going to prepare itself, y'know. Up on your paws and look busy now!"

There were a few groans, but most of the helpers went willingly. Dingeye and Thura were among the back stragglers.

"Huh, I wish we c'd train those pots 'n' pans to scrub 'emselves. Hup there, cauldron, jump in the sink and give yerself a good scourin' now!"

"Or maybe we could get that Martin spirit to wash a few. Owch!"

Dingeye had not realized Thrugg was still within hearing range.

6

Earlier that morning a somber pall hung over the fortress of Salamandastron. Mara lay abed for as long as she could before rising to make her way down to the dining hall. Urthstripe sat in his large chair with Sergeant Sapwood and Big Oxeye on either side of him. Mara sidled in and took a seat at the far end of the big table next to Pikkle; Klitch and Goffa sat on her other side. Usually there would be lots of good-natured joking and chatter over the plain fare, but today breakfast was a dismal affair; silence hung broodingly over the assembly.

Pikkle passed Mara a bowl of wild oatmeal porridge and a beaker of sage tea, keeping his voice to a whisper as he said, "Jolly lot, aren't they, wot? I say, old gel, did you get an awful tickin' off from Lord Urthstripe last night?"

Mara's appetite had deserted her. She dabbed at the porridge with a crust of ryebread. "Oh, it was much the same as usual. One word led to another and I ran off to bed in the end because I couldn't stick it."

Klitch leaned over, the sly blue eyes he had inherited from his father Ferahgo now radiating candor and sympathy. "You didn't get into trouble because of Goffa and me, did you?"

The young badger maid shrugged. "It was nothing to do with you, Klitch. I just get tired of being pushed and bossed like a silly infant around here."

"Did you father shout at you?" Goffa refilled his bowl from a nearby serving dish.

Pikkle wiped his bowl with ryebread. "He's not her father."

Klitch stole a quick glance up the table at Urthstripe. "Then why does Mara have to do as he says? I wouldn't, me and Goffa do as we please—nobeast gives us orders!"

Urthstripe sat looking at his untouched breakfast. Mara had not even acknowledged him this morning. One part of him longed to be friends with her, but the other half detested what he was seeing: a fine young badger maid, gossiping with a ferret and a weasel as if they were lifelong friends. The badger Lord caught the weasel stealing a glance at him. The creature had light blue eyes, shining as honest as a newborn infant. Some faraway faint memory was struggling to surface within Urthstripe's brain, but then it was wiped away as Oxeye nudged him and nodded down the table.

"That chap could charm the bally birds out of the trees with his baby-blue peepers. Still, I'd hate ter be the jolly old bird that fell into his claws. What d'you say, M'lud?"

A deep growl issued from Urthstripe's cavernous chest. "I once knew a searat who could sing like a lark, beautiful ballads. He used to sing to his victims as he cut them up. Vermin are vermin, no matter what—I've learned that much. Sapwood, I cannot stand the sight of those two at my table any longer. Give them provisions and get them clear of my mountain. I'll feel easier when they've gone!"

The hare Sergeant stood up and threw a salute. "Yes, sir. I'll hescort 'em ter the door pers'nally."

The forty odd hares who lived at Salamandastron watched in silence as Sapwood made his way down the table. He nodded to Mara and Pikkle before turning to Klitch and Goffa. "Hare you finished with your vittles, you two?"

Klitch sniggered as he did an impression of the Sergeant's voice. "Yes, we have, hactually!"

The hare kept his face impassive and his voice level. "Right ho, then if you'd hallow me to show you out."

"Show them out?" Mara placed a paw on Sapwood's arm. "But these are my friends, Sergeant!"

Sapwood stood stiffly to attention, avoiding her eyes. "Lord Urthstripe says they must leave. Don't worry, missie, they'll be given 'aversack rations and sent on their way unharmed. Come on, foller me, you two. Lively now!"

Goffa and Klitch rose, the latter smiling ruefully at Mara. "We'll be fine, don't bother your head about us. I wish you luck with Urthstripe. Goodbye, Mara. Maybe we'll meet again someday."

As Sapwood led them the length of the dining hall Mara could stand the tension no longer. The badger maid knew that Urthstripe loved and cared for her, as she did for him, but he was becoming like a dictator to her, ruling her life, saying how she should behave and conduct herself. Now in his usual heavy-pawed way he had insulted her newfound friends. It was too much! Without thinking, Mara suddenly found herself shouting angrily over the hushed assembly at Urthstripe:

"Go on, send my friends away. It's your mountain. You can do as you like and everybeast has to obey!"

Every hare present jumped in their seats as the badger Lord's paws crashed forcefully on the tabletop.

"Mara, go to your room!"

But Mara was already up and hurrying from the hall,

her mind finally made up as to what she would do. "I won't go to that room anymore. I'm leaving this mountain to go with my friends, and you can't stop me!"

Windpaw leaped up to intercept Mara, but Urthstripe shook his head. "Let her go!"

Pikkle dashed after his companion. "Mara, I say, wait, I'm comin' with you!"

When they had gone, Sapwood returned to his chair. The tough hare gazed imploringly at Urthstripe, whose face was set in a stony stare at Mara's empty seat. "She's gone, sir—'er an' Pikkle. Should I bring 'em back?"

Urthstripe looked away, swiftly brushing a tear from his eye with a heavy paw. "No, I must let her go. She is not happy here anymore."

Big Oxeye stood up. The huge hare saluted his Lord. "Beggin' yer leave, sah! With or without permission from you, me an' old Sappers here are goin' ter follow 'em. Watch that they don't get themselves in some bally scrape or other, keep an eye on 'em. Wot?"

Urthstripe grasped both their paws. "Thank you, my friends!"

Snatching a light throwing lance apiece from a weapon rack, Sapwood and Oxeye set off an an easy lope on the track of Mara and Pikkle. Urthstripe went to his forge. All that day the mountain interior resounded with the pounding and banging of his forge hammers, and chunks of red hot metal showered sparks as he battered them as flat as dead leaves.

Hiding among the dunes to the south of Salamandastron, Klitch and Goffa watched Mara and Pikkle getting nearer as they followed the trail.

Klitch nudged his companion. "They'll be here any moment, so listen. Don't you say a word—leave the talking to me. My plan has worked well so far."

51

Goffa patted the two haversacks of food that lay nearby. "Your father won't think so. Two bags o' food isn't really badger's treasure, is it?"

He flinched slightly as Klitch elbowed him sharply in the ribs. "If brains were acorns you'd be a dead oak!" There was a sneer in the weasel's voice. "We've been inside the mountain, we've seen for ourselves, there's about forty fighting hares and Urthstripe, and they're not there for nothing. I'll bet my tail they're guarding a treasure. Now I've given Ferahgo an extra move in the game—I'm providing him with a hostage, Lord Urthstripe's own precious little Mara. We could have done without that hare Pikkle, but if she wants to bring him along, the more the merrier!"

The light of understanding dawned in Goffa's eyes. "You're right! By the claw, you're a clever one, Klitch!"

Without taking his eyes from the two approaching creatures, the young weasel muttered fiercely, "Right, Goffa, I am clever. I'm smarter than Farran, Dethbrush, Migroo or any of that deadheaded bunch. That's why Ferahgo allows me to spy for him. But what my father doesn't realize is that he's getting old and I'm still young. I'll show him who's the more cunning one day soon. Stow it now, here they are!"

As Mara and Pikkle breasted the hill, Klitch feigned surprise. He turned to them, his open blue eyes shining happily. "Mara, Pikkle! What are you two doing here?"

Pikkle let his ears flop forward comically. "What ho, you chaps. Two more recruits for your rovin' band!"

Mara nodded agreement, her face alight with the joy of freedom. "I've done it, left Salamandastron for good! As you can see, Pikkle came with me. He's my only friend."

Klitch grasped her paw warmly. "Well, you've got two more good pals now—me and Goffa. We'll stick by you like true companions. Isn't that right, Goffa?"

The ferret leaned on his spear, echoing the words. "True companions!"

Mara could still see Salamandastron rising tall and grim in the distance. She looked away, banishing thoughts of it from her mind. Taking in her immediate surroundings, the badger maid quivered with delight. They were in a small hollow amid the dunes, basking in the heat of a fresh summer day. Beyond the grass-tufted hilltops she could see a distant mountain range rearing up ahead of them. It was framed majestically against a cloudless sky of vivid blue. Her heart sang within at the prospect of boundless freedom.

"Oh, isn't it exciting, Klitch! From now on Pikkle and I are going to be just like you two, traveling where we want, sleeping beneath the stars, eating when we feel like, and no one to boss or push us around. We're free!"

Goffa pulled a face and grunted. "Where's yer food?"

Pikkle spread his paws, chuckling. "Ask Mara the gallopin' badger there. She was in such a bally rush that she dashed off without a jolly crumb. Had to follow her, of course, so I didn't wait to stock up with tucker. But here we are, hale an' hungry!"

"You never brought anything?" Klitch looked concerned.

Mara waggled her paws in a carefree manner. "No, not a single scone. Still, I suppose we'll find something."

Goffa hefted his spear meaningly. "You mean you didn't even bring a weapon between you?"

"No weapons, eh!" Klitch's look of concern deepened.

Pikkle sat and drew doodles in the sand. "Who needs moldy ol' weapons? I mean, I can't see enemies to fight with round here. Wot, wot?"

The blue-eyed young weasel sat down beside him. "I wouldn't take it so lightly if I were you, Pikkle. Alone out in this country and unarmed, you never know what

53

might happen. Mara, haven't you got anything that could be used as a bribe, something to buy your way with, perhaps a piece of badger treasure?"

"Badger treasure, what d'you mean, Klitch?" Mara was puzzled by the odd question.

The weasel shrugged as if it were not really important. "Oh, you know, gold or silver trinkets, medallions maybe, or jewels and such. I thought all badgers had some sort of treasure stowed away."

Mara scratched her stripes thoughtfully. "Hmm, I can't recall ever seeing treasure at Salamandastron. Can you, Pikkle?"

"Me? No, not a bloomin' bauble, old gel!"

Klitch smiled shrewdly. "I'll bet old Urthstripe has loads of it hidden away somewhere, but he wouldn't tell you about it, Mara. Oh no, he'd be more at home ordering and shoving you about like a slave. I reckon that he thinks any treasure stowed away in the mountain is his and none of your business, because you're too young to know about such things. But forgive me, you must be hungry. We'll share our supplies with you. Let's have an early lunch—your first one as a free creature, Mara, and you, Pikkle."

They gratefully accepted the wheatcakes, cheese and apples from the packs that had been given to the weasel and the ferret.

Pikkle fell upon the food with his usual good appetite. "That's what friends are for, wot! Jolly good chaps, these two. What d'you say, Mara m' gel?"

Mara lowered her voice as she munched an apple. "You're right, Pikkle. D'you know, I don't feel as much of a young one as I used to be. Perhaps it's because Klitch treats us as equals and not underlings. Some of the things he said have made me think. All that secrecy about not allowing other creatures inside the mountain—maybe Urthstripe does have something to hide. I'll bet he does have a hidden treasure. Not that I'm bothered about it; he can keep his moldy old treasure for all I care."

They missed the knowing wink that passed from Klitch to Goffa.

The weasel tossed the haversack across to Mara. "Here, have some cheese. Help yourself, friend!"

7

The muted boom of the great Joseph Bell signaled the twilight hour over Redwall Abbey. Blackbirds, song thrushes and the last larks descending warbled their final melodies to the closing day. Abbess Vale was about to knock on the gatehouse door when Faith Spinney swung it silently open.

The hedgehog lady placed a paw to her mouth. "Hush, little Dumble is sleeping here tonight. I've just put him down in the spare bed. Let's take a stroll round the orchard. We can talk in peace there."

Latching the door carefully, Faith sighed in relief. "My spikes! I don't know which is the worser, grown hedgehogs or baby dormice. My old Tudd an' Dumble been a-playin' together—you should've seen 'em both larkin' an' sportin' about. They're a right couple o' pawfuls an' no mistake! Played themselves to a stan'still they did. My Tudd fell fast asleep in the rockin' chair an' Dumble curled up on the floor. They's both sleepin' now, bless 'em!"

The grass beneath them was still warm from the summer sun as they strolled paw in paw toward the pond. The Abbess sniffed the air, peering at the sky.

"The weather should be fine tomorrow for our Name-day, Faith. How are the preparations going?"

"Everythin' is done to a turn, Vale. Don't you fret yourself. My Tudd's been helpin' Burrley mole bring up the finest of drinks from the cellars — strawberry cordial, new cider, dandelion an' burdock, damson wine an' the finest barrel of October ale tasted in ten seasons. Tudd 'n' Burrley should know, they been a-tastin' it enough today. Now I don't mind sayin', young Samkim an' Arula have been a regular pair o' goodbeasts, helpin' Friar Bellows out wi' the bakin' an' cookin' like they were born in a kitchen."

The Abbess raised her eyebrows. "It's nice to hear a creature with a good word to say for those two. I take it you've forgiven them for the bow and arrow incident?"

"Bless their 'earts, yes." Faith chuckled. "Young uns are only young once, more's the pity. They're both nice liddle wags, so they are. They don't mean a body any real harm."

Abbess Vale watched the trout flap its tail on the surface, setting up ripples over the still pondwater. "What's your opinion of those two stoats? Can we trust them to behave properly?"

"Oh, you mean Dingeye an' Thura. They'm just a silly ol' pair o' stoats. I wouldn't worry about 'em, Vale."

The Abbess steered her friend around the pond edge. "I hope you're right, Faith."

A lantern was lit in the first-floor dormitory. Brother Hollyberry, Sister Nasturtium and Thrugann the otter sat together on the side of a bed. Grouped around them on the floor the young ones sat, wrapped in their blankets, eating thick slices of new Abbeybread spread with cornflower butter and elderberry jam and sipping from beakers of hot dandelion cordial. Samkim and Arula had brought the two stoats with them.

"Gwaw! This jam's luvverly," Thura commented. "I could eat ten o' these, easily!"

Arula held up a paw. "Thurr be a-storytellen, 'ushed naow."

Thura took a sip of hot cordial and scorched his tongue. "Yowch! That's 'ot, mucker. Wot's a-story-tellen?"

Dingeye flicked him on the end of his nose. "Shut up, bottlebrain. It's a story. I like stories."

Brother Hollyberry leaned forward, scanning the eager young faces as he drew out his voice in a deep whisper. "Whooooo waaaants a storeeeeeeee?"

The young ones giggled and hugged each other excitedly. They elongated their voices as they chanted back, "Weeee waaaant a storeeeeee pleeeeeeeease!"

The old Infirmary keeper took a sip of his drink and started.

"Old travelers tell, at the midnight bell,
When the nightdark covers all,
Mid the falling snow, when the cold winds blow,
Of the ghost that walks Redwall . . ."

A baby mole emitted a gruff squeak and hid trembling beneath his blanket. "Burrhoo, oi be gurtly afeared o' goasters!"

A small fat otter joined him. "I'm afeared too. 'Old on ter me, matey. They won't get us'ns!"

When silence had been restored, Hollyberry continued:

"Yes, the ghost that haunts the stairways goes
   slowly on his beat,
Moaning low in the moonlight's glow.
'Give me young ones to eat!' "

Several young mice squealed and dived beneath the

bed, and Thura's beaker rattled nervously against his teeth as he tried to drink some cordial. "I'm g-g-g-glad I ain't a young un, mucker!"

Dingeye whacked him soundly on the head. "Belt up an' lissen frogsbum!"

The storyteller continued his grisly tale.

"Then one night as the lightning was flashing
And the thunder was crashing out, *boomz!*
The beastly phantom came a-haunting
Into this very room.
When up stood a young one, pale as the ghost,
And to the spirit said,
'How dare you moan round here at night
And wake me from my bed!'
The ghost sprang at him with a cry:
'Whoohoo I'll eat you whole!'
The pale mouse laughed as he replied,
'You'll need a great big bowl!
For I am Martin the Warrior,
The spirit of Redwall,
Whilst I protect this Abbey,
You'll eat nobeast at all!' "

The mice beneath the bed raised a cheer at the name of their hero. "Hooray! Good old Martin. What did he do, Brother?"

Hollyberry stood, drawing a long ladle from his habit sleeve.

"Then Martin drew his trusty sword
And chopped that ghost apart.
He sliced his nose, he carved his ears,
He whacked its legs and head,
He chopped its claws, he hacked its jaws,
Then to the ghost he said:
'Be sure to brush up all your bits,

Goodnight, I'm off to bed!' "

Applause and relieved laughter greeted the fitting end of the ghost of Redwall. Creatures were settling down to await the next story when Thrugann mischievously tossed a crust of jam-smeared bread into Dingeye's lap and whooped, "Oo dear, look out, it's the ghost's tail. Oohoo!"

The panic-stricken stoat bowled Thura and Arula tip over tail as he leapt up, startled. It was some time before the laughter subsided and order was restored. Dingeye brushed the floor with his paws, laughing nervously as he searched.

"Haha, that weren't no ghost's tail at all, haha, it was a trick."

Thura had scoffed the crust. He clipped Dingeye's ears smartly. "Of course it was the ghost's tail, noddle'ead. It's vanished, ain't it? On'y a real ghost tail could vanish!"

Dingeye stared at the empty floor and shuddered. "Never shoulda come t' this Redhall place, mucker!"

Suddenly Sister Nasturtium's clear voice cut across them. She was staring at the wall and reciting:

"When night meets day, stand clear away,
Beware the Abbey then.
Stay close beside the rampart wall,
Await the moment when
The flame of storm will strike my blade
To aid the badger Lord,
And bring back to Redwall one day
A guardian and a sword."

In the hush that followed, Brother Hollyberry shook the sleeve of Nasturtium, who was sitting staring, as if in a trance. "Sister, what is it? Are you all right?"

She blinked and looked about her. "Oh dear, have I

done it again? Goodness only knows what I've been saying. Was it something dreadful?''

Thrugann placed a protective paw about her shoulders. "No, no, 'twas only some ol' poetry, Sister— nothin' for you to get upset over. You look tired. Come on, it's bed for you. In fact, it's bed for all you young uns too, otherwise you'll sleep right through Nameday tomorrow an' miss it!''

That night Samkim fell immediately into a deep sleep and dreamed a strange dream. In the dream he was walking into Great Hall. He went up to the huge tapestry hanging from the wall. The likeness of Martin the Warrior seemed to stand out from the rest of the skillful weave; he was clad in his armor, holding his sword lightly, and a friendly smile lit up his brave features. Without warning he tossed the sword. It twirled once in the air and sped from the tapestry, burying its point in a crack between the stones at Samkim's side. The young squirrel felt no fear. Without knowing why, he withdrew the sword from the floor and held it out, offering it back to the Warrior of Redwall. Martin took it. Though his lips did not move, Samkim could hear his voice:

"Squirrel, mouse—it makes no difference, you are a Redwaller, Samkim. Be brave and courageous, true to your friends. One day you will return my sword again and give this Abbey another guardian. Beware the vermin, seek out the White One.''

Thrugg crept up from the kitchens. Sleep did not come easily to the burly otter, particularly with the knowledge that there was a huge pot of shrimp and bulrush soup, flavored with watercress and hotroot pepper, simmering gently on the embers of the kitchen fire. Thrugg could not rest until he had sampled it. Slipping down to the kitchen in his voluminous white nightshirt, the big otter cut a curious figure. He consumed two bowls of his favorite soup, smacked his lips, yawned and added more hotroot pepper to the pot before stealing off back to his bed. Crossing Great Hall he was surprised to see Samkim. The young squirrel stood illuminated by a shaft of moonlight in front of the tapestry. Thrugg had seen sleepwalkers before and he knew what to do. Strolling up, he lifted Samkim easily in his strong paws.

The young squirrel opened his eyes and stared at Thrugg. "Are you the White One?"

Thrugg glanced at his long white nightshirt and grinned. "Aye, that's me matey, the White Un."

Samkim snuggled down in Thrugg's arms murmuring happily. "Oh, that's good. I was seeking you." He closed his eyes and went instantly into a deep sleep.

Back at the dormitory, Thrugg deposited him gently in his bed. "Strike me sails, he ain't no lightweight. All that carryin' has set me appetite off again. I'll just nip back down an' see if'n that there soup tastes better with the pepper I added."

8

The moon over the dunes made hollows of darkness against the dun-colored sand, which stood out in stark relief, still radiating warmth from the hot day into the soft summer night.

At first Feadle thought his eyes were deceiving him, but as he peered into the moon-shadowed dunes he distinguished the smartly dressed figure of Klitch hurrying toward the camp. Filling his lungs with air, Feadle roared at the top of his voice. "Master, see, it's your son Klitch and he's alone!"

Roused rudely from his slumbers, the weasel Chieftain hissed upward at the hapless sentry, "Wormbrain! Couldn't you shout any louder to advertise our presence to the entire countryside?"

Sickear scrabbled for balance, wakened by the sudden shout.

Feadle steadied him as he whispered back in an exaggerated tone, "But, Master, you said to let you know—"

A well-aimed pebble struck him stingingly on the eartip, followed by Ferahgo's voice, heavy with contempt: "Feadle, you useless toad, get down here. Sickear, you stay up there and keep your wits about you."

The Assassin sat with his son, apart from the rest and out of hearing. He nodded his head approvingly as Klitch made his report, then commented, "I knew there was something to those tales of a hollow mountain and the badger's treasure. But you say you didn't see any of it. How d'you know it's there, you sly young fiend?"

Klitch's blue eyes twinkled in the darkness. "Hah! It's there all right, you old murderer. That badger, Mara, she let slip about it in conversation. She'd know where the treasure of Salamandastron is hidden, mark my words."

"Where is she now?"

"Back in the dunes there with her friend, a hare name Pikkle. Goffa's keeping an eye on them while I'm away. No need to worry, they were sleeping like babies when I left them to come here."

"Well done, Klitch. Now we know exactly where the mountain is. The next question is how to get in there and grab the treasure."

Klitch toyed with the sword that hung by his side. "It won't be easy. I've told you, the place is a fortress, besides which there's more than twoscore of hares—proper battle-trained fighters, not like the helpless creatures we're used to. But the main one is that badger, Lord Urthstripe. I've never seen a beast so big and fierce. He's a real warrior. I'd hate to have to go up against him!"

Ferahgo's long skinning knife appeared under Klitch's nose. "You leave him to me, I've dealt with big badgers before. Oh, they're fierce fighters, sure enough, but they lack cunning and suffer from silly little things, like honor and conscience. Now you get off back to your new comrades and guide them over this way, to me. There's more than one way of frying a frog. Off you go, you young backstabber!"

Klitch vanished amid the night-washed dunes, unaware of the two shadowy forms at the side of a hill.

Sergeant Sapwood and Big Oxeye had followed him. Though they had not heard what passed between Klitch and Ferahgo, they were not slow in realizing that the large vermin horde camped in the foothills spelled death and destruction. The young weasel loped past the pair, not knowing they were within a hairsbreadth of him. Oxeye hefted the light throwing lance, feeling its balance as he eyed the receding Klitch.

"D'you know, I could pin the filthy little blighter through his neck from here, even though the blinkin' light's bad, wot."

The Sergeant restrained his friend's throwing paw. "Steady in the ranks, you'd blow the gaff. Now there's dirty work apaw, we've got ter use our brainboxes. I reckons if one o' us reports back to Lord Urthstripe, the other c'n follow yonder weasel an' watch out for new hintelligence. You go back ter the mountain, and I'll foller the weasel."

"That's what I like about you, Sarge," Oxeye chuckled good-humoredly, "always ready to vote on a democratic decision, wot?"

Big Oxeye held up his paws defensively as Sapwood crouched into a sparring position. "Pax! I was only jokin'. You're quite right, of course. I'll go back an' sound the jolly old alarm at Salamandastron, and you stick close to young Pikkle an' Mara. We both know this country like the backs of our paws; shouldn't be any bother trackin' one another if we need to make contact. OK?"

After a silent shake of paws they split up, going their separate ways into the night-shaded dunes.

An early fly landed on Mara's eyelid. She shooed it off with a dozy paw as she awakened to peachgold dawn stealing softly over the sleeping dunes. The land lay in a pool of calm serenity; the sand, now still and cool, awaited sun-warmed day. Somewhere a lark began trilling as it fluttered its morning ascent into the airy heights.

Pikkle opened one eye and swiftly closed it again. "It's no use tryin' ter wake me up, I'm fast a bally sleep."

The badger maid gathered a double pawful of sand and began trickling it onto the tip of her friend's nose. He sneezed and sat up straight, his long ears springing to attention. "Is it that late already, by the fur! My old tummyclock tells me there should be brekkers around. Hope it's something nice, wot!"

Goffa pulled himself upright on his spear haft. "You ate it all last night, greedyguts!"

"Greedyguts y'self, sir." Pikkle brushed sand from his coat. "I didn't notice you stintin' your belly when it came to puttin' food in it. Matter o' fact, I began to think you'd had news of a ten-season famine an' you were packin' it away just in case."

Goffa scowled nastily, testing his spearpoint. "You mind your mouth, you great overgrown rabbit . . ."

"Here, here, what's all this, friends fighting already?" As Klitch brushed past Goffa he dug an open claw in his back and shot him an angry glance. Turning to Mara and Pikkle, his eyes switched to open blue wonderment. "Now then, pals, what's all the quarreling about?"

"No quarrel really." Pikkle laughed. "I merely made inquiries about breakfast. Old Goffa must've got out the wrong side of the sandhill this mornin'—he accused me of scoffin' all the rations last night. Blinkin' cheek! Do I look like a scoffer, Klitch? Go on, be honest, don't spare m' feelin's."

The blue-eyed weasel upended the empty haversacks. "Actually you do, Pikkle, but it's no use falling out over it. The point is that we've run out of food."

Mara licked sand grains from her dry lips. "Not even an apple and I've got a dreadful thirst!"

She thought for a fleeting moment of the cool dark dining room inside the mountain, the tables laid with plain wholesome food and flagons of cold cider, green-sap milk and mint tea. Thrusting the memory from her mind, she looked around. "Well, I only know the country north and west of here. It's much the same as this: mountains, foothills, dunes and sandhills running to the shores. We won't find much food in that direction. What about that way, down south?"

Klitch shook his head. "That's the way we came up here. There's a broad stream in the far south, but between that and here there's a big area of swampland that we had to skirt. The place is overrun with big toads, and it's a pretty bad bet, I'd say."

Pikkle's stomach made a loud audible growl. He patted it. "Yes I know, old lad, but you'll just have ter wait until we find some tucker. Come on, chaps. Anybeast got an idea which way we should go to relieve the jolly old pangs?"

Klitch winked at Goffa. "I suggest we carry on into the foothills over to the east, what do you think, Goffa?"

"Foothills, yeh, good idea!" the ferret agreed readily.

Mara looked east to the distant foothills, with the mountain range rising green and grayish blue behind them. "Do you think we'll find food there, Klitch?"

The weasel patted her shoulder and started walking east. "It's a good chance. Streams usually run down from mountains and stuff always grows by them— plants, roots, berry bushes."

Goffa followed Klitch. "He's good at findin' food."

Pikkle gave Mara a shove in their direction. "Then what're we waitin' for? Lead us t' the berrybushes, chums."

Food had been passed up to Sickear in the lookout post. It was not much—a pawful of berries, a crust of bread

67

and some water—but he ate it gratefully, saving a little of the water to bathe his clawed shoulder.

The hot summer morning wore on, Sickear rubbing his eyes to stay awake as he kept watch, while below the lookout rock normal camp routine went on. Foraging and hunting parties came and went. Keeping away from Salamandastron, they moved south and stalked the swampland fringes for toads, frogs and birds. When these were not available there were always plants and roots.

Though everybeast feared Ferahgo, there were one or two who doubted the wisdom of his trek north. Forgrin the fox and Raptail the searat were two such creatures. They carried the breadsack, doling out stale bread to the horde.

A ferret named Bateye knocked his crust of bread against a rock, muttering complaints under his breath: "Lookit this—bread they calls it. More like stone it is!"

Forgrin rooted about in the breadsack, his voice mocking. "Oh dearie me, did yew 'ear that, Raptail? Pore ol' Bateye's bread ain't fresh. 'Ang on a bit, mate, and I'll see if there's any cake in 'ere. Now which would yew like, Yer 'Ighness, the sort wi' plums in or the cake wi' cream atop of it?"

Bateye raised his paw to fling the bread at Forgrin. "Yah shaddap, yer grinnin' idjit . . ."

There was a whirring swish as Ferahgo's skinning knife zipped between Forgrin and Raptail to pierce the crust held in Bateye's paw. The blood drained from the ferret's narrow face as the Assassin strode forward and picked up the knife with the crust fixed to its blade.

"Something wrong with your bread, Bateye?"

The ferret sat, staring up into the smiling blue eyes, then shook his head in vigorous denial. "No, master, norra thing. The bread's jus' fine, thank yer!"

"Excellent! Then let's see you eat it all up now!"

Ferahgo smiled wickedly, holding the bread transfixed upon his knife as Bateye tried to eat it under his gaze.

Bateye was no longer young, he had teeth missing, and the rock-hard dry crust cut his gums, but he ate on doggedly, too scared to stop.

Ferahgo watched him intently and commented, "What's that noise? Has one of your teeth broken? Oh look, it's fallen out. Tut-tut, Bateye. You should have taken better care of those molars, and cleaned them with a soft twig every morning. Still, eating that bread will strengthen them. What do you say?"

Bateye tried to speak around the knife blade and the stale dried bread filling his mouth, but he was only able to produce a strangled noise.

"I understand, friend." Ferahgo nodded sympathetically. "You'd like more. Forgrin, Raptail, give me more bread out of that sack. This poor ferret is still hungry."

Forgrin's jaw tightened at the wanton cruelty of Ferahgo, but he obeyed. Just as Raptail was about to pass Ferahgo the bread, a stoat called Dewnose came running up.

"Master, Sickear says to come quick, he's spotted somethin' that you should see!"

Flicking the blade from Bateye's open mouth, the Assassin ran to the lookout rock and scaled it nimbly. Sickear moved over on the perch to make room, his claw pointing.

"Over there, Master. It's Klitch an' Goffa with two others!"

"Yes, I see. Good work, Sickear!"

"But look, can you see, Master, just behind 'em in the hills, there's a hare followin' them."

"Hmm, so there is. I wonder if the badger knows we're here, or is that just a lone hare spying on us? We'll soon find out."

Pikkle shielded his eyes from the midday glare as he

viewed the mountainous country before them. "Oh corks! How much farther do we go? I'm absolutely whacked!"

"Too much to eat last night, Pikkle, that's your trouble." Klitch shook his head reprovingly. "Look, it's not much farther now. Why don't you and Mara rest here awhile with Goffa, and I'll go on ahead and scout the land. How does that sound?"

Pikkle flung himself gratefully on the ground. "Absolutely top-hole, old lad. You carry on bein' the jolly intrepid scout, and we'll flop down here!"

Mara did not argue, she was glad of the rest. Goffa merely nodded to Klitch and sat moodily, some distance from Mara and Pikkle. The badger maid rested her back against a rock and closed her eyes.

Suddenly a voice nearby whispered urgently, "Missie, don't turn round, stay has you are. You an' Pikkle 'ave got ter get away from 'ere sharpish. It's a trap!"

Startled, Mara opened her eyes and leaned around the rock. "Sergeant Sapwood, what are you doing here?"

Goffa sprang up. He came dashing over, spear at the ready. "Wot's goin' on 'ere? Who are you talki—"

Sapwood leaped out in front of him, poised for action. With a yell the ferret thrust the spear forward. Sapwood neatly sidestepped, kicking the spear adrift with his long hind legs. Goffa tried to make a grab for it but he was confronted by the champion boxing hare of Salamandastron. In swift succession two neat left pawhooks thudded to the side of his head, followed by a powerful straight right paw, smack dab on his chin. Goffa crumpled to the ground, senseless.

Pikkle came dashing over, puzzlement and concern on his face. "I say, steady on, Sappers ol' boy . . ."

Sergeant Sapwood seized him by the ear. "Liddle

70

block'eads, there's a whole harmy of vermin jus' over yon 'ill. Yore in a trap. Run for yore lives!''

A yelling horde of Ferahgo's creatures came charging over the hill in front of them. Sapwood threw an imploring glance at Mara, then snatched his javelin from behind the rock and thrust it into her paws.

"Too late, missie, but run. Y'might 'ave a chance, both of you. I'll lead 'em off!''

9

The Nameday celebrations at Redwall Abbey were in full swing. Early that morning they had started with the young ones marching round to the orchard, where they were met by Thrugg. As there was no badger to challenge them, the big otter had disguised himself, striping his face black and white and garbing himself with dusty old gray drapes. He shook a ladle at them as if it were a club and called out the challenge,

"What want you here, young beast, young beast,
What want you here at my feast, my feast?"

Two young mousemaids, Turzel and Blossom, stood forward. They danced around Thrugg as they chanted,

"O stripedog, great guardian, some food for us all,
For we are good young ones who live at Redwall!"

Thrugg appeared fearsome and waved his ladle at them.

"Some food, you say. Nay nay, away,
Unless our good Abbess says it is Nameday!"

It fell traditionally to Dumble, being the youngest, to call upon the Abbess to open the feast. He was pushed forward, his head wreathed in a posy of flowers and a willow wand in his paw. Twice he forgot his words as he waved the willow wand, but finally he plucked up confidence and got it right, the Sisters and Brothers laughing and applauding his babyspeech.

"Kind muvva, gudd muvva, er, er, O pleeze tell this
    beast
Dat this is our Nameday, an', an', an' we wanna
    feast!"

Every creature cheered aloud as Abbess Vale came forward, dressed in her best ceremonial habit, and declaimed loudly:

"Fie on you, great guardian, for can you not see,
These young ones are hungry, and they are with
    me."

All the young ones shouted at Thrugg:

"So stand aside and let us pass!"

Thrugg stood to one side as they dashed cheering to the tables. Samkim took Thrugg's paw and led him to the feast.

"Mr. Thrugg, I dreamed about you last night."

"Hohoho, I'll bet you did an' all, young un!"

"Mr. Thrugg, why does everybeast call you great guardian?"

"Oh, that's only on Nameday, Samkim, when I'm dressed up as a badger. In the old days the Abbey badger was often called guardian. It was usually a female badger, like a great mother to Redwallers she was. Why do you ask?"

But the excitement of the feast had gripped Samkim, and he ran to his place at table between Arula and the two stoats, knotting a napkin about his neck as he called out, "Hey, Mrs. Spinney, are those apple turnovers hot? Pass me one, will you please. Oho, look at our Great Hall cake, Arula. It's the best one in all Mossflower, isn't it, Friar Bellows?"

Farther down the table, the Foremole and his crew were setting to with a will.

"Yurr, Grunel, pass oi some damsen pudden, hurr hurr!"

"Moi o moi, wot wunnerful unnycream. Oi spreads it on ever'think."

"Gurrout, you'm be a-spreaden et on moi veggible pastie!"

"Yurr, zurr hotter, you'm been at this soup agin?"

Bremmun was demonstrating a special traveling hare snack to two openmouthed fieldmice. "When I was your age I saw a traveling hare do this when he visited us one Nameday. Hares are real gluttons. Watch! First he took a good flat apple turnover like this—pass me that meadowcream—then he spread it thick and stuck a pair of blackberry tarts on it, like this. Next he ladled it with honey, so, then he placed a huge slice of hazelnut and pear flan on top and ate the lot. Just like this! Mmmfff, snnninch, grooff!"

Dingeye, his face shrouded in whipped strawberry cream, was bolting down candied chestnuts and mintcream wafers at the same time. Thura was dipping a hot vegetable pastie into honeyed plums and woodland trifle, stopping now and then to gulp down great swigs of dandelion and burdock.

"Phwaw! Mucker! This is the life. Good ol' Redwall, that's wot I say!"

"Yer right there, mucker. It was almost worth washin' all those greasy pans for, an' gettin' a bath too!"

"Nothin's worth gettin' a bath for, bubblenose. Yowch! That's me paw yore tryin' to eat!"

Arula watched the two stoats glowering at each other. The little molemaid took her nose out of a slice of Great Hall cake long enough to chuckle.

"Oi must tell Froir Bellers about that un. Stoatpaw pudden, hurrhurr! Yurr, Dumble, get you'm nose out'n moi drink!"

The infant dormouse guzzled the last of Arula's cider and started making inroads upon the Abbess's elderberry wine. "I'm firsty, turrible firsty!"

Burrley mole and Tudd Spinney had cornered a great heap of cheeses and October ale, which they sampled judiciously.

"Ho, Maister Tudd, try'ee big yeller cheese wi' chesknutters innit. Et be a gurt fav'rite o' moin."

The old hedgehog blew the foam off a flagon of ale. "Hmm, nice 'n' nutty. 'Ave some o' my special fieldwhite cheese wi' celery an' onion—very tasty wi' that oatbread."

A challenge was thrown out by Thrugg's sister Thrugann: which of them could eat a bowl of the shrimp and bulrush soup with the most hotroot pepper in it. Thrugg threw a pawful in his bowl and started spooning it down. Thrugann promptly put two pawfuls into her soup and went at it with her eyes streaming. Not to be outdone, Thrugg added a full ladle of the pepper to his, whereupon Thrugann tipped the full peppersack over the top of her bowl. With tears gushing from their reddened eyes, both otters spooned away bravely until the Abbess called out, "I declare a draw, the winners, Thrugg and Thrugann!"

Both otters bolted from the table and immersed their heads in an open cask of old cider. Amid the laughter from the tables, the sound of Thrugg and Thrugann sucking in massive drafts of cider to cool their burning mouths could be heard all over the orchard.

Brother Hollyberry tipped both the bowls into his own and spooned the lot down without turning a hair, his only comment being, "Hmm, this soup could do with a little more pepper. I like it good and spicy!"

Friar Bellows sat back and loosened off his waistcord. "Phew, very good, very good! I don't know which is the hardest, preparing it all or trying to eat it all. Pass me a maplecream tart, will you, Brother Hal."

The Brother broke open an oatloaf stuffed with summer salad. "Tut tut, not beginning to flag, are you, Bellows?"

The good Friar sat up straight and quaffed a beaker of mint tea. The maplecream tart disappeared rapidly, even though it was a large plate-sized one.

"Beginning to flag? Listen, my goodmouse, flagging is for young fellers like yourself. I'm one who knows how to keep up a steady pace. Cut me a wedge of that Great Hall cake, please."

Toward the bottom of the table several baby mice and young hedgehogs had secreted a sizable fruit and cream trifle under the table. They sat on the ground, eating it with their paws, out of the sight of older creatures who insisted on them using spoons, and there was trifle everywhere.

"Mmm, 's better wivvout spoons!"

"Heehee, I c'n eat it wiv all four paws. Lookit me!"

By noon most creatures had deserted the festive board and were lying beneath trees and bushes all over the orchard. Dumble and the rest of the infants were snoring loudly in a hammock that Sister Nasturtium had strung between two apple trees. Samkim and Arula joined Brother Hollyberry and Friar Bellows in the shade of a big old maple that grew in the south corner, and Hollyberry yawned and stretched as he settled down to his nap. "Well, Samkim, how are the two stoats enjoying Nameday?"

Samkim's half-open eyes were trying to follow a large bee as it droned lazily toward the flowerbeds. "Oh, those two. Would you believe it, Brother? They're still at the table eating. I'm sure they think there's going to be a famine. Huh, talk about scoff!"

"They'm woant be no gudd for 'ee games this evenin', zurr."

Arula stifled a giggle as she pointed to Friar Bellows. The fat little Friar was lying upon his back, fast asleep, snoring with his mouth wide open. A spider on its thread was directly over his mouth, hanging there. It went into his mouth and blew out again each time he inhaled and exhaled. They all laughed silently, not wanting to wake him.

"If'n Froir doant blow out 'ard enuff, 'ee'll 'ave spider pudden."

Mara and Pikkle dashed off as Sapwood shot away in the opposite direction. Ferahgo and Klitch headed the band that had come over the hill. They had lost the element of surprise, breaking into a charge when they heard Goffa shout.

The Assassin sized up the situation quickly as he breasted the hill. Immediately he called to his followers, "After the hare, get the spy—the other two are cut off!"

Running southward over the dunes, Mara and Pikkle saw to their dismay two ferrets and a fox circling in on them. Ferahgo had sent them in behind on a wide sweep to take Sapwood from the back, and now they were heading straight for the two young ones.

As they closed in, Mara felt a fury rise within her; they had been deceived by false friends. Hurriedly she breathed to Pikkle, passing him the javelin, "Leave the fox to me. You take one of the ferrets, and we'll deal with the other one together!"

The fox carried a pike. He snarled at Mara and came straight for her. Recalling Sapwood's action, she jumped to one side, swept the pike away and struck out hard with both paws. The fox was not expecting such aggression from a young female badger, and there was a resounding crack as both of Mara's forepaws met solidly along the side of his jaw. His eyes expressed surprise for a moment, then turned up until only the whites were showing, and the fox buckled and fell in a limp heap.

Meanwhile, Pikkle ran straight for the two ferrets and laid the first one low by thwacking him hard between the ears with the javelin. It did the trick wonderfully, but the force of the blow snapped the weapon in two halves.

Mara dashed in. Grabbing a pointed half, she brandished it wildly, growling in a dangerous manner, "Come on, Pikkle. Let's see if this vermin can die like a warrior!"

The ferret, who was wielding a dagger, lost his nerve completely—two angry creatures with a broken javelin were closing in on him, their eyes alight with battlefire. With a shriek of fear he dropped the dagger and ran for his life.

Mara picked up the dagger. She was breathing heavily and snarling to herself. "Try to stop me, eh? Just let's see them try!"

Pikkle's ears drooped in amazement. "Good grief, old gel. I never realized you were such a swashbucklin' warrioress!"

The young badger was trembling all over after her first experience of warlike action. "Nor did I, Pikkle, nor did I. It's a frightening thing to have the fighting blood of a badger running through your veins!"

A burst of whooping and shouting from across the dunes announced that many more of Ferahgo's army were coming.

"No time for gossipin' now, chum." Pikkle grabbed Mara's paw. "Come on, we'd best make a run for it—

there's too many for us to cope with, by the sounds of that lot!"

Together they dashed off willy-nilly across the sand-hills.

Sapwood had run off in the opposite direction, with the main pack hard on his heels. The hare Sergeant was an experienced campaigner, and he put on a turn of speed that could not be equaled by his pursuers, knowing that he could not keep running at that rate for any length of time. Glancing over his shoulder, he saw that three front-runners, all weasels, had broken away from the pack and were trying hard to catch up. Smiling grimly to himself, Sapwood dropped out of sight behind a dune, mentally gauging their approach. At exactly the right moment he sprang out in front of them, paws at the ready. Before they could stop, he had laid two of them flat, one with a superb double frontpaw volley to the nose, the other by lashing out with his long hind-legs and catching the weasel square under the chin. The third he mistimed and dealt a glancing blow to the stomach. As he turned to finish the job with a hooking leftpaw, the winded creature swung out with his curved sword and gashed Sapwood's paw heavily. The rest of the hunters were too close now, so Sapwood gave a grunt of pain and took off swiftly, ducking, bobbing and dodging as he ran.

Ferahgo and Klitch stopped running and stood together on top of a dune, Ferahgo watching the main band chasing after Sapwood.

He spat angrily into the sand. "Hellteeth! They're no match for a running hare—he could run and dodge at half that speed and those oafs would never catch him. How are the others doing?"

Klitch stood on tip-paw, scouring the dunes in the other direction. "I can't see them anywhere. They should be able to catch 'em. There's enough of ours chasing those two."

Ferahgo slumped down and began thrusting his skinning knife into the ground in high bad temper. "It's like I've always said, if you want anything doing then do it yourself, don't rely on others. Fools and clods!"

Klitch curled his lip scornfully. "I did all the spying, me and Goffa. We brought them here—all you had to do was surround them."

"You young whelp!" Ferahgo stood up, leveling his knife meaningly. "Are you saying that it was me who let them escape?"

Klitch's sword appeared swiftly; his eyes were hard as blue ice. "I'm just stating the facts, old one!"

The Assassin quivered with rage. He twirled his knife so that he was holding it in a throwing position. "Old one, eh!"

Klitch moved forward, closing in so that the chance of a knife-throw was ruined, his sword point virtually touching Ferahgo's throat. "Aye, old one—and you won't live to be much older if you try anything with that frog-sticker!"

Two pairs of angry challenging blue eyes faced each other for a moment, then Ferahgo snarled and sheathed his blade. "Aaah, what's the use of fighting between ourselves? Where's the profit in that? All our hiding and spying is blown now, so we'll muster the whole horde and march on Salamandastron tonight!"

10

The Redwallers had deserted the feasting table, leaving the two gluttonous stoats, who were loath to leave food uneaten.

"Wahoo, I'm burstin', mucker. Toss me another cob o' that Great Wall cake!"

A half-finished apple turnover fell from Dingeye's mouth as he shoved the remnants of the Great Hall cake in Thura's direction. He belched loudly and poured October ale into his mouth from an oversized jug. "Huh, you're burstin'? Lookit me, stoat! Aaaawww me stummick's like a big bass drum. 'Ow we're goin' ter manage all this scoff atween us is a mystery!"

Cramming the cake into his mouth, Thura reached for a flagon of old blackcurrant wine. "It's our pore upbringin', I tell yer. I can't stop eatin'. 'Ere, I wonder wot Ferahgo'd say if 'e c'd see us now, mucker!"

Dingeye choked on his drink, spraying October ale across the table as he seized another vegetable pastie. "Dontchew dare mention that name! Waddya wanna do, bring bad luck on the pair of us? Don't even think of that blue-eyed villain. Any'ow, stop gabbin' an keep scoffin', mucker. We gotta finish all this lot yet!"

Thura massaged his swollen stomach as he thrust a

ladle into a bowl of meadowcream. "Waaaaw, it's torture, mucker, plain ol' torture!" Sloshing the meadowcream over several redcurrant muffins, he dug his paws into the mixture and continued eating.

"Yer right, it's orful, wicked an' orful." Dingeye dunked the pastie into a bowl of trifle. "Ooever our mothers was, they shouldn't never 'ave brought us up in starvation an' poverty. Life's crool when yer can't stop scoffin', ain't it."

Equipment for the evening games was being set up on the west lawn. Targets, poles, ropes, hoops and other sporting paraphernalia were laid on the pitches where the games would take place. Arula and Samkim were helping Tudd Spinney to knock quoit pegs into the ground when Mrs. Faith Spinney came bustling over, shaking her head with worry and concern.

"Mercy me, they two stoats is still eatin'. You should see 'em, the dreadful gluttons. I've tried stoppin' 'em twice, but they just ignores me. Do somethin', Tudd, afore they kills themselves wi' overfeedin'!"

A party headed by Thrugg strode round to the orchard. He wagged a paw at Arula and Samkim. "Shirkin' yore duty, mateys? Abbess said you was responsible fer those two rascals. Not ter worry, though. Me an' Thruggann will scupper 'em!"

Dingeye and Thura were moaning pitifully, while still pushing food down their overgorged mouths.

"Aaaaoooow! Reach that cheese fer me, mucker!"

"Phwaaaw! It's agony tryin' ter finish all this pie an' custid!"

With a sweep of his paw, Thrugg cleared the remaining food out of their reach, and Thruggann grabbed them by the ears as they strove to climb onto the table.

Bremmun closed his eyes in disgust at the sight of the two bloated stoats. "You stupid greedy beasts, have you not got a grain of sense between you? Remove them to the Infirmary, please."

"Bless yer, kind sir, it's poverty's done this fer us. Aaaaah, me stummick! Don't carry me like that, marm, I beg yer!"

Thrugann slung Dingeye across her shoulders. Thura belched and pleaded with Thrugg as he was treated likewise.

"Don't take us to the 'Firmary, sir. Be a good riverdog an' leave us 'ere ter die peaceful like. Owooo me achin' guts!"

Brother Hollyberry patted them sympathetically. "There there, you can both have a nice lie-down on two soft beds—after I've physicked you, of course."

Two dismayed stoat faces spoke as one. "Fizzicked?"

"Aye, physicked." Hollyberry grinned mischievously. "I've got a compound there made from wild garlic, slippery elm bark, bitter aloe root and squashed dockleaf mixed with nettlejuice and blackweed compound. Two large ladlefuls each and you'll be right as rain!"

"Yaghabarragaroo, 'elp! Oh mercy, sir!"

Sister Nasturtium winked at Samkim. "Oh, I don't know if two large ladlefuls will be enough—by the condition of these poor creatures I'd say three!"

Thrugg kicked open the Infirmary door. "Three it is, then, marm. You knows best. Tudd, Bremmun, you sit on their back paws, me an' Thrugann'll hold the front paws. Samkim, Arula, pinch their noses tight so they opens their mouths proper."

"Yowhooo! Murderers! 'Ave pity, kind Redhallers. 'Elp!"

Hollyberry topped up a ladle with the foul-smelling medicine. "Hush now, my little gluttons. One more shout out of either of you and I'll double the dose!"

The games commenced just before twilight. Samkim

and Arula started off the proceedings by winning the three-pawed race in fine style. There was much laughter and merriment at some of the elder Brothers and Sisters pillowfighting while perched upon a greased pole. The Abbess and Bremmun, who had always excelled at quoits, were amazed at the skill of Baby Dumble—he could throw a quoit more accurately than any grown Abbeydweller and amassed several prizes. Tudd Spinney carried off the honors on the croquet lawn, using his walking stick in place of a mallet. Turzel and Blossom, the two small mousemaids, teamed up with Thrugann to win the relay race around the Abbey grounds, while Friar Bellows and Brother Hal beat all comers at the acorn and stick high-batting contest.

The games were going full swing when Foremole held up a paw, sniffing the air. "Yurr, et smells loik thunner an' loitenen be due!"

Bremmun shook his head. "No, it's only nighttime arriving."

"Nay, nay, lissen 'ee Maister Bremm'n!"

The distant rumble of thunder proved Foremole's instinct correct. On the still-warm evening air a heaviness began to settle, and over to the east the sky lit up in a flash across the treetops of Mossflower. The little ones threw up their paws and began crying, but Sister Nasturtium cheered them up with the suggestion of indoor games in Great Hall.

Faith Spinney seconded the idea. "Come on now, Redwallers. Gather all this sporty gear up and take it to Great Hall. I'll see if I can manage to prepare some liddle goodies for supper—hot honey 'n' nutdip an' cold strawb'rry cordial from the cellars. 'Ow's that?"

The young ones raised a cheer and began collecting the equipment. Samkim and Arula were about to carry in the bows and arrows from an archery butt that had been set up when Bremmun gave them both a stern glance.

"Remember what I said about bows and arrows, you two? Best leave them to me and keep temptation away from your paws. Get that big tug of war rope inside — that'll be a help."

Thunder boomed overhead and lightning cut the sky as drops of rain big as chestnuts began spattering down.

The equipment was all indoors, and Sister Nasturtium and Abbess Vale were going about toweling small wet heads. Tudd Spinny felt in his waistcoat pockets and checked his front headspikes. "Oh, wildflowers 'n' weeds!" He tutted in annoyance. "I gone an' left my glasses on the west wallsteps. I'll get soaked goin' over there for 'em!"

Samkim stepped forward helpfully. "I'll get your glasses, Mr. Spinney. I'm already wet through from carrying sports gear in. Come on, Arula!"

The rain was warm and heavy, pouring straight down without wind or breeze to drift it. Samkim and Arula skipped across to the west wallsteps, splashing their paws in the puddles that were beginning to build up. They found the spectacles where Tudd had said they would be. Both young ones were enjoying the heavy rain, walking slowly back to the Abbey. Unafraid of thunder or lightning, they held their heads back and caught the raindrops in their open mouths. Suddenly there was a massive bang of thunder overhead, a long bright bolt of lightning struck the weathervane on the Abbey roof, and the entire scene lit up with an eerie light. Samkim and Arula stared up at the high roof in awe as they walked toward the Abbey.

"Gosh! Did you see that, Arula?"

"Boi ecky oi did. 'Twere a big un aroight, Sankin!"

There followed a whirring noise overhead. Fearing it was more lightning, Arula threw herself flat, paws covering her head. Samkim shut his eyes tight as something zipped by him.

Sssshhfffttt!

Close by his side a sword had buried itself half its bladelength in the wet lawn. He gasped with shock.

Arula risked a glimpse through her digging claws. "Wot whurr et, more lightenen?"

Samkim tugged the blade free. "It was this. Look, Arula!"

From the red pommel stone to the tight black leather-bound handle and stout silver crosstree hilt, the rain ran down the razor-sharp edges, through the runneled blood channel to a pointed tip keen as a midwinter blizzard. They stared at the sword in awe. It glittered and shone in the downpour, reflecting a lightning bolt over the threshold in a shimmering gleam of whitefire. Samkim held it flat across both his paws.

"The sword of Martin the Warrior!"

Mara and Pikkle heard the thunder rolling in the east as they ran staggering and panting into the twilit dunes. The troops of Ferahgo were still after them. They had spent a long and breathless afternoon being pursued, sometimes hiding among the sandhills for a short breather, other times running flat out across the hill-tops, with their pursuers in plain sight. Mara stumbled and fell, gasping for breath, and Pikkle tried pulling her upright.

"No . . ." She pushed him away. "You go on. . . . Can't run any more. . . . Hare can make it. . . . You go Pikkle . . . please!"

Pikkle stood, shaking his head, his narrow chest heaving. "Not the done thing, old sport. 'Fraid you're stuck with me, wot!"

Then the rain started, slowly at first, but rapidly increasing to a full-fledged downpour. Thunder boomed overhead and lightning flashed across the dunes.

Pikkle looked about. Brushing rainwater from his

eyes, he grinned. "What ho, here's a bit of a chance. See that high straight dune yonder? Look, there's a sort of a thingummy, a tiny scoop-out like a cave at the top. See, that one with the long grass hangin' down over it!" Exerting all his strength, he pulled Mara upright. "Nothin' t' lose, old badgerbonce. Come on!"

They skirted the hill and climbed it from the opposite side where it was not so sheer. The rain lashed and battered at the pair as they crawled over the top and swung down into the small hole at the top of the dune, little more than a ledge with a grass fringe hanging in front of it. Quickly they scooped it deeper until they were able to lie flat and regain their breath, while peering out through the grass curtain in front of them. The deluge had washed out all trace of their pawprints, and night was gathering. Soon they could make out shapes and hear the voices of their hunters as they scoured the ground below.

"Did yer see 'em go this way, Sickear?"

"'Course I did. I told yer."

"Well, where are they now?"

"Search me. This rain's messed everythin' up."

"Ferahgo's goin' to be mad if we go back without 'em."

"Don't remind me. Come on, you lot. Spread out an' get lookin'."

"I'm soaked through!"

"Aaahh, pore ol' you. An' I suppose we're all bone dry? Idiot!"

"Couldn't we make torches to search with? It's dark now."

"What're you goin' to make torches with, nit'ead? Soakin' wet grass, an' who's got tinder an' flint? Not me!"

"Look, why don't you two stop jawin' like ol' frog-wives an' start searchin'?"

In their hide-out the two fugitives were snug and dry.

Pikkle yawned quietly and whispered to Mara. "Well, they won't find us tonight. I'm goin' to take forty winks. Wake me later an' I'll keep sentry. All right?"

Mara nodded and settled down to watch Ferahgo's creatures.

After a while they moved away, rebuking Sickear for bad eyesight and false information. Mara listened to their voices as they faded into the dark and rain of the night.

"Hey, Migroo, they might've gone this way."

"Yah, it's too dark 'n' wet to find anythin' tonight."

"Tell that to the Assassin or that sly little whelp 'e calls son. Just keep searchin', Dewnose. Them's the orders!"

The rumbling of Pikkle Ffolger's stomach wakened him, and he adjusted cramped limbs as he peered through the overhanging grass fringe into the blackness.

"By the fur, I'm famished. Have they gone yet?"

Mara plucked a blade of grass and nibbled on it. "They're well gone. Why don't you try to forget your appetite and go back to sleep? There's not much else we can do in our present position."

Pikkle groaned. His stomach gurgled like streamwater traveling over stones. Mara ruffled his ears sympathetically. "We'll find food when it gets light. You get some shuteye, chum. Go on, I'll keep watch—I'm still wide awake."

Kicking out sand to make more space, Pikkle settled down rather grumpily. After a while Mara could tell by his steady breathing that he had dropped off. She rested her chin in her paws and mentally summed up their plight. They were hunted creatures in strange country, their only protection a hole in the side of a hill. As for weaponry, they were slightly better off, but not much: a broken javelin and an old dagger. Food and water were nonexistent. The rain and the night had provided cover for them both, but she found herself longing for daylight and warm sun. Had Sergeant Sapwood escaped? She fervently hoped that he had. He could carry back news of their predicament to Salamandastron. No! She was never going back there. Mara imagined the righteous justification of Urthstripe and some of the elder hares. Had they not told her? Had she not been warned about vermin? Was she not a foolish young creature?

No, definitely no! But suppose Sapwood had been captured? It would be her duty to get back to the mountain and warn them of the impending menace.

The young badger maid cudgeled her brains weighing up the probabilities of their next move. She felt responsible for Pikkle; he had deserted the mountain with her, his loyalty and friendship were beyond question, and no harm could befall him because of her. Gradually her eyelids began to droop. She blinked half-heartedly, welcoming the approach of slumber.

A rustling noise in the grass overhead caused her to come alert. Suddenly there was a malignant hissing noise and a narrow reptilian head poked its way into the hole, eyes aglitter and tongue snaking out venomously. Mara's paw felt about madly for the dagger as she came fully awake yelling, "Pikkle! Wake up, Pikkle!"

11

All activity within Great Hall had ceased. Redwallers crowded around the long table, eager to catch a glimpse of the legendary weapon. Brother Hollyberry reverently dried it with a soft cloth, then it lay on the tabletop, winking and shining in the lamplight. Outside, the thunder rolled off into the distance, and rain was still pattering thickly against the doors and windowpanes.

Tudd Spinney donned his spectacles and peered closely at the weapon. "The sword of Martin the Warrior! It could be naught else!"

Samkim and Arula had repeated the story of the finding several times over. Samkim could not resist touching the red pommel stone on the swordhandle as he repeated Tudd's words, "The sword of Martin the Warrior!"

Brother Hollyberry took Samkim's face in both paws and stared into the young squirrel's eyes. "And you say it fell from the skies? Are you sure, young un? This isn't just some piece of mischief you are dreaming up, is it?"

"No, Brother, honest! Arula, tell him!"

"Oh, aye, zurr. Sanken doant be a-tellen whoppers. Et be true."

"Well, I for one find it all pretty hard to swallow."

Bremmun snorted. "Granted it is a beautiful sword and it might even be the very one that belonged to Martin, but swords don't just fall out of the sky like rain. There's more to all this, I'm sure. Listen, Samkim young fellow, if this turns out to be some kind of joke, tidying the Infirmary up a bit will be nothing compared to the penalty I'll impose on you—and you, too, Arula!"

"Hold hard a moment, Bremmun, before you say something that you'll regret later. I believe Samkim!" Sister Nasturtium stepped forward, her normally jolly face stern as she placed a paw upon Samkim's shoulder. "I think Martin the Warrior is making his presence felt in our Abbey. Lately I have been saying strange poems and singing songs that I have never even heard before—most of you have heard me. If the spirit of Redwall is trying to tell us something, then the least we can do is listen!"

Abbess Vale lifted her gaze from the shining weapon. "I agree with you, Sister. Brother Hal, as Abbey Recorder and Historian I want you to examine the past records of Redwall. There are many lessons to be learned from the past, and I have no doubt that the old writings will provide a clue to tonight's strange events. You may start first thing tomorrow morning. Meanwhile, we shall lay the sword in front of our great tapestry, close to the picture of Martin. As for the Nameday celebrations, it is getting rather late, I suggest we abandon the indoor games . . ."

A wail of protest arose from the young ones, but the Abbess silenced them with a wave of her paw as she continued, "Tomorrow the weather will most likely be fine, so the games can be held outdoors all day. Is that a satisfactory solution?"

The wailing was quickly replaced by shouts of joy.

Thrugg slapped his rudderlike tail upon the floor. "Righto, me 'earties. Off to your bunks an' get snorin'!"

Brother Hal felt the furrow on his head that Samkim's

arrow had made some time before. He smiled ruefully and caught Samkim and Arula as they passed on their way upstairs. "You young rogues! Never mind, I'll clear up all this mystery for you. I'm going straightaway to my study to take a delve into my records, and I'll work through the night if I have to. Don't worry now. Those ancient scrolls should provide an answer by morning, then you can concentrate on the Nameday games tomorrow. How's that?"

"Thanks, Brother Hal, you're a sport!" Samkim shook him energetically by the paw.

"Aye, thankee, zurr. Et'll stop Bremm'n a-shouten at us'ns."

Brother Hal smiled at them as they scampered off to the dormitory. "Good night, young uns!"

Dingeye woke shortly before dawn. He was pleasantly surprised to find himself feeling quite chipper. Leaning over, he shook Thura. "Hoi, mucker. Are you all right?"

Thura sat up and felt his stomach, then checked his head.

"By the 'ellteeth, mucker, I feels like a newborn stoat!"

Brother Hollyberry muttered in slumber and settled deeper into his armchair. Dingeye held up a cautionary paw. "Ssshh! We don't want ter wake ol' sleepychops up. Come on, let's get out o' this Affirmary."

Silently the two stoats padded out and latched the door carefully. It was quite dark as they descended the stairs. Dingeye was still struck with wonderment at their well-being. "I tell yer, mucker, that fizzick stuff tasted rotten but it's made me feel great. I can't wait till brekkfist to eat some more. That ol' 'Ollyberry sure knows 'is stuff!"

Thura kept a paw on the wall to guide himself down. "Aye, an' 'e tells the truth too. I'm sorry now that I called 'im a toadwallopin' ol' fibber when 'e said to take the fizzick 'cos it was for our own good. 'E was right.''

From the passage at the stair bottom they could see the lights of Great Hall shining through. Dingeye giggled. ''Come on, mucker. We got the place all to ourselves while that lot's abed. Let's get us some vittles.''

The gluttonish duo invaded the nut and honey dip left out for the young ones, swigged down the strawberry cordial and munched a plate of scones they had found.

''This'll 'ave ter do us till brekkfist. Y'd think they'd leave more'n this out. No consideration somebeasts got.''

''Yeh, where's all the Redhall cake an' Octember ale?''

''You wolfed it all, pigbrain!''

''Pigbrain yerself, stoat. 'Ey, lookit all this sporty stuff lyin' about. Sly villains, they was playin' games while we was sick an' dyin' in the Affirmery.''

Dingeye grabbed some hoops and started spinning them at Thura's head. ''Hahaha, roll up an' win a prize!''

His companion retaliated, throwing quoit pegs at him.

Brother Hal sat sipping cold mint tea amid a welter of faded parchments and yellowed scrolls. He scratched at the furrow in his headfur as he scanned a barkpaper manuscript from the time when old Abbot Saxtus was a young mouse.

The sword of Martin the Warrior has been returned to its rightful home, Redwall Abbey. Today Rufe Brushtail, our champion climbing squirrel, took the weapon and climbed to the very point of the Abbey roof. There he has secured the sword to the north pointer of the weathervane. So will Martin's sword rest there in peace as his spirit guides our Abbey. It is my fervent hope that Redwall lead a calm and tranquil existence and that the sword never has to be brought down within my life's seasons.

Hal sat musing as he pondered over the text. "Hmm, dark night, thunder, rain, storm. . . . That's it!" He leaped up, spilling mint tea over his habit. "The big lightning bolt: Samkim said that it struck the weathervane shortly before he found the sword. Of course, the lightning blasted the sword from the weathervane, it slid down the roof and fell point first. By the fur! From what that young un says, it's a good thing he never moved a pace to the right. Falling from that height, the blade would have cleaved him in two!"

The two stoats had found the archery equipment. Disdaining the rounded targets, they took a bow apiece and began firing arrows upward at the high beamed ceiling of Great Hall. Neither was very good at archery.

"Yah, boggleyes, you can't even hit the ceilin'!"

"That's 'cos I was brought up in poverty, mucker. My ol' mum never could afford bows 'n' arrers!"

"Ho, shut up, snotnose. If you ever 'ad a mum she should've tried to shoot yer with a bow 'n' arrer for winjin' an scrinjin'."

"Wowee! Lookit that'n go. Betcher that gets the ceilin'!"

"Never! Look out, it's comin' down on us!"

They leapt out of the way, and the arrow landed quivering in the tabletop. Dingeye loosed off an arrow that barely missed Thura's ear, and he hid beneath the table.

"Wot was that for? 'Twas only an accident!"

"I'll accident you, muckmouth. I was nearly killed then!"

"That's 'cos we never 'ad proper weapons afore,

mucker. Huh, we only 'ad a rusty knife apiece when we was with Ferahgo . . ."

"Belt up, loosegob. Wot've I told yer about mentionin' that hellspawn's name? Come 'ere, I'll show yer 'ow ter fire one o' these weapons proper."

Dingeye bent the bow with both paws, Thura notched a shaft to the string and heaved back with all his might, and between them they stretched the yew-wood bow to its capacity.

"This is the way ter do it mucker," Dingeye breathed excitedly. "Now lerrit go straight. It should go right across this 'all, over the passage an' right up the stairs. Ready . . . fire!"

Brother Hal came racing down the stairs, waving the parchment as he muttered to himself triumphantly, "Ha, solved. I'll show old Bremmun that swords don't fall out of the sky with the rain. There's an explanation for everything, the records prove that. Hoho, just wait until young Samki—"

The ill-timed shaft came zipping out of the darkness and buried itself in Brother Hal's throat. He gave a small gurgling cry and fell to the floor in a limp heap.

The bow dropped from Dingeye's trembling paws. "Gwaw! Look what you've done, you thick idjit!"

Thura let go of the string, and the bow clattered to the floor. "I never done nothin', smartstoat. It was you!"

"Oh, stow the gab. It was both of us then. There! Does that make yer feel any better?"

"No. Do yer think 'e's dead?"

"Well, 'e don't look very lively lyin' there with an arrer through his gizzard, does 'e? I 'spect that'n's deader'n last autumn's leaves."

Thura found the remnant of a scone and began munching it anxiously as he watched the still form of Brother Hal. "Oooooh! What're we goin' t' do, mucker?"

Dingeye picked up the bow and tried to snap it

angrily. The strong wood withstood his puny efforts, so he flung the bow away. It landed close to Brother Hal.

"Stupid fool, couldn't 'e see we was only 'avin' a bit o' sport? Why did 'e come downstairs like that? I tell yer, mucker, the best thing we can do is get well clear of this Redhall place. It's bad luck, anyway. No one's about yet, so we c'n be gone afore they're up an' about. Grab what yer can an' foller me."

Thura was casting about. He found more scones, a pot of honey and a dish of nuts. Dingeye's urgent hiss made him look up.

"By the claw of 'ellfire an' darknight, lookit this!"

Thura's eyes went wide as he saw his companion hold up the sword. "Wow! Wotta sword! Even Ferahgo ain't got one like that!"

Dingeye was too elated to chide him for using the Assassin's name. He waved the great sword aloft. "This is treasure—riches, I tell yer. There ain't another weapon like this in . . . in . . . nowhere!"

In a very short time dawnlight was beginning to streak the eastern sky. The two stoats sneaked from the Abbey and let themselves out by a small wicker gate set in the south wall, then they dashed across the open sward and vanished into the fastnesses of Mossflower Woods.

Unfortunately Samkim was awake by the first light of day. He could not remain in bed with the thought of the previous evening's events; he had to see the sword again to reassure himself he had not been dreaming. Arula was still snoring as he tip-pawed from the dormitory and made his way downstairs. Samkim was in such a hurry that he stumbled over Brother Hal's body and fell. With a cry of horror he rolled over and leapt to his feet, only to trip and fall again. The bowstring had become tangled in his footpaws. He extricated himself and stood up, holding the bow.

Friar Bellows was up at his usual time to start preparing breakfast for the Abbeydwellers. He came bustling down the stairs and froze to a stop on the bottom step, his plump face a mask of horror. Standing in front of him was Samkim with a bow in his paws, and close by lay Brother Hal with an arrow through his throat. The Friar sat down on the stairs with a bump, his voice hoarse with disbelief. "Samkim, what have you done?"

12

Windpaw bound Sapwood's injured paw with a poultice of soothing herbs and a woven ryegrass wrapper. Urthstripe strode up and down the forge cavern like a demented beast. Though the Sergeant had told his tale several times, the badger Lord kept roaring out a steady stream of questions.

"Did they capture Mara or didn't they?"

"I don't think so, sir. I gave 'em the old runabout so's young Mara an' Pikkle could hescape 'em."

"Can't you give me a straight answer, Sergeant? Did they or didn't they! Who was their leader? How many of them are there?"

Sapwood shook his head despairingly as he glanced at Windpaw, Catkin, Starbob, Seawood and Big Oxeye. All the hares knew that Urthstripe had thrown reason to the winds. Oxeye stood between Sapwood and Urthstripe.

"Milord, I suggest y' leave Sapwood alone. Like me, he's told you all he jolly well can. Workin' yourself into a tizzy ain't goin' to help, if y' don't mind me sayin' so. We all know that before the season's much older there's goin' to be a vermin horde knockin' on our front door.

Worryin' over Mara an' shoutin' at Sapwood ain't goin' to solve that, no sir."

Urthstripe stopped pacing and faced Oxeye. Big as he was, the fighting hare quailed slightly under the brooding gaze of Urthstripe the Strong. But he had no need to worry—the badger Lord patted his paw lightly.

"Thank you, Oxeye. You are right. Sapwood old friend, how's your paw coming along?"

"Bandage or no bandage, Hi can still punch me weight, sir."

Urthstripe nodded approvingly. "Good. Now let's get things organized. Oxeye, Starbob, Catkin, take your patrols and seal up all entrances except the front. Windpaw, Seawood, check that the mountain is fully provisioned and see to the water-barrel levels. Sapwood, you come with me. We'll get together some weaponry to provide a warm reception for whatever scum come visiting. I hope that Klitch and his pal are among them—I'd enjoy meeting them again."

So the fortress of Salamandastron started gearing itself up for war.

Ferahgo was readying his horde to march upon Salamandastron by midmorning of the next day. Forgrin the fox and Raptail the rat were seeing to their weapons. Forgrin was using a flat rock to grind a new point upon his long rapier, Raptail was fletching his arrows with leaf flights. As they worked, the two creatures conversed in low tones, keeping silent whenever Ferahgo or Klitch was near.

"D'you know why we're attackin' this badger mountain, mate? I mean, what's the real reason behind it?"

"Yer not supposed to ask that, Forgrin. The Chief sez it'd make a good fortress for us ter use as a base."

The fox licked his paw and tested the point of his rapier. "Huh, he must think we're all as dimwitted as Migroo. A fortress to use as a base, my fangs! That brat of his, Klitch, and his pal Goffa, and that whinin' searat Sickear, they seem ter know somethin' we don't."

Raptail peered down an arrowshaft, checking its straightness. "Aye, that's the lot of a soldier, mate: carry out orders and don't ask questions. But I'm tellin' yer this, I don't fancy gettin' slain in battle fer summat I don't know about!"

"Same 'ere, mate. Though just atwixt you 'n' me, I've kept me lugs ter the ground and I thinks there's some kinda treasure at the bottom o' this. . . . Stow it, 'ere comes trouble!"

Ferahgo and Klitch walked by, and the two soldiers kept their heads down, working busily at their weapons. The Assassin flashed a dangerous smile and nodded his approval. Klitch pawed his short sword, looking about impatiently.

"We've lost the edge of surprise. This army should have moved quicker. Urthstripe will be ready and waiting for us. Tell me, when are you going to make your move?"

Ferahgo played with the gold badger medal hanging around his neck. "Patience, my young backstabber, patience. When Migroo and his hunters get back, then we march."

"But why wait for Migroo and the others? We could leave signs for them to follow."

Ferahgo seated himself on a rock and stared upward, his eyes becoming bluer as they reflected the clear skies above. "What a beautiful summer morning after last night's heavy storm. My son, do you see how wonderfully clear the air is? I like to clear the air before I do anything. Have you noticed a few grumblings and rumblings amongst my army of Corpsemakers? I have. When Migroo returns with the rest, depending on whether or not he has captives with him, I'll use him as a shining example, or a warning. Either way, I'll instill

100

some loyalty into those who murmur behind my back. You'll see."

"Hah, so you say, old one!" Klitch snorted and stalked off moodily.

Ferahgo smiled mockingly as he called after him, "With age comes wisdom. Hotheads are ten for a crust, young one."

At high noon a stoat named Doghead called down from the lookout post, "Migroo an' the huntin' gang comin' in from the south, master!"

Ferahgo tapped Goffa lightly on the side of his heavily swollen face. The ferret winced and cringed. "Laid out by an unarmed hare, eh. You're a bright one. Get Klitch and muster the army together for a march."

By the time Migroo and his hunters reached camp, the entire horde was gathered in one place among the rocks. Ferahgo stood apart from them, his eyes as dangerous as thin blue ice on a deep spring lake.

"Ho there, Migroo. Where've you been?"

The stoat was not the brainiest of creatures. He stood scratching his head as he pondered the odd question. "Chasin' the badger an' the hare, Chief, like you told us to."

Ferahgo smiled indulgently. He was enjoying this. "No no, you've got it wrong, Migroo. I never said chase them. I said capture them and bring them back here. Right?"

The stoat was beginning to feel nervous. He swallowed hard. "That's right, Chief—catcher 'em an' bring them back 'ere, that's wot you said."

The Assassin's smile swept around the watching horde. He let the tension build a little, then shrugged carelessly. "Well, I don't see a badger and a hare, do you, Migroo?"

The stoat backed off, holding out his paws pleadingly. "Arr now, Chief, we wasn't to blame. We tracked

101

'em arf the day an' all night through the dunes in the dark an' the storm. We tried, Chief, 'onest we did, but they just vanished in the night when the rain was 'eavy! Eeeeyahhhh!''

Ferahgo's skinning knife had moved like lightning. Migroo was writhing on the ground, clutching the side of his head. The Warlord wiped his blade on Migroo as he stepped over him. When he spoke to the horde he did not raise his voice, but everybeast heard each word distinctly.

"When I give an order I expect it to be carried out. Migroo here was lucky: he only lost an ear. The next one who disobeys me will lose his head. Oh, I know some of you think Ferahgo is getting old. . . ." Here he winked at Klitch. "Or Ferahgo is losing his grip. Some of you even think Ferahgo is going deaf, so you gossip behind his back. . . ." Ferahgo smiled at Forgrin and Raptail; they blanched visibly as he continued.

"Let me tell you, Corpsemakers, because who knows about me better than myself? I am Ferahgo the Assassin, scourge of all the Southwest Lands, or wherever I choose to set my claw. I was murdering and skinning when most of you were milk-slopping babes. Nobeast can outsmart, outfight or outwit me! Now I am leading you against a mountain fortress to do what you do best, fight! And fight you will, and bleed and die if I say so! You will either end up wealthy and well-fed, or cursing the day you were born . . ."

The Assassin leapt onto a nearby rock and twirled his daggers until they flashed like wheels of light in the sun. His blue eyes twinkled like brilliant twin pits of evil as he threw back his head and roared.

"Death to the enemies of Ferahgo!"

Spears, lances, knives, swords, pikes and bows sprang into the air as the rocks resounded with a fearsome chant that ripped from the throat of each Corpsemaker.

"Fer-ah-go! Fer-ah-go! Death! Death! Fer-ah-go!!!"

As the evil reptilian head pushed its way into the tiny cave Mara searched frantically for the dagger but could not find it. Pikkle Ffolger did. Wakened by Mara's shout, the startled hare rolled onto the dagger and its point stuck sharply into his rear. With an agonized yell Pikkle leaped forward, butting into the reptile's head. It fell backwards with Pikkle clinging to its neck. Locked together, both creatures tumbled out of the cave. Yelling, hissing, snarling and spitting, they half-fell half-rolled down the steep side of the high dune. Throwing caution to the winds, Mara jumped after Pikkle. She landed with a thud in the sand below and was immediately assailed by the tail of a yellow-bellied sand lizard. The creature had its claws locked in Pikkle's fur, while the young hare had it in a good headlock. Neither would release their grip, as they shouted and snarled fiercely at each other.

"Wah! Lemmego, you slimy old reptile."

"Gitcha paws off, rabbit, ksss!"

"Rabbit y'self. You let me go an' I'll let you go!"

"Kkssss! Nah nah, you leggo first. Kksss!"

"Fat chance, scalybonce. You leggo first then I will!"

Mara solved the problem by giving the lizard's tail a sharp tug. To her horror, it came off in her paws. Immediately the creature released Pikkle. As it let go, the lizard turned on Mara and spat at her.

"Kkkkssssss! Look watcha done now, stupid stripedog!"

Mara's quick temper rose. She dealt the lizard a blow that sent it spinning head over claw and flung its tail after it. "Don't you dare spit at me, you filthy reptile! And just call me stripedog once more and I'll give you a few stripes to think about. Who in the name of fur do you think you are?"

The lizard sat up, exposing its bright yellow stomach.

Its bottom lip began to quiver as it picked up its severed tail. "Kksss! Kaahaa! Just looka that, me bestest tail I've ever growed. Kksss! Tooka me seasins t' grow that. Now looka wotcha did. Kaahaakkssss!"

Neither Mara nor Pikkle could feel any sympathy for the lizard.

Pikkle wagged a stern paw at it. "Serves y' right, bally ol' butterbelly. Frightenin' us out of our cave like that!"

Tears popped from the reptile's eyes as it shook the severed tail at them. "Jawot? Kksss, thatsa mine cave. I duggen it. Kksss! Who said a rabbit anna stripe . . . badgerer could use it? Kksss!"

Pikkle advanced a pace, his ears indignantly erect. "Less of the rabbit, chum, or I'll show you what a doubleback harekick looks like!"

Mara intervened to prevent further grappling. "Look, I'm sorry, we didn't know the cave was yours. We only intended spending the night there to shake off our pursuers. You probably saw them searching for us. You should be grateful really, we dug it around a bit and widened it out for you. By the way, my name is Mara and this is Pikkle Ffolger."

The sand lizard sat sulking, rubbing its tail stump. "Call-a me Swinkee. Not pleaseter meetcher tho'. Kkssss! Ruint me cave—'s far too big fer me now. Kaahaa!"

Pikkle sat down alongside the reptile. "Oh, stop blubberin', Stinkee, or whatever y' name is. We'll make the cave smaller if that'll please you, old lad. I say, you don't happen to have a bite of breakfast around, do you?"

Swinkee began scooping out a hollow to bury his beloved tail, all the time muttering and hissing, "Kssss! Breffist be a fatchance round 'ere, kaahaa. Take me seasins an' seasins ter grow more tail likea that one. Kssss!"

Mara tried reasoning with him. "Look, we're completely lost. Do you know Salamandastron, the big badger mountain on the shore? If you do and you could guide us there, we'll give you as much breakfast as you like."

"Kksssss, swampflies, marshworms, good breffist for Swinkee." The sand lizard shot his tongue in and out several times. "Kkssss, I take-a you there for lotsa those. I know mountain."

Pikkle nudged Mara as he addressed the lizard confidently: "Good enough, old sport, wot? We've got loads of jolly old marshflies an' swampworms at the mountain. I expect we could rustle you up a sackful or two. How d'you like 'em, Stinkee—fried, boiled or done up in a salad with lettuce an' whatnot?"

Swinkee pulled a face as he stood up, dusting himself off. "Kksss, not boila fry, lizard like 'em alive so's theya wriggle an' wiggle inna mouth, kkssss, mmmmmm! Folla me!"

The day rose hot and bright over the dune country as they trekked between interminable sandhills behind the lizard, completely baffled at the direction in which they were traveling.

"Pikkle, are you sure this creature is guiding us back home?" Mara kept her voice low.

The hare tore up dandelions by the roots. Passing some to Mara, he munched steadily, spitting out the sandy grit. "Who knows, old gel. We're at his mercy really. He could be leading us any ballywhere. S'pose we'll just have to rely on his greed and the promise of two bagfuls of squigglies. Yuk!"

At midday they halted. Digging in a damp patch of sand produced a small muddy pool at which they drank gratefully. Mara yawned mightily and stretched. It was peaceful and pleasantly warm where they had stopped.

"Whooohuuuh! I hardly slept a wink last night. What about you, Pikkle? Are you tired too?"

"Absoballylutely whacked out, chum. I could sleep on a prickle."

Swinkee stretched himself luxuriously in the sand. "Kksss, you inna my cave last a night. I didn' sleep, kksss. Bester we sleepnow, longways to go yet. Kksssnnrrrr!"

"Well, beat my bush! Look at old Stinkee, he's snorin'." Pikkle gnawed the last of the dandelion roots.

Mara patted a hollow in the sand and laid her head down. "Good idea, I'd say. Give me a shake if you wake first, Pikkle."

An hour had gone by. Pikkle and Mara curled up in the soft sand, sleeping peacefully through the high golden afternoon without as much as a breeze to disturb them. Swinkee's eye popped open and he watched them for a moment. Assuring himself that they were sleeping soundly, he slid away, hissing to himself, "Kksss, pulla my tail off, hit Swinkee, sleep inna my cave, rabbit 'n' stripedog tella me lies 'bout swampflies. I do show 'em, theya mess with lizard nomore, kksss!"

13

The beauty of the soft golden summer morning following the previous night's storm was lost on the inhabitants of Redwall Abbey. Nameday sports had been canceled and sadness and shock hung like a shroud over everything. Samkim sat alone in the Infirmary, numb with disbelief. Was poor Brother Hal actually dead? Who had done the awful deed? The young squirrel knew nothing of what went on outside the Infirmary, as he had been hastily escorted up there by Friar Bellows and Abbess Vale immediately after being discovered by the Brother's body, bow in paw. They had made him promise to stay put and speak to nobeast until investigations were under way.

While the Redwallers took their breakfast outside on the lawn, a meeting was convened in Cavern Hole. In the smaller, more intimate surrounding of the room that was separated from Great Hall by a downward flight of steps, the Abbess, Foremole, Hollyberry, Bremmun and Nasturtium gathered to discuss events. Bremmun pushed away his untouched breakfast.

"Friends, it staggers belief: Brother Hal dead! Where is young Samkim now?"

Abbess Vale held up a paw for silence. "He is confined to the Infirmary. Now, Bremmun, we are all as shocked and saddened by Hal's death as you are, but please let us not say anything in haste or jump to conclusions that we may be sorry about later. So, has anybeast got something to tell us that we do not already know—and let me add, we know little or nothing of what took place, except that poor Hal is no longer with us."

Sister Nasturtium spoke up. "I cannot contribute any evidence, Mother Abbess, but I must say what I feel in my heart. I do not think that there is a single Redwaller who believes that Samkim would be so careless as to endanger another's life. It would be horrible to even think of accusing him."

The Abbess folded her paws into wide habit sleeves. "I agree with you, Sister, and no one has accused him yet."

Bremmun disagreed. "Friar Bellows told me that when he found Samkim standing over Hal with a bow in his paws he said to him, 'Samkim, what have you done?' "

Brother Hollyberry interrupted Bremmun. "Aye, and the young un didn't say a word. It was as if he was struck dumb by the shock of it all. But I have something to tell that may throw some light on things. Those two stoats, Dingeye and Thura—has anybeast seen them this morning, because they weren't in their beds when I woke up."

Foremole stood up decisively. "Hurr, then you'm guddbeasts stay yurr whoil oi go'n foind 'em. May'ap they do know sumthern."

"Vermin!" Bremmun ground his teeth aloud.

The Abbess rapped the tabletop sharply. "Bremmun, there you go again. I can see you are ready to condemn Dingeye and Thura without any proof or evidence. This must stop instantly. Redwall has a reputation for goodwill, justice and fair play. We are here to uphold it!"

Bremmun made a shamefaced apology. To save him further embarrassment, Hollyberry opened a parchment upon the table. "Friar Bellows gave me this. It was in Brother Hal's paw."

They read the record written down long seasons ago and by simple process of deduction came to the same conclusion that Hal had.

Nasturtium spoke for them all. "Well, now we know how the sword of Martin was found by Samkim—the lightning tore it from the weathervane and it fell to earth. To what purpose, I wonder?"

Foremole came trundling back in, shaking his head. "Everybeast be a-searchen for they stoaters, but yurr this. Marthen's gurt swoard be gone too. Oi 'spect enfurmation any moment naow."

Bremmun's angry voice broke the shocked silence. "The great sword of Martin the Warrior gone? Those filthy thieving vermin! They'll pay dearly for this when we lay paws on 'em. Why, I'd like to . . ."

Indignant voices joined the squirrel until the Abbess rapped the tabletop sharply to restore order.

"Silence, please." She held up a paw. "We won't get anywhere shouting and threatening."

There was a knock upon the door and Tudd Spinney entered. "Mornin' to ye all. Sorry I can't say good mornin', 'cos it's not. Foremole, did you check all the wallgate locks last night?"

Foremole nodded vigorously. "Oi allus do, maister, wi'out fail."

Tudd shook his walking stick. "I knew ye did, 'cos you're a good 'n' thorough feller. Well, I've just checked the wallgates an' the east one is unlocked!"

In the silence that followed, Foremole ticked off further information on his paws. "Burr hurr, an' food fer young uns is gone from Gurt 'All, an' thurr be arrers

109

a-sticken in table an' sporty 'quipment tossed all o'er the place."

Abbess Vale stood up. "As soon as we have laid Brother Hal to rest in the grounds, we will organize a party to search for the stoats and bring them back here! Now I must go straightaway to Samkim to tell he has nothing to reproach himself for. He'll need some comforting after the death of poor Hal."

But Arula had been listening at the keyhole and was already on her way to the Infirmary.

The midmorning sun shone down brightly on a sad little ceremony in the grounds of Redwall Abbey. Brother Hal was laid to his final rest amid much mourning. There were wreaths and posies of wild flowers and small tokens from his friends. Thrugann reverently placed a small quill pen in tribute to the Recorder of the Abbey, and Baby Dumble put his favorite straw mousedoll alongside it on the neat heap of earth surrounded by brightly colored pebbles. Mrs. Faith Spinney recited a few lines:

"Your seasons have run their course, old friend.
In your goodlife we were proud to take part,
But in springtimes unborn and summers to come,
You will live in each Redwaller's heart."

While the ceremony took place at the west lawn, a rope snaked downward from a first-floor window at the east side of the Abbey building. Samkim and Arula were down on the ground in a twinkling and running for the east wallgate. Beside a haversack of provisions apiece, Samkim carried a quiver of arrows and the bow that had fired the shaft which struck Brother Hal down. Arula had a big pruning knife and a sling with a pouch of pebbles. They opened the small wallgate quickly and let themselves out into the leafy depths of Mossflower Woods.

After the ceremony, Brother Hollyberry and the Abbess made their way up to the Infirmary. The Abbess dried her eyes on a spotted kerchief.

"Oh, Brother, I can understand how poor Samkim was too upset to attend Brother Hal's last resting. Well, maybe it will be some consolation to him that we've recommended his name to Thrugg as a member of the search party for those two stoats."

The Infirmary door was wide open. Hollyberry entered, looked around the empty room and picked up a pillowcase with a badly scrawled charcoal message written on it:

"The stoats are the ones what did it. We will fetch them back and the sword too. Tell Friar Bellows it was not me. Do not worry, me and Arula will be all right. *Samkim.*"

The Abbess produced a kerchief and wiped her eyes. "Hollyberry, they may be in danger, we cannot let them go alone."

The old Infirmary keeper took the kerchief and dried Vale's eyes. "We have to. I feel that the sword of Martin did not fall from the roof to land at Samkim's side for nothing. He is marked by destiny and the sign from our Abbey spirit. Call off the search party, Vale. Let us put our trust in two young friends and Martin the Warrior."

The sun started its inexorable descent into the horizon far out to sea. At the close of a long hot day the sky remained cloudless. Salamandastron's monolithic rock took on a somber purple aspect against the dusty fawn of the darkening shoreline.

Hares of the Long Patrol watched from the top of the

111

crater. Armed and alert, each one silently surveyed the torchlit horde advancing steadily through the dunes. Myriad pinpricks of light, like a river of stars fallen to earth, were separating in the distance like the horns of some great animal, closing in to surround the mountain.

Ferahgo the Assassin was coming to Salamandastron!

A young female hare named Pennybright swallowed nervously as she fidgeted with the string of her bow. Big Oxeye patted her gently as he passed. "Steady in the ranks there, Penny."

He moved on to another youngster, Shorebuck, who was sorting out his best slingstones. Oxeye nodded approvingly. "That's the ticket, young feller. First battle, is it?"

"Yes, sir. I've decided to choose good stones an' give a good account of m'self to those vermin."

Oxeye grinned. "Did the same m'self when I was a nipper like you."

"D'you think they'll take long gettin' here, sir?" Shorebuck tested his sling with an experimental twirl.

"Don't fret, laddie. When they do, I'll be right by your side."

Shorebuck relaxed slightly, comforted by the veteran fighter's presence. Keeping his eyes on the advancing lights, he murmured, "No sign of Lord Urthstripe yet. Where d'you suppose he is?"

"Oh, he'll be around somewheres, gettin' ready an' whatnot. Stay awake now, supper should be round any moment now. Y'don't want to miss that, wot?"

Oxeye moved on around the vantage points, murmuring encouragement, his solid presence radiating calm and good humor to the fighters of the Long Patrols.

Inside the mountain stronghold of Salamandastron passageways hewn through the living rock led off caves and chambers. Some were lit by torches, others illumi-

112

nated from window slits, giving the entire place the air of some vast primeval warren. At the end of one such corridor a large rock slab had been rolled aside, and lantern light cast a warm glow upon the smooth stone face of the chamber where Urthstripe stood. This was the place where he sought solitude when his mind was troubled. All around the walls the record and history of Salamandastron and its badger Lords was depicted in intricate carvings: Brocktree, Spearlady Gorse, Bluestripe the Wild, Ceteruler the Wise, Boar the Fighter, Sunstripe the Mace . . . they were all there. It was a place of mystery, heavy with the ages of badger lore.

Urthstripe set the lantern on a ledge and picked up a fine pointed chisel. Selecting a clear space on the flat rock wall, he began carving the likeness of himself into the stone. As he cut skillfully into the rock he reached into his forge apron and produced a pawful of herbs. These he sprinkled over the flame-heated sides of the lantern. Soon the cave was filled with a swirling gray smoke that carried with it a smell of autumnal woodlands. The badger Lord began chanting, the words forming in his mind as he gouged trancelike at the wallstone:

"Seas and lifespans, ebbing, flowing,
Past and future merge as one.
Mountain Rulers, coming, going,
Seasons future, seasons gone.
Badger Warriors from the shades
Stand beside me, guide my paw.
O wise Lords and gentle maids,
Restrain my rage, preserve our law."

Sergeant Sapwood left off stacking lances at a concealed window slit on the lower level. He accepted the bowl of hot mushroom and leek soup from a small wiry hare who carried two short swords strapped across his

113

shoulders. Together they sat on the windowledge and took supper, watching the seemingly endless torchlight procession flooding from the dunes into the moonless night.

Sapwood blew on his soup to cool it, his strong face expressionless. "Do you think they 'ope ter scare us, Thistle?"

Bart Thistledown of the Westshore Thistledowns stared languidly down his long aristocratic nose at the lights bobbing and flickering in two prongs toward the mountain. "Actually, it all looks rather pretty, doncha think, Sap. Though if I were those flippin' vermin I'd be gettin' a good night's sleep instead of paradin' round like a flock of fireflies goin' courtin'. Darnfools, if y'ask me, old fellow!"

"Cor you talk luvly, Thistle." Sapwood chuckled admiringly. "Yer a cool one, all right. Hi'll say that for ye."

Thistledown sniffed disdainfully. "Bad form t' get one's ears in an uproar over vermin, wot?"

Klitch shook his head in disapproval. "Well, if they didn't know we were coming before, they certainly know now. All these torches—it's foolish!"

Ferahgo's blue eyes twinkled in the torchlight. "They'll see us all right. I want them to. Can't you see it's a show of strength? Each of our creatures is carrying two torches, and that makes it look like double our numbers. Also, they can see the torchlights, but from this distance they don't know if we're foxes or frogs, ferrets or toads, big or small, badly or well armed. That will have them guessing and worried too. They know we're here, but they won't see us. Now watch this, my young and still wet behind the ears son."

Ferahgo gave a piercing whistle and upended both his torches in the sand, extinguishing them immediately. Every member of the horde followed his example.

All around Salamandastron the lights went out as if by magic.

"Now they know we're here, but they can't see us." Ferahgo settled down in the sand, grinning with satisfaction. "We can sleep until dawn, but they'll have to stay awake and alert."

Klitch dumped his torches head down in the sand. "I still think it's a stupid move. I've told you, these are trained fighters. They know all the tricks in the book."

Of the two weasels, Klitch was to prove right.

"Right, chaps an' chapesses, lights out an' heads down, wot!" Big Oxeye had caught on to Ferahgo's plan. As he watched from the crater top he tossed aside his sling scornfully. "Huh, they must think we came ashore in buckets, brainless buffoons! Seawood, post six sentries. The rest of you can get a bit of jolly old shuteye until dawn."

Lantern shadows flickered around the hidden cave as the badger Lord stirred his powerful frame. The smoke from the herbs had cleared away, and Urthstripe rubbed his eyes and yawned as if coming out of a deep sleep. Casting aside the chisel, he picked up the lantern and held it close to the wall, where it illuminated the fresh carvings. The badger Lord's gruff voice echoed around the cave as he translated the pictures aloud:

"Two badgers. This small one—it's my Mara, I'm sure. This other one, is it me? No, it cannot be. I have stripes, he has none."

The mountain Lord's eyes clouded over. He shook his head as half-forgotten images flitted through his mind.

"Strange, a badger without stripes. . . . Without stripes?"

He blinked, turning his attention back to the wall.

"What's this? Vermin eyes? Yes, they're the eyes of

115

vermin—two pair, probably weasel's. The round thing between them, is it the moon or the sun? No, it has carving on but I cannot see, it is too small and fine. Ah, here is a sword, the weapon of a warrior, and here am I, Urthstripe, Lord of Salamandastron."

Next to the figure of Urthstripe a few lines were written in Badger rune. He narrowed his eyes, studying them.

Faintheart shall be made strong,
But a warrior's fate for the mountain Lord.
Blue eyes brings battle ere long,
Whilst the maid comes of her own accord.
The mount shall be ruled by badger kin,
The sword shall make Mossflower free
The Abbey will take its Guardian in
Far from this rock by the sea.

Urthstripe stood tall, his brooding eyes alight with the knowledge of his own fate. He felt as though the heavy paw of destiny had touched him, but the thought of a coming war seemed to obliterate all feelings of sadness or fear.

Sapwood's voice cut into his thoughts as it boomed hollowly along the chamber passage, "It's three hours t' dawn, sir. Those vermin are all haround us, surroundin' the mountain. Everybeast is in position, waitin' on your word, shall Hi tell 'em yore comin', sir?"

The badger Lord unfastened his forge apron. "They will see me in the hour of dawn, Sergeant, and I will see them. Then we will take a look at this vermin horde in good plain morning light. Lay out my armor, helm, sword and spear!"

14

Dingeye and Thura headed south through Mossflower Woods. They had a good head start and made the most of it, knowing that once Brother Hal's body was discovered, together with the loss of the sword, pursuit by the creatures of Redwall would be inevitable. The forest was tall, green and silent, save for the rustle of leaves and trill of birdsong.

Dingeye had been forging ahead, slashing and chopping at fern and nettle with his newly acquired weapon. As midday drew near, Thura was lagging noticeably. His companion wiped the blade of the wondrous sword on his sleeve as he waited impatiently for him, calling back through the serried columns of treetrunks, "Move yerself, mucker. Cummon, stir yer stumps, stoatnose!"

Thura wiped his brow. Leaning against an oak, he breathed heavily. "I've got t' rest, Ding. Don't know wot's wrong wi' me. I feels all done in. Must've been that bath they made me take."

Dingeye sneered and took a swipe at a passing butterfly with the sword, admiring the flashing green lights as its blade glinted in the sunlight filtering through the emerald canopy. "Garn! I got bathed, too, an' it didn't 'urt me. Now get yer paws a-movin', or I'll leave yer be'ind. 'Urry up!"

Thura's face was an unhealthy grayish pallor, his limbs trembled and sweat beaded on his nosetip as he stumbled to keep up, calling out to his comrade, "Slow down, mucker. You wouldn't leave me 'ere ter be catchered by that lot from Redhall. 'Ere, carry the vittles an' I'll be able to get along a mite better."

"Carry vittles?" Dingeye pulled a lip and slashed moodily at a young rowan tree. "Huh, not likely. You took 'em, you carry 'em. I've got me paws full luggin' this 'ere sword around. Tell yer wot, though, we'll stop awhile an' 'ave lunch. That'll make less food ter carry."

Gratefully Thura let the sack of provisions drop as he collapsed in a heap at the edge of a small clearing. Dingeye immediately set about stuffing himself with honey, bread and nuts from the sack, ignoring Thura's pitiful state.

"Lissen, we can't stop 'ere too long, they'll be on our trail by now. Still, we've escaped before an' we c'n do it again. We'll stick to this forest—it's better'n flatlands, more cover."

Thura curled into a ball, shivering uncontrollably, his teeth chattering and his tail quivering fitfully. Dingeye stopped eating and prodded him.

"Hah, yer wobblin' about like a baldy beetle there. Just look at yer, mucker. Wot's the matter?"

Thura's head went up and down as he stammered a reply. "S-s-sick! I-I-I'm s-s-sick, feel b-b-b-bad!"

Instinctively Dingeye drew away from him. "Is it a fever? 'Ave yer got a fever? Huh, you look awful!"

"H-h-h-elp me!" Thura stretched out a trembling paw.

Dingeye shouldered the sack. "Oh, come on then, I'll carry the vittles. But I'm not carryin' you, stoat. I don't wanna catch no fever." He took a few paces and looked back angrily at Thura curled up on the woodland floor.

"Well, are yer comin' or aren't yer, 'cos I'm not 'angin' round 'ere waitin' for yer!"

Thura made no reply. Dingeye sniffed moodily. "All right then, you stop 'ere awhile till yer feelin' better. I won't go too fast so that y'can catch up with me."

Still receiving no reply from his companion, he set off into the forest, traveling south and slightly west, talking aloud to reassure himself. "Must be somethin' he's et, greedy ol' toad. Prob'ly catch me up ter night when 'e gets hungry again."

The trail of the two stoats was not difficult to follow. Samkim and Arula could see plainly the slashed and damaged vegetation which Dingeye had hacked at with the sword. Despite the urgency of their mission, neither of the two young ones could help noticing the beauty of Mossflower, draped in summer green and studded with small islands of color from flowering bush and shrub. Their paws made little or no sound as they padded along over the carpet of soft brown leaf loam. Samkim pointed ahead to where a strip of bark had been wantonly sliced from the trunk of a white willow, exposing the pale sapped wood beneath.

"Easy to see which way they went. Look at that."

Arula nodded. "Urr, Foremole'd tan thurr 'ides for doen that to a livin' tree. Ho urr, they'm surely two nastybeasts."

Samkim touched the trunk, noting the dampness of sap on his paw. "If we travel a little faster we may catch them up by late afternoon. They can't be too far ahead. Come on, Arula."

"No need to worry, young Redwallers, heh heh heh!"

The thin reedy voice had come from nowhere. Samkim and Arula halted, staring at the leafy screen about them.

The voice spoke again. "Worry, hurry, that's all some

119

creatures do. No time to live to a ripe old age. Look at me—I can't count the summers I've seen and I'm fit as a flea. Heh heh heh!"

Samkim fitted an arrow to his bowstring. "Show yourself!"

A bed of tall ferns stirred and a woodvole stepped into view. He was small and thin, dressed in a long smock of brown barkcloth, and his face was framed by the biggest white beard they had ever beheld on any creature—it fuzzed out like a cloud, and only his bright black eyes were visible through it. The woodvole laughed and cut a little caper. He was astonishingly agile for such an ancient creature.

"Heh heh heh! You can put the bow down. I'm not going to hurt you, Redwaller. How do I know you're a Redwaller? Easy! You talk with the accent of an Abbeydweller. I'm Furgle the Hermit. I live here all alone—always have done, can't stand the company of any creature for too long, prefer my own. I suppose you're tracking the two stoats who came by here earlier?"

"You'm seen 'em then, zurr?"

Furgle did an angry little dance around Arula. "Why can't moles ever learn to speak properly? Seen them! Of course I did, two evil smelly vermin, slashing away at my woods as if they owned them. You don't need to hurry to catch those two, though."

Samkim bowed politely to the hermit. "My name is Samkim. This is Arula. You are right, of course—we are both from Redwall Abbey. Why do you say that we have no need to hurry?"

Furgle waited until Samkim had unnotched his arrow. "Because one of them is very ill. He won't go much further. I've never been ill a day in my life. Come on then, Redwallers. I'll go along with you—I know Mossflower better than you ever will. By the oak and the ash, I'll give that stoat a piece of my mind when I meet him. How dare he go about chopping up my woodlands!"

Without further ado the woodvole set off. In a short while both Samkim and Arula were having difficulty keeping up with the energetic pace he set.

An hour's swift journey found them on the edge of a clearing.

Arula sighted Thura lying curled up. "Lookum o'er thurr. 'Ee must be the sick un!"

"Wait!" Furgle restrained them both from running over to Thura. "You can never tell with vermin. Give me an arrow, Samkim. We'll see if he's sick or shamming—better careful than careless I always say, generally to myself though."

Furgle snapped the point from the arrow and tied a pad of leaves in its place, then returned it to Samkim. "Fire that at the creature, young squirrel."

Samkim shot the shaft perfectly. It thudded against Thura's back and bounced off onto the grass. The stoat made no move.

"As I thought, he's finished." The hermit nodded knowingly.

The two young ones dashed over to the body. Furgle was right: Thura was freshly dead. Samkim rolled the stoat over. "Dead? I can't believe it. Only yesterday he was as lively as you or I."

"Humm, ee'm dead aroight. Deader'n 'ee black acorn." Arula scratched her head with a huge digging claw.

Furgle pulled them away from the body. "Don't get too close—that stoat died of some form of fever or ague. Well, it was nice meeting you, but now I must go about my business. If you are going to bury him then do it quickly, but try not to touch him. Er, sorry, there's some urgent business I must attend to. See you later. Goodbye."

121

In the twinkling of an eye he had vanished back into the depths of Mossflower. Samkim and Arula stood looking at each other, slightly disappointed at Furgle's abrupt departure.

"Burr, yon owd un doant 'ang about, do 'ee?"

Samkim shook his head. "Not the action of a true forest dweller, I'd say. Still, I suppose he had his reasons. Now, we'll bury this one and track his friend Dingeye. Huh, some friend, leaving his pal here to die like that. Can't see the sword anywhere—Dingeye must have it. Arula, where are you?"

The little molemaid was swiftly excavating a tunnel beside Thura's body. A shower of dark earth flew upwards as she dug in with powerful blunt claws. Before long she vanished into the hole, and the ground trembled and heaved alongside the dead stoat. Samkim blinked with surprise as she emerged from the ground near Thura's ears. Arula dusted herself down.

"Thurr, that be done! Jus' tip'm in with 'ee bow, Sanken."

Samkim levered the body over with his bow. It plopped onto the tunnel top and the earth gave way. Arula covered it with the earth she had pushed out from the excavation.

"Best oi c'n do fer 'ee, pore stoater, tho' 'ee'm wurra bad lot."

Though the lunch at Redwall had only been a light summer salad and some blackberry scones, Friar Bellows found himself weary and perspiring. He left the Abbey kitchens and went to sit out by the pond where it was cool. The fat mouse took off his cap and apron and mopped his brow with a dock leaf. Thrugg came over, shaking out his shrimp net.

"Avast there, ol' Bellers. No scones to bake for teatime?"

The Friar sat down rather heavily, shaking his head.

"Oh, scones. I'll get to 'em later. Very good, very g— D'you know, Thrugg, I feel terribly dizzy today."

Thrugg sat down beside him. "I 'spect it's wi' workin' around those hot ovens, matey."

"No, I never lit the ovens today. Brrrr! It's cold out here!"

The jovial otter looked at him quizzically. "Cold? It's the middle of summer, me 'eartie. I don't know as 'ow y'can say it's cold when you're all asweat."

Bellows lay back and wiped his whiskers. "You're right. I'm sweating but I feel cold. Those scones, must get the ovens lit. Mrs. Spinney'll help me with the mixin'. . . . Very good, very good. . . . Hmmmm."

Brother Hollyberry was shaking a blanket from the Infirmary window to freshen it when Thrugg called up to him, "Ahoy there, Brother. Friar Bellows ain't lookin' too chipper. D'you want me to tote him up to sickbay so's you can give the pore mouse a look over?"

Hollyberry folded the blanket neatly. "Bring him up, Thrugg, there's a good fellow."

When Thrugg had gone, Hollyberry turned to a very downcast young hedgehog sitting on the edge of one of the beds.

"Now close your eyes and open your mouth, young Brinkle. Be brave, this physic will make you feel better and stop all that shivering and sweating. You'll be right as rain by teatime, believe me, young feller."

Tudd Spinney found his old friend Burrley Mole seated with his back to a barrel of October ale down in the wine cellars. He shook his stick disapprovingly. "You been oversamplin' of our October ale again, Burrley?"

The mole's normally bright eyes lacked luster. He waved a hefty digging claw at his hedgehog companion. "Hummm! Go 'way, Tudd. Oi feels orful an' drefful, nor a drop'n of 'ee Nextober ale 'as passed moi lips t'day!"

Tudd heaved Burrley up onto his paws. "C'mon, ol' mate. May'ap yore sickenin' for summat. Let's git you up to the 'Firmary."

By evening the Infirmary was full. Abbess Vale and Hollyberry were discussing using one of the upper galleries of the Abbey as a sickbay when Baby Dumble began his interminable tugging upon her habit.

"Muvva Vale, Muvva Vale, there's a funny old un wiv a cloud stucked on 'is face at the main gate. Wantsa see you, Muvva!"

The Abbess pried Dumble free from her gown. "Yes yes, Dumble. Now go and play like a good little dormouse. I'll be down as soon as I can."

However, there was no need for the Abbess to go to the main gate. Mrs. Faith Spinney had opened it to the stranger, and she brought him to the upper gallery.

"Vale, my dear, this is Furgle Woodvole the Hermit. Would you believe, he met Samkim and Arula today. I think he wants to speak with you."

Abbess Vale took Furgle's paw. "So good of you to come with news of our young ones, Mr. Furgle. You must be tired and hungry coming such a long way. Come with me and I'll see you're fed and rested. Mrs. Spinney, would you take over here with Brother Hollyberry while I see to our visitor."

Seated in the privacy of the Abbess's room, Furgle took elderberry wine and plumcake with relish. When he had satisfied his hunger he turned to the Abbess with a look of concern upon his face.

"You look like a sensible lady, Abbess. I've got something serious to say to you, so listen carefully."

Vale's paws plucked nervously at her sleeve. "Is it

124

Samkim or Arula? Oh please, Mr. Furgle, tell me that they're all right!"

The hermit refilled his beaker with the dark red wine. "Oh, they're fine, madam, just fine. It's the stoat I've come to tell you about—one of the two that were here at Redwall. This very day at sometime before noon he dropped dead. I've gone over all the possibilities on the way to your Abbey. I'm certain now: by the look of that creature he died from Dryditch Fever!"

The Abbess's paws knotted into the hem of her sleeve and her eyes were wide with fright as she breathed the terrible name. "Dryditch Fever! Are you sure, Mr. Furgle?"

The woodland recluse nodded his head sadly. "I wish I weren't, Abbess, but it's Dryditch Fever all right!"

15

Mara was awakened by something heavy descending upon her. The air was filled with wild gleeful croaking as she tried to stand but fell flat with the smothering weight. Her voice sounded muffled as she called out. "What's going on? Pikkle, wake up!"

Beside her she felt Pikkle stirring into action. "Phwaw! I say, what's apaw? This thing stinks!"

Mara managed to push him flat. She lay still a moment as she tried to make some sense of the situation. Instantly it became clear and the icy paw of fear gripped her. They were both enveloped in the meshes of a sprawling net fashioned from tough dried reed-grass and weighted all around with boulders. Through the small apertures she could see literally hundreds of large toads; the slimy creatures were waddling and hopping about in a primitive victory dance, their baggy throats puffing and swelling as they croaked a horrid tuneless chant. Most of them were armed with tridents or a curious type of flail with stone-tipped thongs.

The sand lizard Swinkee leaped triumphantly forward, brandishing the dagger and broken javelin that had been their only weapons. Thrusting his leering face

126

close to the net, he slithered his tongue in and out as he watched the plight of Pikkle and Mara.

"Ksss! Howja feel now? Kaha kaha! Want ta pull me tail off, steal me den, abeat me up? Kksss!"

Mara was about to say that they had not harmed him, but she thought better of it. Unknowingly they had made a dangerous enemy. She tried reasoning with Swinkee. "I'm sorry about what happened. We didn't mean to upset you. We promised to reward you if you took us back home."

"Kksss! Liarssss!" The lizard spat through the meshes at her. "Youa don't fool Swinkee. Kahaha! I got plenty swampflies 'n' marshworms off King Glagweb inna trade for you. Swinkee-a like revenge. Kksss!"

Pikkle pawed at the net in helpless fury. "You're an absolute bounder, Stinkee. D'you hear me? If I could get out of this confounded shrimp trap I'd raise a blister on your noggin that wouldn't go down in a season!"

Before they could exchange further insults, the lizard was swept aside by a massively bloated toad, red-eyed and covered in repulsive yellow warts which blotched its slime-green skin from end to end. The toad prodded a long trident through the meshes, narrowly missing their eyes. "Thrrruk! Foodslaves be silent, krrik! Or you die!"

"Best do as he says—I think he means it!" Mara whispered under her breath to Pikkle.

The lizard bowed fawningly before the massive toad. "Kksss, Swinkee bring you gooda trade King Glagweb."

The King of the toads nodded ponderously and waved his trident. Two smaller toads came forward, carrying between them a sack which moved with a wriggling, writhing motion.

Swinkee snatched it from them and backed off, bowing and scraping. "Kkss, kaha, swampflies, marshworms, no need t' counta them, Swinkee trust great King, always good to-a do trade with."

Dragging the sack off into the dunes, he waved to Mara and Pikkle. "Kahahaha, bye bye, Foodslaves. Kksss!"

The badger maid and the young hare were made to march with the net still over them. Stumbling and spitting sand, they struggled across the dunes, surrounded by hopping, croaking toads who were only too willing to jab at them with tridents or lash out with wicked flails, should they fall or attempt to stop. Some of the smaller toads thought it was good fun to sit on the trailing net ends and be towed along. Pikkle was soon exhausted, but Mara put out all her strength to aid her friend. Holding the net up so that he could walk freely, she bunched her muscles and dragged the whole thing along on her own, ignoring the trident and flail stings, impervious to the sand and stones that were thrown at her by the mocking amphibians. Pikkle crouched low, doing his best to keep her footpaws from being snared or tripped in the net.

Night had long fallen over the dunes, and the captives were still lugging the enormous weight. Mara was forced now to travel on all fours; the strain of standing upright had proved too much. Pikkle crawled doggedly at her side. Blinded by sand and smarting from the cuts and blows of goading weapons, the young ones plowed wearily onward, oblivious of where they were bound, hoping only to be allowed to stop and rest. It gradually filtered through to their numbed senses that they were traveling along flat damp ground—there were tussocks of grass and patches of mud.

One of the toads produced a conch shell. Puffing out its throat, the creature blew into it. There was an answering call from up ahead and lights began to show.

King Glagweb prodded Mara cruelly with his trident. "Krrroik! Move, stripedog. Hurry, krrrik! Nearly there!"

When they reached their destination the two captives flopped gratefully to the soggy ground, panting with exertion. Other toads, carrying lanterns full of fireflies, came waddling over to inspect the prisoners. One firefly settled on Pikkle's ear, which was sticking out of the netting.

Pikkle gave a yelp of pain. "Yowch! That blighter bit me!"

King Glagweb laid about with the handle of his trident, scattering the onlookers as he called out to his guard, "Krroikl! Get these Foodslaves into the pit. Krrrk!"

The net was roughly dragged for a short distance then tipped by a score of guards. Mara and Pikkle were upended into a deep dank hole. They splashed pawsfirst into muddy water almost to their middles. Squelching to a low ledge at one side, the two friends slumped down together.

Covered in sludge and mud, they lay waiting until the sounds of the toad guards retreated. Pikkle immediately jumped up and tried to scale the slippery clay sides of the pit, but slid back hopelessly.

There was a murmur of voices from the darkness, one louder than the rest.

"You're wasting time and strength trying to get out. Don't try again. If the guards come back we'll all be punished."

Mara felt about until her paw encountered short muddy fur. "Who are you, what are you doing here?"

The shape of a small creature loomed up out of the gloom. "We're prisoners, Foodslaves, just like you. What name do they call you?"

"I am Mara of Salamandastron. This is my friend Pikkle Ffolger. He also comes from the mountain."

129

The small creature offered his paw. "I am Nordo, only son of Log-a-Log. My father is leader of Guosssom, the Guerrilla Union of South Stream Shrews of Mossflower. There are thirty-four of us all told down here."

Mara and Pikkle shook Nordo's paw.

Pikkle pawed sludge from his ear in disgust. "Please t' meet you, Nordo. Hah, Foodslaves indeed. We'd be filthy if we attempted to serve 'em food in this bally state!"

Several shrew voices piped up. "Oh, you won't be servin' food, matey. You *are* the food!"

"Aye, the mud'll roast off pretty easy in a cookin' fire!"

"Foodslave's only good for one thing matey. Food!"

Mara was horrified. "You mean they intend to eat us?"

Nordo led them to a small cave scooped out in the pitside. He sat them down and explained.

"Glagweb and his tribe are cannibal toads. If there are no captives they eat the weaker ones of their own kind—you wouldn't believe some of the stories about King Glagweb and his band. At the moment we are lucky; yesterday we numbered forty, but they took six of us last night. We have a temporary reprieve. I heard some of the guards talking today, and it seems that we are to be kept and fed until the King's Feastday, then it's our turn."

Nordo held up a paw. "I know what you're going to ask me next: when is the Feastday? Sorry, I don't know—your guess is as good as mine. But while there's life there's hope, eh. At least we'll be given food for a while."

"And then jolly well served up at a party." Pikkle gulped. "What a nice surprise. Makes a chap feel wanted, wot, wot?"

Mara could not stand in the enclosed space, but she

clenched her paws and growled fiercely, "I'd like to see them try to eat me. I'd give them a few bodies of their own to cook before they got me on the table. Nordo, why do you all wait down here doing nothing? Can't you attempt some kind of escape instead of just sitting here waiting for those filthy creatures to eat you?"

Nordo drew them close and whispered, "That's exactly what we are doing. Are you with us?"

Mara and Pikkle clasped his paw in the darkness.

"We're with you, all the way!"

"Just say the jolly ol' word an' we'll stick t' you like slime on a toad's back, if you'll pardon the pun, old lad!"

Nordo chuckled grimly. "Good! Let me explain. We have a messenger. When it is daylight if you look up you may see a wren fly over. That is Leaflad. He is a friend of the shrews, so keep a watchout for him. The day he drops an acorn into this hole, that's the day we escape from here."

"You mean you're going to break out with an acorn?" Pikkle Ffolger scratched his nose.

Mara slapped his paw. "Stop fooling, Ffolger, and listen to what our friend has to say. Sorry, Nordo. Carry on."

"Right. When the acorn drops in it means that my father and his shrews will attack from the river south of here. They will have to act quickly and drive the toads back beyond this hole. It is our job to defend ourselves until help arrives."

Mara nodded. "How will we do that?"

"Simple really. The cave we are sitting in was dug by us to prevent the toads hooking us out when they want us. While we were digging this cave and others like it, we found lots of good heavy throwing pebbles in the mud. So we stockpiled them and tore up our jerkins to make slings. That's how we'll defend ourselves until the shrew warriors can get us out of this pit."

"Krrike! Hey down there, here's food for you. Eat it all up now. Kraahaahaa!"

As they piled out of the cave they were hit by a pile of watercress, roots, tubers and dandelions that the guards had thrown down. Mara gathered them and heaved them into the cave while they were still dry and edible.

"As you said, Nordo, while there's life there's hope, and we need food to stay alive, so let's eat up and keep our hopes high!"

Pikkle mumbled through a mouthful of roots, "'Sright old gel, couldn't have said it better m'self, wot!"

BOOK TWO

Warriors and
Monsters

Hazy sunlight pierced a pale-washed dawn, sending streaks of gold lancing to banish the sea mists over Salamandastron. Urthstripe the Strong strode boldly out onto the sands in front of his mountain with ten hares at his back. The badger Lord looked every inch what he was—a true warrior—clad in shining metal greaves and breastplate with a plumed and visored headgarb fringed in fine chainmail. Across his back a mighty double-hilted war sword was strapped; resting easily in his right paw was his famed spear, which weighed more than a grown hare and was tipped by a long double-edged blade with ornate iron crosstrees a third of the way down its length. He threw back his head and bellowed out the badger Lord's challenge in a voice like rolling thunder.

"Eulaliaaaa! I am Urthstripe the Strong, Ruler of the mountain! Who dares trespass on my domain?"

A white flag appeared from behind some rocks on the shore, followed by the call of a high-pitched voice: "Flag of truce, flag of truce. My master would parley with you!" Raptail the rat showed himself, waving the flag furiously.

Behind the visor Urthstripe's eyes glittered in anticipation. "Urthstripe does not parley with vermin, he buries them!"

A tall blue-eyed weasel stood up behind Raptail. His voice carried neither menace nor challenge as he sidled forward. "I am called Ferahgo. We have no need to fight each other, Lord Urthstripe. Besides, if I did want to fight, you would lose sorely. I see you have only ten hares at your back."

Urthstripe had gone silent. He stared hard at Ferahgo, as if trying hard to call up something from the depths of memory. Sunlight flashed upon the badger medallion around the weasel's neck, causing it to glimmer like fire, and his blue eyes opened wide in a disarming smile. The badger Lord peered at Ferahgo through the slitted visor; voices were calling dimly down the corridors of his mind, too distant for him to make sense of. The harder he looked the more the blue-eyed weasel with the golden medal seemed to confuse him. Urthstripe shook his head and lifted the visor.

"Ferahgo, Ferahgo . . . where have I heard that name before?" He banged the spearshaft down, bringing himself back to normality. "Hear me, Ferahgo. There may be only a few warriors at my back, but there are many more inside my mountain."

The Assassin stopped a few paces from the badger Lord and waved his claws once in the air. In a trice the rocks were bristling with armed vermin behind him. He turned right and left to wave his claws again. They flooded onto the sands of the shore and stood like a pestilence of evil weeds sprung there by magic: line upon line of ferrets, stoats, weasels, rats and foxes, each one armed to the fangs. Banners of blood red and standards decorated with skins, hanks of beast hair and skulls swayed in the light breeze.

Ferahgo turned to Urthstripe with a confident smirk. "You have thirty more fighting hares inside, I know. The odds would be well over fivescore to one. But let us

136

not talk of fighting. I am a visitor to this country—
where is your famous hospitality? Invite me into your
mountain and let me look around, we will talk . . ."

"Never! I do not allow vermin into Salamandastron!"

As he was speaking, Urthstripe noticed the front
ranks of the horde advancing slowly. Behind him he
heard the slither of arrows being drawn from quivers.
Sapwood and the ten hares were readying themselves
for trouble.

Ferahgo shook his head. "You say you never allow
vermin into your mountain, yet my son Klitch and his
friend Goffa took breakfast with you not so long ago."

The point of Urthstripe's spear had been gradually
tilting. Now it dropped, centered on Ferahgo's midriff a
breath away. The Assassin took a cautious step back.

Urthstripe's short patience was worn exceedingly
thin. "Leave Mossflower country, weasel, or you and
your scum will die here. I am tired of talking. Take your
face out of my sight. You offend me!"

Ferahgo was not short of nerve. He spat scornfully in
the sand. "Your mountain is surrounded, badger. If it
comes to war there is no way you can win. What do you
say to that?"

But Urthstripe was finished talking, except for one
word.

"Eulaliaaaa!"

There was a deadly hiss of shafts as ten of the advancing enemy were cut down by the Long Patrol arrows.
Ferahgo leaped to one side roaring, "Charge!"

The horde swept forward over the bodies of the fallen
toward the badger and his ten hares. The hares dropped behind another ten who had been waiting to back
them up with bows ready. They fired into the yelling
horde as their comrades fitted fresh arrows to their
bows and let loose another quick volley. Carried on by
the lust for battle, Urthstripe, instead of retreating into
the safety of the mountain, flung himself forward into

the foe. A burly ferret wielding a pike charged Urthstripe. The badger's spear took him through the chest and lifted him like a rag doll, hurling him into the seething horde. A weasel flung himself on Urthstripe's back and stabbed the big badger between greave and breastplate. Urthstripe slew him with the backward stroke of a huge mailed paw. Three hares were down—two to spears, one to slingshot.

"I'll try an' get Lord Urthstripe away," Sapwood called out to Oxeye. "Keep the entrance open till we gets back!"

Oxeye coolly notched an arrow to his bow and felled a fox. "Righty ho, but put a move on, Sap. We can't keep up this bally performance all day. Dearie me, what a chap has t' do for these badger Lords!"

Sapwood dropped his bow and tore out into the melee. Punching, kicking, butting and hooking, he made it to the badger's side.

"Cook sez breakfast's gettin' cold, sir. Hare you comin' in."

An ill-timed thrust from a vermin spear missed Urthstripe but knocked Sapwood senseless on the rebound as his head met the blunt end of the spearbutt. Urthstripe grabbed the hare in one paw and slung him over his shoulder as he fought his way back to the entrance. Suddenly Klitch appeared in front of him, brandishing his short sword. The badger turned as he thrust, taking the blade in his arm. Burdened as he was with Sapwood, the badger Lord stood for a moment glaring at the young weasel. Tearing the sword from his arm, he stood on it and snapped the blade, snarling angrily, "Better luck next time, brat. We'll meet again. Eulaliaaa!"

Urthstripe went hurtling through the melee like a juggernaut. Scattering bodies right and left, he pounded through to the entrance, dropping the unconscious Sapwood into the paws of two waiting hares as he roared out orders.

"Oxeye, get your hares inside. I'll block off the entrance!"

Within seconds the hares had ducked into the passage and Urthstripe threw his weight against a mighty boulder. The stone rolled into place, sealing the mountain from the horde outside. The badger Lord drove a large oak wedge into its base with a mallet.

Oxeye leaned on his bow, watching him. "Not very friendly those chaps, sir. I take it they want to fight us, wot?"

Urthstripe licked blood from his shoulder and grinned at the irrepressible hare. "Good enough, Oxeye you old battler. We'll give them a fight, one that we can talk about in the winters to come, when we're sitting round the fire growing old and lazy."

Big Oxeye checked his empty quiver. "Don't mind me sayin' so, M'lud, but there won't be too many around to grow old after this fight's finished!"

16

Dryditch Fever!

The awful name was enough to chill the heart of any creature. A hasty conference was called by the Abbey elders—Abbess Vale, Bremmun, Faith Spinney and Brother Hollyberry, with Furgle the Hermit sitting in on the proceedings. Abbess Vale addressed them.

"Friends, if something is not done swiftly this dreadful fever may wipe us all out. Brother Hollyberry, as Infirmary Keeper do you have any knowledge of this illness?"

Hollyberry pursed his lips. "Mother Abbess, my skills are simple and very limited; tummyaches, headaches, scratches and wounds are what I am used to. I have had a quick look through my medical books, and the opinion of most former Infirmary Keepers is that there is no sure cure for Dryditch Fever. I can keep it under a certain amount of control with my own remedies, but alas I cannot cure it."

"Flowers of Icetor, heh heh heh! But that's only an old mousewives' tale. Heh heh heh, Flowers of Icetor indeed!"

They all turned and stared at Furgle. The woodland Hermit shrugged as he did a small hopskip.

"Never needed anything myself—medicines, pah! Though when I was young my grandma used to say that the only thing which could cure Dryditch Fever was the Flowers of Icetor, boiled in fresh springwater. I think she was mad, of course. Quite mad!"

Faith Spinney shook her paw severely at Furgle. "Show some respect for your elders. My grandma used to say the same thing, Flowers of Icetor from the mountains of the north. Now I recalls her words, she always said that they could cure most anythin'. But who knows where the mountains of the north are? Mercy me, no right-thinkin' Redwaller ever goes north. That's badlands. 'Tis a hard and hostile region we know little about."

"Mousewives' tale or no, we've got to give it a try." Bremmun stood up officiously. "I'll go this very day, see if I don't."

Thrugg had been standing nearby waiting to speak with Hollyberry. He pressed Bremmun back down into his chair. "No, matey, you're too old and long in the tooth t' be climbin' northern mountains. I'll go. Oh, Hollyberry, yore wanted up in the Affirmery—two more creatures just been took poorly."

Mrs. Faith Spinney was very fond of Thrugg. She patted his paw. "Oh, you are a brave creature, Thrugg. We must send somebeast with you to help you on your quest."

Thrugg shuffled awkwardly. "Bless yer, marm, but I'll be fine steerin' a lone course. Every spare pair o' paws will be needed 'ere at Redwall to cope with the fever. 'Sides, I'm mortal feared of bein' sick, so I'd best find this flower quick like. What's it called again, Furgle?"

"Heh heh. Icetor, you great ignoramus—Flowers of Icetor. Though as to where you'll find it or the north mountains is a mystery to me."

Thrugg took hold of Furgle in his brawny paws and

lifted him easily on to the tabletop. "Hark t' me, wood-vole. You ever call me iggeramius agin an' you'll be goin' for a swim in the pond, fully dressed. Yore so clever, but not clever enough t' see the answer to your own question. Where's the north mountains? Why, in the North, o' course. There's a path right outside this 'ere Abbey leadin' north, an' I intends takin' it. Flowers of Icetor, eh. Don't you fret yore spikes, Mrs. Spinney—ol' Thrugg will bring back bouquets of 'em! I ain't never seen no Flowers of Icetor, but I 'spect if they're so val'ble an' rare I'll know those blossoms as soon as I claps eyes on 'em. Mountain's in the north, flowers is on the mountain—what more does a beast need t' know? You leave it t' me, mates!"

The big otter's logic was so strong and straight-forward that he received a hearty round of applause. Everybeast was in agreement, Thrugg was the otter for the job; in fact, the questing light in Thrugg's eye discouraged any fainthearted disagreement.

Being a beast of his word and a creature of action, Thrugg set out without delay, taking with him his throwing sling and pebbles and a large haversack of food. Night had long fallen when he was waved off along the north path from the Abbey gates by a contingent of his Redwall friends.

"Goodbye and good luck, Thrugg!"

"Ho urr, you'm taken good care of 'ee'self."

"Hurry back with the flowers, matey!"

"Do be careful, Mr. Thrugg!"

The gates shut behind him as the otter strode out boldly along the dusty brown path to the north.

Thrugg had not been walking long when he began hearing sounds from the woodlands on his right. He tied a big pebble into his sling. Whoever was trailing him would be called sharply to account if they tried anything. A pale sliver of moon illuminated the path and woodlands dimly as the otter watched the small bushes and shrubs moving not far from where he trod; his hidden follower was trying hard to keep pace with him. Smiling grimly to himself, he twirled his sling meaningfully and stopped. The other stopped too. Suddenly a juniper bush began shaking and thrashing madly and a squeaky little voice cut through the night silence.

"Elpelpelp! Mista Thugg, it's a serpink, a serpink got me!" The voice could belong to only one creature: Baby Dumble.

Thrugg hurled himself into the woodland and pounced upon the bush, ripping leaves and branches as he shouted, "Belay, matey. Don't be afrighted—Thrugg's 'ere!"

The infant dormouse was trapped in the coils of a fully grown grass snake. Though not poisonous, the creature was trying to squeeze the life from Dumble. Thrugg gripped it by the throat and dealt it a powerful blow with his loaded sling. It was knocked senseless in a trice. Baby Dumble's face had an unhealthy bluish pallor and his cheeks were puffed out as he tried to breathe. Sudden shock had paralyzed him.

The big otter turned the tiny dormouse upside down and dealt him a hefty whack on his bottom. It was a drastic but surefire remedy. Dumble let out a yell that resounded through the woodlands, "Waaaahooooohh!"

A short while later he was seated happily on a fallen tree, eating a candied chestnut from the otter's haversack as he watched Thrugg tying the snake in an intricate knot around a sapling.

"You stringy ol' rascal, 'ow dare you try ter choke my liddle matey? Y'can stay there till you learn some manners!"

Dumble chuckled. "Thatsa way, Mista Thugg. Tie d'serpink up!"

Thrugg narrowed his eyes severely and squatted in front of Dumble. "Never mind the serpink, matey. What in the name of jib booms are you doin' followin' me?"

"Wanna come wiv you to norf mountings, Mista Thugg."

"Do you now! Well, you lissen ter me, young dormouse. It's back to yer bunk in Redwall Abbey for you. Now come on!"

Dumble burst into floods of tears. "No no, don't wanna go! Dumble get sick an' die wiv feeva. Me fright'ned."

Thrugg shouldered his haversack and stood undecided with the tearful Dumble gazing beseechingly up at him.

"You my matey, Mista Thugg. You not let Dumble get sicked inna Habbey. We find niceflowers together. Yeh?"

Thrugg picked up the infant in one paw and set him atop the haversack. "All right, you liddle rogue. I couldn't think of ye lyin' sick back there. I'm as feared of the fever as you are. Shove your paw through the straps up there an' get some sleep, then we'll find these Iceflowers t'gether."

Off they went up the path, the big otter having his patience sorely tried by the infant dormouse.

"Good ol' Mista Thugg. You're my bes' matey, aren't you?"

"Oh aye. Now you git t' sleep an' stop gabbin'."

"I go t'sleep now. G'night, Mista Thugg."

"Good night!"

"See you inna mornin'."

"Aye, now be quiet!"

"I quiet now. Dumble quiet."

"Well, I should 'ope you are!"

"Oh I are."

"Be quiet, d'you 'ear me. Be quiet!"

144

"Dumble quiet. You de one makin' alla noise, Mista Thugg."

Since dawn King Glagweb had been peering over the edge of the pit, watching Mara intently. The toad guards heaved a massive load of tubers and roots down to the captives. There was even some fruit among it—a few apples, some half-ripe hazelnuts and late strawberries. Nordo and his shrews gathered it into the little wallcaves, keeping the hazelnuts to one side as sling material.

As Pikkle helped to gather up the food he called to Mara, "You've got a royal admirer there, old gel, wot? I think he fancies you on toast with an apple in your jolly mouth."

Mara shook a paw at the King of toads. "Go away, you fat sloppy swamp-walloper!"

"Kroikl! Silence stripedog, Glagweb is King, Krrk!" Glagweb flung a hazelnut savagely at her. "Not fat or sloppy. I punish you when the time comes. Grrk!"

Mara flung the nut back, scoring a direct hit on Glagweb's nose. "Why not come down here and punish me now if you dare, fathead. Or should I say your royal splodginess!"

Glagweb waddled about the edge of the pit, quivering with rage, his eyes bulging and his throat pulsing wildly.

"Grrroak! I will eat your heart!"

"Hah!" Mara curled her lip scornfully. "Eat my heart? You couldn't eat mud if it hit you in the mouth. Here!" She flung a pawful of slime. It splattered into the Toadking's open mouth. The creatures in the pit had to scramble for cover as the toad guards hurled pebbles down at them.

Glagweb went into an insane rage, spitting slime as he croaked venomously at the badger maid, "Krrikl! I wait no longer. You have angered me, and soon you will all die. Kroik! I will make your deaths so slow and painful you will plead to be eaten. Grakk!"

After the toads had gone, Mara apologized to the other captives.

"I'm sorry I lost my temper and hastened your deaths, but I couldn't stand that loathsome toad staring at me."

Nordo wiped mud from an apple and bit into it. "What's the difference? We're all going to die anyway. Probably better sooner than later—get it over with."

Pikkle nibbled at a strawberry reflectively. "I don't know whether to stuff m'self and give those toads a good scoff, or bally well starve so they won't have much to chew on. What d'you think, Nordo ol' lad?"

"As I said, Pikkle—makes no difference. Once you're dead then that's it, fat or thin."

"Here, what's all this?" Mara put a paw around Nordo's shoulders. "You talk as if the end is inevitable. Where's your famous fighting spirit of the Guosssom?"

Nordo sat down heavily in the mud and slapped his paws in it. "Look at this—mud, slime, sludge, everywhere! Trapped in a pit like frogs in a barrel, forced to live in this filth. I can't take it anymore, living like a wriggling swamp insect!" He yelled hoarsely and threw himself at the pit walls, slipping and sliding as he tried to claw his way upward.

A grass noose snaked down without warning and settled over Nordo's shoulders. Suddenly the pit edge was alive with a mob of toads croaking and hopping gleefully as Glagweb waved his trident and bellowed loudly, "Krrrrokk! Now we eat 'em, one by one. Gurrrrkk!"

Pikkle dived forward and grabbed Nordo's footpaws. "Come on, chaps. Don't let the scurvy knaves take him!"

Mara waded forward and seized the rope. Several

shrews hurried to help her, and the badger maid called to them, "Pull! Pull with all your might!"

On the topside of the pit toads attached themselves to the rope and hauled frantically.

"Krruuuukk! Heave! If you want food, heave!" Glagweb shouted at them.

The toughened grass rope stretched and squeaked taut as creatures at both ends bent their backs into the tug-of-war.

Two young shrews named Scraggle and Wikk climbed over the heads of the others and began attacking the rope with their bare teeth.

Pikkle smiled grimly. "That's the stuff ter give the troops, lads. Bite away!"

Several toads leaned over the edge and prodded with their tridents, but they were driven back with a volley of mudballs from the pit below. Scraggle and Wikk bit furiously into the straining rope, spitting dried grass left and right as their sharp teeth worked on the fibers.

The rope parted with a loud *snap*!

On top the toads went staggering back and landed in a heap on Glagweb. He thrust at them cruelly with his trident.

"Krrrrekk! Off, fools. Get off the King!"

Mara, Pikkle and Nordo fell back into the pit in a splashing deluge of watery mud. Still clinging to the severed half of the rope, a pile of shrews fell in on top of them. Through the slime and sludge they laughed aloud at their victory.

"We won! We won! Hooray!"

"I say, good show, you chaps. That'll teach old Glag guts, wot?"

An arrow came streaking down and pierced Scraggle's paw. Glagweb appeared at the pit edge with several toad archers.

"Krrrg! Kill! Kill them all!"

Mara felt something hit her between the ears. She

clapped a paw to her head and caught the object. From the corner of her eye she caught sight of a wren zooming overhead.

Holding up the acorn, she roared aloud, "Look, it's the acorn! Eulaliaaaaa!"

Immediately, the battle cries of the Guosssom shrews reached their ears. Nordo dived into a wallcave, avoiding arrows as he threw slings and stones forward, lifting his head in an answering war shout to his father's warriors who were pressing up from the riverbank.

"Logalogalogalogalog!"

An arrow zipped between Pikkle's ears as he flung off a rounded stone from his sling. There was a satisfying thud as it caught a toad guard in the throat. Toads were everywhere, swinging their vicious flails and thrusting with tridents. Fierce-eyed Guosssom warriors, their heads bound in bright-colored cloths, leapt to the fray, parrying and riposting with their short fencing rapiers.

"Yahaa, 'sdeath to you, scumback!"

"On guard! One, two, slay!"

Mara and the rest whirled stones upward with as much speed and force as they could muster, dodging arrows and ducking long pike thrusts from the toads on top. King Glagweb turned back and forth, trying to divide his attention between the prisoners in the pit and the advancing Guosssom shrews. The element of surprise was working well. The shrews drove the toad masses backwards mercilessly, pushing them into the flames of their own cooking fires as they did. Log-a-log, the fierce-eyed leader of the shrews, fought like a mad beast, throwing himself onto several toads at a time, regardless of danger. Bleeding from a dozen trident and flail cuts, he fought wildly with tooth and rapier, all the time booming out in his gruff bass voice:

"I'm coming, Nordo my son. Logalogalogalogalog!"

Several shrews had been slain by the toads, but the

losses on King Glagweb's side were far heavier. The toads were beginning to lose heart. They still fought on, but they were pushed into retreat by the ferocity of the Guosssom attack.

Down in the pit there were four dead shrews, but the prisoners never stopped for a moment. The upward hail of stones was so fast and thick that they felled many toads. Mara leapt out of the cave she had been slinging from, heaving and throwing anything that came within reach of her paws. For a second she glimpsed the snarling features of King Glagweb, then he retreated from the edge.

"Mara, he's gettin' away," Pikkle's voice called out to her over the melee. "The tridents—over there!"

Two toad guards had been knocked down into the pit. They lay dead in the deep watery mud, still holding their tridents. Immediately, Mara sensed what Pikkle meant.

Snatching the two tridents, she used them as climbing spikes. Paw over paw, up the side of the pit she went, using the tridents to haul herself up, thrusting them deep into the slippery sides and exerting all of her huge strength she thrust her way up to the top. Flailing with the tridents, she sent two toads hurtling into the pit before she took off after Glagweb.

The King of the toads wobbled and hopped through the swamps. Toad warriors less ponderous than himself passed him on both sides as they fled from the wrath of the Guosssom fighters.

"Krrruk! Worms, deserters, come back and help your King!" Glagweb spat at the toads. Chancing a look back, he saw Mara coming after him. The Toadking's throat bulged with terror as he tried to go faster. The badger maid was a frightening sight, her eyes red with rage, foam flecking her jaws she hurtled forward regardless of brush or sapling. Glagweb froze with horror, the strength draining from his flabby limbs as the young badger threw herself through the air and pounced upon him.

The Log-a-log and several of his crew came dashing up as Mara lifted Glagweb from the ground bodily, both her paws locked around his throat. He dangled helplessly, croaking feebly as his legs tried to reach the ground.

Mara found herself suddenly borne down beneath the weight of half a dozen shrews. Blinded by her warlike badger spirit, she turned to fight with them as her prisoner was wrested out of her grasp. Log-a-log's rapier touched her throat.

"Be still, young badger. Leave this one to us. He is our longtime enemy, and we will deal with him. Come and watch!"

The toad camp had been destroyed, and those who had not fled were slain. Pikkle, Nordo and the others were hauled up out of the pit. Shrew warriors gathered round the pit edge as Glagweb was dragged forward. He snarled and spat at all about him. Log-a-log took little notice of Glagweb's anger as he unceremoniously kicked the Toadking down into the pit. Two shrews nearby loosed the mouth of a sack and something flashed down to join the toad in the pit. The shrew leader smiled.

"So then, Toadking, you end up in your own pit—the same pit that you kept my shrews in so that you could eat them. Other creatures are flesh-eaters too. Take, for instance, the pike that has just been thrown in there with you. He is only half-grown, but fierce. Why don't you try to eat him, Glagweb? Once he is hungry enough he is going to try to eat you. I call that justice, Toadking—eat or be eaten. Goodbye."

Glagweb recoiled to the side of the pit, trying to avoid

the ominous dorsal fin that stuck out of the muddy water as the pike cruised the pit bottom. Looking for food.

Farther down from the toad camp lay the South Stream. Moored on the bank were fifteen huge logs, each one hollowed into a long dugout. The shrews sat in pairs along the length of each log; Mara and Pikkle were seated in the prow of the leading log with Nordo and his father. The dugouts pushed out from the bank and the shrews paddled them out into the center of the broad stream which meandered to the southeast.

"Where are you from, Mara?" Log-a-log questioned Mara as they rode the stream.

"From the mountain called Salamandastron, sir. Do you know how we can get back to there?"

The shrew nodded. "It is a long journey, but I know the way. I am Log-a-log of all these waters. The South Stream has many tributaries, and I know them all like the back of my paw. I will take you to the mountain, but first you must come with me. I have other plans for you at the moment."

Pikkle smiled coyly. "Other plans, eh? Give us a hint, Log-a-thing."

The grim expression on Log-a-log's face wilted Pikkle. He turned aside muttering, "Hmph. Only asked. No harm in jolly well askin', is there? Wonder what shrew tucker tastes like. I could eat a toad."

17

Dingeye got over the loss of his comrade Thura with surprising speed. At first he had grown nostalgic and even wept a bit, but then he remembered how stupid and insulting Thura could be, all the times Thura had stolen food from him, and the arguments that invariably ended up in fighting. As he traveled south and west under the canopy of Mossflower, Dingeye reconciled and justified himself aloud to the lonely thicknesses of the silent green forest.

"Yah, serves 'im right. Anyhow, maybe Thura's got better and gone off on his own. That stoat never really liked me, 'e weren't no proper mucker. Bad luck to him, I says. Besides all that, who needs a mucker wi' a sword like this'n?"

He swung the fabulous blade and chopped off an overhanging branch. It fell, tangling his paws and tripping him. Growling curses, he slashed and hacked at the offending branch.

"Yowhoo! Yaha! Owch, that 'urt!"

Dingeye's clumsy attack on the harmless foliage had caused him to wound himself on the left footpaw with the razor-keen sword. He dropped the weapon and sat rocking back and forth as he tried to bend double and lick his injured limb.

"Urgh! That'll be Thura, wherever 'e is, wishin' bad luck on me, 'is old mucker who never did 'im any wrong nor wished him ill, not once. That Thura was allus a nasty one!"

Casting about, he found a large dockleaf and improvised a dressing for the paw. Staunching the blood with a pawful of leaf mold, he bound the lot with a thin weed stem. Using the sword as a walking stick, he set off again, gnawing on a wrinkled apple and feeling sorry for himself.

"Just fancy, bein' wished bad fortune by me mucker who's deserted me. Life's 'ard an' cruel fer a pore stoat who's all alone an' wounded."

Samkim and Arula had also encountered an unlucky setback. Tracking steadily, the pair were making good progress when they came to an area that Dingeye had not chopped at with his sword. Casting about this way and that, they hunted for signs that would help them to pick up the stoat's trail. Arula rummaged about in a yew thicket until Samkim gave an excited shout:

"Over here, Arula. Look, blood!"

The young mole scurried across to find her friend sitting among a heap of slashed twigs and branches. He pointed to the scarlet stains on the leaves.

"He's been here, all right. See the stoat pawprints— who else could it be? I suspect this is his blood too. Yes, Dingeye's passed this way. What d'you think?"

Arula turned the leaves over with heavy digging claws. "Yurr, so 'e 'as. Oi wunner wot yon stoater wurr a-bleedin' for, Sanken?"

The young squirrel wiped his paws on the ground. "Who knows? Dingeye can't be too far ahead now, though. What d'you say we rest here awhile and have a meal, then we can put on a good forced march and catch him up?"

Arula agreed readily at the mention of food. "Ho urr, gudd idea. Oi'm fair famishered. But us'ns sit o'er thurr, away from all this stoater bludd."

They sat in a sunlit patch between a lilac clump and a thicket of lupins. Samkim allowed Arula to choose the fare. She unpacked strawberry jam turnovers and black-currant cordial from the haversacks. Spreading a napkin, she laid the food out. "Thurr, that do look noice."

First one wasp came. It settled on Samkim's turnover until he brushed it away. Soon there were several wasps trying to light on the sweet jammy turnovers. Others buzzed and hummed around the little flask of cordial. Arula flicked one of the insects as it went for the jam around her mouth. "Gurroff, 'ee pesky wosper!"

The wasp attacked and stung her.

"Burrhoo! 'Ee wosper stungen oi!"

Samkim flailed about at the wasps with his bow, thwacking about as he punctuated each swing with angry words. "Go away, little nuisances! Be off with you—scoot!"

Unwittingly the bow whipped into the lupins, demolishing the wasp nest that was built in the forks of three stems. In a trice the air was filled with maddened wasps. They hummed and buzzed about the young ones' heads in a maddened frenzy. The two friends leapt up, beating frantically at the stinging cloud of insects.

"Quick, run for it before we're stung to death!"

"Whoohurr, they'm all o'er the place. Leave oi alone, wospers!"

Abandoning their meal, Samkim and Arula dashed off among the trees, pursued by an army of wasps.

"Owch! Yowch! Look for cover, Arula! Look for cover!"

"Hooh! Ooh! Oi doant see nuthin' but pesky wospers!"

A burly hedgehog appeared out of nowhere and began catching wasps with a net on a stick and eating them with great relish. "Hoho hoho, lookit yew tew. Don't like wasps, do yer?"

Samkim beat furiously at the insects as he shrieked out in panic to the newcomer, who was obviously enjoying himself: "Yaaah! This is no time for chitchat, mister. Do something!"

The hedgehog snapped at a passing wasp and caught it in his mouth. He chewed on it as he spoke.

"Tchah! Naught like a good crunchy wasp, 'cepting fer a big fat bee, o' course. Come on then, yew tew. Foller Spriggat."

They ran after him, wailing and yelling in pain, with the wasps still in hot pursuit. Spriggat stopped at the edge of a small woodland tarn. Pointing to the little lake, he urged them into the water and plucked two hollow reeds.

"Hoho hoho. Never see'd nothin' like it in me born days—critters afeared o' wasps. Come on, cullies. In y' go. Best duck under an' breathe through these reeds. 'Urry now!"

Grabbing a reed apiece, the two young ones hurled themselves into the water. Submerging themselves totally, they fixed the reeds in their mouths and sucked greedily for air.

Spriggat carried on dining off wasps. Impervious to stings, he ate the buzzing insects by the pawful, only stopping now and then to winkle out wings that were caught between his teeth.

"Come to Spriggat, me crunchy liddle beauties. There's plenty o' room for you all in me good ol' tummy!"

From beneath the clear waters of the small sunlit pool Samkim and Arula watched the hedgehog gorging

155

himself on wasps until the buzzing horde thinned out and flew off back to their damaged nest. When the wasps had gone, Spriggat hauled the young ones dripping from the pool. They looked a sorry sight, soaked and covered in lumps.

"Well, curl me spikes, lookit yew tew. I wouldn't give a moldy acorn for the pair of ye. See this bank mud? Well, if you plaster it all over y'selves it'll stop the stingin'."

Rolling over in the sticky black mud, they coated themselves with it. Strangely enough, it relieved the stings immediately. Looking like two mud dollies, they introduced themselves, telling the hedgehog of their quest.

He nodded knowingly. "I seen that daft stoat earlier, limpin' an' hobblin' along an' talkin' to hisself like a worried wart. No mind, ol' Spriggat'll put y'back on his trail. Least a body could do for bringin' me such a good dinner o' wasps."

There was a slight buzzing noise from the hedgehog's stomach. He gave it a sharp pat and it stopped.

"'Scuse me. Now if yew tew will take a tip from Spriggat you'll set there awhile an' let that mud dry hard, then it'll peel off an' take all the stings with it."

Samkim and Arula sat in an open patch of sunlight. As the mud dried they watched the strange hedgehog taking wasps one by one from his catching net and scrunching them down as if he were at a banquet.

A blow from a spearbutt laid Dingeye flat. Half-stunned, he looked up. Dethbrush the fox and his six tracker rats held him pinned to the ground with the points of their spears. The fox kicked the sword from his nerveless paws, and Dingeye whimpered with fright. There was neither pity or mercy in the cold eyes of the trackers and their leader.

"Where's Thura? Tell me and I'll make your dying easy." The fox's tone was harsh and commanding.

"Thura's dead. 'E died of the sickness. I saw it meself, sir. Oh, you ain't goin' ter kill me, are you?"

"Ferahgo has a long paw," Dethbrush sneered as he kicked the quivering stoat. "You thought you'd escaped us didn't you. Poor fool!"

Dingeye moaned as a spearpoint prodded his injured paw. "I was goin' back to Ferahgo, sir. On me oath I was. See that sword? I was bringin' it to him as a gift. On me 'onour!"

Dethbrush picked up the sword, admiring its cold lethal beauty. "Honour? Don't talk to me of honour, Dingeye. Me and my trackers have wasted nearly a full season searching for you and your mucker. Nobeast escapes Ferahgo the Assassin. You should know that by now. Guess what he told me to do when I caught up with you?"

Dingeye gulped. His throat had gone dry and he could scarce get the words out. "Prob'ly said to f-fetch me back . . ."

The fox smiled mirthlessly at his trembling victim. "Wrong, Dingeye. He said to fetch your head back on a spearpoint."

The sword swung once, its blade flashing in the sunlight.

Dethbrush wiped the blade on Dingeye's carcass. "Leave him; one head's no good without the other. I think Lord Ferahgo will be happy to receive this sword as a gift from an old departed friend. Come on, it's a long and hard trek back to the Assassin's camp."

The battle for Salamandastron was under way. Massed behind sand barriers and rocks, the hordes of Ferahgo sent flaming arrows up at the mountain. Vegetation and crops that had been cultivated on the crevices and ledges of the fortress were soon blackened stubble, burned to the bare rock by hundreds upon hundreds of blazing shafts.

Ferahgo stood in plain view, well out of range, Klitch at his side.

From one of the high slitted rock windows Bart Thistledown brushed drifting black ash from his face as he notched a shaft to his bowstring, murmuring to himself. "Move, you rotten blighter. Come on, just ten paces closer and I'll put one right between your bonny blue eyes, wot!"

Starbob fixed an arrow to his bow and sighted on a ferret who was standing up to take a shot. "Wastin' your time, Barty old lad. Take the nearest available target, like our friend down there, for instance . . ."

Straining the bow taut, Starbob let fly. The arrow zipped down and took the ferret in his chest. He fell backwards, releasing his fire arrow straight up. Starbob gave a grunt of satisfaction.

"Good oh! I say, look, the scoundrel's arrow came straight down and wounded that rat next to him. Two for the price of one. Not bad, eh?"

Barty twanged off his arrow and turned away, ignoring the death cry of the stoat below that he had hit. "Not too fussy on this snipin' game. Open warfare's much better, more team spirit in it, doncha know."

"Move aside there, hares!"

They both shifted from the position as Urthstripe stood at the opening. He strung a massive bow and placed a quiver of arrows within handy reach, each one as long and thick as a short spear. The badger Lord spat on his paws and rubbed them together. "Right, let's open this party up properly!"

Klitch sighed as he drew patterns in the sand with a spearpoint, his face the picture of boredom. "So this is it, the grand attack plan: chuck a few fire arrows at the mountain then sit about and snipe at each other all season. You've really outdone yourself this time, old one."

Ferahgo watched the fire arrows hissing through the air. "Have you got any better ideas, clever snout?"

"At least I got to stick the big badger with my sword!" The young weasel curled his lip contemptuously.

"So you did, Klitch, so you did. Now you're short one pretty little sword. Urthstripe pulled it out of himself as if it was a sewing needle and snapped it in half. What a clever young weasel. Brilliant strategy on your part, eh? Now why don't you leave things to your elders and betters?"

Klitch kept the spear ready lest the Assassin's paws should stray to the long knives strapped across his chest. "You may be my elder, but you'll never be my better. Come on, let's hear about your brilliant strategy, Father."

Having run out of arrows, Goffa decided to stand in the rear awhile with Klitch. He was crossing the beach, exactly in line with Ferahgo, when a huge arrow hit him like a thunderbolt, sending his body crashing into the two weasels. Quickly they leapt up and ran farther back, scrambling behind an outcrop of rocks.

Ferahgo laughed, his blue eyes shining merrily at the narrow escape. "Hellsteeth and Darkgates! That thing was meant for me! Pity about your friend Goffa."

Klitch peered out at the dreadful sight. The arrow had gone through Goffa a full half-length into the sand. Keeping his bored look, Klitch leaned back against the rocks.

"Friend? That dim-witted idiot? He was only my lackey, though I'd never have ordered him to save your skin. Come on, tell me how you plan to conquer this mountain."

Some of the more venturesome members of the vermin

159

horde were slowly advancing closer to the mountain, under the hail of burning arrows. Big Oxeye watched them from the top of the crater. Seawood and Pennybright were with him, and all three leaned on a wooden prop which held back a pile of boulders. Oxeye pointed a paw straight down, closing one eye as he sighted along it.

"Hmmm, about two spearlengths more should do the trick. Come on, you idle vermin, move y'selves. Righto, chaps, that's it, all paws to the log now!"

The three hares leaned down heavily on the wood.

The vermin on the shore beneath Salamandastron heard the rumble from above. Some moved quickly, others were not so alert. Over half of them were slain by the huge slabs and boulders that cascaded down the mountainside. A cheer went up from Oxeye and his comrades when they saw the effect of their avalanche. Yells of rage and curses arose from the attackers on the shore as they redoubled their volleys of burning arrows.

In the late afternoon Ferahgo called Raptail to him. The Assassin winked at Klitch.

"Now I'll show you how I became ruler of all the Southwest Lands, little weasel. Raptail, send Doghead, Crabeyes, Dewnose and Badtooth to me. Oh, and ask Farran the Poisoner to come too."

Raptail blanched visibly as he bowed to Ferahgo. Nobeast, not even the Assassin himself, liked to do business with Farran the Poisoner. The black fox was not even part of the horde, he merely followed at a short distance, going and coming as he pleased. Raptail trotted off to do his master's bidding, dodging around rocks and behind sand barriers.

Farran sat alone at the edge of the tideline, watching the waves ebb and flow. Raptail did his level best to keep in full view, not wishing to be seen trying to sneak up on Farran the Poisoner. Wading into the sea, he drew alongside the black fox and delivered the message.

"Sir, my master Ferahgo wishes to speak with you. He is camped in the rocks north of here. Will you attend, sir?"

Raptail's body shivered nervously as he stood staring into the pale amber eyes of Farran. Nobeast had ever heard the Poisoner speak. The sunlight did not glint off Farran's fur; it was soot-black with no luster whatsoever. The pale eyes stared hypnotically at Raptail from a face dark as the depths of midnight. All the horrific whispered tales he had heard of Farran loomed large. Was it true that he could kill with a long stare? Raptail fervently believed it was as he stood transfixed by the Poisoner's eyes.

"W-w-will you attend, sir? F-F-Ferahgo wishes to know."

Unblinking, Farran stared at him a moment longer then nodded once. That was enough. Raptail bowed so low that his snout went underwater. "Th-th-thank you, sir!"

He took off like a startled fawn, splashing through the waves and dashing across the shore. Farran's sinister eyes followed his course expressionlessly. Slowly the black fox stood up and buckled on his belt of adderskin. Pouches hung from the belt, small sacks made from the skins of bats. What they contained only he knew. Moving like a silent stormcloud shadow, he padded noiselessly over the sand.

Seated at the outermost edge of his camp, away from the horde, Ferahgo outlined his plan to Klitch and the four creatures he had selected as Captains.

"Siege! No mad charges, paw-to-paw battles or out-and-out fighting—a siege is the thing that will conquer the mountain. Sooner or later the badger and his hares will run out of arrows, spears, javelins and boulders. I have him bottled up inside his mountain; he cannot leave. We have superior numbers and time on our side. Nobeast is coming to his rescue. All we have to do is snipe from safety and wait him out. Now, there is one question, can anybeast guess what it is?"

"Food and water!" Klitch answered.

Ferahgo chuckled at his son's quickness. "Right. Someday you may turn out half as clever as your father. Food and drink—how much have they got and how long will it last them, that's the question!"

Crabeyes was an ex-searat. His eyes shifted constantly, never staying still. He held up a paw. "Master, they might 'ave vittles enough ter last them fer seasons to come. Admitted they can't get out while we've got 'em surrounded, but if they 'ave enough food 'n' drink they could stay snug in there forever."

Badtooth, a large fat stoat, agreed with him. "Crabeyes is right, Master. If they 'ave enough supplies we could die of old age waitin' out 'ere on this shore."

Ferahgo pawed at the gold medal on his neck. His blue eyes shone happily as he unfolded his master stroke. "But we won't die of old age. Neither will Urthstripe and his fighters. They will die pretty soon now of something else."

There was a sharp intake of breath from Klitch and the four Captains as the shadow of Farran fell across them. Hurriedly they moved aside to make room for him, each one shivering with fear as he passed them. Farran chose his own place, directly in front of the Assassin.

Blue eyes met amber ones as they faced each other.

Ferahgo smiled ingratiatingly. "Well well, the Poisoner meets the Assassin—what a combination. But we have worked together in the past, Farran, and I have always rewarded you well, have I not?"

The black fox merely nodded once in acknowledgment.

Ferahgo averted his eyes, knowing the danger in Farran's constant stare. He took out his skinning knife and whetted it slowly against a rock, speaking as he did.

"Friend Farran, if I were to launch a nighttime attack on the mountain, could you slip through the lines and find a way in?"

Farran nodded once. That was enough for Ferahgo.

"Good! Once you were inside it would be up to you to find the food and drinking water. I imagine that the mountain will be a honeycomb of passages and side-cuts, but you could find the larders no matter how many chambers and corridors you had to explore, eh, Farran? When you do, I want everything eatable or drinkable to be poisoned with your most deadly fluids. No creature is to be left alive in Salamandastron."

Farran nodded then held out a paw. Ferahgo understood. Standing alongside the Poisoner, he drew close to his ear and whispered in a voice so low that none of the others heard: "Your fee is half the badger's treasure. Is it a bargain?"

Farran's nod was final; the pact was sealed. He gave Ferahgo one long last glance, then padded off silently.

There was a loud sigh of relief when he had gone. Ferahgo turned to the others. "Now do you think my plan will work?"

They all nodded agreement, even Klitch.

Ferahgo sheathed his skinning knife. "Then tonight is the night. Here is what you must do . . ."

18

"Towels, more towels. Damp them down with rose-water, please!"

Brother Hollyberry bustled about the beds that had been set up in the upper gallery, mopping a brow here, administering a dose there, tucking blankets in firmer.

"Please lie still, Burrley. Plenty of cool drinks and sweat it out under those blankets, there's a good mole!"

Sister Nasturtium looked up from the table where she was working with bowl and pestle and wiped her brow. "We're running low on dried motherwort and lemon verbena, Brother. This is the last of it I'm using."

Thrugann put aside a napkin she was dipping in rosewater. "Leave that t' me, Sister. I'll take a trip into Mossflower Woods right now an' gather some. Anythin' else you need while I'm in the woodlands, Brother?"

Hollyberry scratched his chin. "Hmm, nightshade berries—light red ones if you can, the dark red berries are far too squashy. Perhaps you can take a look around for Dumble while you're there, Thrugann."

"That liddle snippet." The otterlady shook her head and chuckled. "I told you once nor a dozen times he's gone off with that brother of mine. Dumble an' Thrugg are close as peas in a pod, you take my word for it."

"Oh, I do hope you're right." Abbess Vale left off laying out clean sheets and sat down on the side of a truckle bed.

A small mole named Droony took a large sucking swig of cold mint tea and half sat up.

"Oh, she'm be roight, marm, never'ee fear. Oi see'd Dumble meself, just afore 'ee went off, an' 'ee said as ee'd fetch me back Oicetor Flowern t' make oi better, so 'im did, hurr."

Sister Nasturtium ground the pestle hard into the bowl. "Droony, you naughty liddle creature, why did you not tell us this before now?"

The small mole let his head fall back on to the pillow. "Oi'm surry, Sister Aspersium, oi wurr sick as an owd frog."

Nasturtium hurried over and drew the blankets gently up to his chin. She wiped the furry little brow with a napkin. "Yes of course you were, Droony. I didn't mean to be sharp with you. Forgive me."

She sat down on the edge of the bed and mopped her own brow. "Whew! Is it hot in here, or is it just me?"

Faith Spinney felt her forehead. "Are you all right, m'dear? My, you do look frazzled."

Nasturtium stood up, swaying a little. "Silly me, complaining of the heat. Now all of a sudden I feel quite cold!"

Abbess Vale placed a paw about her shoulders. "Good job I've just made up this fresh bed, Sister. Time you had a rest—you're a patient from now on."

Droony waved a limp paw at Nasturtium. "Plenty o' roseywater an' medsin furr 'ee, Sister. Naow you'm lie abed an' go t' sleep. Do 'ee gudd!"

"Thank you, Doctor Droony." Hollyberry smiled as he mopped the little mole's brow. "Now how about taking a bit of your own advice and trying to get some sleep?"

The Abbess and Faith Spinney folded a sheet together, worry and concern showing through the weariness on their faces.

"Oh, Faith, do you think Thrugg will get the Flowers of Icetor?"

"There there, Vale. I'm sure he will. Mr. Thrugg is a good otter. I 'ope he's takin' good care of Baby Dumble."

Thrugg and Baby Dumble were in fine form, composing songs as they marched northward on the old path.

"O give me a road to walk along,
    An' a bite of food or two,
I'll tramp an' eat the livelong day,
    My liddle friend, with you."

Dumble rummaged in the haversack and found a vegetable pastie. Passing it down to Thrugg, the infant dormouse threw back his head and sang uproariously loudly:

"O, I'll sit on top'a Mista Thugg
    An' give 'm food to scoff,
'Cos he's my great big matey an'
    'E won't let me fall off!"

Thrugg munched the pastie as he thought of his next verse.

"O, Dumble is a scallywag,
    Fat as a liddle frog.
He's eaten so much vittles,
    He's 'eavier than a hog!"

166

Dumble selected an apple and began polishing it on Thrugg's head. As he did he chanced to look back down the road. Dumble's eyes widened, then he turned them ahead again, this time singing in a low urgent voice:

"O Mista Thugg, don't turn around,
 And don't you cause a fuss.
There's four ol' foxes wiv big sticks—
 I fink they're followin' us!"

Keeping his paws in front, Thrugg fitted a stone to his sling. "Let's see what these coves want then, matey."

He halted and stood in the center of the path as the four foxes approached. They were roving beggars who haunted the path, waiting for helpless travelers or any easy prey that came their way. Two of them carried rusty swords, the other two were armed with cudgels.

"Good summer day to ye, mates!" the brawny otter greeted them.

The foxes exchanged knowing smiles. One stepped forward. "Top o' the summer to ye, yer 'onner. What's in the 'avvysack?"

Thrugg grinned cheerfully at the raggedy fox. "Four unconscious foxes with their tails chopped off who tried stealin' our vittles. Why do you ask?"

"Hee hee, we've got a funny un 'ere mates!" one of the foxes sniggered.

Another fox drew his sword, testing the edge with his paw.

"Yeh, wonder if 'e's tough as 'e's funny?"

Thrugg twirled his sling ominously. "Why don't you come an' find out, mudface?"

The first fox saw that the big otter was no easy proposition, so he adopted a whining tone. "Now be reasonable, friend. We're not lookin' fer trouble. You wouldn't begrudge four starvin' creatures a bite, would yer?"

Thrugg took a step toward him. "Begrudge a starvin'

creature a bite? Not me, matey. You come 'ere an' I'll bite you anytime. Now listen, you lot: be off with you. Go an' scare some crows."

The fourth fox pulled out his rusty sword and began swinging it. "Yah, we're four to one. Gerrim, lads!"

Baby Dumble let out a terrified squeak. Suddenly Thrugg realized that he could not fight and look after the infant; escape was the only solution.

"Hold tight, Dumble. 'Ere we go!" Bulling through the foxes, Thrugg bowled them aside as he rushed off the path into the woods. Dodging and ducking, he skirted tree and bush with the outraged cries of his pursuers ringing behind him.

An idea began to form in Thrugg's head. He put on an extra burst of speed to gain a little time.

The foxes stumbled and bumped into each other as they hurried into the woodlands. They ran a short distance and halted. Thrugg was lost to sight.

"The coward, 'e's 'idin' somewheres!"

"Yeh, spread out an' search. We'll find 'im."

"Hee hee, roasted dormouse—ages since I tasted that. Ringworm, you go with Splidge. Me an' Blitch'll fan out the other way."

They had not been searching long when the one called Ringworm spotted their quarry. He gave a low secret whistle to the others. When they came he cautioned silence, pointing forward as he whispered, "Ssshh! There they are, mates—'idin' be'ind that there bush. See the liddle brat settin' on top of the 'avvy-sack?"

Sure enough, the haversack and the back of Baby Dumble were visible above the spread of a thick clump of willowherb.

"Now let's do this quiet like. Sneak up an' jump 'em!"

"Yeh, good idea. Clubs 'n' swords ready. Let's go!"

Within feet of the vegetation they threw caution to

the winds and leapt at the clump of willowherb, stabbing and striking.

Whack! Bonk! Thwack! Thud!

Four foxes lay senseless on the ground, half in and half out of the clump of rosebay willowherb.

Seated atop the haversack, which was strapped to a low sycamore branch that dipped into the willowherb, Baby Dumble looked as if he were still perched on his friend's shoulders. The trick had worked perfectly! The infant dormouse shouted excitedly: "Mista Thugg! Did ya biff th' foxes, Mista Thugg!"

Thrugg stood over the prostrate foxes, twirling his heavy stone-loaded sling. "Aye, matey, I raised lumps like duck eggs on the villains!"

The big otter disarmed the foxes, throwing their weapons off into the surrounding shrubbery. Breaking off a whippy willow switch, he revived them with a few smarting cuts. "Come on, hearties. Snooze time's over. Up on yer paws!"

Each contributing a shoulder, the four foxes were made to bear the haversack with Dumble sitting on it between them. Thrugg walked behind as they trekked along the north path, making sure they did not flag or lag with his willow switch. By nightfall the foxes were sore, hungry, weary and in tears. Thrugg had driven them a fair distance, even at double speed through a ford where pike lurked.

"Waaahahhooh!" The fox named Ringworm bawled unashamedly. "A pike bit me back there. It ain't fair!"

Thrugg waggled the cane under his nose. "Stop moanin', mate. You won't die, though maybe the pike will. Righty-ho then, you scruffy bandits, 'ad enough?"

"Oh, let us go, sir. We've 'ad enough!" The foxes collapsed weeping in the road.

Dumble took charge. Swishing the cane perilously close to them, he made them repeat extravagant promises never to be naughty, to help other creatures and to get a good wash every night. Thrugg chuckled at the sight of the infant dormouse making sure each fox repeated his lines word for word. The otter then took out his sling and loaded it.

"Right, me lucky lads, I'm goin' to count ten. Then if I can still see you I'm comin' after you. We need porters for tomorrow, see. One, two, three . . ."

Before he had reached seven the four foxes were rapidly vanishing into the distance down the dusky path.

Thrugg and Dumble camped at the edge of the path that night, beside two curiously shaped stones known to travelers as "the otter and his wife" because of their odd contours. Seated by a merry little fire they had a good supper of beechnut scones, cherry cake and cider.

Thrugg stirred the flames with a stick as he ruminated. "Harr, who knows what lies beyond the 'orizon tomorrer, matey."

Baby Dumble also picked up a stick and prodded the fire, nodding his head seriously as he imitated his big otter friend. "Oh harr, matey. Might be more foxes an' serpinks. But you stick wiv Dumble, Mista Thugg. I'll take care of ya."

Stifling his laughter, Thrugg tossed his warm jerkin at the infant. "You liddle villain, I'll take care of you if you're not asleep soon. Wrap y'self in that there jerkin."

The quarter-moon hung like a golden sickle in the summer night. Hardly a breeze stirred the mantle of the woodlands as the two adventurers settled down to rest by the fire's glowing embers.

19

The Guosssom shrew flotilla cut off down sidestreams and weaved its course along barely navigable waterways shrouded by hanging vegetation from tree, bush and foliage. Mara and Pikkle had lost all sense of direction, but the voyage was soothing and the quiet waters transmitted a sense of tranquillity. The young badger maid lay across the prow, half asleep as she watched sunlight dappling through a tunnel of willows onto the barely rippling waters. Dragonflies hummed and once a kingfisher flashed past like a brilliant jewel. Her sense of urgency over returning to Salamandastron waned as, lulled by the steady dip and fall of shrew paddles, she was overcome by lassitude and slipped into the realm of sleep.

The treetrunk boats drifted to rest with a slight bump against a bank overhung by lavender, willow and rowan. Nordo cupped his paws and gave a short call.

"Logalogalog, Guosssom home!"

Only half awake, Mara and Pikkle were escorted through a tunnel in the bankside which opened out into a well-lit and spacious cave. All around them shrews were bustling hither and thither, carrying food from earth ovens to long shelves around the side of the cave which served as tables.

"I say, this is more like it, wot?" Pikkle rubbed his paws together in anticipation. "Shrew tucker and loads of it, by the look of things. Lead on, old Log-a-thing!"

Log-a-log and Nordo seated them at a semicircular ledge. Immediately as they had sat down, a large fat shrew, accompanied by two small thin ones, approached them with a scowl on his face. He prodded Mara and Pikkle roughly.

"You've taken our places. Those seats are for Guosssom shrews, not for ragtag stripedogs an' rabbits!"

Before either of them could say anything, Log-a-log gave the fat shrew a sharp shove. "Mind your manners, Tubgutt. These are my friends. Go and sit at the other end with your pals, do you hear me?"

Log-a-log's paw strayed to the rapier at his side. Nordo stood beside his father, grim-jawed and ready for trouble. Tubgutt gave them a surly glance and retreated to the seats at the other side of the table, muttering something to the two thin shrews, who nodded and sniggered rudely.

The shrew fare was excellent, starting with shrimp and watercress soup, then on to an admirable salad served with soft white bankcheese, and after that there was a magnificent pastie of chestnuts, mushrooms and leeks, followed by hot spiced apple pudding. The two friends did the food full justice, washing it down with beakers of sweet shrewbeer.

Log-a-log watched Pikkle eating and shook his head in amazement. "Witherin' waterweeds! Where do you put it all, Pikkle?"

The young hare demolished his second portion of apple pudding and licked the spoon clean. "No bother, old Log-a-thing. Scoffin' is me fav'rite sport, wot!"

"Rabbits can't scoff, it takes a shrew to do real scoffin'." The loud remark came from Tubgutt, who was sneering openly at them across the table.

Pikkle chuckled as he waved his spoon. "Maybe rabbits can't scoff, m' fat friend, but I'm Pikkle Ffolger, a hare from Salamandastron, and I'll scoff you under the table any day in the season!"

Tubgutt stood up, his face dark with temper. "Nobeast can outscoff Tubgutt of the Guosssom!"

Pikkle turned to Log-a-log. "May I?"

Log-a-log nodded. "Certainly, Pikkle. But watch out for Tubgutt—he's sly. I've noticed that he was waiting to challenge you, so he has hardly touched any food."

Pikkle shrugged. "Well, I only did a quick practice scoff m'self."

A table that was formed from an old oak stump in the center of the cave was cleared. Seated at it, Pikkle and Tubgutt faced each other as Log-a-log stated the rules.

"Do both contestants agree to hot spiced apple pudding?"

Both the protagonists nodded and picked up their spoons.

Log-a-log waved a paw to the servers as he continued, "It is a contest to a pawstill, then. Bowley the cook will count the dishes emptied by each creature. Shrewbeer may be drunk while eating. No half-finished dishes will count, and no throwing food on the floor or hiding it in clothing. First one unable to raise his spoon from the bowl must admit defeat. Make it a good clean scoff and best of luck to you both. Spoons ready . . . then begin!"

Servers fought their way to the table through the throng of Guerrilla Shrews packing round the two contestants. Steaming hot spiced apple puddings were stacked at its center as hare ate against shrew. Tubgutt went to it in a rush, spooning out three bowls of pudding in record time, his fat jaws working madly as the spoon plowed up and down in a blur. Pikkle paced himself, eating slow but big mouthfuls, chewing each morsel with relish. A large contingent of the shrews began cheering for Tubgutt. Mara stood between Log-a-log and Nordo, viewing the proceedings from a ledge some distance away.

Tubgutt had downed five bowls to Pikkle's two. Nordo was beginning to look worried.

"That Tubgutt—look at the speed of him! He's picking up his sixth bowl. What's the matter with Pikkle? He's awfully slow, Mara."

The badger maid merely smiled. "Don't fret yourself. Pikkle can hold his own with creatures twice his size. He's eating slowly because he's enjoying it. Tubgutt may be fast, but he's no Pikkle Ffolger. You watch!"

Back at the table, Pikkle licked his spoon clean, quaffed down a beaker of shrewbeer and began on his third pudding. "Absolutely delicious pud, wot? You must tell cook to give me the recipe. Old Tubbyguts is enjoyin' it, too, aren't you old lad? My my, you are a messy eater, Tubbyguts!"

With pudding festooning his chin and apple smeared across his face, the fat shrew lifted his head and glared at Pikkle. "The name's Tubgutt, hare, and I'll make you sorry you ever went into a contest against me!"

"Sorry, old chap? One could never be sorry with all this beautiful scoff about. May I pour you some more shrewbeer?"

At the end of his eighth bowl Tubgutt began to slow down. He put the bowl aside and reached for another. Bowley the cook rapped his paw with a ladle.

"Bowl not finished there. Still puddin' in it, see."

"Never mind, chum." Pikkle grabbed the bowl from Tubgutt. "You carry on—I'll finish it. Waste not want not, that's what we always say back at the mountain!"

Pikkle was becoming very popular with the shrews. His good humor and impeccable table manners endeared him to them. The Gousssom began to cheer support for the young hare.

"Come on, Pik. Slow and easy does the trick!"

"I'll bet a barrel of shrewbeer he beats Tubgutt!"

"I'll take that bet. Tubgutt's eaten nine, he's only on his sixth."

"I'll bet my sword the mountain hare wins. He's a good un!"

The banter went back and forth as the two contestants battled on. Tubgutt undid his belt and leaned back. A look of disgust crossed his face as he picked up his eleventh pudding and dug a spoon halfheartedly into it. Pikkle now had eight empty bowls to his credit and was halfway through his ninth. The incorrigible hare drank another beaker of shrewbeer, wiped his lips delicately on a napkin and winked at his opponent.

"Good stuff this. I say, Tubbyguts, don't take that one—it looks bigger than the rest. Leave it for me. Try that little one—it only looks half full, wot!"

On his thirteenth pudding Tubgutt stopped. He was breathing heavily and his mouth hung slackly open. The two little thin shrews fanned him with napkins and gave him a beaker of shrewbeer, but he pushed it away with a flabby paw.

Mara nudged Nordo. "Now watch Pikkle really take off!"

The young hare now had eleven empty bowls to his credit. He licked his spoon shiny clean and selected a twelfth.

"Tubbyguts old pal, you've gone green. I must say, you looked much better your other color. Pass another pudden, will you?"

With the spoon halfway to his lips, Tubgutt's stomach heaved and his paw went limp. The spoon clattered back into the bowl.

A hushed silence fell over the onlookers.

Completely ignoring his fellow contestant, Pikkle pol-

175

ished off the twelfth pudding and chose another as he licked his spoon.

Bowley the cook watched Tubgutt carefully. "Can you raise spoon or paw, shrew?"

Tubgutt collapsed, his head squelching into the pudding in front of him. Pikkle blinked and tut-tutted at his table manners. "Is he finished already? Ah well, never mind, Tubbygutts. It's not the victory but playin' the jolly old game that counts. Anybeast want to take his place?"

A wild cheer went up from the shrews. Log-a-log laughed heartily. "Well done, Pikkle! I liked that little joke about anyone else taking Tubgutt's place. Good, eh, Mara?"

Mara gave Log-a-log a blank look. "That was no joke. Pikkle meant it. Look, he's on his sixteenth!"

The Guosssom shrews were laughing, patting Pikkle's back and cheering him to the echo. Bowley the cook held Pikkle's paw aloft.

"The winner by a clear four bowls of pudding, Pikkle the hare from Salamandastron is the champion!"

Amid the cheering and applause Pikkle smiled modestly, trying to pull his spooning paw from Bowley's grasp. "Steady on, chaps. Leggo me paw will you, Bowley old lad. It's bad form to stop a fellow in mid-scoff!"

Covered by a blanket, Pikkle lay on a ledge, snoring loudly. Mara sat with Log-a-log and his son Nordo. The other shrews had retired for the night.

Though Mara had been glad to escape Salamandastron she could not reconcile herself to the idea of Urthstripe being besieged along with the hares inside the mountain. A sudden yearning to be back there, giving what aid she could, caused the young badger maid to turn to the shrew leader.

"Log-a-log, I want to thank you and your tribe for

rescuing us and showing us the hospitality of your home, but I am anxious to go back to Salamandastron. I have told you about what will be happening there, so why can I not go?"

"All in good time, Mara. All in good time." Log-a-log patted her paw. "When you do go, the Guosssom warriors and I will be with you. I have crossed swords with this Klitch you speak of—aye, and his father Ferahgo. The blue-eyed ones are our enemies; we would wear out logboats traveling to fight against them."

Mara nodded. "Then why do we not go now?"

Log-a-log took a sip of shrewbeer from his tankard. "Because I need you to do something for me. Listen and I will tell you. I am leader of the Guosssom because I am the strongest; that is the only thing that keeps our tribe together without the Blackstone. The Guosssom will follow the shrew who holds the Blackstone—it is sacred to us shrews. I held the Blackstone from the time it was passed to me by my father, who got it from his father before him. It makes the holder undisputed leader of all shrews. Well, one day when my son Nordo was little he took it from around my neck as I slept. I did not worry too much because Nordo was a baby who liked to play with the Blackstone. I let him, thinking that one day it would be his by right. However, Nordo lost the stone. I took the blame on myself, not wanting him to be shunned by the Guosssom, and since then I have been leader only by my authority and fighting skills."

"Where did Nordo lose the Blackstone?" Mara could not help interrupting. "And how does it concern me?"

Nordo took up the story from his father. "You must understand our ways, Mara. The importance of the Blackstone is great in our tribe. Without it my father leads only by his strength; if he possesses the stone then he is leader not only by his toughness, but by Guosssom law. . . . But let me tell you my story. "One of the tributaries of the Great South Stream leads out on

177

to a large lake, so big it is like an inland sea. I drifted out there in a little logboat that my father made for me—actually I fell asleep and the logboat took its own course. The oars were lost overboard as I slept. I drifted around on the big lake for more than two days, then I sighted an island near its center. Paddling with my paws, I made it to the island. There I searched the woods, looking for suitable wood to make oars so that I could row back home. Having no knife or sword, I could not cut wood. I searched all day without success. When night fell I went to sleep in the woods. It was like a dream. I was suddenly wakened by a dreadful roar. A huge white creature stood over me. It was terrifying, more ghost than fur or blood. It had hold of the Blackstone. I screamed and ran off, leaving the Blackstone and the broken thong that it had hung from. The ghost had it. I made it back to my little logboat and drifted round until the evening of the next day, when I was found by my father and a search party who were scouring the lake with the big logboat fleet. Since then no shrew has been near the big lake or the island where the ghost lives. But with you along I might be able to get the Blackstone."

"I don't understand. Why must you have me along?" Mara scratched her head in puzzlement.

Log-a-log spoke then, keeping his voice low. "Because you are a badger, and the ghost that haunts the island of the big lake is a badger also, a huge white one without stripes!"

20

Samkim and Arula sat in the late afternoon sun peeling the mud from themselves. Spriggat had proved correct: the stings came out with the mud. The young squirrel picked the last of it from his tail bush.

"That mud is marvelous stuff, Arula. Look, there's not a sting on me and scarcely a lump. I feel great."

"Ho urr, an' oi loikwoise. 'Tis champeen mud, as 'ee say. Oi wunner whurr Maister Spriggat be agone to?"

They had been so preoccupied with bankmud and stings that neither of them had noticed the curious hedgehog's disappearance.

Samkim rubbed his back energetically against the rough bark of a hornbeam tree. "Ooh, that feels good. I expect old Spriggat's about somewhere. No need to worry over him—he can take care of himself all right."

"Hohohoh! That I can, young feller m'lad. Here's yer tucker bags." Spriggat materialized out of the woods and tossed the two haversacks upon the bank. He was picking wasp wings from his teeth again. "I been back yonder 'mid the lupins and found these. Mmmtk! Found that broken waspnest too. I'm full as a stuffed duck. There's nothin' in all the woodlands like a good feed o' buzzers, no sir."

Samkim and Arula checked their supplies. Most of the food was intact. They thanked him and sat down to share a small flask of October ale with their new-found friend.

Spriggat swigged at the flask, a slow smile spreading across his snout. "Hoho, this be prime stuff. 'Tober ale, ye call it. An 'og could get use to a drink like this, I tell ye! Oh, by the by, young uns, I picked up the tracks of that stoat with your sword—not too far from 'ere, travelin' south an' west. If you feels up to it we can start trackin' right away."

No further encouragement was needed. The two friends shouldered their haversacks and weapons. Spriggat was not a fast traveler; he was slow but exceedingly thorough.

"Not too long till dusk now. See 'ere? Swordpoint's been stuck in the ground—usin' it as a walkin' stick, the rascal is. Look, this is a smear of blood from a wound on the bole of this elm."

Samkin watched the hedgehog carefully. He was a master of trail and woodcraft, and without him it would have been nigh on impossible to follow Dingeye's track. His wisdom and experience were proving invaluable in their search.

Spriggat noticed their wonderment and laughed good-naturedly. "Hohohoh. Never fret, I'll learn ye, young uns. 'Tis no disgrace to be shown a trick or two. I had t' learn the 'ard way. . . ." He paused to pluck a dragonfly from mid-flight and gobble it up. "Hmm, that'n were a longways from his stream. Tasty though. Now what were I sayin'? Oh aye, yew tew watch an' take notice, an' soon you'll 'ave young 'eads on old shoulders."

"Doant'ee mean owd 'eads on young shoulders, zurr?" Arula corrected him.

"Hohohoh, so I do. You're a bright un, Arula. A quick learner, eh!"

In the depths of the woodlands, dusk overtook the trackers swiftly, the sunset in the west casting darkness between the haphazard columns of trees.

Spriggat held up a cautionary paw. "Camp yonder beneath that three-topped oak. Mind now, no fire tonight—we be dangerous close to your enemy. I can smell somethin' I don't likes on th' breeze. Yew tew bide by the oak and get supper ready. I won't be gone long."

Before they could reply he had melted into the undergrowth ahead of them. Samkim and Arula squatted beneath the sheltering boughs of the oak and set out a simple supper of oatcake and apple, uncorking a small flask of elderberry wine for their absent friend.

They had long eaten supper and were dozing on the soft moss at the base of the oak when a snap of wood caused them to come alert. Spriggat stood beside them with both halves of the dead twig in his paws.

"Hohohoh, a lesson learned is a lesson remembered, I 'opes. Never both go asleep together, always 'ave one on guard an' t'other sleepin'—that way yew tew will never be sneaked up on, like I just did. What's this? Mmm, tastes good!"

Samkim refused the proffered flask, letting the hedgehog drink as much as he liked. "It's elderberry wine, Mr. Spriggat, made at Redwall Abbey. Keep the flask and drink it all. What did you find out there?"

Spriggat caught a droning gnat neatly with a flick of his head. He chewed it reflectively. "Gnats ain't nearly good as wasps 'n' bees—too acid-tastin'. Now, where were I? Oh aye, what did I find? Well, I'll tell yew tew, that were a strange scent I caught on the breeze a while back. 'Twas death! Aye, death an' other things . . . the whiff of rats—can't mistake that stench—fox, too, though I can't be certain o' that . . ."

181

Arula rocked back and forth impatiently. "Burrhoo, Maister Spriggat, wot did 'ee find out'n thurr?"

"No sight fer yew tew t'be lookin' upon, young uns." Spriggat took a sip of wine and smacked his lips appreciatively. "It were the stoat, but his 'ead was chopped clear off! Most likely done wi' that sword you're a-seekin'."

Samkim was shocked that the sword of Martin the Warrior should have been put to such base use as murder. "Nobeast could use Martin's blade so foully. It's dreadful! The sword of our Abbey Warrior was only ever lifted to defend the right and good in fair combat. How could anybeast treat it in such a wicked way?"

The old hedgehog shook his head at the young squirrel's innocence. "Ye've a lot to learn, laddie. There's no magic in any weapon. That sword may be used for good or evil; it all depends on the creature who wields it. C'mon now, sleep. We've got a full day ahead tomorrow. Rats 'n' foxes ain't as careless about their tracks as that pore silly stoat were."

That night Samkim's head was full of dreams. Martin the Warrior appeared, and there was the rolling hiss of great waters. Shadowy figures fought battles across the paths of his mind, great lumbering mist-shrouded creatures . . . badgers! The voice of the Warrior echoed all around:

"Courage, Samkim, courage. Follow and find my sword, for destiny lies heavy upon you. Trust Spriggat, and take care of Arula. I am with you, no matter how far you may roam. Do not lose heart. Remember the words of Spriggat: the sword may be used for good or evil by the creature who wields it . . ."

The dawn was shrouded in a curtain of drizzle, though the thick woodlands offered fair protection. After a hasty breakfast the three searchers set off, Spriggat

leading them on a course that skirted the headless carcass of Dingeye. Still following a southwest trail, they
pushed on until midmorning, when they halted in an
open sward. The rain had ceased though the sky overhead was gray with rolling clouds.

Spriggat cast about. "Hohohoh, whoever is carryin'
yon blade couldn't resist a chop at this wild mint—I
smelled it soon as we got 'ere. Look, see the cut stems?
That sword is leavin' its own trail. It's as if it knows yew
tew is follerin' it."

"Yurr et be a very swingable sword," Arula agreed.
"Sharp, too, hurr."

Two rabbits popped up from the ferns at the edge of
the sward and began chattering simultaneously.

"Stupid sword, stupid fox, stupid rats!"

"Weren't chopping mint, y'know. Oh no, oh no!"

"Trying to chop us. By the burrow, they were!"

"Hope you haven't got any silly ideas about chopping
rabbits?"

Their heads bobbed up and down as they spoke.
They ran two paces back, turned and ran two paces
forward all the time they were talking, alternately
showing their white bobtails and scared faces.

Samkim shouldered his bow to show they meant no
harm. He spread his paws wide and smiled openly.
"Don't fear, friends. We're not the kind of creatures
who go about chopping up rabbits. I'm Samkim of
Redwall, this is Arula and he is Spriggat the wasp-eater.
We won't harm you."

The two rabbits stopped hopping about and bared
their teeth in what they hoped was a fearsome grimace.

"Harm us, hah! Don't you know I'm Fangslayer?"

"No you're not. I'm Fangslayer. You were Fangslayer
yesterday. You can be Deatheye today."

"All right. Listen here, you're talking to Deatheye
now, so watch yourself, you scruffy squirrel, moldy
mole and hairless hog!"

The moldy mole picked up a hazel twig and took an angry pace forward. "Naow lookit yurr, bunnies, you'm moind yurr manners or oi'll tan 'ee fur wi' this stick, hurr urr, so oi will!"

The two rabbits hugged each other and yelled aloud in panic. "Mummy, Mummy, the mole's going to beat us with a stick!"

A large fat female rabbit waddled out of the undergrowth some distance away and began berating the two rabbits. "Clarence, Clarissa, what have I told you about speaking to strange creatures? Get back to the burrow immediately!"

The rabbits stamped their paws petulantly. "Oh, Mummy, we're Fangslayer and Deatheye, not Clarence and Clarissa."

She bustled over and seized them by their ears. "I'll give you Fangslayer and Deatheye, you naughty bunnies. Didn't I tell you to stop inside the burrow after being chased by that horrid fox and those smelly rats?" She tweaked their ears until they yelped. "Well, didn't I?"

Spriggat made a courtly old-fashioned bow to her. "You'll excuse me, marm, but we won't harm your young uns. Did you say that a fox and six rats came by this way today?"

She turned on the hedgehog with a mixture of temper and impatience. "That's right, an evil-looking fox and six filthy rats. The fox had a sword too. Would you credit it, he tried to chop up my little Clarence and Clarissa, the ruffian! What are the woods coming to? As for you three, be off with you. Beating little bunnies with sticks! Have you nothing better to do with yourselves? Now clear off, go on! The other lot went that way, southwest. You tell that fox if you see him that I'll give him a piece of my mind when he passes this way again, verminous villain!"

She receded into the woodland, shaking the two rabbits by their ears and carrying on at them in a motherly way. "Straight to bed. That'll teach you two. And no lunch for either of you until you learn to behave properly. Fangeye and Deathslayer indeed. Behaving like two little savages!"

"Waaah, leggo my ears, Mummy!"

"Wahahaaah! Don't want to go to rotten ol' bed, Mummy!"

When they had stopped laughing, Spriggat ate a passing butterfly. "Huh, all wings an' no taste, those things. Well, yew tew, I 'opes all the enemies you meet be as 'armless as those, though if you stood lissenin' t' that mummy rabbit for long she'd wear you to bits wi' 'er tongue. Right, young uns. Let's press on."

As soon as darkness had fallen on the previous night, Ferahgo put his plan into operation. The horde went charging towards Salamandastron, chanting as they brandished their weapons.

"Fer-ah-go! Kill! Kill! Kill! Ferahgoooooo!"

In the dining hall, Urthstripe sat with Sapwood and Oxeye taking supper. The sounds of the war chant reached their ears. Oxeye sighed wearily as he put down his beaker.

"Night attack, sah. Shall we just block all openin's an' sit doggo in here? They can't harm us, and all that's required is a score of defenders round the crater rim. We can relieve them through the night, wot?"

But Urthstripe was loath to sit still while there was the faintest chance of battle. He pushed aside his chair. "What? Sit in here while those scum crawl all over my mountain? Never! This is the ideal time to set up a few surprises for Ferahgo. Follow me. We'll need long poles, archers, and oil too. Have that big barrel from my forge brought up to the crater top."

Ferahgo, perched upon a low rock with Klitch and Crab-eyes, watched the masses climbing the outer rocks of the mountainous front face of Salamandastron. Dog-head the stoat captain ignited a torch, and others began lighting their torches from it. Soon the mountain was ablaze with twinkling lights as the attackers sought to find openings in the rocks that would lead them into the mountain. Dewnose had led three ferrets ahead of the rest. They were almost halfway up when one of them yelled, "Over 'ere! There's an openin', a sorta window cut into the rocks!"

They scrambled to get in, Dewnose leading the way.

"Evening, chaps. Nice night to learn flyin', wot?"

Bart Thistledown and Pennybright thrust forward with their long poles. Dewnose saw what was happening too late. The poles hit him square in the chest and he shot outward with a scream.

"No, don't. . . . Yeeeaaaggghhh!"

Together with one of the ferrets who had squeezed in the window aperture with him, he went sailing into outer space. All over the mountain similar flying lessons were taking place.

Down below, Klitch roared up at the crowds of soldiers who were trying to scramble back down, "Up! Keep going. Get to the top, you worthless cowards!" He ran forward, climbing upward and belaboring all about him with his spearbutt. "Come on, follow me, I'm not scared!"

Ferahgo urged the attackers up, keeping the assault centered on the seaward side of the mountain. This way he hoped that Farran would have a clear path on the landward side.

Crabeyes unslung his bow. "Shall I get the archers firin', Master?"

"Addlebrain!" The Assassin pushed him aside scornfully. "They can't see anything to fire at. We'd be killing our own. Tell them to light more torches. Climb up there with 'em, and see if you can't fire some arrows from close range into those slits they're pushing the poles out of."

Sapwood clad himself in old rags and climbed out on to the mountain face. The bold hare moved about freely in his disguise. A weasel carrying a torch and shaking a pike climbed level with him. The Sergeant dispatched him with a swinging left-paw uppercut, the weasel's lifeless body bouncing like a broken doll as it hit the ledges on its way down. Another weasel raised his spear at Sapwood as he balanced precariously.

"Hoi! You're not one of u—Aaaarrgghhhh!"

The boxing hare merely banged his paws down on the weasel's footpaws and the unfortunate spear-carrier danced painfully on empty space for a second before plunging shoreward. Sapwood spat on his paws and went in search of others.

On the shoreward rim of the crater, Urthstripe and Oxeye were tipping the barrel of forge oil over a heap of large boulders. When the barrel was empty the badger Lord kicked away the wedge holding the boulders back. With a loud rumble they bounced off down the mountainside, and Urthstripe flung the empty barrel after them with a wild laugh.

Climbing nimbly, Klitch was almost halfway up the mountain.

A ferret named Frang grabbed his paw. "Sir, what's that noise?"

"Noise?" Klitch pushed him savagely away. "It's the sound of battle, you fool. Keep climbing!"

Farther up, a rat gave a half-scream as the first of the boulders ground him flat, the flames from his torch setting him ablaze as he rumbled downward. Now the boulders were smashing into the topmost attackers, killing them instantly and igniting into huge fireballs as they touched the blazing torches which they had carried on Ferahgo's orders.

Crabeyes and the troops who had just started their climb came dashing back down.

"Master, get out of the way!" The Captain yelled as he passed Ferahgo.

Ferahgo took one backward glance at the mountain as he fled. The front face of Salamandastron was lit up bright as day, and rocks roared with the wind fanning their flames as the blazing boulders cracked and burst, sending death and devastation widespread among the shrieking horde of the Assassin. Above it all could be heard the booming laughter and exultant warshout of Urthstripe, Lord of Salamandastron.

"Hahahaha! Eulaliaaaaaa!"

Farran the Poisoner slid noiselessly over the far topside of the crater. Without pause he made his way down and into the corridors of the mountain fortress. The first door he came to he opened silently, and he looked inside. Nothing there. Shutting the door, he turned around to find himself face-to-face with Windpaw. The female hare was hurrying up toward the crater top with a supply of oil-soaked arrows. Swifter than her eye could follow, Farran flicked out a dagger made from greenhart wood and thrust the poisoned tip into the side of her neck. Windpaw did not even have a chance to call for help. She died instantly, her face in an agonized grimace. Moving like a flickering lamp shadow, Farran slid effortlessly down the passage, checking a cave here, opening a chamber there, until he found what he wanted. The water barrels were arranged along one wall, ten huge oaken tun vats. The black fox sighed almost lovingly as he lifted the lid of one and took a sip. Cool and sweet, rainwater and clear springwater mixed—it was perfect, but not for long.

Carefully uncorking a green glass vial, the Poisoner

went about his deadly work, dividing the contents of the vial evenly between the ten barrels. It was the work of a moment, then he was gone.

Slipping off down the corridor, he descended a rough-hewn flight of rock stairs to the lower level. Farran spent considerable time checking the rooms on this level; they were all armory chambers. The pale eyes showed no emotion, but he knew that he was wasting valuable time. Down the next flight of stairs he went in his search for the foodstore. Unfortunately, every room he went into was a dormitory. Taking a long spiral stairway, he found himself in the dining room. Farran knew then that the foodstore would be somewhere close by, near to the kitchens.

It was quiet inside at the base level of Salamandastron; the rock walls shut off all noise from the outside. The Poisoner padded softly about until he found the kitchen entrance. His amber eyes flickered slightly at the sight of the food laid out there for the next morning's breakfast. Ferahgo had never fed his army this well.

Washing his paws meticulously, the black fox seated himself and ate his fill. Oatcakes, warm and fresh from the ovens—he spread them with comb honey and chewed them with relish, washing them down with gulps of old golden cider; summer vegetable pasties and beechnut crumble, crusty brown bread with mountain cheese—the black fox sampled each one in turn. When he had finished, Farran wiped his lips daintily on a napkin and set about poisoning it all.

Having finished in the kitchen, he sought out the storeroom that led off it. Sacks of flour, vegetable racks, apple boxes, salad bins, nut containers—nothing escaped the deadly potions of Farran the Poisoner. A scattering of powder here, a few drops of liquid there . . . it was accomplished with his evil, but natural skill.

21

Midmorning was cloudy, but promising to clear up later. Thrugg and Dumble had been wakened by the dawn drizzle. The otter sat the little dormouse in the top of the haversack and covered his head with the flap. Shouldering the lot, he strode off northward.

"Better on the move than sittin' round gettin' a wet bottom, eh, matey. Come on, give ol' Thrugg a song t' keep his paws goin'."

Anybeast on the road at that time would have marveled at the sight of the big otter stepping out with a singing haversack strapped to his back. Dumble sang his dormouse song.

"There's no roof mouse, nor chimbley mouse,
No winder mouse or floor mouse,
An' I ain't gotta nokker on me nose,
    but I'm a likkle dormouse.
There's a fieldmouse anna 'arvest mouse,
An 'edgemouse an' prob'ly a shoremouse,
But I'm the bestest of the lot,
'Cos I'm a likkle dormouse.
Ohahaha an' heeheehee,
Yes I'm a likkle dormouse.

So I'll eat me dinner an' grow big,
An' then I'll be enor-mouse!"

"Ahoy up there, don't yer know no songs about
otters, matey?"

By noon the weather had cleared. White clouds scud-
ded across a sunny blue sky on the light breeze.
Dumble was freed from the haversack. He skipped
along at Thrugg's side, enjoying the freedom of the
open road. The otter slowed down, placing a restraining paw on his small friend.

"Whoa there, shipmate. What's that sittin' in the road
up ahead?"

The shapeless mass lying on the path some distance
ahead started moving awkwardly to one side, making
for the thinning forest on the right. Dumble skipped
round Thrugg and began racing toward the object.

"Dumble, come back 'ere, you liddle thick 'ead!"
Thrugg roared out as the infant dashed toward the
thing.

But Dumble had a good head start and plunged
onward, ignoring his friend's shouts. Thrugg stamped
his paws down hard several times; but then, deciding it
was useless, he gave chase.

It was a falcon, a season fledged and of no great size.
The bird flopped about with its right wing hanging
awkwardly as it struggled to seek shelter in the thinning
woodlands at the path's east side. Dumble cut off its
escape and squatted in front of it, holding out a friendly
paw.

"Aaahhh, poor birdie, is your wing 'urted?"

The falcon halted, its fierce golden eyes distending as
it hissed a warning through its dangerous hooked beak:

"Kaarrhzz! Stan' oot o' mah way, bairn, or I'll mak'
dead meat o' ye."

The little dormouse chuckled and tossed a piece of

candied chestnut in front of the savage creature. "Dumble won't 'urt you. 'Ave some food. It's nice . . ."

The bird hopped to the nut and devoured it hungrily. Thrugg arrived just then. He decided Dumble and the falcon were too close to each other for him to intervene. Holding his breath anxiously, the otter stood to one side. The bird cocked its head and squinted at him through one eye.

"Hauld yer wheesht, riverdog! Hey, canna this wee bairn no onnerstand me? Does he not know he's in peril? Ah'm no a sparrow, ye ken. Ah'm a falcon!"

When Thrugg had got the meaning of the bird's high northland accent he replied, "Oh, I can see you're a falcon all right, matey. Lookit me, I'm an otter. An' I hopes you don't mean my liddle pal any harm, 'cos I'd hate to 'ave ter slay you with this 'ere sling!" The big otter twirled his loaded sling meaningfully.

Dumble held out his paw, offering the falcon more bits of candied chestnut. The bird ate them gently, keeping a wary eye on Thrugg and talking conversationally.

"Aye, Ah catch yer drift. We're both warriors the noo. Ach! Ye've no need tae be feared for the wee yin, Ah couldnae hurt a fly wi' mah wing breaked an' hurtin' like 'tis. Mind, though, Ah'm a falcon, not an eedjit, an' Ah'd no be slow in givin' a guid account of mahsel', even to a big bonnie laddie the like o' you!"

Thrugg unshouldered his pack and sat down, smiling good-naturedly. "Call it quits then, matey. You don't hurt us an' we won't hurt you. I'm Thrugg an' this is Dumble. We're from Redwall." He set out oatcake and cheese in three portions.

The falcon relaxed as all three set to eating lunch. "Ah'm beholden to yer for the guid food, Thrugg. Mah name is Rocangus, only son o' Mactalon, Laird O' the High Crags. Och aye, mah home is in the great northern mountains, a braw place tae live. Ah was lost an' driven by the wind some days ago, and had tae land in yon woods, ye ken. 'Twas there the crows set upon me. Ach! They're a sair lot o' cowards. Ten o' them it took tae bring me down. That's how mah wing was breakit."

Thrugg took a careful look at the wing. Rocangus stood still, bravely bearing up under the otter's searching paw.

"You're got a fractured bone there, shipmate. Still, I don't suppose one more passenger will break me old back. Come along with us. We're bound for the mountains of the north in search of the Flowers of Icetor."

Rocangus looked incredulously at him. "Ach, ye mean Ah'm stuck wi' two landbound dunderheads lookin' for the Flowers of Icetor an' Ah cannae fly?"

Dumble stroked the falcon's back. "Come wiv us, 'Ocangus. Mista Thugg is a good carrier, y'know."

Thrugg searched out bindweed, motherwort and pine resin. He made a compound and bound the injured wing, using a willow twig and wild rhubarb fibers to secure the dressing.

"There, that'll do the trick! Once that pine resin sets firm, the wort 'n' weed will do their work. Don't try to move that there wing, mate. The more you keep it still the quicker it'll heal up. Now, young Rocangus, you can be our navigator. Which way is it to the north mountains?"

The young falcon held the wing stiffly at his side as he pointed into the woodlands to the northeast. "Yonder, though Ah'm no certain sure. 'Tis different when a bird's no up in the sky, ye ken. Still, dinna fash yersel'. We'll get there all right."

Dumble refused to ride in the haversack. He trotted along at Thrugg's side. Despite his pleas, Rocangus was made to perch on top of the haversack on Thrugg's back. Latching his powerful talons into the straps, he hung on gamely.

"If mah faither could see me now he'd kick mah tailfeathers. Intae the woods wi' ye, Thrugg, ya great bonnie riverdog!"

The curious-looking trio struck northeast into the far tip of the Mossflower woodlands.

The trees were beginning to thin out into flat bush-strewn country, and by midafternoon they had covered a fair distance. Dumble found ripe blackberries and a tree thick with small soft pears, so they stocked up on both. Thrugg rested awhile, watching both the young creatures feeding each other the choicest berries; their faces, both whisker and beak, were heavily stained with the purple juice.

The otter hefted the pack up onto his back, calling to Rocangus, "Up on yore perch, matey. There's plenty o' daylight left yet."

The falcon nodded toward a thick grove of pine and spruce ahead. "Keep your wits aboot ye, Thrugg. That's crow territory!"

The afternoon was hot and still. Thrugg cast a glance at the grove. Placing Dumble on his left side, he slipped loose his sling, testing the thongs as he loaded a flat pebble into it. There was no sign of crows circling in the air above the trees, but the trio took no chances. They traveled cautiously, keeping hidden among the low brush, fern clumps and any cover the land could afford. Giving the pine grove a wide berth, they went in a curving line, moving at a moderate pace, not too slowly or too quickly, knowing the crows would be down upon them if they betrayed their presence by unnecessary noise. Even Dumble was aware of their precarious position. Every now and then he would give his friends a wink and hold a paw up to his lips as they trekked along in silence.

Everything went well, until the little dormouse stepped on a thistle.

194

"Wowhoo! I stood onna fissle, Mista Thrugg. Ouch!"

The pine- and sprucetops rustled, loud cawing cut the still air, and ragged black shapes came flapping out of the grove.

Rocangus gave a shrill cry. "Ach! It's crows. We're for it, laddies!"

The sandy bed of a dried stream formed a depression in the land ahead of them. Thrugg grabbed Dumble by his smock and made a dash for it. The running otter was soon spotted by the crows. Winging swiftly, they came after him as he ran heavy-laden for the streambed. Calling harshly to each other, the crows zoomed down at Thrugg's back. Rocangus dealt the first one a savage rip with his curved beak as it tried to latch its claws into the back of Thrugg's neck. Whisker over tail, the otter threw himself into the shallow bottom. Throwing off the haversack, he brained a low-flying crow with his loaded sling. Loosing off the stone, he watched another crow fall crazily amid a jumble of tailfeathers as the pebble struck it. Thrugg's fighting blood was up now. Standing tall, he whirled the sling, roaring out the Abbey warcry:

"Redwaaaalll! Come on, you lousy-feathered fleabags. I'm Thrugg, the Warrior of the Waterways! Redwaaaaalllll!"

Little Dumble tugged the thistle from his footpad, seized a long stick which lay nearby and stood alongside the haversack where Rocangus was perched, ready with beak and talon. Together they sang out their battle calls.

"I'm Dumble from Reedddwwaaaaallll!"

"Ah'm Rocangus, son o' the great Laird Mactalon! Kreeegaaarr!"

Two crows landed and came hopskipping fiercely toward Dumble, their vicious beaks like dirty yellow daggers. Dumble thwacked out hard, cracking the spindly legs of the first one. Rocangus bowled the other one

over, tearing madly at it with his hooked beak. Thrugg
took several sharp pecks in his back. Laying one crow
senseless with a hefty smack of his rudder-like tail, he
whirled about, kicking one high in a cloud of black
feathers as he thudded the loaded sling into the chest of
another. Rocangus was scrabbling in the sand against
three more crows, ripping with his talons and stabbing
with his beak. He did not see the crow that pecked
Dumble's paw. The little dormouse squeaked with pain
and dropped his stick. Immediately two huge crows
seized him and began bearing him aloft. He hovered in
the air, shrieking.

"Mista Thuuuuuggg!"

With a bellow of rage, the brawny otter grabbed the
haversack by its straps. Swinging it round, he threw the
laden pack and smashed the two crows out of the air.

Dumble fell, did a tumble and snatched up his stick.
Falling on the two crows, he beat them mercilessly,
pounding beaks, tails, legs and wings furiously. "Ya
nasty ol' crones, takin' Dumble up inna sky!"

The three friends fought so fiercely that they drove
off the crows. The birds cawed angrily, perching on low
bushes and performing a curious hopskip dance on the
ground as they chanted, "Krak krak, yah yah, killa
beast, eata mouse, killa 'ookbeak!"

From the slight cover of the streambed Rocangus stood
with Thrugg and Dumble, watching the performance.

"Have ye ever seen sich a bunch o' cowards?" The
falcon clacked his beak contemptuously. "If mah wing
was better Ah'd go o'er there an' send 'em weepin' tae
their mammies!"

Thrugg wrapped a hasty dressing round Dumble's
pecked paw. "They'll be back, mate. You can bet on it.
They're just gettin' their nerve up agin. Look, there's
more o' the villains comin' out o' the pines."

Dumble brandished his stick in a warlike manner.

196

"Let them come, Mista Thugg. Dumble'll smack their bottoms wiv this big stick!"

Rocangus set his beak in a grim line. "Ah've nae doubt ye will, laddie, but they crows can come doon like leaves in autumn wind. Yon's only a few of 'em!"

"Stand by, mates. Here they come agin!"

"Aye, an' there's more o' the blaggards circlin' in from behind!"

"Come on, crones. Dumble's ready. Redwaaaaalllll!"

Skimming low over the grass, the crows came winging in to the attack. Thrugg blinded the first four with double pawfuls of dry sand. A crow was about to land on top of his head with beak open ready to bite, when Dumble thrust the stick straight down its throat. Four crows flung themselves upon Rocangus; all that could be seen was an explosion of black feathers mottled with the brown ones of the falcon as they fought with mad savagery. Two more landed and attacked Thrugg from behind. Again his ruddered tail came into heavy action, breaking the neck of one bird. The other shot backwards, stunned by a kick from his backpaw. Dumble's stick broke across an enemy head. He snatched up both halves and went at the landing crows like a miniature thunderstorm. The crows were beginning to win by sheer weight of numbers. They swooped in and landed in gangs upon the three friends until none of them could be seen under the mass of black feathers, beaks and scratching claws. Dumble screamed in pain as a beak pecked him hard between his ears.

Suddenly Thrugg could stand it no more. The sound of the infant dormouse being tormented by the crows drove him into a towering rage. Kicking, butting and punching birds, he arose from the tangle with blood dripping from his bared teeth. Fighting his way across the dry streambed, he grabbed hold of Dumble and Rocangus. Standing in front of them, he hefted the laden haversack in both paws and began swinging it like some terrible engine of destruction. Crows exploded into the air, wing over beak over tail over tip. Dark feathers showered the air, together with beak fragments and broken claws. The haversack was a thudding, banging, swishing blur of destruction as Thrugg's head went back and his mouth opened like a scarlet cavern.

"Redwaaaaaaaaallllll!!!"

The crows fled, some hopping, others flapping as they fought each other to get away from Thrugg's mighty retaliation.

As late afternoon faded into evening, the three companions sat tending to each other's wounds.

Thrugg winced as Rocangus dug a beak fragment from his back. "Ouch! Go easy there, you feathered fiend!"

"Hah, stop grievin', planktail. Ye'll live. Haud still while Ah get this crowclaw out o' yer thick heid."

Baby Dumble was counting his war wounds. "Two, free, six, nine, twennyfifteen. Wow, that's a lot!"

"Aye, an' that's a lot out there, matey. Look!"

They followed the direction of Thrugg's pointing paw. Halfway between the pinegrove and the streambed the land was black with crows. They crowded together like beetles in a cellar.

Thrugg sat down with his back against the sun-dried bank. "Nobeast could fight off that many, Rocangus. We're done for."

The falcon preened his tattered breastfeathers. "Aye, but by the crag we'll go oot a-fightin'!"

Dumble searched in the sand of the streambed. "I wanna new stick to fight more crones wiv!"

Slowly the sun began sinking in the west. The sky was a warm peach color with dove-gray pennants of cloud showing silver underbellies. Heatwaves still shimmered in the distance.

Thrugg sat awhile, gazing sadly at the beauty of it all. "Hmm, it ain't too bad for an' old streamdog like me. I've had a good innin's an' enjoyed meself. But you two young uns, I wish you could've seen more seasons to yore string afore you 'ave to go. Still an' all, we're all good mateys, so we'll take a load of 'em with us an' go out in the good company of each other."

Dumble had found a stick. He peered over the bank, wrinkling his nose, fearless in his babyish innocence. "Why are all the crones quiet, 'Ocangus?"

The young falcon winced as he settled his fractured wing right. "Ye'd best hope those birds stay quiet, laddie. When the beasties start up their chantin' again, that's when they'll come for us."

"Can Dumble have some squashy blackb'rries an' pears, Mista Thugg?"

Thrugg undid the haversack that he had used as a flail upon the bodies of many crows. The once tasty contents were squashed flat. "Bless yer 'eart, liddle un, 'course you can. 'Elp yourself." The otter sat with a sad smile on his face, watching Dumble eat.

Rocangus touched his paw with the uninjured wing. "Dinna worry, streamdog, we'll give yon birds a battle tae remember and sing aboot—those that are left alive."

The last gleam of twilight was showing on the horizon when the massed army of crows began to chant themselves into a frenzy. It echoed dirgelike across the deserted countryside.

22

A half-moon hung in a sky of aquamarine. Paddles dipped noiselessly into the high-banked waters as two logboats threaded their way down a tributary far from the Great South Stream. Both craft were loaded to the gunwales with Guosssom shrews. Mara and Pikkle traveled in the front vessel. They had been going since dawn, sailing along an intricate network of backwaters. Beside them Log-a-log and Nordo checked the barkcloth charts showing the route.

"How much farther before we're there, Nordo?" Mara murmured sleepily.

"We should get there by dawn, with any luck. Get some sleep, you two. We're running downstream—put your paddles up."

Pikkle looked around. Save for the watch shrews, all the others had settled down to catch some rest. He patted his stomach. "Bit of tucker wouldn't go amiss, wot! How's a chap supposed to sleep when the old tum starts growlin' an' keepin' him awake, that's what I'd like t' know!"

Reaching into a sack that was stowed in the bows, Log-a-log passed two large round flat objects to the hare. "Try these, Pikkle. They're shrews' long-voyage hardtack biscuits. They might have been baked quite a few seasons ago but they're full of nourishment. You should enjoy them."

"Oof!" Pikkle attempted to bite into one and came away nursing his mouth. "Nearly bust all me molars. What're these things made of—stone? I'll bet even old Tubbyguts couldn't get his jaws around one of these things. I say, Mara, try bitin' one of these. Go on!"

The badger maid pushed away the proffered hardtack biscuit. "Not me. I value my teeth—save 'em to sling at the ghost badger."

Pikkle shuddered and dropped the biscuit. It landed with a clatter in the bottom of the boat. "Oh, thanks a lot, big-mouthed badger. First I can't eat these bally biscuits and now you've gone an' put me off sleepin' for the night with your talk of ghosts. Bit of a bad show all round, I'd say, robbin' a chap of appetite an' sleep!"

Mara fell asleep to the sounds of Pikkle chuntering away indignantly to himself.

She woke in the early dawn light. The logboats were traveling rapidly downstream, bumping and speeding over small rapids as the Guosssom shrew steerbeasts maneuvered them skillfully along the risky waterway. The high steep banks on both sides flashed by. Now and then Nordo would call out for everybeast to duck an overhanging tree. Pikkle was wide awake and ashen-faced as he gripped the sides of the boat, pleading for a reduced speed.

"I say, chaps. Be good eggs an' tell the jolly old Cap'n to slow down a bit, will you? Whoooo! All this uppin' an' downin', speedin' an' bumpin' – I feel quite queasy."

The shrews who were fending the banks off with their paddles made the most of Pikkle's discomfort by ribbing him aloud.

"Try some cold custard and cabbage for breakfast, mate. Haha!"

"Or some warm oatmeal mixed with black treacle an' carrots!"

"How about a stale vegetable pastie with sour cream over it!"

Pikkle lay in the bottom of the boat, clasping his stomach. "Mercy, chaps! Shut up, you shameful shrews. Take pity on a feller, please! Cold custard 'n' cabbage. . . . Bloouurrpp!"

"Hold tight, all paws! It's the lake!"

Mara clasped the sides tightly as the stream took a sharp downward curve. The boats shot forward on a wild helter-skelter ride. Bows forward, they plunged down. Suddenly an immense splash and a great bow wave drenched everybeast, then the two longboats rocked gently on the broad surface of a great lake.

"Never again!" Pikkle wailed piteously. "All this for a bletherin' Blackstone. You chaps must be off your bally rockers. Blackstone, my aunt's whiskers! Once this hare gets his paws on dry ground he's finished boatin' for good!"

Mara stared about her in amazement. They were on the edges of a fantastic body of water—it was a veritable inland sea. The fresh morning sunlight beamed down upon tideless waters whose only movement was the outgoing ripples set up by the logboats' entry into them. As far as any eye could see, there was water, leagues of it, with no sign of island or shore on the distant horizon. To the left and right of them the broad expanse was sheltered by fringed forest with trees, bushes, shrubs and plants dipping their foliage into the water. It was vast and beautiful in its silent serenity; stillness reigned everywhere.

Log-a-log smiled at the badger maid's wide-eyed expression. "How's that for a sight on a lovely summer morning, miss?"

202

Mara could only shake her head in silent admiration of the scene.

"I say, you chaps, this is a bit more like it, wot? I'm feelin' much better now. Break out the brekkers, send in the scoff!"

They breakfasted on the open lake, though this time not on emergency rations. There was plumcake, honey-oat scones, mushroom salad and sparkling new cider.

Pikkle ate his using a hardtack biscuit as a plate. As he munched he stared about. "Well, give us a clue, boys. Where's the jolly old island hidin'?"

Log-a-log pointed straight out. "Two days rowing that way."

After breakfast they took up their paddles and began the long voyage to the island. At first Mara's paws felt stiff and awkward, but she was soon rowing as well as anyone and joining in the lusty shrew boatsongs that helped keep the rhythm of the paddles steady. Pikkle stoutly denied he had ever felt sick and sang as loudly as the rest.

"I'll sing you a song of the river-o,
Where the water's clean and clear,
And the long fast Guosssom logboats go.
We're the shrews that know no fear,
So bend your back and use those paws.
From gravel bank to sandy shores,
Your cares and woes will disappear,
Just sitting paddling here.
Guossssssssssom. . . . Guossssssssssom!
I'll sing you a song of the river-o.
It belongs to me and you.
O'er deeps and shallows we'll both go,
With the finest Guosssom crew,
When other creatures bound to land
Will not feel half so free or grand,

Or know the water shrews' great skill.
So paddle with goodwill.
Guosssssssssom. . . . Guosssssssssssom!"

In the early noontide the two logboats were still out on the lake. Nothing could be seen on all sides save water; sky and lake met on all horizons. The paddles dipped steadily in and out of the water with short powerful strokes.

Nordo noted the sun's position and called a refreshment period. Lots of shrews dipped cupped paws into the lake and drank with relish. Mara followed suit gingerly, but found to her surprise that it was cold and sweet. Pikkle dabbled his paws in the water.

"I say, old Log-a-thing, how deep is this bally lake?"

Log-a-log smiled mischievously. "Hmm, let me see. It comes two-thirds of the way up a boat or halfway up a duck."

"Oh, I see." Pikkle nodded understandingly. "Now hang on a bally moment, old shrew. Who are you tryin' to fool?"

Nordo laughed. "Watershrews always say that to landlubbers. Actually nobeast knows how deep this lake is, though my grandfather tried to plumb it when he was Log-a-log, and he said it was bottomless."

Pikkle turned faintly pale around the gills. "D'you hear that, Mara? Bottomless! That means there's nothin' beneath this boat for goodness knows how deep but water. Oh corks, I knew I shouldn't have come!"

Mara smiled. "Have a nap Pikkle, you'll feel better."

"Hah, listen to the creature! Better, she says. I've never felt so absobloominlutely awful in me li—What was that?"

Log-a-log came alert. "What was what?"

"Over there, sort of a big splash!" Pikkle pointed.

Nordo was about to say something when Log-a-log shot him a warning glance and shook his head. "Oh, that. It was probably a fish jumping. They do that a lot."

Pikkle held on to the boat's side. "Well, I wish they'd bally well stop. It makes a chap nervous, wot!"

"There it goes again. That's no fish jumping!" A shrew paddler stood up behind them, his normally bass voice shrill and frightened.

The crews of both boats shuffled their paws restlessly and began murmuring among themselves. Log-a-log banged a paddle noisily on the prow of his logboat.

"Silence, back there. It was a fish, I saw it myself. Now stop that old mousewives' scuttlebutt and get your lunches eaten!"

Mara looked to her left. A rippling wave was building up some distance away, but it was coming toward the boats. She pointed. "That looks a bit big for one fish; it must be a shoal of them."

One of the shrews stared accusingly at Log-a-log. "You shouldn't have banged your paddle on the boat like that. It's heard you and it's coming for us. It's coming, I tell you!"

From the other boat Tubgutt could be heard yelling accusations: "It's those two, the badger and the hare. They've brought bad luck down on us all!"

Others started shouting as panic set in with the advance of the rippling wave toward the two boats.

"Back the way we came, shrews. Paddle for land!"

"It's the Deepcoiler, mates!"

"Turn back, let us off these boats!"

"If it's the Deepcoiler we're all deadbeasts!"

Log-a-log drew his rapier, rapping out commands over the hubbub. "Silence and sit down, fools, or you'll turn these boats over! If you want to save yourselves sit tight and shut up!"

The rippling hump of water had been building up as it approached the boats. Subdued by Log-a-log's authority, every creature in the boats sat silent and still. Paws gripped paddles tightly, mouths shut tight as vices, fur stood stiff on every back. With little warning the sunlit noontide surface of the immense lake had become a place of horror and dread. Every eye was fixed on the noiseless traveling swell. It was scarce more than three boat-lengths from them when there was a whoosh of water, and something long and scaly slapped the top of the lake. Both craft rose on the swell as the logboats rode the wave.

Mara moved then. Craning over the side, she looked down into the translucent blue-green depths and saw the thing as it passed underneath both vessels. It was enormous!

She had missed seeing the creature's head, but she watched in fascinated terror as the length of its body slipped harmlessly by, a mere paw's-length beneath the surface, round and thick as the trunk of a tree, dark green with slate-gray blotches. Trailing waterweeds clung to the heavily scaled mass of the leviathan; rippling sidefins powered it through the water as its length kept on passing . . . and passing. The pointed tailtip scraped the boat's underside and then it was gone, far down into the fathomless depths of the silent lake.

The badger maid breathed a long sigh of relief and mopped the beads of sweat that stood out on her nose. "By the rocks of Salamandastron! What was that?"

Nordo unclenched his paws from the paddle with a visible effort. "What you just saw was a monster—Guosssom shrews call it the Deepcoiler, though nobeast has ever set eyes on it until now."

Pikkle sat with his eyes wide as saucers and his ears rigid. "Well, let's hope we jolly well live to tell about it. Oh, corks an' catkins! I knew I should never have gone sailin'. At least when you're on bally old dry land you can run away, but stuck out here on a floatin' log, it's a bit much, you chaps!"

206

"Deepcoiler was an old shrew tale," Log-a-log explained to Mara and Pikkle somewhat apologetically, "a story to frighten naughty little ones who wanted to go paddling alone; though in the time of my forefathers there were stories of logboats and whole crews lost in mysterious circumstances out on this great lake. As for myself, I never believed in the thing, but now I have seen it with my own eyes, how can I doubt it? I am sorry that this peril has been brought upon you by me and my son."

The boats were floating side by side. Tubgutt snarled across, "D'you hear that, shrews? He's sorry. We might all be dead meat by tonight, but Log-a-log's sorry! Log-a-log? He's not a proper Log-a-log. Where's the Blackstone that should be hanging round his neck? We don't have to take orders from him! I say we make for the shore!"

Mutinous murmurs started arising from both crews.

"Tubgutt's right, without the Blackstone he's just an impostor!"

"I say we elect another leader!"

"Aye, Tubgutt for leader. He'll get us out of this!"

The fat shrew stood up with a triumphant sneer and faced the shrew leader. "Find yourself another name, shrew. You're Log-a-log no more. I'm the new Guosssom leader now. Right?"

All the shrews were frightened at the thought of being out on the lake where Deepcoiler lurked. Tubgutt's plan to strike for land caught on immediately. Rather shamefacedly they murmured agreement with Tubgutt, though they kept their eyes averted from Log-a-log, who had always been a good and fair leader.

Log-a-log touched his rapier hilt as he gazed coolly across at Tubgutt. "We'll settle this once and for all. You name the time and the place, shrew."

Tubgutt quailed under Log-a-log's stare, but he put on a brave front and began blustering. "There'll be no fighting to the death around here or on land. I'm the newly elected leader now. The moment we get to shore you're banished from the Guosssom—you and your son!"

Fussing busily about, Tugbutt sat down and picked up his paddle. "Hear me now. As your newly elected leader, I say we put about and paddle for land."

"Make one move and you're fishbait, shrew!" Mara had been moving gradually along the boat until she was level with Tubgutt in the other boat. She stood within easy reach of him, brandishing a paddle close to his head.

"Did you hear that?" The fat shrew appealed to his new followers. "This stranger is going to kill your new leader. Get her, shrews. Put the stripedog over the side. She and the hare are the cause of all this trouble. Seize them!"

With lightning agility Log-a-log leapt into the other logboat and was on Tubgutt, his rapier point tickling the fat shrew's throat. "Mutiny and incitement to murder, eh, Tubgutt? You'll face a full council of our Guosssom comrades when we return home. Mara and Pikkle helped our shrews and my son to escape the toads' prison pit; they are honored guests. I've allowed you enough leeway, Tubgutt. Myself I don't care for, but when you threaten the life of Guosssom friends, that's mutiny on the open waters. You there, and you Rivak—get some line and bind this rascal tight and sit him in the stern. I'll deal with him when the time is right."

Log-a-log's speedy victory over Tugbutt, combined with his tough, authoritative air, turned the tide in his favor. The two shrews grabbed the struggling Tubgutt and tied him up.

Log-a-log sheathed his weapon and turned to both crews. "I'm still Log-a-log here, Blackstone or not.

Anybeast who thinks he's shrew enough to challenge me, let him do it now!"

There was a momentary silence, then a big tough-looking shrew stood up and made his way along to stand by the leader. "Anyone who challenges Log-a-log challenges me too. He's always been fair and just to all of us!"

Nordo stood up with Mara and Pikkle. He spoke for all three: "We stand with Log-a-log!"

An old shrew with long whiskers waved his paddle. "Good old Log-a-log! Old? What'm I talkin' about, he's only a young snip compared t' me, heeheehee!"

Other voices now made themselves heard . . .

"Aye, Log-a-log's always been a good un. I like him!"

"Me too. He's always played square with young an' old. What d'you say, shrews?"

The crews of both logboats raised a mighty cheer for Log-a-log as he vaulted back into the boat with Nordo.

"Hooray for Log-a-log, leader of the Guosssom. Hooray!"

"I say, chaps, d'you mind sittin' down or we'll all end up in the flippin' drink. Wot, wot!"

The rest of the day passed by uneventfully. The sun set over the west lakeside horizon in crimson glory as the hot summer day came to an end. The shrews shipped paddles, ate supper and settled down as best they could for the night. Lying awake in the bows of the lead craft, Log-a-log passed Mara a jug of sweetmaple cordial.

"Mara, I want to thank you and Pikkle for backing me—you especially. The way you crept up on Tubgutt was very brave. He had a lot of the others ready to follow him. I know he lost a lot of face in the contest with Pikkle, but out here on the water with everybeast terrified by Deepcoiler they were ready to follow Tubgutt because he was all for turning back. Fear is a great motivator; it was touch and go there for a while.

You could have quite easily got a rapier between your ribs back there. You are a true friend, Mara. I will never forget what you did for me."

The badger maid pretended to yawn and snuggle down, embarrassed by Log-a-log's praise for her. "Oh, that's what pals are for. Now go to sleep, you old water-walloper."

Stilled for the night, the two logboats rocked gently on the calm surface of the vast lake.

23

"Yew tew better keep quiet, they're just up ahead o' us."

Samkim and Arula peered into the night-shaded woodlands.

"How far ahead, Spriggat?"

The old hedgehog sat down beside them. "Oh, no more'n half a good paw-stretch. Leave 'em awhile yet. Let the vermin git a-snorin', then we'll pay 'em a visit, eh?"

Samkim's eyes lit up eagerly. "A night ambush! How about that, Arula?"

"Ho urr, oi'm a reg'lar terror in 'ee dark if'n oi ain't asleep."

They chewed oatcake and apples as Spriggat outlined his plan. "I scouted up ahead an' nearly fell over 'em. They were settin' camp sou'west o' here. Now 'earken to me. In about an hour they should be well asleep, so 'ere's what we do. Split up an' go three ways so we can come at 'em from different angles. The rats shouldn't put up much of a fight—they're only trackers. It's the fox I'm worried about—that one looks like a trained fighter. Moreover, the villain's got your sword close to paw. Staves is the best t' deal with the like o' him.

Arula, lend me that carvin' knife you carries, and I'll cut us two good poles. Samkim, you can unstring your bow and make use of that. I'll signal by makin' a cricket chirrup. Like this—chrrrk! Got that? When you 'ears that noise you charge into that camp yellin' like a badger wi' a bee down his ear. Scream, shout, holler, an' whack all about you good an' hard, an' make straight for the fox. He'll be sleepin' closest to the fire. Don't give the scum a chance to go for that sword. We'll be there, all three of us, whackin' away. Don't stop! Wallop the beast flat into the ground, 'cos he'll slay us all three if'n he gets 'alf a chance."

Samkim unstrung his bow and tested its heft to find the best end. "Never fear, Mr. Spriggat. We'll be right there with you, thwacking!"

Arula seconded her friend. "Ho aye, zurr. You'm cut oi a gurt stowt pole an' oi'll wopp 'ee foxer till 'ee 'm flatter'n a pancake, boi ecky oi will!"

Spriggat shook paws with them. "Good! Now you take a li'l nap whilst I cuts a couple o' staves."

Under a burgeoning three-part moon they set off through the woodland, slipping silently along amid the shadowed treetrunks and undergrowth. Samkim padded carefully, thrilled at the prospect of regaining the sword of Martin the Warrior for his Abbey. Somewhere a nightjar warbled among the foliage and a woodpigeon cooed on the breeze high in the trees. Arula's eyes twinkled in the moonlight as she waggled a hefty yew stave.

Spriggat turned and held up his stave. "Hush now. Samkim, you go to the right. Arula, you take the left. I know they ain't posted sentries, may'aps they think themselves safe deep in these woods. Yew tew travel curvin' inward, take a good thirty long paces, then stop, get those staves ready an' wait on my cricket chirrup. Good luck an' good 'untin', young uns!"

"Twenty-eight, twenty-nine, thirty—that's it." Samkim halted among some junipers and peered in at the firelit camp. The rats lay about, wrapped in their cloaks, but over by the glowing embers he could see Dethbrush. The fox was resting in an upright position, his back against a log. The sword lay close to his paw, glimmering in the light of the dying campfire. There were woodpigeon feathers and bones scattered about. The young squirrel shuddered. How vermin could kill and eat birds—the very idea caused revulsion within him.

"Chrrrk!"

At the sound of Spriggat's call, Samkim leapt forward, yelling, "Yahaa! Death to the vermin! Redwaaaaalll!"

The cricket close by the fire that had chirruped shot beneath the log and hid. Arula was marching slowly along. Counting had never been her strong point.

"Urr, twenny-foiv, nointy-two, thurty-four. Boo urr! Wozzat?" She went charging in waving her stave. "Boi okey, give 'em vinniger! Redwaaaaalllhooouuurrrrr!"

At the same time, Spriggat dashed in and collided with a rat who had leapt up at the noise.

The pandemonium was total. Set off by a real cricket call that proved to be a false alarm, the ambush went awry. Dethbrush jumped up to see two of his rats being belaboured by a squirrel and a hedgehog. He was only halfway up when a mole with a yew stave chased a screeching rat past him, counting as it went, "Twennynoin, take that 'ee vermin! Seventy-'leven, oi'll wack 'ee! Fifty-foiv, sixteen-two . . . wot's next? Take that 'n' that 'n' that!"

The other three rats milled about, bumping into each other.

Thinking they were under invasion from a much larger force, Dethbrush decided to escape with all speed. He hissed under his breath to the three rats:

"Quick, over here. Scatter the fire and run that way, through there!"

Grabbing the sword, Dethbrush helped the rats scatter flame and glowing embers all over the clearing with their spears. They took off through the trees, running southwest after the fox.

Blinded by smoke and burning woodpigeon feathers, Arula whacked away at the log where Dethbrush had rested. "Nointy-seven, thurty-eight. Oi'll teach 'ee a lessing, ho urr!"

Spriggat caught the end of the stave and pulled her away. "It went wrong, we made a mess o' it! Quickly, afore the woods go up in flame, put out the fires!"

Swiftly they cut beaters of green juniper and lupin and set about tackling the blazes that were springing up all about the edges of the forest clearing. Each creature beat furiously, knowing their lives depended on putting out the woodland fire. Hot dry summer was the worst of all possible times to be caught in a woodland blaze, and once established it could devastate a whole wood, burning unchecked. Coughing and spluttering, their faces blackened by smoke, eyes red-rimmed and sore, they fought each fresh outbreak until the flames were subdued.

Spriggat kicked dust on a spark as he leaned heavily on Arula. "Whoof! I'm gettin' too long-seasoned for this sort o' game. Where's Samkim?"

"Over here, look what I've caught!" The young squirrel tugged a limping snarling rat. He had his bowstring looped about the creature's neck. "I must have whacked him good and broke his footpaw. He didn't manage to escape with the others."

Spriggat dealt the unfortunate rat a hefty cuff and pressed some lupins into his claw. "Fire-raiser, eh? Don't snarl at me like that, you scum. Take that." He gave the rat another good buffet.

"Right, get beating, go on! All round this clearing until there's no more chance of a burn-up. And just let me find one spark, that's all, just one—I'll give you such a beating that the lumps'll have lumps on top o' them!"

Arula took the bow. Playing the rat on the attached bowstring like a fish on a line, she kept him going around the clearing, hunting for any traces of sparks they had missed.

Exhausted, Samkim and Spriggat sat down on the log. The young squirrel expressed his disappointment.

"Well, we made a right old frog's dinner of that. You must have chirruped like a cricket too early. Arula wasn't in position and I was barely ready. What made you do it, Spriggat?"

The cricket trundled out from under the log, chirruped twice at them and waddled off angrily into the night.

Samkim covered his eyes, realizing what had happened. "Oh no!"

Spriggat golloped a passing moth and began chuckling. "Ohohoho! Thank ye kindly, Samkim. 'Tis a tribute to my realistic cricket chirrup. Ohohohohohahaha!"

The hedgehog's laughter was infectious. Soon the three of them were doubled up pounding the log with their paws.

"Ahahahaha! Ooh dear! And there was Arula, countin' and whackin'. Ninety-seven, fifty-eight, twenty-three, take that an' that, hahaha. An' you ran smackbang into that rat. Oh heeheehee! You should see the way your snout's swelled up. Whoohahahaha!"

"Hurr hurr hurr hurr! An' thurr wurr oi, beatin' up a log, hurrhurr. It wurr a gudd job 'ee log were dead, or oi'da killed et, hurr!"

When the laughter had died down, Samkim kicked the dust gloomily. "Aye, but the fox got away with our sword. What's to laugh at about that? He could be anywhere by now."

Arula had the solution. She reeled in the rat on the bowstring. "Hurr naow lissen, vurmen. Whurr be 'ee fox gone to? You'm best arnswer oi afore oi get turrible mad!"

The rat sneered at Arula and remained silent. Spriggat smiled pitifully at the creature.

"I 'opes you don't talk, rat. Tell you why. See yon mole, she weren't foolin' when she said she were mad. Take it from us, she is mad, ain't she, Samkim?"

The young squirrel nodded, straight-faced and serious. "Mad? I'll say she is. Remember the last rat she caught, Spriggat? Dearie me, I dread to think about that poor creature."

The rat began to look twitchy. Spriggat shook his head sadly. "On my oath, I 'opes never to see that done to a livin' creature again, 'specially the bit with the three squashed frogs an' those maggoty apples. Ugh! Sickens me t' think of it."

The rat tried to limp away, but Arula reeled him in on the bowstring until their faces were almost touching. She put her head on one side and grinned insanely at him.

"Oh, oi likes bein' mad, oi do! Sanken, can 'ee get oi sum big wurms, smelly mud an' dedd wuddbeetles. Oi got a noice idea, hurr."

The rat went limp. He fell to the ground blubbering, "No, please, don't be mad with me! The fox's name is Dethbrush an' he's got five others with him—tracker rats like myself. We're not killers, I swear it. Dethbrush serves in the horde of Lord Ferahgo the Assassin. We were going to the South Stream to journey by water to the west shore and join up with Ferahgo. We were sent to bring back Dingeye an' Thura, but they're both dead. Dethbrush is takin' the sword as a gift to Ferahgo. That's all I know, I promise you. Don't hurt me, please!"

Arula looked crestfallen. "Doant say you'll take us'ns an' show us 'ee way, pleeze. Oi wants to 'ave moi fun!"

Tears streamed from the rat's eyes as he beseeched Samkim, "I'll show you every footpaw of the way. I'll show you—only please keep the mad mole away from me, sir."

"Oh well, all right." Samkim shrugged. "Tie him up to a tree for the night, Arula, he can show us the way as soon as it's light."

Samkim and Spriggat slept sitting against the log, but Arula was enjoying her new role as the terror of the woodlands. She snuggled up to the quivering rat, who was bound paw and claw to an elm.

"Goo' noit, ratface. Doant wake oi up, it makes oi mad."

"No sleep for you yet, friend," Spriggat called across to Arula. "First watch is yours. Remember what I said, always post a watch through the night. Samkim can take second and I'll take the dawn watch—an ol' grubber like meself needs his sleep. Hope stayin' awake doesn't make ye too mad."

"Hurr, 'spect moi matey 'ere will tell 'ee if'n oi gets mad."

The rat slumped in his bonds and gave a despairing sob.

That night Samkim dreamt of Martin the Warrior. The spirit of Redwall held both his empty paws forth pleadingly. "Give me back my sword, Samkim. Do not let others use it for evil."

24

Though his pale eyes showed no emotion, Farran the Poisoner knew he was in a dangerous position. Urthstripe and his fighters had returned from the fray; outside, the mountain was strewn with lifeless carcasses and groaning wounded. Ferahgo had called off his horde of Corpsemakers. Their losses were considerable, though not enough to make any great dent in numbers. Farran crouched in a dark corner of the passage between storeroom and dining hall, silently cursing the ill fortune that had caused his escape route to be cut off. From his hiding place the Poisoner could hear the badger Lord and his hares as they entered the dining hall. They talked of the battle they had won on the slopes of Salamandastron.

"Sapwood, I never gave permission for you to fight outside. You could have been killed by those rolling fire boulders."

"Not me, sir. Hi was well out the way by the time they started. Paw-ter-paw combat is me best style, beggin' y' pardon, but this shootin' arrows hout of winder slits an' rollin' boulders, that haint fer the like o' me. Face t' face with the enemy his wot I fancy. That's the way I fights best, sir."

"I know you do, Sergeant. From all I hear you gave a good account of yourself out there—but ask me before you do anything like that in future."

"Good fight though, wasn't it, sir?" The squeaky voice of a hare, no more than a leveret, reached the ears of Farran.

"Indeed it was, young Shorebuck. How do you feel after your first battle?"

"Tip-top, m'lud! I say, is that breakfast laid out for us? I'm jolly well starvin'."

Urthstripe chuckled good-humoredly. "I never knew a young hare that wasn't always hungry. Go to it, Shorebuck. Seeing as it was your first fight, you shall be the first to take breakfast."

Farran's pale eyes lit up momentarily. He listened to the young hare intently.

"Good show! Thank you, sir. Mmm, oatcakes, an' they're still a bit warm. Pass me the honey, Sergeant."

"Git it y'self, you young rip. I ain't waitin' on you tail 'n' paw."

Urthstripe's voice cut in again. "Oxeye, did we suffer any losses or injuries?"

"None reported, sah! A jolly old bloodless victory, wot? Though Windpaw never showed up at roll call after the skirmish. Still, I suppose she's got her head down in some quiet corner. That hare c'd sleep on a bally clothesline."

The next sound to reach Farran was that of a pottery bowl smashing on the floor and a chair falling over.

' Shorebuck, what's the matter, old lad?" Bart Thistledown's voice came through loud and urgent. "I say, looks like he's chokin' on a bit of scone. Lend a paw, you chaps!'

For the first time Farran showed some sign of emotion. His paw struck the rock wall of his hiding place in disappointment. He had made the mixture too strong, his poison was working far too speedily. Other voices crowded in on the fox's ears.

"Give him somethin' t' drink, clear his throat!"

"No, hold him upside down, shake him and pound his back!"

"I can't, sir. The pore young un's all doubled up like . . ."

"Out of my way, Sergeant! Here, give him to me. Shorebuck! Shorebuck! Come on, young feller. Stand up straight!"

"Stand aside, chaps. Let Seawood through. He's a healer!"

There was a momentary silence, then Urthstripe's anxious tones rang through the dining hall.

"What's the matter with him, Seawood?"

A pause followed, then Seawood's voice came through. He was sobbing softly. "He's dead! Young Shorebuck is dead, sir!"

"Dead? Surely not. Can't you do something—herbs, a potion?"

"It's too late. Can't you see, sir! Look at the way his poor face is all twisted, and his body doubled up tight an' stiff. It's poison. I'd recognize it anywhere. Shorebuck's been poisoned!"

"It must have been somethin' he's eaten, sir. The pore liddle feller was right as rain a moment ago."

"Spot on, Sarge. He dashed t' that breakfast board like a bally young trooper after his first fight . . ."

Urthstripe's voice boomed through the dining hall. "Get away from that table! Don't touch the food!"

Ferahgo tossed his knife high in the air and caught it by the handle. He was in good spirits.

"Haha, what's thirty or forty creatures slain? There's always more where they came from. That's what soldiers are for, to kill or be killed. What's the matter with your face, backstabber?"

Klitch sat to one side with the four Captains, a scowl hovering around his blue eyes. "The whole thing was a waste of good fighting creatures."

Ferahgo flicked the knife. It stuck in the ground near his son's paw. "Oh dear dear. Friends of yours, were they? Are you sad because they were killed in the battle?"

Klitch ignored the dagger a fraction away from his footpaw. "Don't worry, old one, I'm not going soft. I couldn't give a split acorn whether your whole horde lives or dies. I just think that getting Farran inside the mountain could have been done easier, with a whole lot less killed."

Doghead, a stoat Captain, was about to agree with Klitch when he saw the wicked smile forming in the blue eyes of the Assassin. Doghead looked at the ground and kept his comments to himself.

Ferahgo retrieved his knife, waggling it under Klitch's nose. "It's not important what a wet-behind-the-ears weasel like you thinks, my son. I'm your old daddy, Ferahgo the Assassin, and only what I think counts around here. Tell him, you Captains: won't life be easier once the badger and his hares are dead from Farran's poison and we're lords of the mountain? Surely that's worth the lives of a few ragtailed scavengers?"

Badtooth the other stoat nodded. "The Master's right, Klitch. If Farran does the job proper then it was a good plan."

Without another word, Klitch jumped up and stalked off in high bad mood.

Ferahgo winked at the four Captains. "It's a sad thing, being young and thinking you're clever like that. No one can outthink the old Master. Remember that if he ever starts talking to you behind my back. I'll let him live because he's my son, but anyone who plots with him I'll kill stone dead—after skinning them alive, of course. Now, the next move! If Farran shows up and

221

says they're all poisoned inside the mountain, we'll hack a way in and take over the place."

Crabeyes the rat Captain held up a paw respectfully. "But he should have been well out of there by now, Master. What happens if he doesn't show up?"

Ferahgo sheathed his knife and winked at Crabeyes.

"That means he's still inside there. Oh, don't worry. Farran has never let me down. He'll poison them all, make no mistake. But then, I've become worried over Mister Farran of late. Maybe he's getting greedy and wants all the badger's treasure for himself . . ."

"Badger's treasure?" Crabeyes sounded surprised.

Ferahgo patted his back and smiled broadly. "Badger's treasure, friends. Didn't I tell you? That's why I made you Captains. It will be too much for one; I need four good loyal comrades to share the treasure with—you four. Keep it to yourselves, though. Don't tell the others. When we take Salamandastron I'll make you rich beyond your dreams. We'll be five kings together . . ."

The Assassin watched the joyous greed shining from all four faces. He had them hooked. His tone dropped slightly. "There's just one thing, however. Farran wants all the treasure for himself. The Poisoner has got to be removed."

Greed turned to apprehension on the Captains' faces, but Ferahgo had them like clay in his paws.

"Have you ever seen the treasure of the badger Lords? I know for a fact that the center of that mountain is packed with gold, silver, jewels, armor, swords, encrusted shields and all manner of wonderful weapons. Just think, if you owned a fifth part of all that, every creature in the land would be bowing their heads and fighting to kiss your footpaws. Once the badger and his hares are dead, all that stands in our way is the greedy one, Farran. Now I think that between five warriors like ourselves we could manage to slip a dagger in his ribs while we're congratulating him on a job well done. So it's either get rid of the black fox, or back to the life of an ordinary horde soldier."

Four paws touched that of Ferahgo's. "We're with you, Master!"

The Assassin watched them as they went back to their duties as Captains of his horde. He threw back his head, eyes reflecting the summer blue sky as he laughed aloud.

"Hahahaha! Fools!"

The body of Windpaw lay alongside that of Shorebuck. Big Oxeye gripped his javelin tightly.

"Found her in the top corridors, sah! Slain by a different type of poison. The filthy scum stuck somethin' in her neck—see the mark? Only a tiny wound, but by the swellin' it looks like poison."

Urthstripe's eyes were red-rimmed from tears and wrath. "First it was young Shorebuck. I watched him during the battle—he would have made a great warrior had he lived. Now it is Windpaw, often pretending to be stern, but with a heart as soft as a summer dawn. She always took good care of my Mara. But now she's gone. Gone! And there's some dirty, low vermin going to pay for this, I promise you!"

A party of Long Patrol hares carried the bodies down to the lower caves, where they could lie until such times as proper burial could be given on the shoreline where tide meets land.

Urthstripe sat with Seawood in the empty dining hall. The hare turned out a kerchief containing dead ants.

"Poisoned, all of them—some from the kitchens, some from the foodstore, these two here from the base of the water barrels."

The badger Lord brushed them away with a heavy

paw. "Is there none of our food or drink that has not been contaminated with poison, Seawood?"

"None, sir—or at least none that we know of. Who's goin' to trust any of our supplies? I wouldn't. We're facin' starvation!"

Urthstripe sighed as he covered his eyes with both paws. "Leave me alone now, I must think. Oh, just one thing. Make sure that none of our creatures shows themselves to Ferahgo or his vermin. I want them to think we're all dead, then we'll see what his next move will be."

Sapwood and Oxeye were returning up a flight of spiral stairs hewn into the rock. They were making their way back to the dining hall after laying Shorebuck and Windpaw to their temporary resting place in the lower caves. Bart Thistledown grabbed Oxeye by the paw.

"What was that?"

Oxeye was quick-sighted. He squinted in the direction indicated. "It's a black shadow like a . . . Wait there!" Oxeye bounded up the stairs with an amazing turn of speed. "Hi! You there. Stop!"

The others arrived within seconds.

"What was it, Ox? Did you spot anything?"

The big hare scratched his eartips. "Funny, at first I thought it was a shadow. But I'd swear on a carrot pie that it was a black fox—long sleek vermin with funny eyes."

Urthstripe appeared in the corridor outside the dining hall. "Fox, did you say you'd seen a fox inside the mountain, Oxeye?"

Oxeye was still slightly puzzled. "Er, yes an' no actually."

The badger Lord was in no mood for jesting or riddles. "Stand up straight, sir—ears up, chin in, chest out, shoulders back, paws at an angle of forty-five degrees to the side legfur! That's better. Now answer my question as a hare of the Long Patrol. Did you see a fox?"

Standing correctly to attention, Oxeye faced front as he replied. "Sah! Difficult to tell, sah! Could've been a trick of the light, sah! Looked remarkably like a black fox with odd eyes, sah! If it was, the blighter went that way, to the left along the corridor. End of report. Sah!" Oxeye threw a smart salute and stood awaiting further orders.

Urthstripe paced up and down, musing aloud. "Hmm, quick, dark and sleek, like a shadow . . . slip in and out unnoticed, a fox too. That doesn't sound much like a fighter, more like a creature that does things by stealth, a spy, or a poisoner maybe!"

Sergeant Sapwood clenched his paws. "May Hi ask yer permission to find this 'ere creature, sir?"

But a swift plan had already formulated in Urth-stripe's mind. "Permission denied, Sergeant. I want this poisoner myself, but if we are to capture him we must act with all speed. Right, here's the plan. Split into two groups—Oxeye, you take one group up to the crater top immediately. Keep low so that Ferahgo's army cannot see you. I want that crater top sealed off like a bottleneck so that the fox cannot get away. Sapwood, take the rest and follow him. When you reach the top, pair off in twos and start searching the mountain thoroughly from top to bottom. Wedge off all exits, window slits and the like. If you do the job cor-rectly, the fox will have only one way to run—down! I will be waiting in the cave where Shorebuck and Wind-paw are lying. Off you go now!"

Ferahgo had been searching the base of the mountain, poking, sniffing and prying all around its mighty cir-cumference. A sizable contingent headed by Doghead and Dewnose followed him. They watched as the

Assassin halted at a spot on the north side and marked a cross in the sand with his dagger.

"Here! See the cracks and loose boulders? It's a fault in the rock. This is where we'll tunnel in. Hah! They should have eaten and drunk their fill by now in there. Thirsty work, heaving all those boulders about and defending a mountain against my horde. The poison should be working well, if I know Farran!"

Klitch perched on a rock slightly above his father's head. "Tunnel in? Seems a lot of unnecessary work when we could find a window slit, or even attempt unblocking the main entrance. That'd save a lot of digging."

Ferahgo toyed with the gold medallion around his neck. "Don't worry, Klitch my son, you won't be asked to get your paws dirty. We've got an entire horde to do the job. Have you never heard of the element of surprise? If there is anybeast left alive in there and they still happen to be in fighting form, they'd expect us to try unblocking one of the entrances, but we will be doing the unexpected. Doghead, Dewnose, make a start here. There's loose boulders and lots of wide cracks. Use spears, pikes, knives, swords—anything, but keep them at it."

Farran the Poisoner knew that his mission had failed. All that he desired now was to leave the mountain. But try as he would, the black fox was frustrated at every turn. Salamandastron was virtually alive with determined hares. Fully armed and alert, they scoured every nook and cranny from the top of the crater downward. Farran found himself running before them, down, ever down. Whenever he turned and tried going upward he was cut off by two pairs of angry, determined hares coming from each side. Scurrying along one of the mid-level corridors, he practically bumped into Sapwood. Turning, he dashed off down a flight of stairs with the

Sergeant's voice ringing in his ears. "Run, you poisoner. We're givin' you more of a chance than you gave two pore 'ares. Go on, keep runnin', vermin!"

In desperation Farran concealed himself in a dark corner until Sapwood had passed by, accompanied by Pennybright. The ghost of a smile flitted across Farran's sombre face. Slipping out of his hiding place, he mounted the stairs, only to find himself facing the lance points of Bart Thistledown and Starbob.

Bart tapped his lancepoint on the steps. "Up y'come, laddie. Let's see what you're made of, wot?"

The black fox turned and fled, taking the opposite direction to Sapwood and Pennybright. Behind him he could hear Starbob and Bart. Suddenly the passage ahead of him was cut off by Seawood and a hare called Moonpaw. Drawing his deadly greenhart dagger he backed off, snarling. The two hares made no move to attack, merely covered the bottom of the staircase so that he could not go up. Hugging the opposite wall, Farran slid past them and sped off. As he descended another flight of steps, he could hear four sharp lance tips tapping behind him.

On the ground-level corridor Farran glanced left and right. Two more hares were coming from the left, both with arrows nocked on drawn bowstrings. He ran to the right. Narrowly avoiding two more advancing members of the Long Patrol, the Poisoner went helter-skelter down a long spiral stairway carved into the rock. Tripping and stumbling, he staggered into the final passage leading to the lower caves. Farther along the way hares flooded down silently from another stairway in front of him, while at his back another group came down the spirals he had recently descended.

The sour taste of fear rose in the black fox's mouth. There was just one place left to go: the large cave in front of him.

It was a huge, rough-hewn place with torches placed

plentifully in wall sconces. There was a pair of raised stone slabs at the far end.

Beside the bodies of Shorebuck and Windpaw, Lord Urthstripe stood waiting in the well-lit chamber. He was unarmed, save for a wet strip of linen that had been knotted at one end. Farran's pale eyes watched him warily as the Long Patrol crowded in the cave entrance, blocking any possible way out. The badger Lord pointed to the two lifeless creatures laid out either side of him.

"See how you have murdered my friends, fox? Now the time for reckoning has come. You must face me. Sapwood, provide this vermin with any weapons he needs, then stand back, all of you. Nobeast is to lay paw upon the fox. . . . Nobeast, save me!"

25

As night fell, Thrugg began piling up pebbles. The otter moved stiffly, his whole body aching from the fight earlier that evening. Out on the open land the crows were beginning to stir in the cool night air. One or two were trying out desultory hops and caws.

Rocangus glanced over the bank edge of the dried-out streambed, his fierce eyes watching them keenly. "Och, yon birds are startin' tae work theyselves up again."

Dumble had fallen asleep. He muttered to himself and turned over.

A full moon rose like a dull gold platter. As Thrugg looked up at it, a dark winged shape swooped low out of the night. Grabbing his sling, the otter launched a hasty stone at the bird. It banked and circled, shrilling out angrily, "Ach, ye great lump-haided riverdog, can ye no see Ah'm a falcon?"

Rocangus cocked his head on one side. "Is that ye, Tammbeak?"

The other falcon landed smoothly atop the haversack. "Aye, 'tis. Whit ha' ye done tae yer wing?"

Thrugg stood to one side, listening to the falcons conversing in their quaint northland accent.

"Never ye mind mah wing, Tamm. Will ye lookit yon

229

crows, mah cronies an' mahsel' are sair troubled by them. Are any of oor clan aboot tae lend a talon here?"

"Nae bother. Bide ye here a wee bit. Ah'll bring ye help." Tammbeak shot off into the night sky, screeching at intervals as he flew in a high wide circle.

"Krrreeeekah! Gather ye tae me! Krrreeeekah!"

Rocangus watched him. "Och, it's a braw thing tae be flyin'. Dinna ye fret, Thrugg, yon crows'll soon be sorry they messed wi' the son of the Laird Mactalon."

The cawing and hopping from the crows had increased. They appeared to be working themselves up into a frenzy. Out on the open moonlit land they hobjigged and sang raucously. Thrugg covered the still sleeping Dumble with his jerkin as he watched them anxiously.

"Rocangus, matey, I 'opes yer pals gets here afore those birds charge us. We won't stand a butterfly's chance agin that mob!"

As if on cue, six falcons dropped out of the sky into the streambed.

Thrugg gave a startled jump. "Phew, that was quick!"

A tall, imposing elder with fearsome beak and huge talons folded his massive wings and winked at Thrugg. "Aye, 'twas an' all. Mah clan's speedier on the wing than anything in yonder sky."

Thrugg looked around doubtfully. "But there's only six of you. There's 'undreds of crows out there, beggin' yer pardon o' course."

The big falcon grinned fearsomely. "Ach, dinnae apologize, streamdog. We were searchin' for that young rip, mah son Rocangus, but six braw sojers like us wid be shamed if we couldnae give some crows a guid tanning!"

Rocangus had been standing respectfully to one side. Now he came forward and bowed his head to the Laird.

"Faither, 'tis yersel'. Och, am Ah glad t'see ye. Yon

riverdog is Thrugg, the wee mousey is Dumble. They found me wi' mah wing brokit an' fixed it up. Ah should be flying again soon."

Laird Mactalon inspected the dressing on his son's wing, then proffered a talon to the otter. "Ah'm beholden to ye, Thrugg. Mah son should be thankful he met sich bonny decent creatures as ye an' yer wee friend there. We'll talk some mair later. Sit ye down while Ah deal wi' yonder bunch o' disgraceful birds."

Now the cawing and dancing had increased to fever pitch and the bolder crows were beginning to hop toward the streambed. Laird Mactalon and his clanbirds broke cover. They stood in a line on the banktop and threw back their heads.

"Kreeeekah, tak' nae prisoners, give nae quarter, kreeekah!"

As if by magic, the crows fell silent and ceased dancing. Laird Mactalon and his falcons started walking toward them with a definite warlike swagger, chests puffed and neckfeathers spread wide, their talons crunching the dead bracken as they went. The front crows hopped backwards. Mactalon threw out his bold challenge and walked forward alone ahead of the others.

"Och, come on, laddies. We're no a babbie mouse and a wounded young un, or an earthbound riverdog. See if ye can do any better against us. Ah'm the Laird Mactalon, as well ye know. Ah'll do battle wi' ye on land or in the air. Dinnae keep retreatin'. Whit's the matter? Surely you're no' frighted?"

All the time he was talking, Mactalon had been advancing. With the speed of a whipcrack he suddenly hurled himself into the crows. In the melee that followed, four crows were stretched out by the deadly beak and raking talons of the Laird. The other crows took to the air in an awkward flurry. They were met by the five falcon warriors, who hit them like thunderbolts.

Baby Dumble was awake. He sat on Thrugg's shoulders, wide-eyed as crows fell from the sky like tattered scraps of dark cloth. Eventually the crows made it back to the safety of the pine thicket. They crouched among the trees as the six falcons circled in a warlike aerial display. Between the streambed and the trees, crows dead and injured littered the ground like discarded rags.

Thrugg and Dumble cheered wildly, but Rocangus perched miserably on the haversack, muttering away. "Ach, 'tis a sad thing tae be stuckit here on the ground, by mah eggshell it is. Missin' oot on a scrap the like o' that!"

Landing back in the streambed with his clan members, the Laird contracted and dilated his big golden-flecked eyes as he preened his wing feathers delicately.

"Ah wisht ye could fly, Thrugg. Battlin' in the skies is a grand thing, sure enough. Och, the wee Dumble is awake an' all. How are ye, bairn?"

Dumble offered his paw. "Please ter meetcha, mista."

The rest of the night they spent sleeping in the fragrant heather that grew along the far streambank, safely surrounded by the six falcons. Next morning they were on their way again, trekking northeast. Thrugg raised his head and saw the snowcapped mountains far off, pushing their peaks up at the high blue summer skies.

Rocangus flapped his good wing. "Lookit, 'tis a braw sight. Did ye ever see stones piled so high that winter snow stays atop o' them in summer, Dumble?"

The little dormouse nibbled on a candied chestnut. "I never see'd mountings wiv snow. Goin' ter play in it when us gets there, eh, 'Ocangus?"

Snow would have been of great use to cool fevered brows in Redwall Abbey at that moment. Mrs. Faith Spinney carried up a pail of springwater that had been

232

left in the cellars to stay cold overnight. Trudging up the stairs, she stood to one side as Foremole and two of his crew lugged down a large basket, bumping it on each stair. The Foremole tugged his snout respectfully to her.

"'Scuse oi, marm, but us'ns be goin' to do 'ee washen in 'ee pond. Boi 'okey, oi never did see so much durty washen in moi ol' loif. These yurr diggen claws ain't bin so clean since moi mummy used t' scrub 'em furr oi when oi was a hinfant."

Faith patted their velvety backs. "Bless you all, you're so kind."

Abbess Vale was up to her paws in oatmeal. She mopped it up from the floor and set the bowl upright.

Brother Hollyberry tried to help her, stammering apologetically, "I'm sorry, Vale, it was all my fault. The old paws started shivering and I couldn't stop them. Here, let me clean it up."

Furgle the Hermit approached with a ladleful of dark liquid. "Huh, looks like you're coming down with a touch of Dryditch Fever, too, my friend. Here, get this down you."

Hollyberry took it and pulled a wry face. Droony the little mole watched him and gave a weak smile. "Hurrhurr, naow you'm knows wot yurr own med'sin tastes loik!"

Thrugann bustled in and plonked down a large bunch of fresh herbs on the table. Seeing Hollyberry and Abbess Vale struggling to clean up the oatmeal, she hauled them both up and sat them down on the edge of Droony's bed.

"Tch-tch! Lookit the mess of you two. Let me do that. There's more motherwort, nightshade and dockleaves, though I'm havin' to travel farther afield to get 'em now. Ah well, press on and never weaken, that's an otter motter."

Tudd Spinney sat up on the bedside and found his

walking stick. "D'you know, I do feel a little better this mornin'. P'raps I can get up today an' be of some 'elp around an' about here." He began to stand upright but was pushed back down by his wife as she passed carrying the pail of cold water.

"If you wants to do anythin', my ol' dear, then you just lie still there an' stay out of the way. Lan' sakes, there's enough to do without trippin' over you all day."

Bremmun poked his nose over the bedsheets surrounding his face. "Bah, I'm weak as a brown leaf and fed up lying about. I wonder how Thrugg and little Dumble are going on with their search for those Icetor Flowers?"

Sister Nasturtium was so ill she could not raise her head. She waved a limp paw at Bremmun.

"I dreamed of Thrugg and Dumble last night. . . . Thrugg was sad. . . . Sad for Dumble and—and another young one. Threatening . . . threatening, horrid shapes like . . . like dark birds. . . . But warriors will help Thrugg. . . . Warriors. . . . Martin said so . . ."

"What was that you said, Sister Nasturtium?" Bremmun sat up with an effort.

Faith Spinney plumped the pillows and pressed him back down. "Hush now, she's asleep. Prob'ly just talkin' to herself, pore thing. That nasty ol' Dryditch sickness has hit her worse'n any of us."

26

Two hours before dawn the Deepcoiler came back!

The first thing Mara and Pikkle knew of it was the scream of a lookout shrew, then all was chaos. The quiet surface of the lake exploded into boiling action as the huge creature broke surface between the two boats. They both tipped sideways and though Mara's boat stayed upright the other one overturned.

Shouts and cries of dismay rent the air as a massive head thrust up out of the lake, towering over Mara and Pikkle. It was akin to something from the dawn of time. Fearsome eyes and teeth aglitter, the creature blew out a foul-smelling stream of air and water as it dipped toward them with open jaws. Yelling with fright, they struck at it with their paddles. Nordo and Log-a-log sprang to their assistance. Splintering paddlewood flew everywhere as they battered wildly at the gargantuan head. Hissing balefully, the Deepcoiler flicked out a serpentine tongue. Mara saw the nightmarish cavern of its mouth as the thing came at her, purplish-red, blotched, with horrific rows of serrated teeth framing it.

The badger maid walloped furiously at the tongue with her shattered paddle as Pikkle and the others hammered at the widespread jaws and teeth. The monster veered away, turning its attention upon the capsized boat and its crew. The shrews shrieked as they floundered and struggled in the water, fighting to avoid the lashing coils that pounded the lakewater into a bubbling lather.

Mara could only watch in helpless horror as the scaly behemoth seized a half-drowned shrew in its jaws. Two others were cruelly trapped by the convolutions of its massive body as it twisted about, slamming them against the hull of the overturned boat.

"Help, badger. Help me, please!"

With his paws bound, Tubgutt was bobbing about in the roiling melee, buoyed up by the air trapped in his fur. Mara grabbed the fat shrew and hauled him aboard quickly. Log-a-log, Nordo and the rest of the Guosssom crew drew their rapiers. They leaned over the side, rocking the boat perilously as they stabbed repeatedly at the gigantic bulk that thrashed about between the two logboats.

"Nordo, watch out!" Pikkle hurled himself bodily at the shrew. Cannoning into him, he knocked him out of harm's way just in the nick of time. The flailing tail whipped down mightily on the boat, striking the spot where Nordo had stood a split second before and smashing a large chunk out of the vessel's side.

As suddenly as it had appeared, the Deepcoiler vanished down into the mysterious unfathomed depths of the lake, taking with it three shrews. Instantly the surface was restored to mirrorlike calm. Log-a-log slung out a grappling hook on a line, neatly snagging the upturned boat. Willing Guosssom paws heaved to turn the craft upright. Mara, Pikkle and some others pulled the survivors to safety, some semiconscious, others injured, but all grateful to be alive.

As Mara released Tubgutt from his bonds, Nordo sized up the situation. "Well, we've lost three good shrews and the provisions from the other boat. Just look at the damage to our boat!"

Pikkle was ministering to those he had rescued from the water. "These chaps aren't too badly injured—knocked about a bit, mostly bruises an' cuts. We'll live t' fight another day, lads!"

Tubgutt went down on all fours. Taking Mara's paw, he placed it on his head. "I'm sorry I ever spoke out against you, badger. I owe you my life. From now on I will be at your side. Your friends are my friends and your enemies my enemies, this I swear upon my oath as a Guosssom shrew!"

Mara chuckled to hide her embarrassment. "Thank you, Tubgutt. But I wouldn't try to outscoff Pikkle again, if I were you. Next time you might swell up and explode."

Minutes stretched slowly into hours. Dawn was a long time in coming as the two boats rocked gently on the surface of the great waters. Throughout the night watches everybeast sat awake, too fearful for sleep.

Log-a-log, Nordo and Tubgutt repaired paddles as best as they could. Mara and Pikkle issued a scratch meal from the depleted rations. Other shrews tended to their injured comrades. All through the long night countless worried glances were directed at the silent dark waters, dreading a return attack from the Deep-coiler.

Daylight arrived in rosy mist-shrouded splendor, lifting the spirits of the voyagers. The sun banished wreathing vapors from the lake and a cloudless blue sky heralded another glorious summer day as they paddled over the vast deep. Trailing lines and small nets were thrown out, and they trapped a few trout fry and some fresh-water shrimps. These were cleaned and spread in the sterns to cure by sun-drying. Midafternoon brought with it a cry from the lookout.

"Land ho!"

Log-a-log had been baling out water from the damaged boat. He looked up gratefully and called back, "Where away?"

"It's an island, straight for'ard as we go!"

Mara stood carefully on tip-paw. Sure enough, there was an unmistakable smudge on the horizon that could only be an island of some kind.

Pikkle bobbed up and down at her side. "Well, blow me down with a feather. Is that it? I say, good show! I don't give a frog's hoot how many ghosty ol' badgers live there—take me to it. Anything's better than floatin' about out here waitin' for that blinkin' Deepthingy to work up an appetite again."

Log-a-log scooped busily at the water building up in the bottom of the boat. "Fligg, Rungle, lend a paw here! This is worse than I thought. We've got a crack running halfway under the hull. Huh, we'll be lucky to make land in this leaky tub, though we might stand a chance if we bale fast and paddle even faster!"

Mara took up a paddle and moved to the prow. Nordo, Pikkle and Tubgutt joined her. The badger maid struck out deep and strong.

"Right, come on, Gousssom shrews. Let's see what you're made of. Me and Pikkle are only landlubbers, but I'll wager we can paddle the paws off you idle lot!"

Nordo grinned across at her. "Hah, did you hear that, lads? Come on, let's show these two that we're the sons of the roarin' shrews!"

Paddles plunged deep as the logboat shot forth like an arrow, each shrew defending the reputation of the Guosssom as they bent their backs and rendered a lusty paddling shanty.

238

"Pull, boys, pull!
O, we're the sons of the roarin' shrews
And a logboat is the home we choose.
O, pull, me bullies, pull!
Now we can stamp an' we can fight
An' paddle logboats day and night.
Pull, boys, pull!
I was born in a stream on a stormy day,
So I jumped in a boat and paddled away.
O, pull, me bullies, pull!
A paddle's me son an' a boat's me wife,
An' the open water is me life.
Pull, boys, pull!
O, I can scoff an' outfight you,
I'm the paddlin' son of a roarin' shrew.
O, pull, me bullies, pull!"

Not to be outdone, the crew of the other logboat took
up the shanty and began paddling harder. Soon it had
developed into a full-blooded race. The two boats fairly
skimmed over the waters, paddles flashing and bow
waves throwing up spray.

For all his girth and weight, Tubgutt was a powerful
creature. He dug his paddle long and deep, laughing
aloud at Pikkle's unorthodox but effective methods. The
young hare was like some crazy jack-in-the-box, ears
flopping either side as he bobbed up and down, grunting hard at each paddle stroke and improvising his own
shanty.

"O, I'm a Salamandastron lad,
An' by my reckonin' that's not bad.
Scoff, chaps, scoff!
Now listen, shipmates, while I say
I'd rather scoff than paddle all day.
O, scoff y'villains, scoff!
I don't think that I'd feel so sore

With an apple pudden in each paw.
Scoff, chaps, scoff!
So set me down on good dry earth,
I'll eat an' snooze for all I'm worth.
O, scoff, y'villains, scoff!"

On through the afternoon the two logboats raced,
sometimes neck and neck, but mainly with Mara's boat
in the lead, owing to the formidable strength and staying power of the badger maid and her friends. Because
of the speed they were traveling, the pressure on the
hull of the damaged vessel was causing water to leak in
ever faster. Log-a-log and the bailing party had their
paws full trying to cope with the flow but, caught up in
the spirit of the race, they battled on.

Toward evening the island was beginning to loom
large. Rearing up out of the surrounding deeps, it was a
high, rocky outcrop, fringed on top by foliage, bushes
and overhanging trees. The red sky of eventide sil-
houetted it eerily. Still fearful of Deepcoiler's reappear-
ance, the Guosssom paddled on with their last reserves
of strength, anxious to be ashore.

Log-a-log's boat had settled low in the water. Pikkle
urged the crew on with false cheerfulness. "I say, you
shameful shrews, wallop those paddles a bit faster.
That's the ticket! Keep goin', chaps. Think of all that
lovely land to wiggle your paws on."

The lake was close to lapping over the boat's sides as
they nosed into a rocky inlet. Log-a-log jumped ashore
and leapt onto a broad shelf-like ledge.

"All ashore, Guosssom! Nordo, loop a line over the
stern. Rungle, get one round the bows. We'll haul her
up here and see if we can make the old tub shipshape
again!"

It was dark by the time they had heaved the damaged

logboat up onto the ledge. Both crews sprawled about on the flat rock, resting after the day's labors. A small fire was built and food was shared out. Mara and Pikkle squatted around the fire with Log-a-log and Nordo. They ate shrewbread, yellow cheese and nuts and drank their portion of the remaining shrewbeer. The Guosssom leader settled his back against the cliff which reared up behind him.

"Ah well, we finally made it! In the morning I'll search out some pine resin, wood and clay to repair the boat. Nordo, you'll take a crew and forage for supplies. Don't stray too far, though. Stay within hailing distance of here. Mara my friend, I don't need to tell you what you and Pikkle have to do . . ."

The young hare spoke around a mouthful of cheese and nuts. "Spot on, old lad. We've got to go an' have a chinwag with the bally ghost, I suppose. Honestly, the things a chap has t' do! I don't know which is worse, actually: gettin' scoffed by old Deepthingy, or bein' frightened to death by a spooky spirit."

Mara emptied her beaker and lay back yawning. "No need to worry about that until morning, my old Pikkle. Get some sleep while you can."

Tubgutt came over and lay curled up close to Mara's footpaws like a faithful pet dog. "Where you go, I will too. I'll be there to watch your back tomorrow. You can rely on me."

The camp fell still as the fire dwindled to dying embers. The only sound was that of weary shrews snoring. A myriad host of twinkling stars surrounded the waning moon in the night sky, reflecting into the broad, still waters beneath. The peace that summer darkness brings fell over the slumbering earth.

It was some time shortly after midnight that every-beast on the ledge was dragged into wakefulness by a long echoing howl which boomed about cliff and lake like some sepulchral knell.

"Eeeee. . . . Yoooooo. . . . Laaay. . . . Leeee. . . . Aaaahhhhhh!!!"

Pikkle's ears stood up like two pikestaffs. He leapt across to Mara and grabbed tight hold of her paws.

"Hellteeth and Darkgates! What was that?"

27

Early morning shed its light over the leafy canopy of far Mossflower in the southwest. Spriggat tugged at the bowstring fastened around the tracker rat's neck.

"Stir yer stumps, yew rogue. We've got ter catch up with that fox. Mind now, you play us false an' I'll let 'Rula the mad mole loose on ye. Right, me beauty, for'ard march!"

Off they went, Samkim stifling his laughter as the little molemaid muttered darkly to the trembling rat, "Hoo urr, oi'll chop off'n 'ee tail an' stuff it up 'ee nose, then oi'll fetch some woild ants an' let they darnce in 'ee ears. That's after oi poured gurt globs o' sticky mud o'er 'ee vurrmint 'ead, o' course. Hoo urr, an' harr hoo!"

Convinced that Arula was truly mad, the rat led them on a straight course. This was confirmed from time to time as Spriggat found evidence of the other five trackers and Dethbrush along the way.

There was a short halt at midday for refreshment. Though supplies were running low, they managed a tasty little meal of apples, cheese and some half-disintegrated oatcakes. Spriggat found a ready supply of insects buzzing around the surface of a small patch of marshground. Caked from snout to paw in mud, he wandered happily about, munching gnats, wasps and other winged insects.

"Mmm, a very nice liddle selection 'ereabouts. Very nice!"

The afternoon was well on by the time the rat led them up a hilly rise in the woodland. Samkim held the bowstring lead, walking at the tracker's side. On reaching the peak of the hill, the young squirrel tugged sharply on the string. "Get down, lie still and be quiet!" he commanded the prisoner.

Sensing the need for caution, Arula and Spraggat bellied down, crawling through the loam to join him.

"Yurr, wot be amiss, Sanken?" Arula whispered.

They followed the direction of Samkim's paw as he pointed downhill. Between the thickly wooded side of the slope a glint of running water could be seen below.

"The Great South Stream," Spriggat whispered.

The young squirrel concentrated hard as he sniffed the air. "Aye, that's probably it, but I'm convinced I can smell woodsmoke and hear voices down there. What d'you think, Arula?"

The molemaid moved her head this way and that, wrinkling her dark button nose intently. "Ho urr, you'm roight, woodsmoke an' voices it be."

Samkim pulled an arrow from his quiver and held it point forward at the rat's throat. "This could be a trap. If you've played us false then your seasons are finished as of now, rat!"

The tracker swallowed hard, not daring to shake his head with the arrow tip stinging his gullet. "Dethbrush wouldn't hang about layin' traps, he only wants to get back to Ferahgo as quickly as possible. I told you he'd be followin' the course of the South Stream."

Samkim looked across at the hedgehog. "What do you think, Spriggat?"

The old hedgehog stood up quietly. "Well, we can't

244

lay about 'ere all day, I say we goes down yonder an' investigates. Roll over this way, rat."

The rat complied and was promptly gagged with a mouthful of leaves. Spriggat wound the bowstring under his chin and over his snout, effectively securing the gag and muzzling him.

"Right ho, vermin. Lead on, slow an' easy-like!"

Using the trees as cover, they crept down the hillside toward the stream. Arula drew the heavy pruning knife she had brought with her from Redwall, giving her loaded sling to Spriggat. Samkim gripped the unstrung bow, ready to use it as a stave. As they drew closer the sounds of creatures talking grew louder, though what they were saying the friends could not tell. Spriggat hauled the rat from the cover of an elm trunk and did a short run forward, pushing him into the cover of a yew thicket. Peering between the pole-like branches, he caught sight of a group of creatures arguing heatedly in gruff bass voices.

The hedgehog heaved a sigh of relief. Pushing the rat out in front of him, he called to Samkim and Arula, "It's all right, yew tew. No need to 'ide. They're shrews!"

The shrews on the streambank turned at the sound of Spriggat's voice. Before anybeast could stop him, one of them dashed forward. Drawing his rapier, he ran the tracker rat through the heart.

Realizing what had happened, Spriggat dealt the shrew a hefty crack over the head with his loaded sling, roaring as he laid the creature out senseless. "Yew stupid liddle murderer, couldn't y'see the rat was tied up? 'E was our prisoner, an 'elpless vermin. Yew 'ad no right to slay 'im like that!"

Samkim and Arula had now caught up with Spriggat. Instantly all three were surrounded by shrews with drawn rapiers and heavy wooden paddles. A mean, thin-looking shrew was shouting, "Kill them. It's the rest of the fox's gang. Kill them!"

Without thinking, Samkim threw back his head and yelled, "Redwaaaaaaalllll!"

The shrews held still a moment, surprised by the call. A fat old shrew, gray with many seasons, pushed his way through, belaboring about him with a knobbly blackthorn stick.

"Enough of this killin' talk, can't y'see these beasts aren't vermin? Stand aside, get out o' me way, Gousssom!"

The shrew who had been struck by Spriggat rose, moaning as he nursed a sizable bump between his ears, "Kill the hedgepig. He tried t' murder me. Oooohhhh!"

The old shrew brandished his stick at the speaker. "One more word, Racla, an' I'll raise another lump atop of the one the hog gave to ye. Now then, you lot, put up those weapons. Do as I say or I'll lay about yer with me stick!"

Muttering sullenly, they complied, and the old shrew winked at Samkim.

"I'm Alfoh the Elder. We're a colony of Guosssom shrews—there's tribes of shrews all along this stream, part of the main Guerrilla Union. We pride ourselves on being the most civilized and reasonable of all the Guosssom tribes—that's why we call our group a colony and not a tribe, y' see. But I suppose any shrewband has its loudmouths an' hotheads, like young Racla there. Still, I don't suppose he's altogether to blame after what happened here last night. A fox and five rats mounted a sneak attack here, while we were half asleep. They stole our best logboat an' killed four of our shrews. One of the dead was Racla's brother—that's why he ran the rat through without stoppin' to ask questions. Anyhow, we'll all sit down t'gether an' take a bite an' a sup, then you can tell me your end of the story."

246

Twilight gleamed on the streamwaters. Seated in a large comfortable cavern facing the bank, the three friends related their tale as Alfoh's colony members sat around listening. Hot acorn and chestnut dip was served with arrowroot wafers, a large honeyed plumcake was brought out in their honor, and dandelion wine and redcurrant cordial flowed freely. Spriggat munched away as he longingly watched two dragonflies hovering over the stream outside.

When the friends had finished their narrative Alfoh leaned back in his deep pawchair and nodded. "I saw your sword, it was a most wonderful piece of craftbeastship—badger-made, I'd guess. Now, my friends, what to do about all this? If the fox is a good navigator he will eventually make his way down to the sea, though if he's never sailed these waters before you can take it from me he'll be as lost as a fish up a mountain."

Samkim clasped his paws across a full stomach. "Do you think we'll be able to catch him up?"

Alfoh pondered the question for a moment. "Maybe we could, but there are four ways he could go: down to the sea, into the great lake, or up one of the back creeks that leads to a dead end—all of these routes we could follow and catch up with him. The other way leads under the mountains. No creature would be stupid enough to follow anybeast that way."

Arula blinked. "Whoi be that, zurr?"

Alfoh took a sip of wine and explained, "There are rapids, a giant waterfall and caves. Besides, nobeast knows whether you would come out on the other side of the mountain or keep going down into the earth forever."

Racla touched the lump on his head gingerly; his eyes were hot and angry as he glared at Spriggat. "I'm not sorry I killed that rat. First thing in the morning I'm goin' after the others. The fox is mine; he killed my brother."

Alfoh's paw strayed dangerously near his blackthorn stick. "You'll stay where you are until I give the word, young Racla. Tomorrow we'll take the other three boats and all go together. As for revenge upon the fox, I think Samkim has a prior claim to you. He needs to retrieve the sword for his Abbey. Now let's all get some sleep. We've got a full day ahead of us at dawn."

28

A light breeze from the sea fanned the flames of a small fire among the rocks on the shore by Salamandastron. Klitch and Ferahgo watched each other in the flickering light. They were arguing again. Klitch had scored several points, and his blue eyes twinkled maliciously at his father's show of temper.

"Yah, what do you know?" Ferahgo spat into the flames derisively. "I was leading a horde before you were born. You wouldn't know the back of an army from its front, you snot-nosed little upstart!"

The young weasel grinned, happy that he had his elder upset. "There's only one way to find out, old grayhair—give command of the horde to me. At least I couldn't make a worse mess of things than you're doing."

Ferahgo's eyes blazed with temper. "Worse mess? What worse mess? I've burned all their crops from the mountainside, poisoned all the food and drink they have. And if they're not already dead inside that mountain, now I've got a team tunneling in so that we can make a secret entrance. Go on, smartmouth, tell me what you'd do that's so brilliant?"

"Tunneling in?" Klitch laughed lightly. "Sometimes

you amaze me. Do you realize how thick that mountain is? A butterfly would have more chance trying to knock down an oak tree. When do you expect them to break through—next week, next season, in ten seasons' time, or twenty?"

The Assassin stood upright, his gold medal gleaming in the firelight. "Come with me. I'll show you!"

Midnight had long gone. Ferahgo's diggers were well advanced, but the Assassin's confidence would have wilted had he seen what awaited him inside Salamandastron. Several hares were listening to the banging and pounding from the outside.

Bart Thistledown grinned wryly as he leaned on his lance. "Well, twist my ears. The crafty ol' blue-eyed villain! Who would've thought he could find the old kitchen drain outlet. It was blocked up when I was a leveret."

Big Oxeye took up a heavy spear and held it poised. "Good thing you heard the diggin' an' gruntin', Barty m'lad. What d'you say we dig from this end, give those chaps a bit of help if they're so anxious to come in?"

Sapwood considered this proposition, then shook his head. "Pers'nally Hi'm agin it meself, an' Lord Urthstripe wouldn't be too 'appy about us 'elpin' vermin. Let 'em do their own diggin'. They should be through afore mornin'. We'll just wait 'ere nice 'n' quiet. Penny, you stand by. When I tips yer the wink, run an' fetch 'is Lordship."

Pennybright stifled a youthful giggle. "Righto, Sarge. I can't wait to see what happens when the jolly old vermin break through."

The two Captains, Doghead and Dewnose, were working like madbeasts. They had got about two spearlengths into the rock; the tunnel was going to work. Horde soldiers lined the narrow passage, passing back loose boulders and shields piled high with pebbles and shale. Outside on the moonlit beach, others were disposing of the rubble. Doghead and Dewnose labored hard with iron bars and spearpoints, levering away at the packed mass of stone that blocked the old kitchen drain. Both stoats knew that their lives depended on completing the tunnel; nobeast failed Ferahgo. Together they sweated and strained to prise out a big slab.

"Come on, mate. Pull. We've got it!"

"I'm pullin'. Owow! Me paw's jammed—wait a sec!"

"Migroo, get yerself up 'ere. Squeeze in there an' hold that bar while Dog'ead gets 'is paw loose."

"Owch! OK, I'm free. Now get yer spearpoint in right about 'ere, Migroo. I'll take care of the bar. Watch out, or it'll slide down an' trap yer paws!"

Crabeyes came crawling up the tunnel and pulled their tails. "Outside, you three. The Master an' young Klitch wants to see yer."

They crawled backwards out of the tunnel, scratched, bruised and covered in dust. The Assassin and his son awaited them on the sands. Ferahgo brushed aside their salutes, questioning them anxiously.

"Well, how is it going? Are you nearly through yet?"

Doghead wiped dirt from his eyes and licked his injured paw. "It's just like you said it'd be, Master—all loose rock, none of it solid. We're over two spearlengths in now, shouldn't be too long before we break through."

Ferahgo smiled scornfully, his crinkling blue eyes mocking Klitch. "That sounds like a fine mess, eh, young know-it-all?"

Klitch looked slightly taken aback. "But how did you know it was possible to tunnel at this spot?"

Ferahgo scooped up a pawful of sand and held it under his son's nose. "Kitchen debris, old nutshells, broken bits of pottery—that's how. Sometime or other this has been an outlet. When I checked I could see it wasn't part of the original rock, only stones packed in there to block it off. I was right, you see, cleverpaws. Now do you think that the old one is making a mess of things?"

"How wise of you, Father, you have found a way in." Klitch put on an expression of respect and kept his tone apologetic. "Now, are you going to stand there sneering at me and patting yourself on the back all night, or are you going to break into Salamandastron?"

Ferahgo's blue eyes smiled back and his tone was equally civil. "Raptail, Bateye, take this ignorant infant to one side, will you. Now guard him carefully and don't let him get hurt. Keep him here while his father goes to do the work of a warrior. Klitch is a bit inexperienced for this sort of thing, you know."

Leaving his son fuming under the eyes of the two guards, Ferahgo drew his daggers and rapped out orders.

"Doghead, Dewnose, bring a single torch. The rest of you, get fully armed and follow us. Keep silent in the tunnel . . . or else!"

The flaring light of a brushwood torch threw elongated shadows across the horde members packing up the tunnel behind Ferahgo and his two Captains. Dewnose patted the large slab when they reached the head of the tunnel.

"There's only this big 'un and a bit more behind it, Master, then we should be inside the mountain."

The Assassin sheathed his dagger and grabbed the spear from Dewnose. "Come out of my way, I'll show you how it's done."

The muscles stood out like whipcords on Ferahgo's lean body as he pitted his strength against the slab. It moved and slid. Angling it across the uneven floor, he struck it hard with the spearbutt, cracking it in two halves. "Pass that along and shift it out the way. Move yourselves!"

The Assassin went to work on the remaining rocks with ferocious strength, ripping them out with his bare paws, gouging with dagger and spearpoint. Hastily the rocks were passed back along the lines of hordebeasts jamming the length of the tunnel.

Throwing back a last few small boulders and kicking aside debris, Ferahgo halted abruptly. Licking the edge of his favorite skinning knife, he whispered to Doghead, "We're through! Feel that draft of cold air—that's our first breath of Salamandastron. Keep that torch aside a moment, there's somebeast standing with their back to the entrance. Now listen carefully. Whoever it is I'll stab him and drag him through for you and Dewnose to finish him off, then we're in. Keep silent now and I'll get him."

With the dagger between his teeth, Ferahgo inched quietly forward, his murderous blue eyes shining with joy as he sighted the unprotected back of the creature at the opening. When it came to silent death Ferahgo the Assassin was the acknowledged master. Throwing a paw round the creature's throat from behind, he locked off the windpipe and slid the blade expertly between its ribs. Pulling back in one swift movement, he threw the body to his Captains.

"Finish him off quickly, then follow me!"

Doghead pushed forward, spear in one paw, flaming torch in the other. He turned the creature over to stab it—and screamed. Ferahgo turned, he took one look, gave a strangled sob of horror and shot through the packed ranks for the open beach, kicking and slashing as he went. The body of Farran the Poisoner lay on the tunnel floor, the face a twisted mask of fright, the mouth wedged open wide by the adderskin belt with its poison bags that Urthstripe had forced down the

Poisoner's throat. Thus had the badger Lord dealt with the murderer of his two hares.

The poisoned drinking water was standing by the entrance Ferahgo had made, lined up in cauldrons, boiling hot. As they were wheeled by, Urthstripe tipped each one with his spearbutt, sending scalding water rushing into the tunnel as he roared at the top of his voice:

"Eulaliaaaaaa!"

The hordebeasts packed inside the tunnel fought each other madly in a vain bid to escape the contents of the cauldrons. Spears, swords, pikes and other weaponry hindered them in the darkness as the blistering hot stream gushed out, welling up into a steaming wave. Screams were drowned amid the boiling torrent. Smashed against the rocky walls, the bodies hurtled the length of the narrow aperture to be spewed out on to the beach.

Moonpaw, Starbob, Catkin, Thistle and Seawood climbed back into Salamandastron's east side, throwing the sacks of dandelions, apples, berries and roots ahead of them. Sapwood helped each one in as they clambered through an unblocked window hole. Seawood and Thistle came last, cautioning the Sergeant, "Careful with those two sacks. There's six canteens of fresh water there, Sap."

Sapwood chuckled, patting their backs. "Bless yer ears, mates. Where'd you come by all this lot?"

Thistle nudged him in the ribs and gave a broad wink. "Fancy askin' a Long Patrol Hare a question like that, Sergeant. Did you never have to survive off the land on a long scout?"

Sapwood began blocking the window hole up. "'Course I did. Silly ol' me. Hey, Seawood, the diversion worked a treat. You should've seen Urthstripe. 'Is

Nibs was like a liddle bunny on 'oliday, roarin' an' a-shoutin'. By the fur, the Boss gave those vermints an 'ot old time an' no mistake."

One backpaw, a leg and a large area of Ferahgo's back were painful areas of blistered flesh. He lay stretched on a rock in the dawn light, biting on his knife handle to stop himself crying out. Sickear dabbed seawater gently on the injured weasel, backing off a few paces every time the Assassin winced.

"Water from the sea is all we've got, Master. It smarts, but it cures. We used it for all injuries when I was searattin'."

Klitch was enjoying the whole thing hugely. He leaned down close to his father's face as he mocked him. "Ah then, did the naughty badger roast your bottom, O ruler of all the Southwest and Leader of the Corpsemakers. Never mind then, you leave it to young wet-behind-the-ears Klitch. I'll take charge for a while."

Ferahgo arched his back in agony as the seawater trickled onto it. Sweat beaded on his lips and nose as he gritted around the dagger blade at his grunting son, "Oh yes? And what's your brilliant plan, you little toad?"

Klitch took one of the daggers from his father's discarded belt and tapped the point against his teeth pensively. "Hmmm. Plan? I'm not quite sure yet, but it doesn't involve getting thirty soldiers boiled to death by hot water. But don't you fret your dear old gray head, I'll think of something."

"You bring me the head of that badger, or I'll . . ." Ferahgo struggled to rise but fell back snarling.

"You'll what?" Klitch patted the Assassin's back, none too gently. "You're not in a position to do anything. Give me until nightfall and I'll guarantee I'll have a foolproof plan, one that will make this horde realize that they've been led by the wrong weasel for many seasons now.''

Forgrin the fox emptied a slingbag onto the rocks beside his friend Raptail the rat. "There y'are, mate—whelks, limpets an' a few mussels. They'll taste better'n hard crust an' roots.''

Raptail smashed open a mussel with a stone and ate the contents ravenously. "Couldn't yer find no fish?''

Forgrin scooped a limpet out of its shell into his mouth. "You get them shellfish down yer an' thank yer lucky stars we're still alive, Raptail. It's a good job we was only at the entrance t' that tunnel or we'd be layin' scalded dead by now.''

"It was a stupid plan, a cracked idea, the 'ole thing!'' Raptail chewed with difficulty on a rubbery whelk. "Migroo says that young Klitch is takin' over. What d'you think of 'im?''

The fox spat on a rock and began sharpening his sword. "Think? We're not 'ere ter think, mate. Accordin' to 'Is Majesty Ferahgo, we're just 'ere ter take orders. But between you'n me an' the seashore, I think the time's ripe for Ferahgo to go.''

The rat scratched his nose and stared at the fox. "Go?''

"Aye, go, matey. He's down an' injured. Now's the time to slip a blade across 'is weasely throat, see wot I mean?''

Raptail gouged at a tooth crevice with a grimy claw, realization dawning on him. "Yeh, maybe yore right. Ferahgo couldn't give orders with a slit gizzard, that's fer sure. Say tonight, when it's nice 'n' dark . . . he'll be sleepin' deep then, eh?''

Forgrin tested the edge of his sword on a whelk he had disgorged. "We'll make sure he sleeps deeper than ever . . . tonight.''

256

BOOK THREE

Destinies and Homecomers

29

Thrugg and Dumble had arrived at the mountain stronghold of the Laird Mactalon. They stood shivering among the high rocks, unconscious of the beauties about them.

The Laird Mactalon spread his wings wide at the snowcapped peaks. The setting sun had turned the ice and snow from white to a clear pink.

"Och, 'tis a sight tae gladden yer feathers, laddie!"

Baby Dumble spread his paws, gazing down at his fat little stomach. "I don't avven no fevvers."

"Ach, so ye dinna. Would ye no' like to be a falcon?" Mactalon's wide wing patted him, nearly knocking him over.

The dormouse sniffed as he climbed into Thrugg's haversack, away from the cold. "Sooner be a Dumble!"

Mactalon chuckled fiercely. "Och, awa' wi ye, mousie!" He turned to Thrugg. The otter was stamping his paws to keep warm. "Noo then, mah friend, ye'll be wanting tae get your paws on some Icetor Flow'rs, mah son tells me."

Thrugg swung the haversack to his shoulders. "Yessir, them's the ones—Icetor Flowers. You tell me where they're at an' I'll go an' pick 'em."

"Weel noo, aren't you the bold creature?" Mactalon preened his neck feathers. "Pick them indeed. Yer a braw big riverdog, Thrugg, but yer a long ways frae hame. Icetors only grow aboot the nest of the wild King MacPhearsome. Och, nae bird or beastie ever goes up there, laddie. Yon eagle's a verra unpredictable creature. I wouldnae fancy makin' requests o' him! But if ye be foolish enough tae try, I'll fly up there on the morrow, but you'll have tae climb, as ye have nae wings tae speak of."

Rocangus showed Thrugg and Dumble to a small cavern where they were to spend the night. There was heather and bracken piled up in a corner, but the place was dreadfully cold. Thrugg put some of the bracken to one side, the rest he placed at the cavern entrance. Digging flint and tinder from the haversack, he soon had a small fire going. Rocangus was wary of flames, but the sight of Baby Dumble seated in front of the fire warming his paws soon had the young falcon perched between Thrugg and Dumble, enjoying the welcome heat. Rocangus had some words of advice for the otter.

"Mah faither says ye're going up tae see the Wild King in the mornin'. Be careful, Thrugg. Auld Mac-Phearsome is a giant. Mind yer manners, address him as King or Your Majesty. Och, he has a braw temper that one has. He'd as soon eat ye as look at ye."

Thrugg put more of the sweet-smelling bracken on the fire. "Listen, Rocangus me ol' matey, I'll do whatever it takes to get those Icetor Flowers back to Redwall Abbey. If I've got to pretend to be frightened of some old bird, then so be it."

"Ye have mah admiration, Thrugg, for I know yer not affrighted of anythin'." Rocangus flexed his good wing. "Mind, though, ye'd be well advised tae fear the Wild King. He's the only one who has Icetor Flow'rs an' he doesn't part wi' anythin' lightly. Oh, an' ye'd best leave yer sling wi' me. MacPhearsome won't have any armed bird or beast near his eyrie. That's aboot it, Thrugg. Guid luck to ye. Yer a braw friend an' a bonny river-dog."

Rocangus had conquered his fear of the fire. In fact, he had rather come to like it. The young falcon spent the night feeding the flames with heather and bracken while Thrugg and Baby Dumble slept peacefully in the high snowcapped mountains of the north.

Dawn in the high mountains was a strange sight. Thrugg shivered as he peered into the whiteness. Clouds had descended upon the peaks, turning the whole place into a land of cotton wool. There was no sky, horizon or ground, save for that beneath the otter's paws.

Settling Dumble into the near-empty haversack, Thrugg cautioned him. "Stay put, matey, an' keep yore head down. Ye'll be nice an' warm in there."

The Laird Mactalon flew in low and hovered outside the cave. "A guid mornin' to ye, Thrugg. Are ye ready the noo?"

Thrugg gave his sling to Rocangus. "Ready as I'll ever be. Lead on, Yore Lordship!"

Rocangus stood waving with his good wing, watching them until they were swallowed up in the mists.

It was a perilous journey. Thrugg needed all his strength and sure-pawed skill. Sliding down glacial valleys and ascending slopes of crusted snow, scaling bare freezing rocks, the otter pushed on, keeping Mactalon in sight all the time. Seeking for holds in crevices, Thrugg dug his paws in, hauling himself strenuously upward. Ledges with thick icicles hanging like sets of organ pipes ranged each side of him. Grunting and panting, he watched the falcon ahead flying upward, ever upward. Battling almost blindly through the world of snow, ice and white cloudbanks, the otter often slipped and slid back, but he was always back on the trail immediately, gritting his teeth and wiping away the perspiration that threatened to freeze on his nose and whiskers, ever mindful of the infant dormouse in the haversack strapped to his powerful shoulders. Thrugg lost all sense of time and space as he plugged doggedly onward and upward. It was at the exact moment that he thought he could go on no more that Laird Mactalon wheeled down through the shrouding mist.

"Guid show, laddie. Ye've made it! Yon's the eyrie of King MacPhearsome. Ah'll be waitin' here for ye when you're done. The rest is up to ye now, Thrugg. Ah wish ye the best o' fortune."

Raising his eyes, Thrugg saw the eyrie. Swathed in clouds, it sat on a rocky pinnacle, strewn with heather, bracken, gorse, thistles and branches, all faded, dried and dead. The only living plant that could be seen sprouting through the debris was the Icetor flower, small, delicate, white, starlike, with blue-tinged petals, almost invisible in the surrounding snow, but mysterious and beautiful in its mountain isolation.

Thrugg called up at the nest in a friendly tone, "Ahoy there, Yer Majesty. It's me, Thrugg of Redwall Abbey. I've come to visit the Wild King himself."

There was a crackling of heather and twigs, the nest stirred slightly, then MacPhearsome himself flew out.

The sight completely took Thrugg's breath away. He had not been prepared for something like this. Snow flurried around his head as the great expanse of wings flapped downward and the Wild King landed in front of him. It was an awesome thing to see! The colossal golden eagle towered over Thrugg, two massive feet sinking slightly into the snow, lethal orange-scaled talons digging in for leverage. Each of the heavily feathered golden brown legs was as thick as the otter's body;

the eagle stood rooted on them as if they were twin oaks. The staggering canopy of wings swooshed noisily as the bird folded them both over his mighty back. The head dipped toward Thrugg, lighter brown-gold feathers framing the wild eyes afire with hunting lights.

MacPhearsome opened his curving amber beak, like two bone scimitars parting. "Ah doant like mah breakfast comin' up here tae meet me. Hie awa' an' hide, riverdog. Ah'll come an' hunt for ye!"

Thrugg swallowed hard and stood his ground. "Majesty, I've not come to harm yeh. It's the Flowers of Icetor I'm after. They're needed by my friends at Redwall Abbey, where there's a great sickness."

The eagle King clacked his beak together like steel striking rock. "Aye, so Ah've heard. Yon Mactalon flew up an' told me of this. Yer a tasty-looking beastie, Thrugg o' Redwall. Tell me, pray, why should the MacPhearsome gi'e ye his flow'rs?"

Thrugg took a bold step forward and raised his voice. "Because, O King, there's creatures goin' to die if'n they don't get the medicine made from your Icetor Flowers. You wouldn't want the deaths of honest Redwallers on yer mind, now would Yer Majesty?"

A fierce smile hovered about the Wild King's eyes. "Ah care no' a whit fer beasties that doant live in mah mountains. Ach, it wouldnae bother mah mind a wee bit. Tell me this, Thrugg o' Redwall: whit would ye do if Ah refused tae give ye mah flow'rs. Answer true now, riverdog!"

Thrugg took off the haversack. Placing it carefully to one side, setting his paws apart, he stared the eagle coolly in the eye. "Then if you'll forgive me for sayin', Majesty, I'd fight you for them. The lives of my mateys at the Abbey means a lot ter me, sir."

The golden eagle's raucous laughter set the mountain peaks ringing. He flew up, knocking Thrugg flat with the backdraft from his wings, circling and soaring in and out of the drifting mists. MacPhearsome's ear-splitting screeches of merriment echoed and re-echoed until the very air was full of the sound.

As suddenly as he had started, the Wild King stopped. He landed back on the snow in front of Thrugg and cocked his head, one glittering eye staring at his challenger. "Och weel, Ah've heard everythin' noo. Ye'd fight me? Jings, yer a braw beastie, a'right—Ah'll say that for ye, Thrugg o' Redwall. Mind, yer the on'y livin' creature ever tae stand there an' say that tae the Wild MacPhearsome. Yer friends must mean a great deal to ye, ye bonny riverdog. Fight me? It'd mak' me grieve sair tae eat ye!"

At that Baby Dumble clambered from the haversack and began attacking the golden eagle's leg, or at least one talon of it. "You leave Mista Thugg alone, ya big bully. Dumble fight you!"

One of the formidable talons looped through the infant dormouse's smock and he was swung aloft, close to the golden eagle's huge eye. "Name o' crags! Whit have we here? Ah'm scairt an' affrighted for mah life. Ye wouldnae kill me, would ye, mousie?"

Dumble swung a chubby paw at the eagle King. "Dumble knock you beak off if you 'urt Mista Thugg!"

MacPhearsome plopped him neatly back into Thrugg's outstretched paws, astonishment written on his savage features. "Och, Ah dinnae ken whit they feed ye on at Redwall, but it must be guid tae produce sich braw beasties. Ah'm thinkin' Ah'd best gi'e ye the Icetor Flow'rs afore Ah'm slain by the pair of ye!"

The great golden eagle spread his pinions, beating wildly as snow flew up all around, laughing and screeching in high good humor at his own joke.

On the snowy crag below them the Laird Mactalon pressed a wing hard over his heart to stop its racing beat and sat down flat, glad to be off his trembling legs.

The High King's strange mood had favored Thrugg and Dumble. Instead of MacPhearsome's wrath they were receiving the Icetor Flowers. It was a huge relief for the falcon Chieftain.

30

"Ee. . . . Oo. . . . Lay. . . . Lee. . . . Aaaaaahhhhh!"

Again the loud haunting cry rang through the wooded heights of the lake island above their heads. Shrews sprang up wide-eyed and quivering with fright.

Mara detached Pikkle from her paws and grabbed a paddle. "Whatever that is, it had better keep clear of us because if it comes down on to this ledge I'll brain it, ghost badger or not!"

Nordo piled more driftwood onto the fire. It burned bright, crackling sparks up into the still summer night. By its light Mara looked around at the ashen faces of the Guosssom shrews; even Log-a-log seemed shaken by the unearthly call. The badger maid knew they were close to panic, so she set about dispelling their fears.

"Hah! That's an old trick to keep us awake. Lord Urthstripe used to do things like that at Salamandastron to keep his hares alert, didn't he, Pikkle?" She nudged the young hare sharply. He jumped.

"Ow! Who? What? Oh er, rather, I'll say! Old Thingummy was always runnin' about in his nightshirt scarin' the tail off some chap or other, doncha know. Oh yes! Of course he couldn't frighten me or ol' Mara here, we just snoozed through it all."

Mara backed him up, watching the Guosssom beginning to relax.

"Haha, yes. Remember he terrified Bart Thistledown and the poor fellow fell backward into a pot of hot vegetable soup? Hahaha!"

"Hohoho, will I ever forget it, chum?" Pikkle slapped his sides as he expanded on the tale. "There was ol' Barty with the pan stuck to his bottom, chargin' about yellin' blue murder!"

The shrews began smiling and tittering. Soon they were rocking with laughter as Pikkle continued with the comical incident.

"Hahahaha! Dearie me, I tell you, fellers, Barty was the only one among us who'd never look at vegetable soup again. He's eaten nothin' but jolly old porridge from that day t' this. If ever you ask him to tell you the tale. . . . Hahahaha! Shall I tell y' wot he says . . . ? Heeheehee! He says, 'Don't mention the tale—it was cooked to a turn!' Ohohoho! Tail, tale, cooked to a turn—get it?"

Reciting stories and telling jokes, the two friends continued into the night until the incident was all but forgotten. Log-a-log posted sentries on the rock ledge, the fire was stoked up higher and gradually the shrews dozed off one by one. Mara lay watching the fire; Pikkle lay some distance away, though he could still see his friend's face in the firelight. She looked sad. Softly the young hare called across to her, "I say, old gel, what's up? Y' look like a wet wallflower on a windy day."

The badger maid sighed and closed her eyes. "All those stories we told, Pikkle—lies, the whole lot. I wish it *had* been like that back at Salamandastron. I'd never have left. Ah well, let's get some sleep. Goodnight, Pikkle."

Pikkle watched as a single teardrop oozed from his friend's closed eyelid.

"I say, steady on. Maybe we did tell a blinkin' pack of

fibs, but it certainly calmed down those shrew chapp-
ies. Look, they're fast asleep, the lot o' them, just like
we should be. G'night Mara ol' gel, happy dreams,
wot?"

Log-a-log roused them as he threw more wood on the
fire. It had been light for nearly three hours. "Come on,
you lot. Roll me log, are you going to doze there all
day?"

Breakfast was a hasty affair of meager rations. Preparations for the day were mapped out by the shrew
leader. Log-a-log elected to go with Nordo and the
foraging party, saying he would search for logboat
repairing materials while they gathered what food the
island had to offer. Six shrews were to remain behind
on the ledge to guard the boats and keep the fire going.

Mara and Pikkle studiously avoided mentioning the
nature of their quest, so as not to upset the others.
Arming themselves with rapiers and slings, and
accompanied by Tubgutt, as promised, they climbed up
the cliffs to the woodlands above and struck out for
the center of the island, leaving the Guosssom to their
chores.

It was a thickly wooded island. Small birds twittered in
the foliage, sunlight shafted through the leaves of
beech, elm, oak, ash, sycamore and cedar, tracing patterns of light and shade on the pretty forest flowers
carpeting the ground. Pikkle found a cherry tree in full
fruit and they sat beneath it, eating the softest dark red
cherries. Apples and pears too grew in profusion.

Pikkle flicked a cherry stone in the air. "I say, this is
all rather nice, chaps. A body could get used to this,
the blinkin' place is a paradise. Look, there's a sweet-
chestnut tree—beech and hazelnut as well. Flop my
ears, if a ghost does live here he must be a blinkin'

268

well-fed old spook. Yowch! Go easy with those cherry stones, Mara!"

"What are you gabbling on about, Ffolger?" The badger maid looked at him quizzically.

"Gabblin'? I'm not gabblin', m'dear gel. Just quit chuckin' jolly ol' cherry stones at me, that's all."

Mara indicated a small heap of cherry pits at her side. "I've not thrown a one. Mine are here—see?"

Pikkle clapped a paw to his eye. "Yowch! Now listen, old Tubthing, throw one more cherry stone at me an' I'll squidge a cherry right on your bally nose!"

Tubgutt was a serious shrew, not given to practical jokes. "I don't throw pips at other creatures, Pikkle. Don't blame me!"

"Yowch! Well, who the—ow! There goes another one!"

Mara looked up swiftly and caught a glance of a fleeting grayish creature flitting through the treetops. "Aha! There's somebeast up there. Come on. It went that way!"

Dashing between the close-growing trunks, they chased after the shadowy figure, but it was a pointless exercise; whatever it was had them easily outdistanced. The three friends stopped in a small clearing, panting from the hard run. A pool of crystal-clear water provided them with a refreshing drink.

As they drank, Pikkle watched the treetops reflected in the surface of the water. Leaning close to Mara, he whispered, "It's back again. The bally thing's watchin' us from the top of that beech tree yonder. What'll we do?"

Mara kept her face down and her paws cupped as she drank water. "Ah yes, I see it now. Pay no attention. We'll let its own curiosity get the better of it. Look, it's coming lower."

Traveling in small jerky runs, the creature was moving down the beech trunk toward the ground.

Tubgutt watched the reflection in the pool with Mara and Pikkle.

"What do you suggest we do now, Mara? It's down on the grass."

Now Mara had lost the reflected picture, she took a quick glance over her shoulder. The creature had started moving across the clearing behind them.

"It's a squirrel!" the badger maid hissed to her friends. "When I give the word we must move fast, cut it off from the trees and surround it in this clearing. Pikkle, you're the fastest—get behind it. Tubgutt, go to the left. I'll go to the right. That way the only place it will have left to run will be straight into this pool. Ready . . . Go!"

The plan worked neatly. Dashing out, they had the squirrel boxed in. As they moved closer, it backed toward the pool. It was a female, incredibly small and thin, traces of its former red showing beneath the fur that was heavily grayed with age. She stood with her back to the water, baring toothless gums at them. Mara held out her paws in a sign of peace.

"I am Mara, this is Pikkle, and Tubgutt. We mean you no harm. Why were you throwing cherry stones at us? I could understand if you were a young playful squirrel, but one of your seasons . . . You surprise me with your infantile behavior."

The ancient creature did not reply. She swayed from side to side, seeking a chance to dash off, but there was no escape likely.

Pikkle stepped closer, wagging a paw at her. "How would you like it if I aimed cherry stones at your bonce, marm? What I mean is, hang it all, can't a chap scoff cherries in peace on this island?"

The squirrel opened her mouth wide and let out a long shrill call.

"Eulaliaaaaaa!"

There followed a silence. Pikkle shook his head disapprovingly. "Is that all you've got to say for yourself, old lady? Dearie me, I can see this conversation's goin' nowhere fast, wot?"

There was a rustling in the woodland at their backs. The squirrel nodded with satisfaction before speaking.

"You'll be sorry you came to this island. It's you who are surrounded now, not me."

A heavy crashing in the undergrowth caused the three friends to turn round. Two badgers came thundering out of the woods, one a female as old as the squirrel, but the other was a huge male, white as driven snow and whirling a big knotted oak club. They roared as they burst into the clearing.

"Eulaliaaaaaa!"

Pikkle and Tubgutt stood openmouthed with shock, but Mara stood forward, a tiny shrew rapier in one paw, twirling a loaded sling in the other. The battle light shone in her eyes.

"I am Mara of Salamandastron! Stay out of the way, old mother. You, white one, come a step closer and I'll slay you!"

The white badger looked for a moment as if he were going to charge forward, but Mara noted the fierceness dim suddenly from his face, and his massive paws quivered as he stood undecided.

"Get in there and fight, Urthwyte!" The old female badger stamped her paw down angrily. "Go on, she's a mere puppy compared to you. Flatten her!"

Mara came forward lightly, poised on ready pawpads, her neckfur bristling, fangs bared. "Aye, come on, Urthwyte. You're a fine big beast. Let's see if you fight as good as you growl!"

Pikkle and Tubgutt stood to one side, out of the whole thing. The confrontation was between two badgers; to get in the way meant certain death. Pikkle, however, noticed as Mara did that the white badger, for

271

all his size and muscle, seemed unwilling to offer battle. The young hare called encouragement to his friend.

"Watch him, Mara. Remember Sergeant Sapwood— dodge and weave. Don't try a paw to paw with this rascal. He's too big!"

Mara was still moving forward.

"Urthwyte, what have we taught you?" The old squirrel chattered angrily. "Kill the creature! Ooooh! Loambudd, kick his tail for him, good 'n' hard!"

As Mara advanced, the older badger, Loambudd, gave Urthwyte a hefty shove in the back.

"Go on, you big lump. Fight!"

The white badger stumbled forward into Mara, accidentally catching her off guard. He closed his eyes, averting his head as he grabbed her. The breath left Mara's body in a great whoosh, two enormous vicelike paws lifted her clear off the ground, and she was pinned helpless in midair, with the great white badger shouting, "Look, just leave me alone, will you? I don't want to fight. Let me be, or I'll squeeze you hard!"

Mara felt as though her whole body was trapped in a mighty press. Her eyes bulged and she fought for breath. Pikkle pushed Tubgutt aside as the shrew ran forward, drawing his rapier. The young hare set his jaw grimly as he thwacked down a loaded sling viciously on the white badger's footpaw.

"Enough of this, y' great bully. Put that maid down this instant!"

It worked like a charm. The big, simple badger dropped Mara in a heap as he hopped about on one leg, rubbing his smarting footpaw. Urthwyte's lower lip jutted resentfully as he muttered, "I'm not a bully. *She's* the bully. Anyway, why are they always trying to make me fight?"

Pikkle patted his head. "There there, old lad. It's not your fault."

The squirrel rushed in, chattering. "You leave him

alone, hare. Who asked you to come to our island in the first place? Go away and leave us in peace!"

Loambudd, the old female badger, went to attend to Mara, rubbing her ribs and patting her back until the badger maid regained her breath. She was very motherly and considerate.

"Stay there, Mara. Lie back and take deep breaths. There's nothing broken. Ashnin, I don't think these creatures mean us any harm."

"Well, they had me surrounded and captured!" The squirrel folded her paws stubbornly.

Pikkle gave her a playful shove. "Oh, go on with you, Granny. You started it by invadin' me with bloomin' cherry stones."

Ashnin gave a cackling laugh. "Good shot, aren't I? Never missed ye once!"

Urthwyte tugged Ashnin's tail, complaining aloud just like a small badger babe, "I'm thirsty. Is it all right to have a drink?"

The old squirrel threw up her paws in mock despair. "Oh go on, you great white tripehound, but don't go drainin' the pond. Leave some for others."

They all sat at the edge of the pool as Urthwyte sucked in great noisy gulps of water like a thirsty babe.

Loambudd shook her head. "Look at him, the son of one of the greatest badger warriors ever to put paw on grass. Ah, but it's not all his fault."

Urthwyte raised his dripping white snout from the water. "I'm hungry. It's well past lunchtime, Nin."

The old squirrel tugged his ear sharply. "Tell me a time when you're not hungry, you big scoffbag."

She turned to the three friends. "I suppose you're all hungry too? D'you want lunch?"

Pikkle bowed gracefully and kissed her wrinkled paw. "Feed us, O beautiful one, and we're yours forever!"

"Oh go on with you, longshanks." She cuffed the

273

young hare's ear lightly. "I can see you'd take more feedin' than a whole army, just by lookin' at yeh."

Loambudd stood up and beckoned them. "Follow me. You'll have to put a move on, though. I put a leek and mushroom pastie in the oven before Ashnin called. I just hope it hasn't burned."

The two badgers and the squirrel lived a short distance from the pool in a beautiful natural cave. Mara looked about admiringly. It was spacious and well ventilated; two long windows had been carved through the rock, which stood like a hump in the forest. Flowers and trailing plants decorated the windowsills, woven rush matting carpeted the cave and there were several large seats carved from dead logs. These were spread with soft barkcloth covers. The rock had been carved in one corner to form a fireplace and a wide oven. In the center of the cave was a fine table of rock slab adorned with bowls of fruit.

They washed their paws in a trough by the entrance and sat round the table as Urthwyte and Loambudd brought the food. Pikkle's eyes lit up and Tubgutt gave a small growl of anticipation. A crisp salad of fennel, hazelnuts, young dandelions and scallions was placed on the table, followed by a giant-sized leek and mushroom pastie, its steaming golden crust adorned with watercress. A large pitcher of cherry cordial and beakers came next, with cold mint-flavored springwater standing by in another jug. Apples baked in honey with dollops of yellow kingcup cream topped the whole thing off, with a wide, flat, sugared plumcake standing by as an extra.

Ashnin and Loambudd ate sparingly, encouraging the younger creatures to have as much as they liked — though little encouragement was needed. Mara ate steadily, but Pikkle, Tubgutt and Urthwyte went at it as though they were facing a ten-season famine.

While they were enjoying the food, Mara noticed a black stone on a leather thong hanging over the fireplace. She nudged Tubgutt.

"Is that Log-a-log's famous Blackstone?"

Tubgutt rose from the table. Going over to the stone, he touched it and bowed low reverently. "Aye, this is the Blackstone of all the South Stream shrews."

Urthwyte leaned back and stretched out. Unlooping the stone and its thong, he swung it back and forth, a mischievous grin hovering on his big face.

"Oh, this? I took it from a shrew who trespassed on our island a long time ago. The little rascal took off like a shot. He must've thought I looked like some kind of ghost in the dark. Ha ha, most creatures do, y'know. I used to play with this stone—dreary-looking old thing, isn't it? You can have it if you like, Mara."

He passed the Blackstone over, noting with a smile the gratitude on her face.

The badger maid accepted the stone, winding the thong around her paw. "Thank you very much, Urthwyte. This stone means a lot to the tribe of Tubgutt, and to the father of the shrew you took it from."

Loambudd served Pikkle a great chunk of pastie. "So that's what two boatloads of shrews came all this way for, a simple black pebble on a string. Well I never. We thought they'd come to settle here—that's why we got Urthwyte to sound his ghost cries last night. I hoped it'd frighten them off."

Ashnin nibbled a fennel leaf, watching Mara with shrewd eyes. "But you never came here just for a piece of stone, missie?"

Mara took a drink of the cool mintwater. "No, I came because Log-a-log the shrew leader wanted me to. Once he gets the Blackstone back, his authority as Guosssom leader will be complete. Then he will take me and Pikkle to the sea in his logboats to help Urthstripe in his fight against Ferahgo."

"Ferahgo the Assassin?"

Urthwyte's voice roared out like thunder as he threw back his big chair and reared up, a picture of massive ferocity, all traces of his former gentleness gone as fury blazed from hot angry eyes set above savagely bared teeth.

Ashnin and Loambudd rushed round the table. They clung to the white badger's paws, trying to pull him back down into his chair. He was yelling at the top of his voice, "Ferahgo the Assassin! Ferahgo the Assassin!"

The three friends helped to calm him down and get him seated. He was shaking and trembling all over, the food in front of him forgotten.

Ashnin slipped a small quantity of powder into a beaker of cherry cordial and gave it to him. "Here, drink this all up and go outside. Take a nap in the clearing and you'll feel better. Go on."

Obediently the big badger drained the cup and shambled off out of the cave. When he had gone, Loambudd seized Mara's paw.

"Urthstripe—you mentioned Urthstripe. Is he alive?"

Mara looked puzzled. "Yes, of course he is. Urthstripe is the badger Lord of Salamandastron. He is a great warrior, and also a stern old guardian. That's why I left Salamandastron."

Loambudd sat back in her chair, shaking her head as she wiped away tears with a distracted paw.

"Urthstripe alive! So, that little striped babe escaped the Assassin somehow. Tell me about him. What does he look like? Is he as big as his brother? Wait, tell me everything, all about my grandson and about yourself, too, young one."

The badger maid related the story of her life and all she recalled of the badger Lord, from the time she became the adopted daughter of the mountain, up until the time she landed with the shrews at the island.

31

Three long shrew logboats shot out into the waters of the Great South Stream. The dawn was gray and overcast with a warm blustery wind coming out of the northeast. In the prow of the lead boat Samkim, Arula and Spriggat sat with their paddles shipped. There was little need for paddling in the fast-flowing current with the wind astern of the vessels.

Arula chuckled with excitement as the sturdy craft skimmed and bobbed over the rushing waters. "Huhurr, boaten beats walken boi arf a season's march!"

Now and then Spriggat would lean to one side and snap at the odd passing winged insect. "Huh, goin' too fast fer an 'og to catch a bite."

Samkim crouched in the prow with Alfoh. Together they scanned ahead for signs of Dethbrush and his five trackers. Spray blew up into the young squirrel's nostrils. It was his first time on a shrew logboat and he found it very exhilarating. Winking across at Alfoh, he called over the rushing stream noise, "This is the life, eh? Makes me wish I was a shrew!"

The elder nodded as he shouted back, "You like it? Good! Your fox would have had to come this way

277

because of the speedy current. We can follow this way until we get below the rapids!''

"Rapids?'' Spriggat gave a squeak of dismay. "You never said anythin' about rapids. Where are they?''

"Up there a piece.'' Alfoh nodded ahead. "Don't worry, they'll come soon enough. I'll pass you the word when they do.''

Frequently the shrews would use their paddles to negotiate a rock or ward off floating driftwood, but the pace was becoming faster all the time and the banks shot by in a blur of green and brown as Alfoh roared out directions and warnings.

"Duck your heads, overhangin' willows comin' up!''

Arula barely made it, receiving a smart clip from a branch.

"Rock to port! Get those paddles lined up!''

Samkim shoved hard with his paddle, feeling the shock run through his paws as it struck stone. He pushed and felt the boat skip out away from the rock.

"Wood stickin' up midstream, paddles to starboard!''

Spriggat and Arula paddled furiously, sighing in relief as they whizzed by a tree trunk that had stuck in the muddy bottom.

Alfoh brought his mouth close to Samkim's ear. "No signs yet, but don't worry, we'll catch the blaggards. Here come the rapids now. Stow yer paddle an' hang on tight!''

Samkim threw his paddle in the logboat bottom, gripping the sides tightly as he heard Alfoh yell out, "Rapids ahead! Stow all paddles an' hang on!''

White water boiled up over the prow, drenching Samkim as the boat dipped and hurtled crazily into a mad world of foaming, writhing waters. At the stern two experienced shrews sculled with their paddles, slewing the craft around jagged rocky outcrops. Arula threw herself into the bottom of the boat, digging claws hiding her eyes in fright.

"Oohurr, oi'm bound t'er be a drownded mole choild afore sunset!" Like a roller coaster the logboat tore through the rapids, sometimes with water gushing over the sides, other times with the hull groaning as it scraped over submerged rock ledges. Sterns up, heads down, the three vessels weaved and twisted with terrifying speed down the perilous watercourse. Samkim was amazed the shrews seemed to take it all in their stride, neither laughing nor looking fearful they battled away with expertise, competence written all over their faces. Finally, after one long watercourse that seemed more like a waterfall than a rapid, they splashed down into a semicircular lagoon with a thick covering of foamy scum lying slowly swirling on its surface. Behind them the rapids crashed and roared in watery chaos. Dipping their paddles, they began pushing on down the wide calm stream. Traveling easily, they felt possessed of an overwhelming tranquillity after the turmoil of the rapids. The sky was still lowering and overcast, wind soughed softly through the sedge at the banks and margins as the three logboats forged ahead.

It was midday when the stream ahead split two ways and Alfoh held up a paw and called out, "Bows into yon middle bank!"

They headed into the tongue of land that protruded at the parting of the stream. Leaping ashore, Alfoh pointed to a high giant hornbeam.

"Mollo, shin up that there hornbeam tree an' scout the lay o' the waters."

A sprightly young shrew bounded forward, but Samkim beat him to it. "Shrews to water but squirrels to trees, my friend!" Like a shaft from a bowstring the young squirrel shot up the towering trunk. Alfoh watched him in amazement. Arula nudged the old shrew.

"Burr, owzat furr cloimen, zurr. 'Ee be a gud'n, our Sanken."

279

The giant hornbeam was so high that it was difficult to see Samkim when he was at the top. With the speed and agility of a born climber he whizzed back down again, leaping lightly to the ground, eager to deliver his news.

"I could see them, I could see them! They've taken that stream on the left!"

Alfoh leapt back into the boat. "Lucky for them. This'n on the right would've taken them into another waterfall and the mountain caves. How far away are they?"

Samkim jumped in beside him. "Only about two hours good paddling I'd say."

The boats pushed off down the left fork of the stream. It sloped slightly and ran straight as a die as far as the eye could see. Alfoh struck out with his paddle.

"Seems they're headed right for the sea, but keep your eyes peeled anyway. You never can tell wi' vermin."

The wind increased. Now dark cloud masses could be seen drifting over from the northeast. Spriggat snapped up a mayfly that had been silly enough to try a landing on his paw.

"Looks like rain's goin' to bucket down afore long!"

Halfway through the afternoon Alfoh peered at the left bank. It was heavily overgrown with willows and bushes. He had been watching out for this particular place.

"Pull over here, shrews. That's it, now back water an' hove to."

Samkim watched intently as the elder inspected the thicketed edge. "What is it, Alfoh? What are you looking for?"

Alfoh slashed at some vegetation with his rapier and

pulled a clump of bush lupin to one side. "Hah! I thought so. Look here!"

It was a hidden side creek, overgrown by bush and tree, which wound its way into thick woodland. Alfoh ponted to recent scrapes in the clay of the bank at water level.

"Aye, that's a fox for ye, always one jump ahead of a grasshopper! The villain knew we'd follow t' get our boat back, so he's sidetracked off down here—though I suspect he doesn't know where he's goin' to. This isn't the way to the sea."

"Whurr do et lead to, zurr Affaloh?" Arula peered up the dim overgrown waterway.

Alfoh scratched his chin. "Only one place it can lead to, Arula: the Great Lake."

It was like paddling through a long green tunnel. The water reflected the trees overhead as they crowded low, and the mossy banks, and everywhere was green. Samkim looked at the faces around him, tinged by the green light. Apart from the muted sound of paddles, they were in a cocoon of verdant silence. Spriggat paddled and snacked upon various winged denizens of the hidden waterway, lifting his eyes as the splash of water on the leaves above announced the arrival of the rain. They ate as they went, passing back oatcakes and small fruit scones preserved in honey and flower syrup.

Arula took gulps of cooling lilac and rosewater from a hollow gourd and passed it to Spriggat. "Yurr, wash'ee flies down, zurr."

All along the waterway there were signs that the fox had passed in the stolen boat—broken branches, bruised plants and scrapes in the mossed banks. The wind increased overhead, howling a dirge through the treetops. The banks started to rise higher and the watercourse flowed faster as it took a downward slope.

Suddenly Alfoh pointed ahead to the stern of a logboat vanishing round a bend. "There they are! Dig those paddles deep. We've got 'em!"

Dethbrush heard the shout. Looking over his shoulder, he called to the five tracker rats, "Paddle for your lives! It's those shrews!"

Other side streams, swollen by the rain, began gushing into the watercourse, and the stolen boat picked up speed, zinging along on its downhill course to the inland lake. Behind it the three logboats raced to catch up.

Dethbrush's boat tipped dangerously and took off into the waters of the Great Lake with a loud splash. It was followed soon after by the Guosssom boats. Now all four were in the open waters. The howling northeast wind whipped the surface into foaming gray waves driven along in a wild slanting downpour of battering rain. Samkim wiped rainwater from his eyes, shielding them with a paw as he tried to keep his sight focused on the boat ahead. The storm drove it powerfully over the wave-crested waters. Up and down bobbed the prow of Samkim's boat, driving deep into the troughs and being lifted high upon the crests. The crew pulled with might and main, until Samkim could see the back of the fox drawing closer.

"We've got 'em, lads. Dig those paddles deep!" With a shrew rapier in his paw, the young squirrel stood balancing as far out on the prow as he could go. "Paddle! Paddle, you water-wallopers!"

Within a third of a boatlength Samkim braced himself and took off with a mighty leap. Hurtling across the water with the waves almost hitting his paws, he sprang across the gap between the two boats to land scrambling for balance on the stern of the fox's boat. A rat raised a paddle at him, but Samkim ducked and thrust in one movement, taking the tracker through his midriff.

Dethbrush turned, brandishing the sword of Martin the Warrior. He advanced on Samkim, calling above the storm, "Come on, I'll carve your gizzard to doll rags! 'S death for you, young un!"

32

Ferahgo lay stretched upon the rock. An old cloak that belonged to him had been soaked in seawater by Sickear and thrown over him to heal his scalded back. He sprawled flat on his stomach, feigning sleep, watching the shoreline through half-open eyes. The Assassin was expecting an attempt upon his life, whether from Klitch or some other source he knew not, but he was certain of one thing: injured leaders were a good target for the rebellious. When his penetrating stare caught the telltale movements far out among the rocks of the shore, he called Sickear to him.

The rat was weary after nursing Ferahgo all day; he lolloped across and threw a desultory salute. "Yes, Master? Can I be of service?"

Ferahgo rose slowly, shaking his head. "No, Sickear, you've done enough for one day. You look tired."

Expecting a reprimand, the rat came to attention. "No, Master, I'm fresh as a daisy. It's my duty to get you well."

The Assassin ruffled the rat's ears good-naturedly. "And a splendid job you've done of it, Sickear. My own mother couldn't have nursed me better. Listen, I'm just going to see what that son of mine is up to. You can have the rest of the night off. Come here, lie down on this rock. It's flat and smooth. Come on now, I won't take no for an answer."

The rat complied somewhat hesitantly, but Ferahgo was right, the rock was cool and smooth. He stretched out on it and yawned. "Thank you, Master."

"Oh, it's the least I could do." Ferahgo's blue eyes smiled lovingly. "Here, let me cover you with this cloak. You wouldn't believe how soft and soothing a drop of your seawater has made it. There, how does that feel?"

Sickear relaxed. "Mmmm, it feels really good, Master."

Ferahgo ducked down and stole off into the rocks. Within moments Sickear was slumbering peacefully, the damp cloak protecting him from the early night breezes that drifted about the darkened shoreline.

Forgrin had sharpened an edge and point upon his sword all afternoon, and Raptail had driven a sharp spike through the top of a wooden cudgel. They crept slowly across the rocks toward the still draped figure lying on the flat stone near the tideline. Of the two, Forgrin was the bolder. He popped up from behind the rocks and bobbed down again.

"See, Rap, not a sentry in sight. I told yer, young Klitch 'as taken charge of the rest. This'll be a piece of pie. You'll see!"

Raptail nodded at the fox and brandished his club. "Listen, mate, I'm scared, I don't mind tellin' yer. Suppose Ferahgo wakes up?"

Forgrin pawed the blade of his sword, grinning at the rat. "I've sent many a beast to sleep wi' this liddle beauty. None of them ever woke up. Come on, let's git it done afore yer nerve runs out altogether!"

Not even daring to breathe, they stole up on the supine figure.

Forgrin felt confident. Standing over the cloak-draped creature, he could not resist a quiet snigger. "Weasel yer way outta this one, weasel!"

He drove the sword downward with both paws. The cloaked figure gave a gasp and went rigid. Raptail thudded two solid blows of his club to the covered head and leapt back.

"Is 'e dead, mate? Stick 'im agin ter make sure!"

"Oh, he's quite dead. There's no need to stick him any more."

The voice was unmistakably that of Ferahgo.

Raptail died with a faint moan as Ferahgo dispatched him with his skinning knife, almost carelessly in passing. Not even bothering to glance at the fallen rat, the Assassin turned to the fox. Forgrin was shaking uncontrollably. The blue eyes looked almost jolly as they smiled through the night at him.

"See, we've killed a rat apiece. You murdered Sickear and I slew Raptail. Now what happens, do you kill a weasel, or do I kill a fox?"

Terror had robbed Forgrin of his power of speech. A gurgling noise escaped his throat as he turned and ran along the beach.

Ferahgo could throw a knife better than any creature. The long skinning knife took Forgrin between the shoulder blades before he had got thirty paces. His eyes were glazing over for the last time as the Assassin retrieved the knife.

"Oh, I forgot to tell you," Ferahgo whispered close to his ear, "this game ends with the weasel killing the fox. Sweet dreams, Forgrin."

Ferahgo's back felt much better. As he strolled along the beach, his brilliant blue eyes lit up with happiness.

Urthstripe watched from the top of the crater with Sapwood and Big Oxeye. Below them on the shore, masses of torchlights were moving away from Salamandastron. Sapwood nodded toward them.

"Hi wonder what they're hup to now, Ox?"

The big hare leaned on his spear. "You tell me, ol' chap, you tell me. From up here it looks remarkably like a flippin' wholesale retreat, wot?"

Urthstripe shook his great striped head. "Ferahgo doesn't give up that easily. He wants us to think it's a retreat. What we've got to figure out is why."

"Why what, sah?"

"Why Ferahgo wants us to think he's retreating. By my stripe, Oxeye, sometimes I think your brain's been scrambled by all the fighting you've done."

Big Oxeye let one ear droop and grinned. "Quite possibly, sah. I often think that m'self. Shall I take a couple of the chaps an' investigate?"

The badger Lord pondered the question for a moment. "Hmm, I'm not overfond of spying—much sooner have a straight battle. But if we want to know what the vermin are up to, I suppose we'd better resort to a bit of intrigue. Sapwood, you and Oxeye go. Take a fast young one with you, in case you have to get a message back here quickly."

Sergeant Sapwood threw a smart salute. "None faster'n young Pennybright, sir. She'll be useful to 'ave halong with us. Come on, Hoxeye ol' pal."

Klitch lay hidden in the rocks, watching the mountain carefully. With him were threescore vermin, personally paw-picked for the mission. The young weasel's blue eyes never left Salamandastron as he explained his plan to them.

"When they see the horde withdrawing it'll puzzle 'em—we're here to attack, not retreat. Urthstripe will do what any leader would do in this case: send out hares to investigate. That's where you lot come in. I want those hares captured—not slain, mind. Dead hares are no good to me; I need live hostages. Are the nets ready, Dragtail?"

287

A tall gaunt ferret whose tail hung limp pointed to the beach. "Ready an' waitin', Klitch. Right in the path taken by our horde."

Klitch held up a paw for silence. "Get down, here come the hares. Three of 'em—just right!"

Oxeye, Sapwood and Pennybright watched as Urthstripe rolled the boulder, closing the main entrance.

Pennybright's eyes shone with admiration. "There's not a creature in the world as strong as Lord Urthstripe. I'll bet twenty of us couldn't budge that boulder."

Sapwood pushed her lightly, urging the young hare onward. "That ain't nothin' to some of the things Hi've seen 'Is Lordship do. Shake a paw, Penny. We ain't got all night."

Padding silently over the sands, the three hares tracked in the direction taken by the main body of the horde.

Klitch spread his soldiers out behind them in a wide half-circle. Striking flint to tinder, he ignited a torch and waved it. Ahead of the three hares sixty more fully armed creatures filed out from the rocks. Fanning out into another semicircle, they trotted swiftly to join up with the others, completely ringing the three hares inside a wide circle that was closing rapidly.

Sergeant Sapwood dropped into a fighting crouch, his eyes glittering pugnaciously. "Nice of 'em to send a welcomin' committee t' meet us, eh, Ox?"

Big Oxeye stood back to back with him, placing Pennybright facing Salamandastron.

"Life ain't always true an' just,
A villainous vermin you can't trust!

"No doubt you've heard that old rhyme, Penny. Well,

here are the jolly old villainous vermin in the fur an' flesh, m' gel."

"They've got us surrounded. What do we do now?" Pennybright gripped her javelin nervously.

Sapwood's reply was calm and reassuring. "Just stick by me an' Hoxeye, missie. We've fought our way out of tighter corners than this'n, believe me."

Now the circle was drawing tight. Klitch stood outside it, his blue eyes shining triumphantly in the torchlight.

"Well well, what have we here? Three bold warriors sent by the badger. No doubt you'll be wanting to fight. Sorry to disappoint you, though."

Oxeye hefted his spear, chuckling with anticipation. "Oh, don't fret, laddie buck, we won't disappoint you. Come on now, step up an' taste some cold steel from Salamandastron. Or haven't y' got the nerve for it, you slimy little weasel?"

Klitch had been stalling for time, but now he saw his soldiers had found the rope ends poking up out of the sand he gave the signal.

"Now!"

They tugged hard and the net was unearthed from just beneath the sand. With a yell they charged inward.

The three hares fought to keep their balance as the heavy twisted fibers of the net appeared through the sand beneath their paws.

In the confusion that followed, Sapwood yelled to Oxeye, "We're trapped. See if y' can get Penny away from 'ere!"

Oxeye dropped his spear, knocking the javelin from Pennybright's paws as the Sergeant lashed out all round at the yelling mob that scrambled forward holding the net high. Exerting his great strength, Big Oxeye grabbed Pennybright and lifted her bodily over his head. Jumping high, he hurled her over the heads of the vermin and the closing net.

"Run for home, gel! Eulaliaaaaa!"

Sapwood went down under the weight of creatures who piled in throwing the coils over him and Oxeye. Seconds later they were clubbed senseless and wrapped in the snares of the fiber mesh.

Pennybright hit the sand in a stumbling run. A stoat managed to grab her, but she bit his paw to the bone and he let go with a squeal of pain. The young hare righted herself and ran flat out for the mountain, the breath sobbing in her throat as she thought of her two friends lying trapped. Glancing over her shoulder, she saw Klitch and Dragtail speeding after her. Sand flew beneath her paws. Three stoats were racing madly, trying to cut her off before she could reach the mountain. An arrow whizzed by Pennybright's head, and Dragtail was notching another shaft on his bowstring. She swerved, ducking left and right. An arrow hummed viciously by, clipping her ear as she went. The mountain loomed large as Pennybright yelled with the last of her lungpower:

"Eulaliaaaaaaa!"

One of the stoats screeched as he went down with a javelin sticking out of him like a flagpole. Bart Thistledown, Moonpaw and Urthstripe came bounding out of the main entrance. Bart unslung his bow and fitted an arrow as he ran. Loosing off the shaft, he sent another stoat limping off with an arrowhead lodged in his paw. The remaining stoat turned tail and ran off, as Urthstripe grabbed Pennybright and swung her up over his shoulder.

Klitch and Dragtail had stopped running; their quarry had escaped. The young weasel hurled a stone at Urthstripe's back as the badger Lord turned to go inside the mountain. It missed and bounced harmlessly off the rocks. He stood paws on hips shouting, "Be sure to watch the shore tomorrow, Urthstripe. See what I'm going to do with your pet bunnies. Hahahaha!"

Urthstripe put his shoulder against the boulder and heaved it back into place. Bart Thistledown poured a small beaker of water from their meager supply and made Pennybright drink it slowly.

"Don't fret, Penny old gel. Losin' a battle doesn't mean we've lost the war."

Ferahgo watched as Klitch directed his soldiers to drive stakes deep into the sand. Keeping his voice casual, the Assassin addressed his son.

"Forgrin and Raptail are both dead. Your little plan failed."

Klitch picked up a mallet and gave one of the stakes a knock. "Oh yes? And what plan was that, old one?"

Ferahgo seized Klitch's paw, holding the mallet still. "The plan to kill me. I killed Forgrin and Raptail."

"Very clever, I'm sure." Klitch wrenched his paw away and went on hammering at the stake. "But I know nothing of any plan to kill you. My plan was to take hostages, and I've done that. If I'd planned to kill you I wouldn't have failed at that either. Out of my way, old weasel!"

Big Oxeye peered through the net holes at Klitch and his soldiers driving stakes into the sand. "What I wouldn't give for two minutes alone with that evil little brat!"

"We fell fer that one, Ox." Sapwood rubbed his head ruefully. "Hi wonder what they're a-cookin' up for us?"

A ferret jabbed a spearbutt at him, laughing nastily. "Wouldn't yer like to know! Well, you 'ave a nice sleep an' you'll find out tomorrer!"

33

The Joseph Bell tolled out mournfully across a quiet summer morning. Mrs. Faith Spinney sat on the west wallsteps, sobbing gently into her flowered apron. Her husband Tudd sat beside her, resting his chin on his walking stick as he stared across the Abbey grounds through tear-dewed eyes.

"Pore old Burrley. I can't believe he's dead. Not Burrley me best cellarmate. Who'll 'elp me to brew October ale an' roll those liddle casks o' berry wine about?"

Faith sniffed loudly as she dried her eyes and stood up. "Oh, that dreadful Dryditch Fever. Wot did we ever do wrong that made fortune visit it upon our Abbey? Pore Mr. Burrley, he were such a gentle ol' mole. Ah well, tears won't make anythin' aright. I'd best make meself busy. There's lunch t' be made an' sickbeasts to care for. Now don't you sit out 'ere too long, my Tudd. Go an' 'ave a nap in your chair. You still ain't well enough t' be out an' about."

Tudd pulled himself up shakily on his walking stick and hobbled alongside Faith toward the Abbey. "I'll go an' set awhile in the cellar among the barrels. That's where me 'n' Burrley sat yarnin' many an 'ot afternoon.

Oh, smash my prickles! I wish it'd been me as was taken, an' not that good ol' mole feller."

The Abbey door opened and Foremole trundled out with his crew, bearing with them the sad little bundle that had been their friend Burrley. Foremole wiped his eyes on a spotted kerchief and tugged his snout respectfully to the two hedgehogs.

"Burr, 'tis a sad morn oi bid 'ee, guddbeasts. Us'ns will 'ave ol' Burrley putten to rest at late noontoid. Will 'ee tell everbeast within 'ee Abbey?"

Tudd patted the bundle and nodded brokenly. "Thankee, Foremole. I'll let 'em all know. They'll want t' be at Burrley's last restin'. He were greatly loved by all."

In the Infirmary and the upper gallery the beds were packed end to end. Abbess Vale and Furgle the Hermit hovered anxiously about Brother Hollyberry's bed, mopping his brow and rubbing his paws. Hollyberry lay still, his old face thin and ashen. Vale pawed her girdle cord distractedly.

"Oh, Furgle, can't you do anything to snap him out of it?"

"I wish I could, Abbess." The woodvole Hermit shrugged helplessly. "Hollyberry is in a deep faint. I know naught of such things. If he goes any deeper we'll surely lose him."

Bremmun levered himself weakly up off his pillows. "Ooooh, I'm aching all over! Don't even think of losing Brother Hollyberry—only he knows how to mix the medicine that's keeping us all alive. If he goes then who will be able to make it?"

Thrugann had been bathing little Droony's brow. She hurried over and hushed Bremmun. "Keep yore voice down, squirrel. These sick creatures got enough t' worry about without you startin' off a panic!"

Abbess Vale grasped the otter's paw beseechingly.

"You'd know how to make the medicine, Thrugann. You collected the herbs for Bremmun. Surely he told you how to blend them together?"

"Oh, Abbess, marm, I only wish he had." Thrugann shook her head sadly. "I can find herbs an' pick 'em, but make 'em into medicine, never!"

Droony the infant mole woke up and began crying. "Whurr be moi ol' nuncle Burrley? Burrhurrhurrhurr."

Thrugann hurried to comfort the little fellow, drying his tears and reassuring him. "There there. Hushabye, mole. Nuncle Burrley's gone away, but you'll see him agin some sunny season."

Abbess Vale swayed slightly, clasped a paw to her face and fell with a bump to the gallery floor. Faith Spinney had just arrived with a jug of soup and some bowls. She set the tray down and hurried across to help her old friend. The Abbess lay senseless.

"Oh, mercy sakes, somebeast 'elp 'er, please!" Faith looked around wildly.

Thrugann swept the frail form up in her strong paws. "Lan' sakes, I knowed this'd 'appen. She's been runnin' about 'ere takin' care of everybeast except 'erself. Furgle, it looks like one o' those faints to me. What d'you think?"

The Hermit needed only one glance to confirm his worst fears. "Lackaday! This is the worst thing that could happen right now."

Thrugann looked around gnawing her lip worriedly. "There's not an empty bed in the whole place for 'er."

"Oh yes there is." Faith Spinney dropped her voice to a whisper. "Burrley's bed is still empty in the dormitory. We'd best take pore Vale down there."

The dormitory was silent. Hastily Thrugann laid Abbess Vale on the bed and dashed around checking on the patients. They had all gone into a deep faint, with the exception of Blossom the mousemaid, who was feebly shaking her comatose sister, Turzel, and weeping softly.

"Wake up, Turzel. Please, please wake up."

There was a pawstep on the stairs. Thrugann and Faith turned to see Furgle standing in the doorway.

"Er, er, the medicine has just run out and er, er. . . ." The Hermit stood fidgeting with an empty medicine bowl in the doorway until Faith Spinney snatched it impatiently from him.

"Goodness me, Mister Furgle, stop stammerin' about. Is there somethin' you've got to tell us?"

He sighed and sat down on the floor. "There'll be another empty bed in the upper gallery. We've just lost Bremmun!"

Thrugann shook her head. "But that ain't possible. I was only talkin' to Bremmun a moment ago. Oh, tell me 'e ain't dead, Furgle!" The Hermit shook his head. "I wish I could, marm. I was wiping his brow when he looked me in the eye and said he was tired, then he just turned on his back and closed his eyes and died."

Faith Spinney sat down on the floor, her face pale and shocked. "Oh dearie me, that means there's only we three an' my Tudd down in the cellars who ain't down with Dryditch Fever. We're all that's left standin' on our paws in Redwall Abbey!"

Thrugann mopped sweat from her brow and sat down on the bed where Abbess Vale lay.

Faith Spinney was at her side in an instant. "Thrugann, are you all right, my dear?"

The otter staggered up and crossed to the window. "Aye, all I need is a breath of fresh air. Help me with this window catch, Mister Furgle, I feel weak as an otter kitten."

"Redwaaaaaaallllll!"

"Great acorns, what was that?" Faith Spinney sat bolt upright on the dormitory floor.

Thrugann flopped down beside her. "Now I know

295

I've got that pesky Dryditch Fever—I'm seein' things. I just saw Baby Dumble go flyin' past that window!"

Furgle jumped up and down, pounding the windowsill. "I can see him too! He's sitting in a haversack and the biggest bird on earth is carrying the thing in its claws!"

Faith Spinney and Thrugann went skeltering down the stairs toward the main door, yelling aloud.

"Murder! Help! A big bird's got Baby Dumble!"

"I don't care 'ow big the bird is, I'll wring its neck if it 'urts one 'air of that infant's liddle 'ead!"

Tudd Spinney hurried up from the cellars and hobskipped on his cane after them. "Ain't things bad enough without an attack of big birds!"

The Wild King MacPhearsome beat the air with his gigantic wings as he set the haversack carefully down on the lawn of Redwall Abbey.

"Oh, ye didnae tell me ye lived in sich a braw nest, Dumble!"

The infant stumbled from the haversack wreathed in Icetor Flowers. "It notta nest, birdie, it's a Habbey called Redwaaaaaalllll!"

In the island cave Mara listened with amazement to the tale that Loambudd told.

"My son Urthound was the strongest and wisest badger in all the Southwest Lands, and his wife Urthrun was famed for her beauty and gentleness. They ruled and protected the Southwest and were loved by all. Urthound's father Urthclaw had been dead many seasons. I was alone and there was trouble in the land, so Urthound took me in his home to live with him. It was autumn and Urthrun had given birth to two beautiful badger babes, male twins—we named them Urthwyte and Urthstripe. The trouble was called Ferahgo the Assassin and his gang of Corpsemakers. He was young and evil, a blue-eyed weasel who murdered for pleasure, with an army of vermin to back him up.

"That winter, the babes were scarce one season old, the snow was deep and the weather hard. If I had known that Ferahgo was in the area of my son's home I would never have gone out into the woodland that day to gather snowdrops. But I think that my son had arranged some sort of meeting with Ferahgo. It was Urthound who asked me to go and gather the snowdrops for his wife, though I know now that he only did it to get me out of his home lest I should attack Ferahgo—I was a mighty fighting badger when I was younger. Be that as it may, off I went into the winter woodlands to gather snowdrops.

"When I returned it was to find an awful scene of Ferahgo's treachery. The beautiful home was wrecked, my son Urthound lay dead, murdered by the blue-eyed one, and his wife Urthrun, too, was terribly slain. Of the two little ones there was only the white one Urthwyte. As for Urthstripe, I never knew what became of him. Did Ferahgo carry him off? Or did he wander away into the woodlands to perish in the winter? I never knew until this day when you came here, Mara. Fate sent you here to let me know that my grandson still lives. I might have known it, he was a tough little thing, more like his grandfather, fierce and warlike. He must have survived somehow.

"Urthwyte is like no other; he can be gentle at times but savage when needs be. I have told him the story of what happened many a time throughout his growing, hoping that someday he might have a chance to avenge the death of his parents. That winter day I fled, taking Urthwyte with me. We wandered the woodlands for many seasons. That is where we met our goodfriend Ashnin—she was the slave of wandering foxes. I fought them off and freed her, then the three of us traveled together, looking for peace and a better life. One summer day many seasons ago we found it here, an island paradise where we lived in safety until now."

Mara touched the old badger lady's paw.

"Why don't you forget the past and stay here, Loambudd?"

"Because you have brought the past walking in through our door and because my grandson and I are both badgers, fighting beasts. Besides, how do you think I could stay here, knowing that kin of mine may be battling for life in the lands by the big sea? When you go, we will go with you, on the day after tomorrow."

Pikkle looked up from his cherry cordial. "Why the day after tomorrow, marm?"

"Because a great storm is brewing: It will hit the lake tomorrow and nothing will be able to get on or off this island all day."

Mara rose. "I must go and tell Log-a-log so that he can pull the logboats up to safety."

The old squirrel, Ashnin, spoke. "That would be wise. The rock ledge they are camped on will be battered by heavy waves when the storm comes. Go and wake Urthwyte. He will haul the boats up to the woodlands for you. Tell your shrew friends to come and visit us until it is time to leave—I would like to know what sort of creatures I will be traveling with to the shores of the great sea."

"You'll be goin' too, marm?" Pikkle was surprised.

The ancient squirrel took a bow and arrows from the chimney corner. "I certainly will, young feller. I've never missed a good fight in my life. I'm a dead shot too!"

Pikkle rubbed his head where the cherry stones had struck. "I can already vouch for that, marm!"

Log-a-log and the Guosssom shrews yelled in alarm when a large white badger head poked over the cliffs at

298

them, until Pikkle came bounding down paw over paw on a rope.

"Panic over, chaps. This is old Urthwotsit, a pal of ours. He's offered to haul the boats up to high ground— apparently there's goin' to be a whizzo storm tomorrow and all this ledge where you're standin' will be underwater. Hey, Mara, come down an' show old Log-a-thing what you've brought for him!"

Mara slid down the rope. Without a word she hung the Blackstone around Log-a-log's neck. Immediately all the Guosssom shrews raised their paws in the air and gave a mighty roar.

"Logalogalogalogalog!"

One by one they filed past their leader, touching the Blackstone and bowing respectfully. There was not a shadow of doubt who the absolute leader of the Guosssom was now. Log-a-log clasped Mara's paws in both of his.

"I will never forget this, Mara." His voice shook with emotion. "No matter what the time, day, or season I am yours to command."

Nordo placed his paws over those of his father. "And I also. Mara, friend, words cannot thank you enough!"

The badger maid smiled at them both. "Then save your words, friends. Show me by your actions when we reach Salamandastron and face the hordes of Ferahgo!"

The white badger was a great source of amazement to the Guosssom. They watched openmouthed as he wrapped his huge paws around the damaged logboat. Bracing himself, Urthwyte gave a single grunt and lifted the entire vessel. He carried it five paces, then deposited it neatly on the trestles they had set up for its repair.

Nordo hesitantly touched the powerful corded muscle and sinew which stood out through the badger's snowy coat. "By the log of my father's boat! It would

299

have taken at least fifteen shrews to even budge one of our craft. You have the strength of a giant, Urthwyte!"

The big badger smiled and swelled out his chest. He was a simple creature and enjoyed the adulation of the shrews.

Loambudd brought him back to earth with a bump as she commented to Nordo, "Aye, my grandson has strength that he has not used yet, but he also has an appetite to match. He could eat your tribe out of house and home. You should try feeding him for a season—he's a bottomless pit, that one."

Log-a-log knew all there was to know about boats. Pikkle sat watching him as he deftly set about repairing the damaged craft. Taking a saw-edged dagger, the shrew leader cut away the damp splintered wood from the boat's side. Working with wet clay and pine pegs, he fitted a neatly cut piece of oak into the space, bedding it with clay and boring the wood with a red-hot rapier until the pegs secured the new piece firmly. Taking a bubbling pan of pine resin from the fire, he brushed on several thick coats, rendering the whole job waterproof.

Pikkle stood back to admire the repair. "I say, good show, wot! I'll bet the old boat'll go as fast as the day it was built now, Log-a-thing."

Log-a-log dipped his brush in the resin pan. "She certainly will, Pikkle my friend. This pine resin is a marvelous glue—they say that two coats of this around the mouth of a hare will stop him chattering and eating too much. Hold still now while I try it on you!"

The entire camp roared with laughter as Log-a-log chased Pikkle round the boat, brandishing the resin brush.

"Gerraway, you moldy ol' shrewfeller," the young hare whooped as he ducked and weaved. "Go an' try that stuff out on old Tubbguts. He needs it more than me!"

Ashnin leaped about, cackling. "Get him, Log-a-log. That Pikkle eats more than Urthwyte an' Tubgutt put together. I should know—it was me who served them lunch today."

34

Through the drenching curtains of storm-blown rain, Alfoh and Arula watched the battle from the logboat as it bucked and pitched on the heaving surface of the Great Lake. Only Samkim's nimbleness of paw was saving him from Dethbrush; the fox was an experienced fighter and used Martin's sword efficiently. Samkim was on the defensive, seeking desperately to parry each slashing blow with his light shrew rapier. The remaining tracker rats clung grimly to the side of the boat, silent spectators to the duel. Steel clashed upon steel. Bobbing up and down with the storm-tossed craft, Samkim held his weapon in both paws, frantically trying to turn the ever-seeking point and edges of the glittering sword. Dethbrush pursued him along the boat's length, hacking and thrusting until the young squirrel was trapped up on the bow with nowhere left to go. Showing his teeth viciously, the fox battered away forcefully at the puny rapier which stood in the way of a death-thrust from the sword. With a sweeping blow he struck at the outstretched weapon—and the rapier snapped off at the hilt with a metallic ping.

"Paddle 'ee boats over," Arula yelled aloud. "'Elp Sanken!"

The three logboats nosed their way across as the Guosssom paddled wildly against the mounting waves.

Reaching instinctively as Dethbrush raised the sword above his head, Samkim kicked out with both footpaws. He caught the fox low in his stomach, sending him sprawling into the bottom of the boat.

Dethbrush pulled himself quickly upright, snarling, "I'll use your tail as a headplume after I've slain you!"

The prow of Alfoh's logboat struck the fox's craft amidships. He tottered, struggling for balance as the other two vessels closed in. Samkim saw his chance. Leaping up, he punched Dethbrush on the jaw, still holding the rapier handle in his paw. A look of surprise crossed the fox's face as he plunged overboard into the rain-lashed waters, still holding the sword.

The Deepcoiler came suddenly, surging up from the depths like a juggernaut into the midst of the maelstrom. The fearsome head crashed through the surface, water rushing from it as the horrible mouth yawned agape.

Dethbrush gave vent to a gurgling wail as the monster's jaws closed across the middle of his body, and the sword fell from his lifeless paws into the water. Without thinking, Samkim flung himself headlong into the water, grabbing the sword as the fox let it go. Arula was only inches from the Deepcoiler's head. Swinging her paddle with both paws, she struck with the strength of panic, belting it in the eye. Immediately the gigantic reptile shot back under the water, Spriggat and Alfoh grabbed Samkim by the ears and heaved him scrabbling back into the logboat.

Without warning the Deepcoiler exploded back to the surface. The four logboats stood upright on their sterns as the mighty beast cleaved the water between them. Every creature aboard the boats was flung into the lake. Amid the driving gales of wind and rain the Deepcoiler began its killing in the crests and valleys of the sweeping waves.

Samkim clung grimly onto the sword. For the second time in as many moments he found himself pulled to safety as Arula dragged him onto the hull of an overturned boat. Screeching and yelling creatures hung on to capsized logboats as the Deepcoiler wreaked its savagery upon them. Coils of awesome thickness lashed and crashed everywhere, and the gray and white foamed lake was tinged with red as rows of razorlike teeth ripped and tore at any moving thing, the thrashing tail stunning, killing and drowning as it whipped about in random savagery.

Spriggat roared in pain as the deadly jaws closed on his back. Samkim cut a chunk from the rearing neck in front of him. The creature hissed, opening its mouth and releasing the hedgehog as it turned its attentions to the young squirrel. Samkim caught one glance of the glittering eyes as the lake monster came at him with open mouth, then recklessly he drove his blade beyond the teeth and into the roof of Deepcoiler's mouth.

"Redwaaaaaalllllll!"

Arula and Alfoh threw themselves upon Samkim, dragging him back as the fearsome jaws closed with a stunning clash of teeth. All three creatures fell back onto the hull in a bundle as with its customary unexpectedness the Deepcoiler submerged.

Samkim fought madly to free himself from the paws of his rescuers, roaring above the storm, "The sword! That thing has taken Martin's sword! Let me go!"

Arula and Alfoh dug their paws into his sodden fur.

"Hurr, yon beastie near got 'ee, too, Sanken, but yore safe naow!"

Out of his mind with frustration and battle lust, Samkim bit fiercely at the paws of his friends. "Let me go, I've got to get the sword! Stupid shrew, blundering mole, let go of me!"

Samkim did not see the paddle that Arula swung at his head until too late. Stars burst inside his brain, then suddenly he was falling through rushing darkness.

It was nighttime when Samkim regained consciousness. The rain had stopped but northeast winds were still sweeping across the lake. He lay on his back at the bottom of a logboat, watching wind-driven columns of cloud scudding across the face of a pale moon. A cool damp cloth was pressed to his head. It lessened the nagging pain which pounded in his temple. Samkim groaned and tried to sit upright.

Alfoh pushed him none too gently back down. "Be still, you wild squirrel. I'm trying to reduce the size of this bump on your skull. How do you feel?"

Samkim closed his eyes, and the throbbing receded slightly. "Ooh! A massive headache, that's all I can feel. What happened, Alfoh? I can't remember much of what went on."

The shrew held a beaker of water as Samkim drank slowly. "Hmm, can't remember, eh? Well, let me refresh your memory, though I don't know whether you'll trust the word of a stupid shrew. Or maybe you'd like to ask the blundering mole?"

Arula leaned over her friend's face and winked broadly. "Blunderin' mole 'ee called oi, hurr hurr. Oi blundered 'ee one o'er yore 'ead wi' moi paddle! Sanken, you'm wurr loik some orful woild beastie. You'm said bad things 'bout us'ns."

The young squirrel winced as memory of the events flooded back. "Arula, and you, Alfoh, I'm very sorry for what I said, but it was the thought of losing Martin's sword like that. Forgive me."

"You'm a mad ol' feller, but you'm moi best matey." The molemaid's homely face creased into a friendly smile.

Arula took over the ministrations with the damp cloth

305

as Alfoh explained what had happened while Samkim had lain unconscious.

"Deepcoiler went straight down and never reappeared, at least not so far. We lost six shrews, all the rats and one boat. I can tell you it wasn't much fun trying to turn three boats upright in that storm and keep you and Spriggat above water at the same time . . ."

Samkim pushed the cloth aside and sat up. "Where is Spriggat? Is he all right?"

Alfoh pointed across to one of the other boats. "He's over there. We can't really see how badly the poor creature is injured. When it gets light we'll check up on him. Don't worry, my Guosssom are attending to him as best as they can. Rest now and try to sleep. Our position is none too good—we lost all the provisions and this wind is driving us along very fast, though to goodness knows where. There's no point in paddling or fighting against things. Lie back and rest—that's all we can do. At least the rain's stopped and that horrible monster hasn't shown up again."

It was a long night. Completely exhausted, wet and shivering in the blustery wind, they curled up in the bottoms of the speeding logboats, trying to ignore waves splashing over the sides as they were rushed on through the gusty darkness.

Samkim was the first to wake at dawn. His headache had cleared up and he felt much better. He lay still awhile, enjoying the light warmth of early sunlight. Alfoh, Arula and the rest were still snoring peacefully as Samkim sat up slowly and looked about. The wind had dropped and the clouds were gone. The lake was calm, mirrorlike and silent, and the three logboats lay side by side, becalmed on the tranquil surface of the great waters. Ripples spread as Samkim dipped his paws to drink the clear lakewater.

"I'd give a whole waspnest fer a drink o' that. C'n yew get some across t' me, young un?"

Spriggat's head lolled against the boatside as he watched Samkim drinking. The young squirrel found a beaker and filled it. Treading carefully, he stepped over sleeping shrews, and the logboat wobbled slightly as he climbed across into the other craft. Cradling the old hedgehog's head in his lap, Samkim held the beaker to his lips.

"Take it easy now, Sprig—just small sips, don't try to gulp it. Well, how are you feeling today, you old flyscoffer?"

Water dribbled from Spriggat's mouth as he smiled wearily. "Yore a good young un an' I don't want to upset ye."

Samkim wiped his friend's mouth. "Why, what's the matter?"

"I'm right sorry I can't stay much longer." Spriggat held feebly on to Samkim's paws as he spoke. "No, be still an' listen t' me! That there monster chewed me up like a fat juicy dragonfly. Don't try to turn me over an' look at me back, Samkim—I'm all broken up." Spriggat moved slightly, screwing up his face in agony. "Uhhhhn! Wish I could've gone with me paws on good dry land. Taint too bad, though. It's a fair morn an' I'm in the arms of a friend."

Arula and Alfoh were awakened by the sound of Samkim sobbing. With the three boatcrews, they watched in silence as the young squirrel sat rocking back and forth. Regardless of the hedgehog's spines, Samkim held Spriggat's limp body as though he were nursing an infant, and tears coursed openly down his face onto the wrinkled old paws.

"He said he was going to find a summer forest, full of wasps and flying insects. Then he just smiled at me and, and . . . Oh, my poor old friend!"

Arula and Alfoh climbed across. Together they held Samkim and Spriggat tightly, letting the support of their strength flow through their paws, united in their grief at the passing of a fatherly creature who had given his all for them.

35

Klitch and Ferahgo, backed by a hundred armed vermin, strode boldly across the sun-warmed sands toward Salamandastron. The golden badger medal bobbed on the Assassin's chest as it reflected the hot summer morning.

Urthstripe watched them from an unblocked windowspace. Resting his huge paws on the sill, his eyes locked on the shining medallion as he tried hard to recall some long-gone event.

The two weasels sat down on the sand within hailing distance of the badger Lord. Food and drink was placed before them by Migroo and Feadle, and they ate and drank noisily, slopping water into the sand and carelessly chewing on bread and a roasted fish from the sea, spitting out bones and throwing away crusts. Ferahgo's blue eyes held a trace of mock pity as he called out to Urthstripe, "What a pity that you can't come and join us, badger. Food and drink must be pretty scarce inside your mountain by now."

Urthstripe tried hard to control his rising temper. "Hear me, scum! The only thing that will be scarce will be your breath if I get my paws around your miserable neck!"

Klitch threw a clay beaker. It smashed against the

rocks as he shouted out contemptuously, "You talk a good fight, stripedog, but words never won wars!"

Swiftly Urthstripe brought up his longbow. Fitting a shaft to its string, he drew it full back. "Here, this is for you, little snotnose!"

Klitch leapt up. Pulling back his jerkin to expose his narrow chest, he challenged the badger. "Fire away. Go on, kill me! But the moment you loose your arrow you will slay two of your own creatures. Look out by the tideline, you great stupid beast!"

Big Oxeye and Sergeant Sapwood lay staked out upon the damp sands below the tideline, and Crabeyes and Badtooth had spears pressed to the throats of the two hares. Urthstripe had to stare long and hard before he understood what was going on. It was a fair distance away, too far for bowshot. The badger Lord slacked his bowstring and withdrew the arrow.

"What do you want?"

"Nothing, really." Klitch sucked a fishbone and flicked it away. "We can sit out here until you all starve to death in there, and just to make things a little more interesting you can watch your two best hares get a good wash each time the tide comes in. At least they'll die clean."

Baffled rage was stamped on the striped features of the badger. "Then tell me what you want of me. What *do* you want?"

Ferahgo took out his long skinning knife and began drawing patterns in the sand. "When we first arrived here we were only after your treasure. But now things have changed, as you can see, so now we want the treasure and your mountain too."

Urthstripe shook his head vehemently. "There is no treasure, weasel, and as for my mountain, you will never have it, no matter what evil plans your twisted minds can think up. You will never be Master of Salamandastron. Never! Do you hear me?"

Klitch chuckled nastily. "Oh we hear you all right, you great windbag. But soon you'll hear from your friends Oxeye and Sapwood. When the sun dries them out and all they have to drink is seawater, then you'll hear them calling for mercy, screaming for a quick death. What'll you do then, eh?"

Oxeye shut his eyes against the midmorning sun. Licking parched lips, he looked across at Sapwood. "Are they still parleyin' up there by the mountain, Sap?"

The Sergeant tried to crane his head, but the rope across his throat pulled tight. He lay back with a sigh. " 'S no good, Hi can't see a thing, Ox, but Hi tell yer, if'n Hi was Urthstripe, Hi'd wipe Klitch an' Ferahgo out as soon as they was close enough an' fergit us two."

Migroo menaced them with his spear. "Shut yer mouths, yew tew!"

Big Oxeye winked at him. "Do me a favor, ol' chap—go an' boil your scabby head!"

"One more word an' I'll run yer through!" The stoat touched Oxeye's throat with the spearpoint.

"Slay away, old lad, slay away." Oxeye closed his eyes again, dismissing Migroo. "But if you harm a single hair of our handsome heads, young Master Klitch'll let his daddy skin you alive, then he'll kill you."

Klitch came striding up and stood over his captives.

Oxeye stared boldly up at him. "Listen, sonny me old weasel, if that chap Migroo kills us, would you be awfully kind and kill him back for us?"

"I wouldn't be so cheerful if I were you." Klitch kicked the big hare savagely. "Urthstripe is leaving both of you here to die. We've given him until dawn tomorrow to make up his mind, but by then a couple of tides will have washed over you and the gulls will be pecking at your corpses."

Oxeye raised his head slightly, smiling insolently at

311

Klitch. "Feedin' the jolly old birds, eh. At least we'll be doin' somethin' useful. What d'you say, Sap?"

"Oh aye, but Hi think I'd sooner feed 'em this 'ere weasel—that's if they haint too fussy wot they eats."

Klitch leaned down and struck Sapwood in the face. The boxing Sergeant wrinkled his battered features scornfully. "You ain't got much of a right, sonny. Try yer left—it might be better. Tell yer wot, why not untie me an' I'll give yer a free boxin' lesson."

Bart Thistledown and Pennybright watched from the top of the crater. Pennybright was very upset, but Bart comforted her in his laconical style. "Now don't be gettin' y'self in a tizzy, young Pen, wot? Oxeye an' Sap look in good form from here. No doubt Milord Urthstripe'll lead a party out an' rescue 'em tonight."

"Oh, Bart, d'you think he will?" Pennybright gnawed her lip anxiously.

"Goes without sayin', young Pen. Bad form not to, y'know. Milord would never give up his jolly old mountain, but he's a good ol' stick—he wouldn't leave two of his best chaps in the clutches of those vermin, you can bet your bally lettuce on that! I say, speak of the badger an' here he comes. Sah!" Bart came smartly to attention as Urthstripe ascended the crater stairs.

"Thistledown, get your weapons ready. There'll be you, Moonpaw, Catkin, Seawood, myself and some others. We're going out tonight to rescue Sergeant Sapwood and Big Oxeye. Penny, you'll stay here and guard the mountain with the rest. No arguments, missie! Bart, one hour after sunset, be ready at the main entrance!"

When Urthstripe had gone, Bart turned to the crestfallen young hare. "See, I told you, Pen—we'll have 'em both back by mornin'. Now now, don't stick your lip out like that, m' gel—makes you look quite ugly. Somebeasts have got to stay here and mind the old place. Cheer up, I'll slay a few for you, eh?"

By late noon the tide was swirling in. Fortunately for the two hares it was not a spring tide. They lay staked out with the water oozing around their backs and paws.

Sapwood shook his head several times. "Cor, it's runnin' down me ears. D'you think it'll come much 'igher? Hi'd 'ate ter be drownded by the sea."

Oxeye strained against the neck rope. "Me, too, Sap. Bad enough a chap gettin' all his back 'n' tail soaked in salt water. Where's old stoatbottom an' his pal got to?"

"Over there, see, sittin' on those rocks an' keepin' their paws dry."

Oxeye turned his head on one side, watching Migroo and Feadle as they sat on the warm dry rocks. The big hare wiggled his paw. "Now don't get too excited, Sap, but I think I've got me bally paw free. Those dimwits prob'ly didn't realize that these ropes are only twisted grass fibers, and the water makes 'em soft 'n' stretchy. Hold fire a tick, there! That's one paw free. Now for the other three. How are you doin', old feller?"

"Workin' on it," Sapwood grunted. "An' less of the 'old feller', you cheeky rogue. You must be at least two seasons older'n me."

"One, actually. What drill d'you think we should follow when we're loose? Personally I think that big hunk o' driftwood looks like a good bet. We'd never make our way through all those vermin back to the mountain—they'd probably stick us so full of bally spears an' arrows we'd look like a couple o' pincushions."

Sapwood wriggled his paws against the softening fibers. "An' what 'as that cob o' driftwood got to do with all this?"

Oxeye sneaked a footpaw loose. "Can't you see? It's an ideal boat. They wouldn't think of you putting to sea. It's the great escape, Sap. You could float up or down the coast apiece, land the driftwood and sneak back to Salamandastron."

The Sergeant shook water from his ear as he looked at his friend through one eye. "Me?"

"Yes, of course you! I simply hate water—can't swim a stroke, y'know. But I've watched you doin' all those sporty exercises—you used to swim like a bally duck, every mornin'."

Sapwood was not very keen on the idea. "Er, 'scuse me, hold feller, but what'll you be doin' while I'm cruisin' round on a cob of driftwood if Hi might ask?"

"Keepin' 'em busy while you escape, you great pugilistic duffer." Oxeye chuckled. "One of us has got t' do it. I'll catch up with you as soon as I've roundly cracked a few heads. Now no arguments, Sergeant. Besides, I outrank you—I'm a lieutenant, y' know. Never use the title an' I hate pullin' rank on a chap, but that's the way the pebble rocks. First we've got to get some weapons— let's see if we can entice ol' thickhead an' his pal over."

Migroo was nodding off nicely in the late noontide heat when Feadle shook him awake.

"Wot are those two hares up to, matey? Listen to 'em!"

Migroo sat up as the two captives started yelling, "Help! Help! There's a big fish over here tryin' to eat us! Yowch! Gerroff! Do somethin', chaps. It's a big fat fish!"

Feadle grabbed his spear. "Did yer 'ear that, mate? A big fat fish!"

Migroo also picked up his spear. "Hoho, just the job fer supper. Don't tell the others. Come on!"

They splashed across through the shallows. Feadle got there first, waving his spear animatedly as he shouted, "Where's the big fat fish?"

Sapwood sprang up right on cue, laying the weasel out with a crashing double pawswing. Migroo pulled up short, alarm on his face as he turned tail and ran off yelling, "Escape! The prisoners are escapin'!"

Oxeye's back had sunk into the wet sand and he had difficulty pulling himself up. Coming free with a sucking squelch, he ran to the driftwood and began tugging it into the water. "Come on, Sap. Hurry up! Get this thing out to sea!"

Between them they lugged the heavy tree limb, tripping and stumbling on branches and twigs as they pushed and towed it into the water.

Scores of vermin came racing across the beach with Klitch and Ferahgo yelling in the rear.

"Get them! Stop those hares!"

"Kill the two of them if you have to, but stop them!"

The driftwood was just beginning to float as Oxeye pushed his friend aboard. The enemy was now in the shallows, racing toward them through the rippling waves. Sapwood turned and grabbed Oxeye's free paw.

"I haint goin' anyplace without you, Ox!"

Big Oxeye shook his head and laughed. "No no, Sap, you sail away. I'll hold 'em off. Have a good trip!" He whacked Sapwood beneath the chin with the butt of the spear he had taken from Feadle. The Sergeant lay stunned on the dead tree limb as Oxeye pushed it out into the current and the waves began to recede, carrying the makeshift craft into deep water.

A skinny ferret had outdistanced the rest. He waded out, swinging a sword. The big hare disarmed him with a single spear thrust. Grabbing the ferret, Oxeye pushed his head beneath the waves as he called out to the advancing foebeasts, his anger renewing the warrior spirit of his strength: "Come on, chaps, who's next for a jolly good bath?"

Sapwood was out of reach of the enemy as the water bore him on a southerly curve. Far behind him Big Oxeye threw himself spear in paw at the foe crowding forward through the waves.

"Eulaliaaaaaaaa!"

36

Dumble sat on the edge of little Droony's bed. The mole listened wide-eyed as the baby dormouse described his flight in great fictitious detail.

"Wizooooo! Right up inna sky we was, anna heagle was frightened, but Dumble wasn't, me laughed, haha! like that."

Brother Hollyberry opened his eyes slowly. "Who's that I hear laughing? Woke me up from a lovely sleep."

Thrugann was caught by surprise. She almost dropped a beaker of Icetor Flower mixture, juggling it in the air as she hooted, "Mercy me! Look, Furgle, it's Brother 'Ollyberry, an' he's waked!"

Furgle clasped his paws together gratefully. "Oh joy! He was first to go into that deadly sleep and the last to come out. Aren't old mousewives tales wonderful? Flowers of Icetor boiled in springwater—who'd have ever thought it?"

Mrs. Faith Spinney trudged up from the Infirmary. She was carrying a trayful of hot hazelnut scones, each one with a blob of buttercream and chestnut on top of it.

"Dearie me, bake, bake, bake! I've done nothing the livelong day but bake since you sleepyheads woke up.

Friar Bellows, when d'you think you'll be fit for kitchen duties again, sir?"

The fat friar hopped nimbly from his bed. "Right now, marm. Are those hot hazelnut scones? Very good, very good. I'm quite partial to a well-baked scone."

Faith rapped his paws. "Then get along wi' you an' bake some, you idle mouse. These are for the big bird. I'm afeared greatly of it meself. Here, Dumble, take these to your friend."

Abbess Vale and the two mousemaids Turzel and Blossom watched chuckling from the dormitory window as Dumble and Droony fed the Wild King MacPhearsome on scones.

"Missus Spinney says don't eat too much, you get heagle's tummyache."

"Yurr, Dumble, let oi give heagle a scone. Burr, 'ere y' are, zurr."

MacPhearsome had never tasted such food in all his wild life among the icy crags. He picked the scones from the infant's paws delicately with his savagely curved beak and wolfed them down, showering the two little heads below with crumbs.

"Och, these vittles are braw eatin', Dumble. Ha' ye nae mair o' those wee veggible pasties the guid hedge-pig lady made?"

Droony squinched his eyes until they nearly disappeared into his small velvety face. "Bohurr, you'm heagle do be a-talken funny loik. Oi carn't unnerstan' a wurd 'ee be sayen, Dumble."

That evening the tables were laid out in the orchard. Friar Bellows, Faith Spinney, Thrugann and Furgle were setting out a scratch feast in honor of the two saviors of Redwall: Dumble and the Wild King Mac-Phearsome. It had all been done on the spur of the moment with what food was available; nonetheless it was a happy and joyous occasion.

317

Perched on a specially chosen log, the great golden eagle and Dumble did full justice to the food from their place of honor. A large basin of moles deeper'n ever tater 'n' turnip 'n' beetroot pie stood steaming in the center of the board, surrounded by woodland salad, yellow and white cheeses and oat farls. Farther out it gave way to candied acorns, hazelnuts and chestnuts arranged around flagons of October ale. Three plumcakes, heavy with honey, stood at strategic points, and between them were heaped platters of bilberry, redcurrant and apple tarts, with bowls of greensap milk and rich buttercup cream. Friar Bellows had invented a special MacPhearsome cake, comprised mainly of damson cream, stiff comb honey, arrowroot shortbread and glazed maple shoots. It was difficult for the Wild King to keep a dignified posture and satisfy his ravenous appetite, so Dumble translated for him as he sank his talons into the special cake.

"Ach, yer a bonnie wee mousie, Dumble—bringin' yer auld pal MacPhearsome tae sich a gran' blow-oot. I'll remember ye fer aye an a', ye wonderfu' bairn."

Abbess Vale wiped Dumble's cream-caked mouth. "What is your friend saying, Dumble?"

The infant chortled. "The heagle says to feed me plumcake so I'll grow all bigga an' strong, wiv cream too."

Tudd Spinney and Droony, his new cellar apprentice, rolled out a keg of elderberry wine.

Foremole removed the head from the keg and bowed graciously. "Yurr, zurr, heagle, dip'n 'ee beak into this woin, hurr hurr!"

Thrugg strode down through the foothills, accompanied by Rocangus. Tammbeak and two other able-looking falcons circled overhead as they began the trek back to Redwall. The Laird Mactalon stood waving goodbye with both wings.

"Mind how ye go, lads. Rocangus, ye young rip, watch yer manners an' be civil tae other beasties. Guid luck walk with ye, Sir Thrugg. Yer a braw riverdog an' Ah'm proud tae call ye fren'."

"Och, mah faither's no' a bad auld stick," Rocangus whispered to Thrugg. "Just o'er fussy."

Thrugg chuckled as he swung his sling. "Listen, matey, d'you think by chance we could drop in on them crows an' whack the features off 'em? Make the journey back to Redwall a bit more interestin', eh?"

Rocangus flexed his good wing. "Ach, yer a wicked riverdog, Thrugg, but et's a braw idea!"

The two logboats were about to be lowered from the cliffs in the early dawn when a scream from the rock ledge below cut the still summer air.

"Eeeeyaaahhh! It's the Deepcoiler!"

Log-a-log's face was ashen. "That's Nordo down on the ledge!"

Urthwyte and Loambudd tore into action. Shoving Mara and Pikkle aside, they grabbed the lowering ropes and scrambled down to the ledge, Mara and Log-a-log following them as soon as the ropes were clear.

Like some grotesquely twisted tree trunk, the reptile lay half in and half out of the water, its tail trailing off into the lake depths and its monstrous head laid flat on the rock ledge.

"Stay clear! It'll kill you all!" Ashnin yelled down after them.

Mara ventured forward cautiously, staring into the wide-open eyes that were glazed over with a milky film. "It's dead!"

Pikkle stood pressed against the rock face with Nordo. "Dead? I wonder what killed the dreadful old blighter?"

Mara moved around the lifeless head until she could touch the cold steel that stood out from the center of the skull. "This is what slew the Deepcoiler. Urthwyte, Loambudd, lend a paw here—we'll get the head on its side and open the mouth."

Between the three of them the badgers managed to push the wet scaly head on its side. It was a repulsive dead weight, and foul-smelling water gushed from the mouth as they prised it open. Urthwyte propped the jaws apart with his club as Mara reached in with both paws. She began tugging. The steel that protruded from the skull waggled back and forth. Loambudd struck the pointed steel with a rock, driving it downward as Mara pulled and tugged with both paws, setting her footpaws against the sides of the fearsome rows of teeth framing the mouth. Finally the object came loose and the badger maid fell backwards onto the rock ledge with a beautiful sword in her paws.

A cry of wonder went up from the shrews crowding the clifftop. Loambudd inspected the head, speculating as Mara washed the fabulous weapon in the lake, "Somebeast stabbed it in the roof of its mouth. The thing must have swum off then and tried to close its jaws. The brain was pierced, because as it forced its mouth shut it drove the sword right up through its head, killing itself. The storm must have washed it up here last night sometime."

Mara held the sword aloft. It glittered and shone in the sunlight, completely undamaged and sharp as any razor's edge. "What do you think, Loambudd? It's too small for a badger, but slightly too large for a shrew to wield. But what a weapon!"

The older badger inspected it. "The beast who carried this must have been a famous warrior. This sword was made by badger skill—I know, I have heard of weapons like this—and nothing can turn or damage the blade."

Pikkle plucked a hair from his tail and split it across the blade. He gave a whistle of amazement. "Well, chaps, I think we should all be grateful to the warrior who slew this horror. Now the lake is safe to sail on!"

The Guosssom raised a mighty cheer and began preparing for the voyage. Urthwyte scaled the cliff and lowered both boats down to the ledge, then supplies were packed on board the vessels. With light hearts the Guosssom took up their paddles. The boats were riding low in the water because of their extra passengers, but two more badgers added considerably to the paddle power as they shot out across the wide lake.

"From lake to the river and down to the sea,
Paddling, paddling, onward go we.
The sun on the water does shine merrily
As away go the logboats like birds wild and free.
So paddle, my brother, I'll sit next to you,
A fine handsome creature, a bold Guosssom shrew.
High sky and deep water are both colored blue.
Our boats like our friends are all solid and true."

The weather stayed fine, and they pushed onward until the island was a mere dot on the horizon behind them. Log-a-log noted the position of the sun and set a further course. Mara could not help noticing the admiring glances everybeast cast at her sword; as she paddled, it lay beside her, sparkling in the sunlight, its beautiful red pommel stone shining above the black bound hilt with its flaring silver crosstrees, the mirrored steel of the blade clear ice-blue, deep blood-channeled, and keenly double-edged down to the awesomely dangerous tip. It was a true warrior's weapon with no unnecessary fancy bits and no sign of weakness in its design; the swordmaker had forged and tempered it with one thing in mind; a stout blade that would serve its owner well in battle. She stared at it hard until a dizziness came over her. Shaking her head, the young badger maid blinked and rubbed her eyes as she glanced out over the lake, then back to the sword. She gave a start. Pikkle noticed her strange behavior.

"What ho, old gel. Are you all right?"

Mara picked up the sword. Bringing it close to her face, she peered at the blade until her breath misted it. "Can you see anything in this blade, Pikkle?"

The young hare took a look and shook his head. "No, not a bally thing. Why d'you ask?"

"I saw the face of a mouse looking at me from the blade, a warrior mouse, fiercer than any fighting badger." Mara kept her voice low so that only he could hear.

Pikkle let one ear droop comically. "You didn't eat any strange fruit or plants on that island, did you? I remember one time I scoffed an old preserved damson I was sick as a frog for a day, and you wouldn't believe the things I saw when I tried shuttin' me eyes . . ."

Mara jabbed him with the end of her paddle. "Don't talk silly, it was nothing like that. I tell you, I'd swear I saw this warrior mouse looking straight at me from the blade of that sword!"

Log-a-log had overheard Mara. He offered an explanation. "What you saw was probably the face of the shrew sitting behind you; the blade was lying at an angle where it caught his reflection and distorted it, what with the sunlight and the movement of the boat. It couldn't be anything else, Mara, believe me."

Mara thought about it for a moment then nodded. "Aye, you're probably right, Log-a-log."

As she resumed paddling she glanced back at the shrew behind her. He was an old Guosssom member with a thin face, one good eye and a flowing gray beard—nothing remotely like the fierce hot-eyed warrior she had seen reflected in the mirrored blade.

Morning gave way to noontide. They ate as they paddled, traveling on without any untoward event.

Urthwyte stood up carefully and stretched his cramped limbs, turning this way and that as he rolled the stiffness out of his thick leg muscles. Suddenly he pointed and cried out, "Over there, to the left, dark shapes in the water!"

Immediately the crews felt a chill of fear run through them. Was there more than one Deepcoiler? Perhaps the monster had a mate that was seeking vengeance for the slaying of its partner.

Log-a-log gave orders for them to ship paddles and be silent. The two logboats lay still and quiet on the waters, some of the Guosssom shrews even holding their breath with apprehension.

When Mara could stand the suspense no longer, she turned to Pikkle. "Come on, Ffolger. You've got good long-sight—up on my shoulders and tell us what you can see."

Nordo and Log-a-log steadied Mara's footpaws as Pikkle climbed up and stretched his lanky frame. "Can't see much, you chaps. 'Fraid it's too far away. Paddle over to the left a bit, please, and maybe then it'll become clear."

Log-a-log gave the order. "Stay where you are in that other boat—no sense in putting two craft in danger. Right, Guosssom, no paddle-splashers now—nice and easy, long deep strokes, paddle over that way."

Still balanced on Mara's shoulders, Pikkle shaded both eyes with a paw, flopping his ears over to add to the shade. The shrews pulled well and strongly; not a spare drop of water fell from their paddle blades as the logboat glided smoothly over the lake, silent as a feather floating on the breeze. Mara stood still as the trunk of a tree as Pikkle narrowed his eyes and strove to make something of the dark shapes that shimmered in the sunlight on the surface. Suddenly his ears stood erect and he muttered out of the side of his mouth, "Log-a-log, old scout, you've got friends out here—somebeast is callin' your name."

The shrew leader looked up. "Calling my name?"

"Oh yes indeed." Pikkle nodded. "Shall I tell you what they're saying?" He threw back his head and shouted, "Logalogalogalog!"

Immediately Log-a-log swung into action, his deep shrew voice roaring out orders:

"It's Guosssom shrews. They need help! You shrews in the other boat, follow us! Bend your backs, dig those paddles deep and pull! Logalogalogalogalog!"

The two logboats raced across the waters, paddles flashing as bow waves churned up and the vessels rocked from side to side. Pikkle leaped down and grabbed up his paddle to match Mara's stroke.

A cheer went up from the crews of the three logboats as Samkim climbed down from the shoulders of Alfoh and Arula.

The young mole patted Samkim's back furiously. "You'm a roight gudd shouter, Sanken. They'm 'eard 'ee, hurr hurr. Lookit, they acomen. Wot think 'ee, Alfoh, zurr?"

Alfoh shook Samkim heartily by the paw. "Best Guosssom call I've ever heard in me whole life. We'll make a boatshrew of you yet, young squirrel!"

There was a moment's pause as the five logboats met on the wide lakewaters. Log-a-log stood in the prow of his boat, displaying the Blackstone strung about his neck. All the five crews bowed low in acknowledgment of the Log-a-log of all the Guosssom, then happy shouting broke out.

"It's Alfoh's colony from the hillbank!"

"Hey, Nordo, you young rip, how's your paddle!"

"Cousin Dwing, you fat old rascal, give me your paw!"

"Bowley—hi, Bowley, are you still poisonin' the lads with your cookin'?"

"Forbun, how are the twins—still growing?"

"I'll say they are, Tubgutt, and they're the image of your sister: fat and idle. Hahahaha!"

Backslapping and paw-shaking went on apace as the shrews were reunited with old friends from the Great South Stream. Samkim was lost for words; he could only stand and stare at the handsomely marked young female badger holding the sword of Martin the Warrior in her paws. Stepping over the side of the boat, he never once took his eyes from hers as he spoke.

"I am Samkim of Redwall Abbey."

"I am Mara of Salamandastron."

They stood staring at one another until Samkim found himself speaking again. This time the words sprang unbidden to his lips. He felt as though he was back in Redwall, standing before the tapestry picture. Images golden with motes of the dust of time floated through his mind like brown leaves drifting over an autumn evening meadow . . . Thrugg the otter dressed as a badger guardian at the Nameday feast . . . the big empty chair in Great Hall where once sat Abbey badgers . . .

"The sword you are holding belongs to Redwall Abbey. It was once the sword of Martin the Warrior, and it was his face you saw in the blade."

Samkim shivered and placed a paw across his mouth, not knowing why he had spoken such words. He felt slightly foolish as he looked into the badger's dark brown eyes. Mara was mystified but she did not question the young squirrel. A sense of calm and quiet happiness stole over her as she placed the beautiful sword into his paws.

"May your sword travel safely back to its Abbey, Samkim of Redwall."

37

Three gnarled apples and half a beaker of water stood on the long dining hall table in Salamandastron. Urthstripe sat in his chair like some brooding mountain spirit, and around the table were thirty-two hares—the full complement of the Long Patrols. Urthstripe's gaze roved about his fighters, finally settling on Pennybright.

"Take these apples and this water, Penny. A sip and an apple apiece for you and the two next youngest in the mountain."

Pennybright was about to object when Bart Thistledown nudged her forward, murmuring under his breath, "Do as your Lord says, Pen. Go on, don't question him when he's in this mood—he's dangerous!"

The young hare did as she was bidden, bobbing a curtsy to the badger Lord as she passed him.

The hares waited in silence until Urthstripe stood. His gruff voice was heavy and doom-laden as he spoke.

"Sergeant Sapwood and Big Oxeye are gone. I could not make out what way they were slain, but there were over a hundred vermin against them. No two hares were with me longer, or served Salamandastron more loyally. First Windpaw and Shorebuck, and now Sapwood and Oxeye. It has come to this, my friends." His paw crashed down on the tabletop. "We are starved and surrounded by a vermin horde, trapped inside our own fortress!"

The booming echoes of the badger Lord's voice died away as he glared down at the tabletop, the dark eyes becoming blood-flecked with rage. His paws clenched and unclenched, and a fleck of foam appeared at the side of his jaw as he pounded the table with each thunderous word.

"My mountain held under siege by a blue-eyed weasel and his brat!"

The chair behind him clattered onto its side as he swept out of the dining hall.

In the shocked hush that followed, Bart Thistledown set the chair upright and commented lightly, "Well, I'm glad I'm not a blue-eyed weasel, chaps. Yes indeed!"

Pennybright shared the water and apples with Lingfur and Barfle on the crater top. They gulped the water down but ate the apples sparingly, making each bite count, chewing hungrily.

Lingfur finished his apple first. "I'm still hungry, Pen. Phwaw! What I wouldn't give for a big beaker of mountain-pear cordial and a plate of hot oat scones with honey to spread thick on 'em!"

Barfle chewed away at the core and apple pips. "Greensap milk I'd like, with hot oatmeal and a whole blackcurrant pie, all to myself."

Penny closed her eyes longingly. "D'you remember those little cheese and onion pasties that Windpaw used to bake? I'd love to have one of those right now, with a flagon of new cold cider that'd been cooling in the bottom caves for two days, all sparkly and light gold!"

"Oh, what did we start talkin' about scoff for?" Lingfur nibbled the soft wooden stalk that his apple had hung from the tree on. "It only makes you even worse hungry than you are now!"

Suddenly a battered and sandswept figure hauled itself wearily over the crater top. It was none other than Big Oxeye, alive and well.

"Cheer up, young Ling. I never knew when you weren't bally well hungry, wot?" His familiar chuckle boomed out around the mountaintop. "Have some pears. They're a bit hard, but I don't suppose a young feedbag like you would care."

The three young hares gave a yell of horror at the ghastly apparition and fled down the crater steps as if a demon were chasing them.

Big Oxeye dropped the two woven reedbags he was carrying and looked down at his sand-crusted body. "Hmph! Suppose if I clapped eyes on me right now I'd be frightened out o' me wits!"

They gathered around the table in the dining hall as Oxeye related his marvelous escape.

"Hoho, you should've seen old Sap, floatin' off t' sea like he was born on the briny with not a care in the world. Next thing, here comes a bunch of those vermin yahoos, right nasty lot I can tell you. So I ups spear an' slays one or three, just t' let 'em know I mean business, doncha know. Blow me, there must've been more than a bally regiment of the stinkers. They stabbed an' whacked at me with cutlasses an' whatnot. As for me, did m' best to give a beastlike account of a Long Patrol scrapper, an' then I tripped and went under the water. D'you know, I could never swim until that moment, as true as I'm here, I tell you, chaps. I went under an' right off started swimmin' like a bloomin' fish under-water. Just kept goin', wot! On an' on I swam until I ran out of jolly old fresh air, so I came up an' there they were, far away, all arguin' an' hackin' at each other like billyoh. So I took a good deep breath, dived an' swam some more—must've done that a dozen times until I got clear away from Ferahgo's lot. From there it was quite simple really, I just rolled meself in the dry sand to give me a coat of camouflage and hoofed it back here. Oh, I stopped off an' gathered a few supplies on the way back—thought you chaps might be gettin' a bit peckish. I say, where's His Nibs old Urthstripe?"

Bart Thistledown pointed a paw upward. "Probably in the forge room beatin' some poor chunk of metal to a powder. He's got one of his rages boilin' up. You'd best go an' report that you're alive, Ox."

Oxeye popped his head round the doorway of the forge room and called out in a loud voice, "Big Oxeye, sah! Reportin' for duty, sah! All present an' correct an' quite alive, contrary to popular rumor, sah!"

The forge was cold and the room deserted. Oxeye wandered about until he noticed one of the window apertures had been unblocked. The big hare sighed with despair at the sight that greeted his eyes as he looked out of the window.

Fully clad in badger war armor, Urthstripe was pounding over the shore towards Ferahgo's encampment. Brandishing his giant battle spear aloft, the badger Lord of Salamandastron hurled out his challenge to the foe:

"Come and meet me, Ferahgo—you and your brat together. I will fight you in paw-to-paw combat or any way you choose! It ends here today, weasel. Come and meet death! I am Urthstripe the Strong, born in the dark of the moon! Lord of the mountain! Slayer of vermin! Eulaliaaaaaaa!"

Migroo had died beneath the spear of Big Oxeye, so the other prisoner guard, Feadle, was held responsible for the escape of the two captives. His lifeless body hung, bound to a stake, in front of the entire horde. Ferahgo put away his killing knife and took out his skinning knife as Urthstripe's roars reached his ears across the beach. Ignoring the weasel he had just slain, he sheathed the knife and issued hasty instructions.

"Crabeyes, station archers in the rocks around where we fight. Badtooth, get forty spearbeasts and be ready to strike whenever you see the badger's back. Klitch, come with me and do as I say!"

Klitch was in a foul mood. He had been responsible for the victories they had won so far, but because of his youth the army was more inclined to obey Ferahgo. Accordingly his father had swiftly assumed position as Master of the horde. Klitch sat sullenly on a rock, curling his lip at Ferahgo.

"Huh, another of your cockeyed plans. It'll end in disaster like all the others, you'll see."

The Assassin dragged his son bodily from the rock and shook him. "Young fool, you don't know everything. I'm going to set up an ambush for the badger. Just watch me and do as I tell you. This will work. I killed the badger Lord of all the Southwest Lands and his wife the same way, seasons before you were ever born. Now get yourself a weapon and follow me!"

As the word spread around Salamandastron, windows and openings were unblocked. The hares crowded to the viewpoints, watching in dismay.

Big Oxeye had assumed command in Urthstripe's absence, and his word was law. "Lord Urthstripe is out to settle this himself. He's challenged the two weasels to double combat. When they meet we must stay here out of it—this is between Urthstripe and the two weasels, a Duel of Chieftains. Not even the vermin of the horde are allowed to interfere in a battle of honor, so stay at your posts and watch. That's an order!"

Down at the tideline, Ferahgo and Klitch stood in a smooth sea-washed area of sand, a semicircle of rocks at their backs. Urthstripe faced them. Raising the visor of his warhelm, he tried hard not to laugh aloud with joy. This was what he wanted, the moment he had been waiting for. Ferahgo had armed himself with a mace and chain in addition to his knives. Klitch wore a short sword and carried a pike. Urthstripe leaned on the haft of his great battle spear; it was half as tall as he himself was, forbiddingly heavy and thick with a leaf-shaped blade and barbed crosstrees jutting out.

The badger nodded at them. "Let us get things straight before we settle this. If you win then the mountain is yours, but you must let my hares leave unharmed. If I win, your army turns around and marches off back to wherever you came from. Agreed?"

Ferahgo pawed the golden medal on his chest and replied levelly, "As Master of the horde, I agree. So does my son."

Klitch swaggered about, jabbing the air with his spear as Urthstripe continued, "Nobeast must interfere—this is a Duel of Chieftains and must be fought under the rules of honor. Agreed?"

"Agreed!" Ferahgo's blue eyes shone with fervor and sincerity.

Urthstripe lowered his helm as he spoke the final words.

"No quarter, no surrender. To the death!"

Under the midafternoon sun the three combatants closed in on each other.

Under that same sun the creatures of Redwall took their ease. Young ones played and tumbled on the lawn while the elders rested in the cool shades of the orchard. The Wild King MacPhearsome perched on a beech stump, sound asleep in the summer heat that he seldom felt among his icy crags and mountain wilderness.

Friar Bellows nodded with admiration. "Very good,

very good. What a magnificent giant of a bird. I'm glad he's sleeping, because while he is he's not eating!"

Tudd Spinney leaned on his stick and chuckled. "Oh, he's got a rare appetite, that one, but I'm a thinkin' that he's entitled to it. We'd all be dead as doornails but for yonder bird. What d'you say, Hollyberry?"

The old Infirmary Keeper had been half dozing off. He shook himself and looked around, blinking. "Oh, er, what? Indeed, whatever you say, Mr. Spinney. I was just wondering whatever became of young Samkim and Arula. I was very fond of those two little rogues, y'know."

Abbess Vale sniffed, brushing away a tear with her habit sleeve. "Oh dear, it seems ages ago since they both sat out here at our Nameday feast. I do hope they are safe. Samkim was a bright-eyed little fellow and Arula was a dear funny mole."

"What's all the fuss about?" Furgle brushed an ant from his paw and lay back in the shade of a spreading pear tree. "When I met them they seemed like two sensible and resourceful young beasts. Maybe they've settled down elsewhere and found a new life for themselves."

"Mr. Furgle, the very idea of it!" Sister Nasturtium chided him. "I know Samkim and Arula and I've lived here with them since they were tiny orphaned dots. They could never be happy in any place except Redwall. I'll wager an apple to an acorn shell they come striding back through that main gate one day. You mark my words, that day will be the happiest day this Abbey has ever known!"

Faith Spinney stood up, brushing off her flowered pinafore. "What about pore Mr. Thrugg? What's to become of him?"

Thrugann stifled a gurgling laugh. "What? You mean that great lump of a brother of mine? I'll bet wherever he is right now he's scoffin' or fightin'. Don't fret yore 'ead over Thrugg, marm—he'd live in the middle of a snowstorm on a duck's back with a daisy in his ear!"

Baby Dumble popped through a gooseberry bush. "Yeh, Mista Thugg my friend. 'E carry me inna 'avvysack an' was gunna fight the heagle. Mista Thugg a brave hotter!"

Foremole gave Dumble a push that sent him rolling downhill. "Hurr well, that be all ter be sayed on that subjeck. Tho' oi do 'opes liddle Sanken an' our 'Rula be safe. Ho yes, zurr."

Safety was the last thing on Samkim and Arula's minds. They sat in a logboat with Mara and Pikkle as it flashed helter-skelter down a long winding stream towards the sea and Salamandastron. The previous night had been spent swapping life stories with their new friends, so each now knew all there was to know about the other. Samkim and Arula felt duty bound to help free Salamandastron and the Mossflower country of vermin; faintheartedness was not their strong suit.

The logboats had traveled without stopping. Under the twin Captaincies of Log-a-log and Alfoh, they pressed onward. Creatures ate, slept and paddled in shifts, and sometime before dawn they had left the Great Lake behind, steering into a long winding arm of the Great South Stream that traveled downhill to the open sea. The paddles chunked steadily as high canyon walls swept by the five logboats, and shrews in the bows watched out for rocks and warded off the tall banks with their paddles and long branches. Bowley the cook and Ashnin passed out food from the goodly supply they had brought from the island, while Nordo made his way skillfully between the vessels with a compound of china clay and slippery elm bark for blistered paddle paws. To any creature on land that saw them passing it would have made a curious sight: five logboats stem to stern, hurtling downstream, laden with three badgers, two squirrels, a mole and a crowd of shrews, roaring out a bass war shanty.

"The Guosssom shrews are off to war,
With our rapiers close to paw.
Woe to him who will not go
To fight the vermin foe.
Logalog Logalog Log-a-log!
Guosssom shrews must live or die
Free beneath the open sky.
Battle on while we have breath,
With no fear of death.
Logalog Logalog Log-a-log!"

38

Ferahgo whirled the mace and chain. The spiked iron ball whistled and hummed as he closed in on Urthstripe's left side. Klitch sneaked in on the right and threw his spear at the badger's head. Urthstripe whirled with a roar, knocking the spear aside with his own weapon as he spun in a circle, catching the mace around the haft of his own spear and heaving Ferahgo bodily onto the sand. Behind the rocks an armed band of treacherous vermin waited until such time as Urthstripe was forced to turn and present his back to them. Scrabbling through the sand to get away, Ferahgo cowered in the shadow of the badger Lord. Urthstripe kicked the mace and chain toward the blue-eyed Assassin.

"Pick it up, weasel!"

Klitch dashed in and slashed at Urthstripe's shoulder. The short sword caught the badger on an open place between shoulder plate and back armor. With a roar Urthstripe wheeled on him, thrusting at the stabbing sword with his mighty battlespear. Ferahgo was still down on the sand as he grabbed the mace and chain. Flinging it, he trapped the badger's footpaws, and Urthstripe toppled and fell with a crash of armor. Klitch ran in with his sword held high, but Urthstripe pulled himself into a sitting position and lashed out. The metal-clad paw caught Klitch in the chest, sending him thudding into the rocks. The young weasel sobbed for breath as he looked down at his own blood, oozing from the deep bruising scratches the armored paw had inflicted.

Ferahgo seized the spear Klitch had dropped and advanced on his opponent. Kicking free of mace and chain, the badger Lord came up off the sand, holding his battle spear crossways like a stave. They clashed, and Ferahgo yelled in dismay as his spear was snapped in two like a brittle straw.

"Klitch, help me, son. Help me!"

All the fight had been knocked out of the young weasel. His blue eyes flooded with tears as he nursed his aching chest. Dragging himself up on the rocks, he spat at the ambush party. "Stop hiding there like a pack of halfwits. Kill the badger!"

Ferahgo had drawn two of his knives. Throwing himself flat, he rolled under Urthstripe's paws, out of the way of the big spear, stabbing at the badger's footpaws viciously until Urthstripe leapt back and dealt him a tremendous kick. The weasel's body left the ground in a somersault as the ambushers came flooding over the rocks, spears ready and bowstrings taut.

Spitting blood from a mouthwound caused by the breaking spear, Urthstripe snarled, "You treacherous scum, come and get me!"

Ferahgo struggled up, gasping hoarsely, "Don't shoot any arrows until I'm out the way!"

"So you don't want to be slain by murderers, eh?" Urthstripe roared with laughter as he went after the Assassin.

The ranks of spears and blades closed in, cutting Ferahgo off from his enemy, but Urthstripe saw nothing in front of him but the terrible joy of battle. Spear

336

flailing, he bulled in among them, yelling as the lust to slay foebeasts took hold of him.

"Eulaliaaaaaaaa!"

Ferrets, stoats, foxes, weasels and rats flew everywhere, stabbed by the giant spearblade, hooked with the crosstrees and hammered senseless by the battering spearbutt. Ferahgo and Klitch danced and leapt on the outskirts of the melee, shouting:

"Get him! Slay the badger!"

"Go on! Get at him! Don't stop!"

Spears, pikes and swords battered at armour and fur as Urthstripe went down beneath the howling mob. There was an immense roar as the badger surged up, throwing bodies into the air, punching, kicking and biting. The helm ripped from his head and his spear lying on the ground, the badger Lord fought insanely against the overwhelming odds. Down he went again. Blades flashed in the sunlight on the churning sands, barely visible beneath the pack of yelling, screeching ambushers. Again they shot in all directions as, scored by countless wounds, Urthstripe rose like a mighty geyser bursting from the ground with a fox between his teeth and a rat in each paw, hurling the lifeless carcasses into the mob, and went at them again, laughing like a beast gone mad.

Like a pack of wild animals they clung to him, bearing him down to the sand once more. Limbs thrashing and teeth slashing, Urthstripe battled on, the armor torn from him, battered and dented into uselessness. Ferahgo and Klitch hugged each other in delight, anticipating the inevitable outcome.

"Blood 'n' thunder, chaps! Eulaliaaaaaa!"

Twoscore well-placed shafts thudded into the ambushers as Big Oxeye and twenty others came charging over the sands, their javelins held short for stabbing action. Straight into the fray they plunged, dealing death wherever their lancepoints found the foe. Completely taken by surprise, the vermin scattered, leaping for the safety of the rocks—but not before Ferahgo and Klitch, who hid among the rocks, calling out frantic commands.

"Get them! Don't let them escape!"

"Finish the badger off!"

Six hares supported the staggering badger Lord. Oxeye and the others backed off swiftly, firing arrows into the rocks to discourage pursuit. Hurrying across the sands toward the mountain, they ducked, returning salvos of arrows and slingstones.

Klitch and Ferahgo laid about them with sword and knife blades.

"Get after them, you lily-livered cowards!"

"Come on, you worthless trash. Charge!"

Oxeye saw them coming and broke his command into three—five shooting arrows, with five behind waiting and another five behind them. As one party fired they fell to the rear, letting the next five loose off their arrows; they fired and went to the rear, leaving the next five to shoot. Urthstripe's paws dragged twin furrows in the sand as they half carried, half pulled him along.

Big Oxeye was moving slowly backwards with his archers, coolly in command of the situation. "Righto, chaps. Fire! Next five, ready, aim, pick y' targets now. Fire! Well done, the Long Patrol. Next five, steady in the ranks there, draw strings . . . and fire!"

The deadly shafts hissed through the air as the ambushers advanced reluctantly. Ferahgo sent another contingent out from the rocks to reinforce the half-hearted ambushers.

"Their arrows are nearly used up—look. Get after them!"

Bart Thistledown muttered to Oxeye as the mountain loomed large, "Bad show this. We'll never get Urthstripe up through that windowspace he climbed out of. What'll we do, Ox?"

The big hare glanced over his shoulder, sizing up the situation. "You'd better dash back, Barty old lad. Tell Penny and the others to unblock one of the big ground-level openings. Off y' go now!"

Ferahgo had followed his ambushers, loping a short distance behind them and yelling a mixture of threats and encouragement. Klitch stayed behind. Standing on one of the high rocks, he surveyed the scene before him. Excitement rose within the young weasel as he called the ferret Dragtail to him.

"Dragtail, come here! See that? They've unblocked a big space near the entrance to the mountain. Go as fast as you can and muster the rest of the horde. We'll never get a better chance than this to conquer Salamandastron. Hurry!"

Oxeye, Bart Thistledown and some others were having difficulties with Urthstripe. They had lifted and pushed him halfway through the long unblocked fissure when the badger Lord began shoving backwards. Half demented, he had partially recovered and wanted to return to the battle.

"Never trust vermin. I should have known—treacherous toads. I'll show them! Where's my spear, Oxeye?"

The hare scrabbled desperately, clutching Urthstripe in an attempt to stop him escaping. "You're in no shape to fight, sah! Wounds 'n' injuries an' so on. Come inside an' rest now, there's a good feller."

Urthstripe sat up on the bottom ledge of the fissure, swaying as he glared groggily at his friend. "Don't talk rubbish, Ox! Day I can't attend a battle I'll . . . I'll . . ." As he crashed over unconscious, Oxeye had the presence of mind to tip Urthstripe inside. He fell backwards over the ledge with a bump, landing in the ground-level corridor. Willing paws gathered round to carry the badger Lord up to his bed, a rush-strewn rock slab in the forge room.

Pennybright stood side by side with Bart Thistledown and Starbob, firing arrows at the advancing horde. She was clearly worried.

"Oh, Barty, what'll we do? Most of the rocks blocking this space were pushed outside—we just levered them out to get Lord Urthstripe inside. It'd take simply ages to reblock this crevice."

Bart Thistledown notched a shaft to his bowstring and dropped a charging rat with unerring accuracy. "Nothing much we can do, Pen. Hold the gap and wait further orders from Oxeye. Hi, Starbob, bring your bows an' lend a paw over here!"

Outside on the shore, Ferahgo's blue eyes gleamed triumphantly as he was swept along toward Salamandastron at the center of his horde of Corpsemakers. Now nothing could stop them.

"Yurr, be this'n anuther o' those gurt lakes?"

"No, it's the jolly old sea, Arula. We've reached the sea!" Pikkle waved his paddle in the air.

The logboats bumped out across a gurgling stream that spanned a short pebbly beach. Mara turned to her right and pointed at the distant flat-topped peak.

"Look, Salamandastron!"

Framed against a reddening evening sky, the badger mountain stood separate from the ranges to the east. Loambudd placed a paw on Urthwyte's shoulder.

"Look at it, grandson. That's where your brother Urthstripe rules."

A tear gathered in the corner of the white badger's honest eye. "Urthstripe, the brother I never knew!"

The logboats bounced as they hit the white-crested waves. Log-a-log shouted orders as they backed water and turned the noses of the vessels into the tide, beginning the wide semicircular tack which would eventually bring them to land on the beach in front of the mountain. As darkness fell they paddled side by side in convoy.

"What's that floatin' up ahead?" Alfoh called across in a gruff whisper.

Log-a-log peered into the darkness as he called to his paddlers, "Take a tack to starboard, watch out for that driftwood ahead!"

A voice rang out from the floating debris of branches. "If yore vermin, I warns yer Hi'll fight fer me life!"

Mara looked at Pikkle in astonishment. Together they echoed one word: "Sapwood!"

The Sergeant was hauled aboard. He hugged Mara and Pikkle, staring over their shoulders at the huge white badger in the other logboat to his left. Pikkle ducked and bobbed, throwing a light friendly blow at Sapwood with his remaining skill and energy. The boxing hare dodged it and rapped him smartly on both ears with a left-right combination as he spoke to Mara.

"Who's the big white badger over there? Strewth, 'e must be as big as 'Is Nibs Urthstripe."

Mara rummaged in a sack of provisions. "Oh, you'll find out soon enough. It's too long a story for tonight—we'll need rest if we're going into battle tomorrow. Here, take this food. I'll bet you're hungry, eh, Sergeant."

"Huh, 'ungry ain't the word, missie. Hi could make a stew o' me own ears an' enjoy it!"

"I say, Sarge, no need for that sort of thing, wot." Pikkle pulled a face and shuddered. "Tuck in and have a good supper, have a nap and wake up bright 'n' breezy tomorrow, eh!"

However, it was some time before Sapwood was allowed to sleep. The shrewd old badger Loambudd questioned him closely about what was going on at

Salamandastron. Later she held a conference across the boat sides with Mara, Urthwyte, Log-a-log and Alfoh.

"From what I gathered off Sapwood, I think that my grandson's mountain is in a perilous position. Our help is sorely needed there. When do you think we'll make land, Log-a-log?"

The shrew leader watched the moonlit wake of his small fleet. "We're running with the current and the wind is behind us. If the weather holds out, we'll probably hit the beach by dawn—though if I put on extra paddlers we could be there in the hour before daylight."

Loambudd did not hesitate. "Then do it right away, my friend. There's not a moment to lose. Now, let's hold a war council and make plans . . ."

Only the rolling night waves were witness to the five logboats cutting speedily through the sea toward Salamandastron. Grim-faced shrews dug their paddles deep, keeping the boats abreast of each other as the leaders conferred urgently.

Salamandastron had been breached—the horde of Ferahgo was within the mountain!

Bart Thistledown and his little band had fought a gallant action. Firing into the oncoming masses until their arrows ran out and thwacking away at vermin bodies, they defended the open fissure heroically until Oxeye sent Seawood and ten others to pull them out. Javelins clashed and slings whirled as they fought a fierce retreating action, having to desert the opening and back off into the maze of tunnels that honeycombed the mountain.

In his forge room at the middle level, Urthstripe lay sorely wounded, bound to his bed by restraining bandages as he hovered between life and death. Ferahgo's Corpsemakers flooded the lower corridors, crowding into caves and chambers—harassed by the hares, who, though overwhelmed by numbers, fought guerrilla style, popping up at intersections and appearing in the most unlikely places to loose arrows at the vermin.

Oxeye was now in sole command of the Long Patrol. He used all his warrior cunning and skill to contain the horde within the lower levels; hares appeared, attacked, then vanished like smoke along the winding tunnels. Big Oxeye used the forge room as his center of operations, issuing instructions as he stayed close to the delirious badger Lord.

"Moonpaw, take Lingfur an' Penny. Stay at the south stairwell an' give 'em blood 'n' vinegar. I'll send a relief as soon as Catkin an' Barfle get back."

Moonpaw took the two younger hares, saluted and set off at a trot for the stairwell. Oxeye watched them go, shaking his head despairingly as he slumped down beside Bart Thistledown. "It's no good, Barty old lad. We can't hold 'em back for ever—there's too many of the vermin."

Wounded and battered from his defense of the opening, Bart grinned lopsidedly through a half-open eye. "No use shiverin' over lost fur, Ox. What'd you sooner die of, old age or battle?"

Oxeye shook his head admiringly. "Battle, I suppose. By the left, Barty, you're a cool one!"

His friend stroked a lancebutt with an injured paw. "Cool nothin' – I'm quiverin' like a jolly jelly inside, but don't tell old Urthstripe that."

Oxeye took a damp cloth and bathed the badger Lord's heated brow. Urthstripe was oblivious to all about him. He lay struggling against the restraining bandages, muttering, "Winter . . . golden medallion . . . cold . . . Father, Mother . . . where are you? . . . White snow, white brother . . . cold!"

The pale moon glinted off Ferahgo's medallion as he

343

sat out on the sands with Klitch. For once father and son were in agreement over their strategy.

Ferahgo drew his skinning knife and pointed at the mountaintop. "I'll take a hundred and get up there; you keep up the attack inside—we'll have them trapped both ways."

Klitch's blue eyes shone gleefully into the night. "You took the words out of my mouth, backstabber. By tomorrow night the mountain will belong to us!"

Ferahgo tapped the knifepoint against his son's chest. "And while you're in there, young one, remember: just keep fighting, don't stop to look for badger treasure. I'll do that when my horde have finished the job."

"*Your* horde?" Klitch turned the knifepoint aside with his spearshaft.

The Assassin twirled the knife deftly. "Yes, *my* horde—and so it will remain while I'm alive!"

The younger weasel leapt up and bounded athletically up the rocks to the opening, turning to address his father before disappearing inside.

"Once again we agree, old one. It is your horde . . . while you're still alive!"

39

In the hour before dawn, Guosssom shrews leapt from the logboats into the shallows, willing paws pushing and tugging as they beached the five vessels on the shore in front of Salamandastron. Samkim and Arula looked up and down the empty beach, paws close to their weapon handles.

"Yurr, Sanken, it be turrible soilent 'ereabouts. Oi wunner where all 'ee vurmints be agone to?"

Sapwood was tracking through the sands. "Not too 'ard to tell Harula. I'm a-thinkin' we might've arrived 'ere too late!"

Loambudd lifted Ashnin lightly from the logboat and set her on dry land. Hefting a paddle, she joined them. "No time for gossip now. Gather round, everybeast!"

Every creature present dropped what they were doing and crowded about the wise old female badger as she rapped out orders.

"Urthwyte, Samkim and Arula—go with Alfoh and his tribe and find out what the position is at the mountain. Pikkle, you go with them and act as runner. The rest of you stay here with me."

Armed with rapiers and paddles, the tribe of Alfoh stole

silently across the shore in the wake of Pikkle and the white badger. Samkim drew the sword of Martin as he hurried along with the frontrunners; Arula waddled alongside him, swinging a loaded sling. Automatically Pikkle made for the main entrance. He groaned softly as he saw the unblocked fissure yawning wide.

"Oh no, it looks like Ferahgo's stinkin' lot have found a way inside!"

At the opening, Samkim held up a paw for silence. "Hist!" Badtooth had taken an arrow in his paw. Hauling himself painfully through the opening, the stoat sought a soft resting place on the sand. He was halfway through the opening when a huge white paw seized him by the throat. Badtooth gave a terrified gurgle as he was dragged out onto the rocks. Samkim held the edge of the sword across his throat, growling viciously, "One false move or a wrong word and you lose your head! Now speak up, what has happened here?"

The unfortunate stoat gulped and whimpered out all he knew. "The horde are in there, tryin' to fight their way through the mountain . . ."

Pikkle grabbed him by the ear. "Where's Ferahgo an' Klitch?"

"Klitch is in there, an' Crabeyes, an' Dragtail an' the rest. I 'aven't clapped eyes on Ferahgo since the attack started, I swear it!"

Urthwyte and Samkim exchanged glances.

"We'll have to take his word for it," the white badger grunted. He knocked the stoat senseless with a sweep of his paw, looking about as if undecided what to do next.

Samkim took charge, coming up with a fast and workable solution. "It's going to be light soon—we'll have to move fast. Pikkle, tell Loambudd that we've gone up the mountain to reinforce those inside. If she brings the rest up through this opening we can mount a two-pronged assault."

Alfoh clapped him on the back. "Good idea. Are you sure you've never done this sort of thing before, young squirrel?"

Samkim shouldered Martin's sword with a wry grin. "There's a first time for everything, matey!"

Pikkle was gone in a spray of loose sand. Strapping his mighty club to his back, Urthwyte began climbing. Arula threw up her paws in resignation as she started the ascent.

"Burrhoo! Oi doant loik 'igh places, bein' naught but 'ee mole. Bohurr, yur goes one cloimbin' young beast."

Dawn broke in roseate splendor over Salamandastron as Mara and Loambudd thundered over the sands with the Guosssom of Log-a-log hard on their heels. Pikkle rested a moment as they surged by him. Eventually he regained his breath and grabbed a paddle.

"I say, chaps. Wait for me!"

Moonpaw was slain defending the stairwell. The gallant hare placed Pennybright and Lingfur behind her. The two young ones thrust either side of Moonpaw with their lances at the ravening pack of vermin that pressed its way forward up the stairs.

Wounded in a dozen places, Moonpaw yelled to the two young ones, "Get back to Oxeye quickly. Tell him to send reinforcements." She gazed for a moment at Pennybright's tearstained face. "Don't stand there gawping, young Pen. Do as I say. Go on!"

Moonpaw had a double-pointed javelin. Wildly she broke it in half over the head of a ferret. Brandishing both halves, she dived headlong into the press of foebeasts, yelling a last warcry.

"Eulaliaaaaaa!"

Breathlessly the two young hares sobbed out their story to Oxeye. He sat them down, keeping his voice calm.

"Well, it looks as if we've lost the lower levels. Sorry I haven't any food or drink to offer you two. Sit there and rest awhile. I say, Barty old thing, how're you feelin'?"

Bart Thistledown flexed his paws. Nodding to two other hares, he picked up his bow and quiver of arrows and limped off. "Oh I suppose I'm about ready for another scuffle, Big Ox. Come on, you chaps—duty calls, an' all that. Oh, if I don't manage t' make it back, you'll know its bye-bye Barty. Under those circumstances you'd be best movin' His Lordship out of here an' up to another chamber, wot? Toodle-oo!"

The sounds of yelling, chanting vermin stamping about inside the mountain was growing louder. Big Oxeye threw a paw about Lingfur's trembling shoulders and chuckled. "Noisy old lot, aren't they?"

In the full flood of bright morning sunlight, Urthwyte's party neared the top of the crater.

Alfoh was staring at something up above as he fitted a rock to his sling. Whirling the weapon, he called out to Samkim, "Look, that's a rat up there. Hey you!"

The rat's head was barely visible, but as Alfoh shouted he turned and showed himself. The slingstone took him under the ear with a distinctive thud. The rat screamed and toppled over the crater top. Instantly there was a mob of vermin, hurling rocks and firing arrows down on them.

"Where did they come from? Who are they?" Ferahgo could be heard yelling from the top of the mountain.

Arula aimed a rock from her sling in the direction of the voice. She was rewarded with a cry from the Assassin.

"Ow, my paw! Kill them, whoever they are!"

A shrew stood to whirl his sling but an arrow took him through the eye and he fell back dead. Urthwyte picked up a sizable boulder and hurled it upward, taking out a rat and injuring a fox.

"Charge! Eulaliaaaaa!" The great white badger went surging forward regardless of arrows and stones.

Samkim and Arula took up the cry. "Forward, Redwaaaaaallll!"

"Logalogalogalogalog!" The shrews broke cover and began scrambling up the rocks, slinging as they went.

Klitch led a band of Corpsemakers along a twisting rock passage toward the stairwell. He trod scornfully on the body of Moonpaw as he mounted the stairs.

"Kill! Kill! Kiiiillll!"

Standing to one side, he let his attack force sweep up the stairs, smiling craftily as he heard the death screams of the front rank who had walked into the range of Bart Thistledown's bows. "Come on, you lucky rabble. It's only a couple of hares. Rush them!"

Big Oxeye picked up a longbow and arrows. Issuing slings and stone pouches to Pennybright and Lingfur, he nodded toward the clamor of battle echoing up through the passage outside.

"Right, hares, up on y' paws. Quick's the word an' sharp's the action. We'll have to go an' give ol' Barty a pull-out. His Lordship'll be safe here until we get back. Young Pen, an' you, Ling, give me a big smile—come on now. That's the ticket. Now yell after me as we go. It's the Loooong Patrooool! Eulaliaaaaa!" Yelling like demons, they sped down the passage to Bart's aid.

Standing at the back of his command, Klitch watched as an ashen-faced Dragtail came running up from the lower levels. The young weasel eyed him cynically.

"Where in the name of Hellgates have you been? It's up here you should be, where the fighting's taking place, not down there in the peace and quiet!"

Dragtail was plainly scared and, breathing heavily, he hooked a paw back down at the lower levels. "Listen to that!"

349

Echoing hollowly up through the rocky corridor the sound reached the young weasel's startled ears.

"Logalogalogalogalog!"

Undecided as what to do, Klitch shrugged and smiled nervously. "Logalog? What's that supposed to mean?"

A well-aimed arrow took Dragtail through the chest as Log-a-log, Mara and Pikkle came hurtling along the passage at the head of a charging Guosssom band.

With a terrified yelp, Klitch took to his heels, fighting his way through the vermin crowding the stairwell until he was safely ensconced in the middle of the pack. Unreasoningly he grabbed a fox by the throat and shouted into his face, "Nobeast told me about this."

The fox was about to reply when one of Big Oxeye's arrows snuffed out his life. Klitch looked wildly about as he moaned, "It's a trap. We're trapped!"

With a stentorian roar Lord Urthstripe burst through the restraining bandages, ripping his huge bulk up from the bed. Seizing a forge hammer, he lumbered off toward the upper levels. From some amazing reserve, the mountain Ruler had dredged up his wild strength; the madness of the warrior badgers was upon him— nobeast could stand in his path now, even despite the fearsome wounds that scarred his giant frame.

Urthwyte's party had gained the summit, and now they were fighting around the top of the crater. Ferahgo stared at the white badger, a wave of fear sweeping across him.

"Kill the white one! Kill him! The one who slays the white badger is a richbeast!"

Twenty crowded round Urthwyte as he battled furiously. Roaring mightily, he swung his oaken club. Samkim forged around the crater top, his sword flashing in the sunlight, leaping, dodging, hacking, thrusting—with Arula covering his back, swinging her loaded sling.

"Goo on, Sanken, urr hurr. Make Redwell proud of 'ee!"

Alfoh and his shrews fought valiantly with rapier, paddle and sling. There was no quarter given; shrew and vermin alike died that day on the heights. The creatures of Ferahgo fought with the ferocity of despair, bemused by the strange force that had scaled the mountain to offer them battle. Seeing his chance, Ferahgo sneaked up on Urthwyte, knowing that if he could slay the white badger the fight would swing his way. Urthwyte had his back to Ferahgo, hammering relentlessly at any creature coming into club range. The Assassin drew both his best knives, the killer and the skinner, and crouched low, bunching his muscles for the spring that would carry him onto the white badger's back, where his blades could feast on the unprotected neck. Nerving himself, he made the spring.

In midair time seemed to stand still. He heard the roar, saw Urthstripe appear in front of him and felt the shock as two fearsome paws caught him in their viselike grip. Ferahgo screamed with shock. Galvanized into action, he began stabbing with both knives, plunging them into the body of the roaring badger Lord.

The massive injuries he had formerly sustained, together with the horrendous wounds of Ferahgo's daggers, now caused Urthstripe's fierce dark eyes to cloud over with deathmist, but his fate was not yet sealed. From the deep wells of strength within his gigantic frame he called up a last mighty surge that would enable him to rid Salamandastron of Ferahgo.

Crushing the blue-eyed weasel to him, Urthstripe leapt from the top of the mountain, yelling his last beloved battle cry:

"Eulaliaaaaaaaaaaaaa!!!"

The knowledge that he had glimpsed his lost brother for a moment hit Urthwyte; the look on his face caused

351

every creature who had followed Ferahgo to lose their nerves completely.

Alfoh pulled Samkim to one side. "Leave him here. Get Arula and my shrews down inside the mountain before he kills us all. Leave him here with the vermin!"

Samkim could readily understand Alfoh's meaning; the sight of the berserk white badger hurling himself bodily at the panic-stricken vermin was enough. Pushing Arula in front of him, the young squirrel followed the Guosssom band down the walkways that spiraled into the heart of Salamandastron.

Pennybright hurried up from the forge room with a quiver of arrows. She passed them to Oxeye.

"These are the last. There are no more!"

Oxeye grinned as he fitted a shaft to his bow. "Good gel. Keep slingin', Penny. Look at young Ling there—he's tossin' rocks like a good un. Want some good news, m'dear? There's a band of shrews an' whatnot attackin' from the lower levels. Listen to this." Oxeye shouted over the melee at the top of his voice. "Duck 'n' weave! Blood 'n' vinegar! Long Patrol's here!" The sound echoed down the rocky stairwell.

A moment later there was an answering call.

"Jab an' move! Give 'em a towsin'! Long Patrol's 'ere too!"

"Good ol' Sapwood." Oxeye's grin spread from ear to ear. "Knew I never sent him on that cruise for nothin'."

Lingfur looked fearfully over his shoulder. "Sir, look out! They're behind us!"

Carrying a heavy paddle and her sling, Arula bowed low. "We'm not behoind 'ee, young un. Us'ns are with 'ee!"

Oxeye stifled a laugh as he shook paws with the molemaid. "Well, thank goodness for that. I'd hate to face a warrior like you, young molemaid."

352

Arula wrinkled her nose. "Thankee koindly, zurr."

"Pleased t' meet you, I'm sure." Oxeye clasped the paws of Samkim and Alfoh gratefully. "But could we leave the introductions until after the war, old lads?"

Samkim immediately liked the big hare. Gripping his sword in both paws, he took up a fighting stance and nodded. "That seems fair enough, sir. Shall we charge?"

Paddles, slings and rapiers waved behind Samkim and Oxeye as the hare tossed aside his bow and picked up a lance.

"Well said, sir! Ready, chaps . . . Then . . . charge!"

"Eulaliaaa! Redwaaaaall! Logalogalogalog!"

Taking up the call, the band at the bottom of the stairwell howled their own battle cries as they charged from their end.

The war was hopelessly lost for the once vaunted horde of Corpsemakers. Klitch killed the two vermin closest to him and fell flat on the stairs, pulling their bodies over his to act as concealment. The rocks echoed with the clangor of battle. Trapped and cut off on the long rambling flight of stairs, the last of the horde fought with desperation, but they were no match for the Guosssom, two badgers and the remaining hares of the Long Patrol. Mara felt herself swept along in the rush. Ahead of her she glimpsed Samkim, his face alight with the madness of battle as he fought his way through the tight-packed ranks of vermin, some of whom were standing dead, having no room to fall. At the center of the turmoil they met, the young squirrel and the badger maid. A sudden silence prevailed. The madness was over, Salamandastron stood free.

Creatures who a moment before had been yelling and slaying stood weary and quiet, as if shamed by the indignity of war. Bodies of friend and foe alike lay strewn on the rocky steps like leaves after an autumn gale.

The voice of young Pennybright echoed hollowly round the scene of carnage: "Oxeye, sir, I want to go out into the sunlight. I don't want to be here!"

Oxeye stroked her ears gently as he gazed around. "Neither do any of us, young Pen. Come on, let's all go out into the fresh air!"

As they climbed out of the opening, Loambudd grasped Mara's paw.

"Ayaaaaaaah!"

The sound that tore from the old badger's throat was like the cry of an animal being slain. She released Mara's paw and went rushing out. The young badger maid was about to call after her when she, too, saw what had made Loambudd cry out. As fast as she could she ran after her.

Urthstripe the Strong lay with his paws still clutching Ferahgo the Assassin. Both were dead. On all fours beside the two bodies was Urthwyte, weeping like a baby, his paws bruised and cut from the wild rushing descent he had made from the mountaintop to be with his brother.

Loambudd unlocked the dead badger Lord's paws from around Ferahgo. As she removed the golden medallion from the weasel's neck, Sapwood and Oxeye approached her and bowed low.

"Can we be of help, Lady?"

She turned the Assassin's carcass over with her footpaw. "Take this worthless thing and cast it into the sea. It does not deserve a resting place like any decent creature."

Blinded by hot tears, Mara watched as Loambudd placed the medallion about Urthwyte's snowy neck.

"This belonged to my father and to your father. It

should have been worn by your brother Urthstripe. It now belongs to you, my grandson. Wear it proudly."

Mara knelt and clasped the big battle-scarred paws of the fallen badger Lord. Words tumbled out with her tears. "I came back too late. Now it is past the time when I could tell you what is in my heart. I have ranged far and wide to be back home here with you, and in that time I have slowly understood what you tried to teach me—you who were ever true to your own code of honor and duty. To everybeast you were Urthstripe the Strong, Lord of the mountain; so will your name be always remembered. You cannot hear me now, but I wish to add one more name to your title."

The young badger maid took both the lifeless paws and placed them on her bowed head as she spoke a single word:

"Father!"

Klitch lay still, listening until the victors had departed. Beneath the slain bodies it was hot and airless. His tongue clove to the roof of a dry mouth, parched from battle, thirst and the fear of discovery. The silence became total, oppressive, like the weight of the two creatures he had slain lying on top of him. Pushing and kicking, he freed himself from the carcasses and sneaked off up the stairs. His only hope now was to gain the crater top and slip away over the east rim while his enemies rested on the sands at the west side of the mountain.

The young weasel took several wrong turns as he roamed the passages and upper galleries, seeking an exit. Panic was beginning to set in. Fearing the return and possible vengeance of his foes, Klitch ran desperately. Some passages ended in a blank rock face, others opened out into caves and chambers. He padded along, silently cursing Ferahgo's stupidity and the bumbling horde that had followed blindly on such an

355

addle-brained enterprise. Licking bone-dry lips with a parched tongue, Klitch stumbled along a passage that opened out into a cool dark cave. Feeling his way around the rocky walls, he sobbed raggedly. Was there no way out of this accursed mountain, no way back to the good lands of the Southwest where he could terrorize the creatures that had been subdued by his father? Surely they would know that he was the son of Ferahgo the Assassin and learn to fear him as they had feared the old one.

Klitch's footpaw stubbed against something hollow and wooden in the gloom. He hopped painfully, biting his lip to keep from crying out. When the pain receded he looked more closely. There were several of the objects. He tapped their sides.

Barrels!

Pulling one over, Klitch was rewarded by the swishing sound of dregs swilling about. The top was open. The young weasel smiled in the darkness; maybe now his luck was beginning to change. The water sloshed out of the open barrel on to the rocky floor, and Klitch went down on all fours and lapped gratefully at it. The cool liquid refreshed him, lending a new sense of purpose and resolve to the Assassin's son.

Standing upright, Klitch squared his narrow shoulders and strode out of the cave purposefully, fear receding as he mentally planned a campaign of terror that would mark his return to the Southwest Lands.

Now every passage and corridor appeared light and airy, and the way to the top was clear. His bright blue eyes gleamed confidently—yes, this was the day luck had returned to him. Up ahead he could see the bright summer morning and the catwalk to the crater top.

An unexpected stomach twinge caused him to double up. He stood still a moment until it passed. Straightening up, he smiled. There, the pain was gone—nothing was going to ruin his newfound luck. Mounting the catwalk, he started to run for the crater top and freedom.

Twice, thrice, he was stopped by the sudden lightning bolts of pain that lanced through him, but each time he recovered and hastened upward.

Now Klitch was going slower, his limbs became numb—it was like wading through deep cold water. The young weasel blinked. Why had the day become foggy and dark? Finally he made the top and lay down upon the edge of the crater, fighting off the dizziness and agonizing lances stabbing through his body. Klitch doubled up and wedged himself between two rocks. He would sleep here awhile until he felt better. Fixed in this position he could not roll over the mountain edge as he slept. Nothing was going to ruin his good luck . . . The once bright blue eyes clouded over and went dim as he slipped into an endless dark dream.

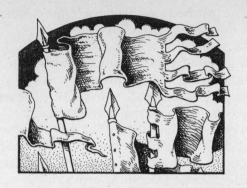

40

Two days had passed, two days of sadness and hard work. Salamandastron was cleared of the horrifying debris of war. Pennants waved from lances fixed in the sands of the shoreline—these were the graves of hares and shrews who had fallen in the struggle to free the mountain—and farther along in an unmarked place the carcasses of Ferahgo's horde found their last resting place. Now was the time to bring light and fresh food to the rocky fortress by the sea. Parties were sent out to forage, others worked on the slopes, unblocking window spaces and replanting the mountain terraces with flowers, crops and trees.

Deep in the cellars Arula had discovered a fault in the rock. She supervised a band of shrews as they levered, chiseled and chipped at the fissure. The young mole-maid had smelt water below, a cold clear spring of good fresh drinking water. It would make the mountain invulnerable to siege, giving an endless supply of the most precious of liquids. She shook paws with Log-a-log and Alfoh as they watched the spring gurgle gently through the hole they had sweated to cut into the living stone.

"Hurr hurr, it baint no 'Tober ale, guddbeasts, but oi wager 'ee taste just as gudd, hurr hurr!"

There remained one last sad duty, to install the body of Urthstripe with his predecessors.

Samkim was requested to be at the ceremony, wearing the sword of Martin the Warrior strapped across his shoulders. He carried a lantern, lighting the way for the three badgers who bore the mountain Lord. Big Oxeye and Sergeant Sapwood walked with them, giving Samkim directions to the spot.

Urthwyte pushed back the slab to the secret cave. Samkim gazed around at the rock walls covered in mysterious badger carvings and pictures. Sapwood sniffed and wiped a paw roughly across his eyes as he peered at the last carving.

"This 'ere was graven by 'Is Lordship 'imself. See, there 'e is, an' there's you, Lord Urthwyte. 'Ere's young Master Samkim, too, an' the sword. Though Hi can't read the writin' my friend Urthstripe carved there."

Loambudd could, however. Samkim held the lantern as she silently scanned the high ancient badger script. When she had finished reading she turned to them.

"This was written for me alone to read; that is why I am not pictured on the wall. I alone must keep the awful and joyful secrets written here until Urthwyte can be instructed as Lord of Salamandastron. There is one thing I can tell you, however: Urthstripe my grandson wishes to rest beneath emllor—where that is I cannot say. Do any of you know?"

The lantern light flickered about the walls as they looked at each other.

"Emllor?" Big Oxeye shrugged. "There's no place in this mountain with such a name."

Samkim wandered about the chamber, repeating the name to himself. "Emllor, emllor."

359

At the far end of the cave the wall was smooth but blank; there was no writing on it. Samkim ran his paw across it and leapt back in surprise. "Look, this is not stone!"

It was a curtain made from some rough woven material. Pebbles and sand had been fixed to it with pine resin, giving the effect of a rock wall. Urthwyte moved it carefully to one side. An awesome sight greeted the eyes of the onlookers. Seated on a rock throne was the crumbling skeleton of a badger clad in full war armor. The alcove behind the curtain was semicircular in shape, marred by a huge boulder that bulged out on one side. "The writing says that is the last remains of old Lord Brocktree, first badger Lord of Salamandastron." Loambudd's voice echoed around the cave.

Sapwood touched the dusty mailed pawguards reverently. "Hi'll bet this old Lord knows where emllor is, but he ain't tellin' us, hare you, sir?"

Mara stood staring at the skeleton of Lord Brocktree. When the feeling of awe had passed she noticed something. Hurrying forward, she examined the wall at one side of the throne. "His paw seems to be pointing this way. Look!"

An oblong plate of copper was fixed into the rock. It was green and dulled with age. Loambudd wet it and scoured the surface with sand until it gleamed dully. Bringing her face close, she inspected it carefully. "It's just a smooth metal plate—there's nothing written on it."

They sat on the floor, facing the plate. Oxeye turned to the entrance where Urthstripe's body lay waiting.

"Poor old Lordship, looks like you'll never get to emllor."

Mara stared at the copper plate long and hard. "Pass me that lantern, please, Samkim."

The young squirrel did as he was bid. Mara placed it

on the arm of the throne next to the skeletal paw. "Who's got good eyes?"

Sapwood raised his paw. "S'pose my peepers are good as anybeast's."

"Then sit right here and tell me what you see, Sergeant."

Mara moved out and Sapwood took her place. He sat staring at the burnished metal as it shone dully in the lantern light. "Well, bob me tail! I can see words— letters, I mean—though I don't know what they says. Never learned writin'. Too busy teachin' meself other things—fighting' an'—"

"Samkim," Loambudd interrupted, "give him your sword. Sapwood, can you scrape the word on the floor here?"

"Certainly, marm."

It was badger script. Loambudd said the word triumphantly:

"Emllor!"

Loambudd placed her paw on the plate, then moved precisely in a straight line across the chamber. Her paw smacked hard upon the rock bulge to one side of the throne.

"Give me the lantern. It's right here! See this word carved on the boulder? It is directly opposite the plate so that it reflects in the metal, backwards, of course— like all mirror images it is the wrong way round. It's not emllor, it's rollme."

Urthwyte looked puzzled. He began repeating the word over and over, fast at first but then slower: "Rollme, rollme, ro . . . llm . . . e, r . . . oll . . . me . . . Roll me!" Striding heavily over to the boulder, he stretched his powerful paws to its sides, grunting as he cautioned his friends, "Stand out of the way!"

Mara knew that Urthwyte was a badger of immense strength, but she doubted that even he could shift such a formidable chunk of rock. She was about to move

361

forward and offer her help when Loambudd placed a restraining paw about her. "Watch him, Mara. He will do it."

Planting his legs square like two tree trunks, Urthwyte threw his weight against the boulder. Cords of sinew stood out from his snowy hide as the muscles of the great white badger bulged, and his teeth ground together like millstones. Growling savagely as the blood rose to his eyes, Urthwyte grabbed the boulder and gouged deep at it with both paws. His whole body shook and trembled with the staggering effort. Riveting his whole being on the boulder, Urthwyte let out a whooshing roar and heaved.

Wide-eyed with awe, Oxeye grabbed Sapwood's paw. "By the blazin' thunder! He's not rolled it . . . he's lifted the thing!"

Urthwyte stamped a full three paces before letting the huge boulder drop. The thud shook the entire cavern. The boulder had rested in a hole. Holding the lantern between them, Mara and Samkim lay flat on the floor, gazing down at the treasure of the badger Lords of Salamandastron.

Pearls from the depths of the sea; silver cups and gold plates; and weapons, fabulous arms forged by the badger Lords of old—longswords, sabers, rapiers, strange curved swords, shields, spears, pikes, daggers and lances—made from the most precious woods and metals, lay in a glittering heap, cascading over the massive sets of ancient badger armor, studded with stones that shone and twinkled, scarlet, ultramarine, turquoise, amber and obsidian jet. Their lights reflected in Mara's eyes as her mind went back to the day when Klitch tried to wheedle information out of her in the dunes.

"So there is a badger Lords' treasure after all!"

Urthstripe was lowered down in his full ceremonial

battle armor to lie there as he had wished, an eternal guardian.

41

"Ho, the good ol' Abbey. Anybeast 'ome? Redwaaaaaallll!"

Mrs. Faith Spinney jumped up and down like a fat little jack-in-the-box on the north ramparts, peering across the battlements each time a leap carried her that high.

"Stickle my ol' spikes, it's Mister Thrugg! Bless 'im, it's Mister Thrugg!"

Thrugann leaned on the parapet, shaking her head. "Oh, it's that harum-scarum brother o' mine. I could tell that if he were two country leagues away. Ahoy there, trouble. What took you so long, an' who are all those hungry-lookin' birds?"

Looking very much the returning hero, Thrugg strode jauntily up the road, wearing a cap he had taken from a fighting weasel who had picked on the wrong otter. In the cap was a splendid falcon feather. Thrugg swept it off and bowed low, grinning like a mole at a picnic.

"Good afternoon to ye, ladies. Meet me mates, Rocangus, Tammbeak, Winghye an' Rantaclaw. I trust yer all well an' shipshape."

Mrs. Spinney was overjoyed. Thrugann opened the

gates impassively. "You look like a rovin' riverdog in that hat, Thrugg Otter."

Flourishing the hat elegantly, Thrugg kissed his sister's paws affectionately, declaiming aloud, tongue in cheek, to the whole of Redwall:

"You was never out o' my thoughts, sister dear, an' all the time I was freezin' in the mountains, battlin' crows an livin' lower than a lame toad, there was one question that I made me way back here to ask yer."

Thrugann sniffed slightly, and wiping her eyes on her tunic, she asked in an apologetically tender voice, "What was that, brother o' mine?"

"What's fer tea? Me an' me mates is fair famished!"

The four falcons joined the crowd of Redwallers who had flooded out to greet them, laughing uproariously as they watched Thrugg fleeing across the Abbey grounds with Thrugann, hard on his heels, swinging a twig broom.

"You bottlenosed rogue, I'll give yer tea. You'll get a taste of this when I catch up with ye!"

Later that day Abbess Vale watched fondly as Thrugg dandled Baby Dumble on his knee while he plowed his way through a buffet teatime meal, specially set up on the gatehouse steps for him and his four falcon guests. Baby Dumble told the most atrocious lies about his epic flight in the haversack—how he had rescued the eagle from some far bigger birds and how he had pushed MacPhearsome's wings up and down to keep him flying when he was weary. Thrugg and the four falcons tried their level best to keep straight faces.

Dumble glared suspiciously about at them. "Och, yer no laughin' at the bonny Dumble, are ye?" He had begun affecting a smattering of Northland into his speech.

The Wild King MacPhearsome, perched on his favorite log in the orchard, nodding his approval as the falcons circled above, dipping their wings in tribute to him.

"Aye, they're a grand bunch o' laddies, nae doot!"

As evening drew on, Dumble was carried off snoring to his bed by Thrugann. Thrugg sat relaxing with a flagon of October ale, glad to be back safe in his beloved Abbey. A deputation of Redwallers attended as Tudd Spinney presented the otter with a specially carved bowl and spoon of applewood. The old hedgehog twirled his stick awkwardly as he made the presentation speech.

"Er, oh dearie me, I'm not much at words, but this is a liddle gift from us all to you, Thrugg. Redwall owes its life to you. It's all carved pretty, like, wi' your name an' so on, an' Friar Bellows says as he'll fill it with shrimp an' bulrush 'otroot soup any time you pleases. So er, 'ere 'tis, an' thank ye!"

Three rousing cheers went up for Thrugg. He hid his head with embarrassment, placing the bowl over his blushing face. "Thank ye, mateys. Thank ye kindly, but 't weren't nothin', you'da did the same fer me, an' I knows it!"

Late that night they all sat together in the orchard around a small fire. The summer was drawing to a close and nights were getting chilly. Brother Hollyberry held out his mug for more hot spiced cider, and Foremole filled it from a big black kettle, eyeing the laden apple trees as he did.

"Burr, 'twill soon be toim fer 'arvestin'. 'Ee arples do make a noice drop o' cider for next summertide."

Hollyberry blew on the steaming drink and sipped reflectively. "Aye, the seasons turn and the fruit ripens well, old friend. Oh dear me, I wish that young Samkim and Arula were back with us, I do miss those two scamps."

Foremole poured himself a mug of the hot spiced cider. "You'm roight thurr, zurr Berry'olly. 'Tis not fittin' furr a young moley maid t' be gone so long. Burr hurr, no taint."

Sister Nasturtium had been sitting staring long into the flames. In the silence that followed she sang:

"Bring me back a squirrel carrying my blade,
Bring me back a little mole, a pretty fair young maid,
Bring me back a speedy one with hunger and long
     ears,
And a Redwall Guardian to watch us through the
     years."

Nasturtium shook herself and sat up straight. "My goodness, there I go again, singing silly songs that I know naught of. I am sorry!"

"Nay nay, Aspershum, doant 'ee 'pologize." Foremole patted her paw. "That wurr Marthen 'ee Wurrier."

Abbess Vale stirred the fire with a twig. Sparks drifted upward to dissolve in the night. "Thank the seasons for that! Now I can stop worrying over those two young ones. If Martin says they're coming back, that's good enough for me. I'll post lookouts on the ramparts tomorrow as soon as it's light."

High above Mossflower Woods the moon shone down over Redwall, and the fire burned to embers as everybeast about it dozed in drowsy contentment.

The sun burned through to the shores of Salamandastron, dispelling the wreaths of sea mist to reveal the Guosssom shrews standing side by side with the hares of the Long Patrol. All eyes were on the front entrance, and a hubbub arose as the boulder was rolled to one side, revealing Loambudd, her head garlanded in a wreath of wildflowers. She was clothed in a magnificent robe of blue. She stepped aside and silence fell as the procession emerged from the mountain.

As honored guests from far Redwall, Samkim and Arula led the line, the young squirrel holding aloft the sword of Martin, the molemaid bearing a shrew paddle wound about with ivy. Behind them walked the shrew leaders, Log-a-log and Alfoh, green cloaks about their shoulders, paws resting on sheathed rapiers. Then came Mara and Pikkle—the badger maid in a decorated smock of rich autumn brown, carrying a large bouquet of late roses upon a lancetip. Pikkle in light sandy-yellow, bearing a hare longbow and a quiver of gray-flighted arrows. Ashnin walked behind them, wearing a splendid cloak adorned with sea shells. Urthwyte was flanked by Sapwood and Oxeye. They were the last to emerge.

Now that Urthstripe lay at rest clad in his best cere-monial armor, the great white badger was wearing his brother's old fighting armor. It had been retrieved from the shoreline where he fought his last great battle. The armor had been restored, rebeaten and burnished at Urthstripe's forge by Urthwyte himself.

He looked every inch the true warrior now, and it shone from his eyes and face, told in every movement of his giant limbs as he strode easily out in front of the assembly. The sun bounced and glimmered off snow-white fur and glittering metal as Oxeye presented him with his own huge oaken club and Sapwood knelt and placed his head beneath Urthwyte's free paw.

"This is my grandson," Loambudd's voice rang out majestically. "His grandsire was Urthclaw, his father Urthound and his brother Urthstripe the Strong. He stands before you this day and for all the time until his seasons have run, Ruler of the mountain! Commander of the Long Patrols! Warrior Lord of Salamandastron! Salute Urthwyte the Mighty!"

Lances, bows, rapiers and paddles went up like a sea of weaponry.

"Eulaliaaaaaaaaaa!"

All creatures alike yelled the mountain war cry until the very rocks rang and the clear morning air was filled with the swelling sound. Salamandastron had a new badger Lord.

After the ceremony there was a meal spread out upon the shore. It was good solid food, but quite plain. Salamandastron being a warriors' place, even the best of cooks there could never match the skills of Redwall creatures at preparing a festive board.

They sat among the rocks and sprawled on the sand, happily sharing the homely fare. Arula, Pikkle and Nordo were building a likeness of Salamandastron from the sea-damped sand. Alfoh and Ashnin perched on a low rock watching them.

The wise old shrew smiled wistfully. "Look at them playing at sandcastles like a proper bunch of young uns. Arula, what about a tunnel entrance?"

The young molemaid touched a heavy digging claw to her nose. "Thankee, zurr Alfoh. Oi'll do that straightways, hurr hurr."

Arula vanished in a spray of flying sand as Ashnin shook her head in wonderment. "They bounce right back like springy little branches. That's a good thing, Alfoh. It helps them to forget all the hardships, warfare and slaying they've been through. Look at young Samkim sitting alone down there by the sea. I wonder what he's thinking of. He's been very quiet all morning."

Samkim was staring at the logboats moored above the tideline. The sword of Martin lay beside him. He made no move to join the others, staying alone and apart from everybeast.

369

Still clad in her new smock, Mara approached the solitary young squirrel. She sat beside him, gazing out at the sea pensively. Without looking at her, Samkim began to voice his thoughts. It soon developed into a conversation, though they both avoided each other's eyes.

"The season is dying, Mara. I feel that summer is gone and the autumn is upon us. The leaves will turn gold and brown."

"So they will, Samkim. Nobeast can stop the turn of the seasons. I think you are lonely and far from home. What is Redwall like in the autumn?"

"Oh, it's a happy place to be at anytime. Autumn is harvest time: the fruits and crops are gathered in, October ale is made, chestnuts are candied in honey. We sit up late in Cavern Hole around a great fire, enjoying supper and listening to the stories and songs of bygone days. The mornings are quiet and misty. Leaves rustle in Mossflower Woods, and you can feel the dew on the grass between your paws, smell the bread and cakes being baked in the kitchens, lie in the orchard on a sunny afternoon and eat a russet apple or a ripe purple plum. Oh yes, Redwall is like no other place."

"You must love your home very much, Samkim."

"Aye, the Abbey is everything to me. What about you, Mara? Salamandastron is a fine place—don't you like being here?"

The badger maid ran dry sand from the rocks through her paws. "It is all I can remember—I grew up with the mountain. This morning I feel that I have a certain fondness for it, but I can never make it my home again. There are too many unhappy memories hovering around it. Lord Urthstripe put his mark upon that mountain. The graves of creatures we knew look lonely here by the great sea, and it will take a lot of healing. Time alone can do it, though I would not be happy staying here to grow old. Even today I noticed the change in Urthwyte—he is becoming a badger Lord. The life here is not for me."

"Then what will you do, Mara? Where will you go?"

"I will follow my dream."

"Ah! The dream you dreamed last night of Martin the Warrior?"

"Samkim, how did you know . . . ?"

"Because I, too, had a dream. Martin came to me also. He told me to stay apart from the others today and I would see the Guardian of Redwall Abbey come to me. Is it you, Mara?"

The badger maid turned and looked at him. "Martin said in my dream that this was my destiny. He told me that I will be happy at Redwall, happier than ever before."

Samkim took hold of her paw. "So you will be. Come on, let us go home, Mara of Redwall!"

42

Though the season was well advanced, Abbess Vale stoically refused to hold any Nameday feast. Each day she had posted lookouts on the ramparts, and they watched until torches were lit and lanterns shone with the onset of night. Through sunny days, cloudy days, and days when soft drizzle and mist hung low over woodlands, the vigil continued, still with no sign of Samkim or Arula returning.

Sitting in the gatehouse one windy morning, Abbess Vale and Faith Spinney took hot mint tea and nutscones with cream as they embroidered a bedquilt together.

Faith took the spectacles from the end of her nose and massaged her eye corners gently. "My ol' eyes get tired pretty quick these days, Vale. 'Spect it'll be with standin' out on yon wall all yesternoon."

The Abbess looked rather severely over the top of her glasses. "Faith, what have I told you? There are lots of younger ones happy to do lookout duty—you have no need to be up on the ramparts in all weathers."

The hedgehog lady poured more tea for Vale. "But I wants to be first to see 'em. 'Sides, it keeps me out of

Dumble's way. That infant's become a reg'lar liddle terror."

"Indeed he has." The Abbess nodded in agreement as she picked up a stitch. "Everywhere I turn he's following me, bullying away in his north country speech for a Nameday feast."

"The Hautumn of the Heagle, you mean." Faith chuckled.

Vale threw her paws up to her ears. "Honestly, if I hear that name once more I'll tan the little villain's tail!"

The little villain in question was hatching a conspiracy, together with Thrugg, MacPhearsome, Friar Bellows and several others. It had been brewing for three days. Secret meetings in the cellars with Foremole and Tudd Spinney standing guard, clandestine gatherings in the dormitory with Brother Hollyberry watching the door, and whispered conferences in the orchard were becoming the order of the day at Redwall. Dumble made the participants swear deathly oaths that Abbess Vale and Mrs. Faith Spinney should not know a thing until the time was ripe.

The kitchen fires burned late, heating the ovens as extra cakes, pies, flans and pasties were baked to a golden turn. Bands of moles plundered the orchard regularly, and young ones were seen coming and going, muttering furtively to each other as they covered for others who wheeled great cheeses from the storerooms, lugged forward big barrels of October ale and strawberry cordial from the cellars and grunted beneath mysterious bulky sacks as they strove to move them in secret.

Around lunchtime the wind dropped, and so did Abbess Vale's head. She fell asleep in the armchair by the fire. Faith Spinney covered her with the quilt they had been working on and stole quietly out of the gate-house.

The sun was breaking through scudding cloud masses as the Wild King MacPhearsome flapped his wings and did a short run. The golden eagle nearly collided with Faith as she came out of the gatehouse. He pulled up short and stalked off huffily to the start of his intended launch. Faith followed him.

"Sorry, Your Majesty. Did I disturb your exercises?"

MacPhearsome sniffed the air, hopping from one foot to the other. "Och no, wee lady, Ah'm just off for a stretch o' the wings, ye ken. Mah fithers need a guid wind rufflin' 'em."

Swaying from side to side, he dashed forward and launched himself into the air. Faith shook her head in bewilderment as she watched the huge bird soar gracefully.

"Whatever you say, I'm sure! Dearie me, I wish I could understand one single word from that bird's beak."

Hollyberry watched from the sickbay window, explaining the scene to Foremole, who was sitting on a bed tucking into a huge wedge of yellow celery-studded cheese.

"He's about to start his second run now—hold on, he's talking to Faith Spinney. I can't hear what he's saying. There he goes, up into the air! Faith's looking up and saying something. Let's hope MacPhearsome hasn't given the game away to her."

Foremole wrinkled his nose. "Missus Spinney doant unnerstand heagly burds. They'm can't talken propply. Doant 'ee wurry, zurr Berry'olly."

The five shrew logboats were on a broad open expanse of the Great South Stream. Mara sat side by side with Samkim, paddling steadily, as well as any two shrews.

The badger maid could hear Arula telling Pikkle of Redwall feasts as they sat paddling in the prow of the boat opposite.

Pikkle kept interrupting with what could only be described as groans of delight at the mention of each fresh dish.

"Yurr, an' then they takes the meddyo cream an'—"

"Whoo, my growlin' tummy! Don't tell me, let me guess, they take the jolly old meadowcream an' spread it thick over the damson pudden an' chuck lots of those candied chestnuts on top, wot?"

Arula blinked earnestly, shaking her head in amazement. "Bohurr aye. But 'ow did 'ee knoaw, zurr Ffloger?"

Pikkle rubbed his stomach. "The name's Ffolger, ol' thing, not Ffloger—an' if it's absoballylutely anythin' to do with tucker, you can bet an acorn to a boulder that a Ffolger'll know about it. We're professional gluttons, y' see."

Mara splashed him with her paddle. "I can vouch for that, Arula!"

"Back water, ship paddles! Bows 'n' slings at the ready, Guosssom!"

Mara looked up to see a massive bird of prey beating its wide wings close to the water as it sped towards the logboats. Swiftly she brandished her paddle in the air as Samkim drew his sword and stood by her.

Log-a-log roared out further orders: "Don't fire until it tries to attack—it may not be hunting!"

The great bird soared over them, brushing Mara and Samkim with a wingtip as it mounted into the air and wheeled in a circle. "Ach, yer braw beasties the noo, but if ye fire one arra' Ah'm a-coming doon tae mak' ye regret it!"

Pikkle put down his paddle and scratched his ears. "What in the name of the crazy cuckoo is the chap burbling on about? Can anybeast tell me?"

Alfoh placed a paw across Pikkle's mouth. "Wait, I think he's trying to tell us something. The bird certainly doesn't mean us any harm or he'd have attacked by now. Hi! You up there! We're the Guosssom shrews. Who are you and where are you from?"

The golden eagle dived, screeching like a siren.

"Redwaaaaaaaallllll!"

Samkim leapt up, waving his sword as he yelled out the reply:

"Redwaaaaalllllll!"

The eagle wheeled slowly then flapped off at a leisurely clip, turning off north to follow the course of another channel.

Samkim quivered with excitement as he picked up his paddle. "Did you hear that, Mara? Come on, Guardian, paddle! I'm sure he wants us to follow him. What do you say, Log-a-log?"

The shrew leader took up his paddle. "I think you're right. He's certainly traveling in the right direction—that branch stream will make a good shortcut, now I come to think about it. Right, let's follow the bird. Up paddles, Guosssom. Take the watercourse on the portside. We've got a new navigator to take us to Samkim's home!"

"Beating up the river, paddling down the stream,
Find me a berth, lads, somewhere I can dream,
Still quiet waters there, where the lilies float,
Cool and green, dark and clean, there I'll moor this
     boat.
Oho, you old paddle, you have made me sore,
Bent all my back and wearied all my paw.
Pull me into harbor, there I'll make my thanks,
Lie by the river, slumber on the banks.
Where the willow's leaning o'er
And the waters kiss the shore,
That's the place that I will rest, linger evermore."

376

"Abbess, marm, Missus Spinney, would you please get in the cart!" Thrugg stood with the harness about his shoulders, and the little green Abbey cart stood waiting on its four small wheels. Abbess Vale and Faith Spinney had been roused when it was barely dawn and hustled out of gatehouse and Abbey dormitory by Tudd and Sister Nasturtium. They stood hastily dressed on the lawn.

Thrugg looked over his shoulder at them. "Come on, ladies. Stir yore paws. Hop in the cart an' we'll go a nice ride down the path, eh?"

Faith Spinney fussed with her cloak fastener. "Mercy me, Mr. Thrugg, whatever for?"

The otter snorted impatiently. "For some o' those violets an' saxifrage wot grows in the churchyard of old Saint Ninian's, of course! I've told ye, Brother' Olly-berry needs 'em fer a new batch o' physick. Now come on, Marms. We can't be lettin' 'im down, can we?"

Reluctantly the two friends climbed into the cart, plumping themselves on the cushions that had been placed on the seats specially for them.

"But why must we go now—it's barely dawn?" Abbess Vale shook her head.

Tudd Spinney opened the main gate and waved the cart out onto the path. "That's the best time for violets 'n' saxifrage, so I'm told. Off you goes now, gels. 'Ave a nice time!"

Faith wagged a severe paw at her husband. "Tudd Spinney, you ol' fibber. What's got into you, sendin' us off like this? I'm sure there's lots of spry young uns who could pick plants better'n us two old creatures."

Thrugg jogged off south down the path through the mists of the rising dawn. "Aha, that's where yore wrong, marm. 'Ollyberry says them young uns don't know lupins from lilacs. He says that you an' the Abbess 'ave the beauty of experience."

Mightily flattered, Abbess Vale arched her neck and

fluttered her eyelids. "Hollyberry isn't given to untruths, Faith. He could be right!"

Behind them, Tudd Spinney slammed the door and hobbled across the lawn, waving his stick. "Stir yore stumps now, good Redwallers. They've gone. Let's get busy!"

The sun heralded the day, palely at first but gradually bursting through into a heavy golden autumn radiance. Faith Spinney looked up at the dark evergreens and golden brown leaves turning crisp on the boughs, the dappling patterns of light and shade through the foliage making her blink as they trundled along.

"Oh well, we've got a fair 'n' pretty day for whatever it is we're supposed to be a-doin' of, Vale."

The Abbess folded her paws into the wide habit sleeves. "Violets and saxifrage, my paw! There's something going on back at Redwall, or I'm a frog. Isn't that right, Thrugg?"

"Don't croak too loud, marm. Saint Ninian's is a fair ol' way yet. Why don't you two ladies 'ave a nap and catch up on yore sleep. I'll tip ye the word when we gets there."

The logboats had been pulled ashore at the nearest point MacPhearsome could manage; now the rest of the journey was mainly a good stout march through woodland. They ate supper and slept through the early evening on the banks of the stream.

Two hours after midnight, Log-a-log had disguised the five boats with branches and fern for safekeeping. He roused them and they broke camp. Lighting lanterns, they struck off into the depths of Mossflower. Samkim and Arula led, watching the dark shape of MacPhearsome whenever it could be seen above the treetops.

Arula drew in a deep breath. "Booharr, smell 'at, Sanken. 'Tis loiken the smell of 'ome!"

Samkim sniffed gratefully. "I know what you mean, Arula."

Mara plucked a sycamore leaf, peering hard into the woodland. "Trees, Pikkle—I've never seen so many trees. It's so silent and peaceful, too, not hot and bare and sandy like the shore by Salamandastron. I could grow to like these woods."

"I could grow t' like any place where there's a scrap of tucker about, old gel. It's bally ages since we had supper, I'm starvin'."

In the same hour of dawn that the cart left Redwall, the travelers emerged from the woods onto the path. Though the going was easier, there were many who were weary from marching all night. The irrepressible Pikkle kept everybeast going by improvising a silly ditty.

"I'd give my left ear an' raise a cheer
For a plate of woodland pie,
And as for a pudden, if it was a good un,
I'd give my best right eye.
I'd give a paw to get my jaw
Around a fat fruitcake.
For a dumplin' stew, my tail could go too.
I mean, for goodness sake,
If I saw a pastie, I wouldn't get nasty
I'd trade it for my nose.
And if I couldn't smell, I'd just say 'Well,
I'd rather have one of those.'
So take my heart and leave me that tart,
But my mouth I won't take off,
Because, I plead, it's a mouth I'll need
To eat all that bally scoff!"

The burgeoning sunlight lifting flagging spirits, they

stepped out with a will, the golden eagle flying low in front of them as they chanted aloud.

"Redwall! Log-a-log! Redwall! Guosssom! Redwall! Log-a-log! Redwall! Guosssom!"

Abbess Vale rubbed her eyes and looked about suspiciously. It was midmorning and they were still bumping along the dusty brown path in the cart. She rapped on the side sharply.

"Thrugg, where are you taking us? I haven't been this far for seasons, but I recognize the country. We're well past Saint Ninian's!"

Thrugg muttered something unintelligible under his breath and quickened his pace. Faith Spinney awakened suddenly.

"Eh, what's that, m'dear? What's a Log-a-log?"

The jolting of the cart was not doing much for Vale's mood. "Log-a-log? I never said anything about a Log-a-log. What are you chunnering on about, Faith Spinney?"

Faith held up a paw. "Stop, please, Mr. Thrugg. Sssshh, listen!"

Thrugg halted the cart. All three creatures listened carefully. On the still morning air the sound drifted up to them from farther down beyond a bend in the path.

"Redwall! Log-a-log! Redwall! Guosssom!"

Slow to catch on, Faith Spinney shook her head. "What sort of beast d'you reckon a Gossen is, Vale? Who's making all that noise, anyway?"

A large smile was spreading across the Abbess's face. She leaned over and patted Thrugg on the back. "It's Arula and Samkim, I know it is. Forward with all speed, Thrugg. Charge!"

As they rounded the bend, Samkim saw the cloud of dust approaching and heard the rattle of the cart.

Ever vigilant, Log-a-log yelled out to his shrews, "Bows and slings ready, somebeast is coming this way fast!"

380

But Samkim and Arula had recognized Thrugg and the occupants of the cart, who were standing up, cloaks flying in the breeze. "It's the Abbess and Mrs. Spinney and Thrugg! Good old Thrugg! Come on Arula!"

They dashed off toward the oncoming cart, Faith Spinney could be heard crying shrilly, "Oh, my dears, it's Samkim an' Arula! Oh, my spikes! Oh, those young rascals! Oh, see them, Vale, see them. An' young Master Samkim a-wavin' that great sword aloft! My life an' great acorns! 'Tis the sword of Martin! Look, he's brought it back to us!"

Everybeast cheered wildly and tears sprang unbidden to the eyes of Abbess Vale at the sight of the young squirrel, now a fully fledged warrior wielding the great blade in the sunlight.

Thrugg made the little cart bounce and leap from the path as he dashed at top speed, laughing wildly. "Haharr haharr, I knew it were you two young villains. Samkim! Arula! It's me yer old matey Thruggo!"

Arula made the dust fairly fly as she pounded along the path. "Habbess, marm! Missus Spinnsey! 'Tis oi, 'Rula the moleymaid!"

Laughing, weeping, gasping for breath, they met in a rush.

For one so old and frail, the Abbess turned out to be a mighty hugger. She clutched Samkim, completely winding him as she yelled down his ear, "Samkim, Samkim. I knew you'd come back someday!"

Faith Spinney was kissing Arula and boxing her ears at the same time. "Oh, you liddle rip. Welcome back, m'dear! Now don't you ever stray from that Abbey again, d'you 'ear me!"

Thrugg wiped the dust from his face and patted their backs heftily. "Yore a sight fer otter's eyes, young uns! I'll wager you've some good ol' tales an' yarns to spin about adventures an' travels!"

The Abbess had managed to compose herself. She

placed her paws around Samkim and Arula, protecting them from the curious Redwallers. "There will be ample time for the telling of tales later. Perhaps we'd better greet all these new guests they've brought to our Abbey."

Mara had purposefully fallen to the back of the crowd. Slightly embarrassed and unsure of herself, she listened to the Abbey ladies as they met the others.

"So good to meet you, Mr. Log-a-log, and you, Mr. Alfoh. Thank you for bringing our young ones safely back to us. Oh dear, there are such a lot of you and we haven't prepared anything, but you are welcome to come back to Redwall Abbey with us, all of you. Samkim, Arula, will you lead these good creatures to Redwall, please. I'm sure you'll excuse us, Mrs. Spinney and I have to get back before you and see what we can arrange in the way of lunch. Thrugg, turn this cart round and get us back to the Abbey with all speed! Faith, don't stand there fussing, get in the cart—quickly!"

The shrews set up a mighty cheer as Thrugg galloped off up the path, towing the cart behind him.

Early noon saw the Guosssom outside the Abbey gate. They met with a very embarrassed Abbess and Faith, who were sitting resignedly in the cart. Abbess Vale threw up her paws in despair.

"We're locked out, Samkim. We've banged, yelled and shouted but nobeast answers. Thrugg has gone round to the back wall to see if he can climb over somehow."

Faith Spinney threw her apron over her face. "Oh, the shame of it, m'dears. Locked out of our own Abbey, and here you all are without a welcome, dusty an' hungered!"

"Excuse me, but may I be of help?"

Abbess Vale looked up into the deep brown eyes of a

beautiful young badger maid. She was completely taken aback. "Oh, Samkim! Oh, why didn't you tell me?"

The badger maid patted the Abbess's paw lightly. "My name is Mara."

"Mara—a good name for such a lovely creature." Vale clasped the badger maid's paw tightly. "Yes, I am sure you could be of help, Mara."

Striding slowly over to the gateway door, Mara raised her paw and dealt it a flat blow. The sound boomed out as she called, "Open these gates in the name of your Abbess!"

Immediately the hinges creaked as the gateway door swung open.

It was a joyous shock. Every creature in the Abbey crowded on to the lawn in front of the main entrance, cheering them to the echo. Faith and Abbess Vale were bewildered until Thrugg stepped forward and bowed.

"Forgive our liddle surprise, ladies. They let me in by the north wallgate. King MacPhearsome has been watchin' Samkim's approach for the past three days. No need t' worry yore 'eads, just step this way, if y' please!"

Samkim and Arula were borne shoulder-high, and the young squirrel waving Martin's sword cheered as loudly as anybeast. Paw in paw, Mara and the Abbess headed the procession.

In the center of the orchard a feast had been laid out.

Pikkle gazed at it in openmouthed delight. "Well, flop my ears! I've heard of tucker, but I never thought I'd live to see such a bally spread as this!"

Dumble appeared from beneath a table, his high northland accent forgotten as he clung to the Abbess's robe, staring around at the army of strange shrews.

"It's a Nameday, Muvva. Wot we gunna call it?"

The Abbess looked fondly at Mara and Pikkle standing next to Arula and Samkim.

"The Autumn of the Homecomers. What else could we call it?"

43

The Feast of the Autumn of the Homecomers was an event long to be remembered in the annals of Redwall Abbey. For the first time in many long seasons the big badger's chair that had remained empty for so long had a badger sitting in it: Mara, Guardian of Redwall.

Friar Bellows, clad in a smart new white apron and cook's hat, stood ladle in paw on top of a barrel of cowslip cordial where all present could see him. The fat mouse coughed importantly.

"Er, ahem, ahem! Your attention please, friends. Very good, very good! Now, er, as most of you are new guests to our Nameday table, the Abbess has asked me to say a word or two."

Vale chuckled quietly as she whispered to Alfoh, "I never asked Bellows to say anything, but he will!"

The Redwall Friar continued his speech, warming to the subject. "It is indeed unusual to see such visitors joining us. I've never catered for a royal golden eagle, four falcons, a badger and a veritable army of shrews, to say nothing of a hare—"

"I never told you to say nothing of me, old chap," Pikkle chipped in.

Bellows shot him a glare. "Er, quite, very good.

Where was I? Ah yes. Welcome to Redwall—our Abbey is yours. Join us in good cheer upon this happy day. Eat, be merry and enjoy the bounty of the season, though I don't know whether our food will suit you all as my helpers and I have never had to feed such a strange assembly. Yes, very good!"

Droony ducked his head beneath the tablecloth and called out, "Hurr, then give you'm jaw a rest an' let 'em try 'ee vittles!"

There was a general roar of laughter. Amid the jollity, Mara stood up and rescued the red-faced Friar.

"I am sure the food will suit us all, Friar Bellows. It looks too good for words. The fame of you and your kitchen staff is a legend throughout Mossflower. We intend to do this feast full justice. Abbess, I believe it is customary for you to say grace at these occasions. Would you be so kind?"

Abbess Vale recited the Abbey grace as they all bowed their heads.

"Squirrels, otters, hedgehogs, mice,
Moles with fur like sable,
Gathered in good spirits all,
Round the festive table.
Sit we down to eat and drink.
Friends, before we do, let's think,
Fruit of forest, field and banks,
To the seasons we give thanks."

Amid a clatter of bowls and spoons, the feast began. Tables had been joined together to form a large cross shape, and there were five centerpieces. A Redwall jubilee trifle of pears, damsons, greensap cream and hazelnut truffle was on the north end. Opposite at the south trestle stood a magnificent blackcurrant pudding, swimming in a peach-covered cream of whisked beech-nut and strawberry topped off with a sugar-preserved sprig of maple. The east side was graced by a high wobbling redcurrant jelly with flaked almond and chestnut suspended inside like a sunset snowstorm, and it was wreathed in yellow-piped meadowcream. At the west board was a golden honey-crusted confection of latticed pastry with mintcream and candied chestnuts oozing from it onto a bed of purple plums. In the center stood a wide diamond of sweet arrowroot shortcake with all the fruits of the summer piled on it, fixed there by stiff comb honey blended with a purée of apple and raspberry. Salads of ten different kinds ranged amid the wedges of white, yellow and beige cheeses, studded with nuts, herbs and celery. Oatfarls, cottage loaves and batons of ryebread, all hot from the ovens with their crusts gleaming brown, lay scattered between vegetable flans, shrimp and hotroot soup and massive deeper 'n' ever turnip 'n' tater 'n' beetroot pies beloved by moles. Redcurrant tarts, bilberry scones, plumcakes, latticed apple pies, strawberry flans and damson puddings radiated out into patterns, dotted by bowls of nutcream, meadowcream, Abbeycream, rosecream and buttercup fondant. Pitchers, flagons and jugs overflowing with October ale, strawberry cordial, dandelion and burdock, berry wine and cowslip cordial jostled for position amidst bowls of warm scented rosewater and embroidered napkins standing by for sticky paws.

"Hey, Nordo, what do you think of our shrimp an' hotroot soup, matey?

"Whooh! It's hot! Pass the October ale, please."

"Yurr, you'm sample some o' 'ee deeper 'n' ever pie, zurr heagle."

"Och, as soon as Ah get mah beak free o' this trifle, laddie."

"Righto, Dumble me old scout, load in the cheese an' salad. Now you start at this side of the loaf and I'll start at the other side. That's the ticket—meet you in the middle, wot?"

"D'you likes ches'nut an' celery cheese, Mr. Log-a-log? Just try a piece atop of yore vegetable flan."

"Mmm! It was worth paddling all that way for, Mr. Spinney—and I think I'll dream of your October ale for the rest of my life. Alfoh, what's that you're eating?"

"Bilberry scone with meadowcream. The Friar's going to give me the recipe—very civilized indeed. Now then, young mole, don't fall into that deeper pie thing."

"Hurr hurr, zurr. That be the bestest part, fallen in 'ee pie, then oi c'n eat moi ways out o' et!"

"Oh, look out, Thrugann and Brother Hollyberry have started a shrimp-and-hotroot-soup-eating competition. Just look at that pepper they're putting into it!"

"I say, chaps, any room for another jolly old contestant?"

"Steady on, Pikkle Ffolger. You're in the middle of a pie-eatin' contest with me."

"Haha, so I am, Tubbyguts old lad. Hold the soup—I'll be with you as soon as I've dealt with this Guosssom glutton."

"Ach, yon skinny lang-legged laddie is a braw scoffer. Ah'd hate him tae visit mah nest for a season. Pass some o' those candied chestnuts, will ye, Tammbeak."

"Awa', yer no doin' sae bad yersel' for an injured falcon, if ye'd tak' yer beak out o' yon trifle an' look at yersel', Rocangus!"

The son of Laird Mactalon did take his beak out of the trifle long enough to rip away the dressing from his wing. He flexed it and gave a wild whoop. "Kaaney! Mah wing's workin' again. Thrugg, yer a bonny riverdog!"

Immediately he was in the air, circling and soaring around the high spire and redstone turret of the Abbey. Wheeling out, he swooped down and glided majestically over the heads of the revellers in the orchard as they cheered and hurrahed.

Abbess Vale smiled contentedly at her old friend. "My my, Faith, they are enjoying themselves. I do hope we don't run short of anything."

"Humph!" Friar Bellows leaned over between them. "Short, did you say? You should see the supper spread I've laid out in Great Hall—it would feed an army through a hard winter."

Mara shook the fat mouse solemnly by the paw. "Thank you, Friar Bellows, you have done our Abbey proud."

Abbess Vale smiled as she grasped the badger maid's paw.

"Did you hear that, Samkim? She said 'Our Abbey.' Do you think she will stay here as Guardian?"

"I'm certain, Abbess. Martin the Warrior said it should be so."

Vale sat back in her chair, folding her paws into the habit sleeves as her eyelids began to droop. "You must forgive me, it has been a long day and I need to take a little nap. Samkim, I always knew you would come back. You have returned Martin's sword, and tomorrow the Wild King MacPhearsome will restore it to its place on the weathervane. There it will stay to watch over our Abbey. My heart is glad, because not only did you bring the sword, you brought us our beautiful badger, Mara. Heroes Samkim—we were never short of them: Thrugg, little Dumble, Arula and yourself, brave creatures all! What more could an old one like me desire than to rest here with Redwallers enjoying themselves in good health, peace and happiness . . ."

The young squirrel and the badger maid sat watching the Abbess of Redwall as she slept quietly, surrounded by her friends in the orchard on a high sunny afternoon in the Autumn of the Homecomers.

44

The great Joseph Bell pealed out mellowly over the warm spring evening as an old mole grandmother made her way slowly over to the small cheery fire that glowed by the beechlog in the orchard. The infant mole was toasting a chestnut on a stick at the fire, and his friend the dormouse elder was dozing.

Taking the little mole by his paw, the grandmother whispered, "Come on, Burrem, et be yurr bedtoime long since, bring thoi chesknutter with 'ee."

Paw in paw they strolled back toward the Abbey dormitories, the old one questioning her grandson.

"Wurr et a gudd story, Burrem?"

The infant trundled along, nodding. "Hoo urr, it serpintly wurr, tho' oi thinks that ol' dormouser be a gurt fibber, Granmurr."

She stopped and wagged a heavy digging claw at him. "Gurr, maister Dumble b'aint no fibber, you 'pologize roight naow, young un!"

The infant mole smiled winningly at her. "Oi 'pologizes, Granmurr 'rula. You wurr in 'ee story so it must be 'onest true, burr aye!"

Old Arula patted his velvety head. "You'm forgived, young ripscullywag."

They continued walking to the Abbey.

"Whoi does Maister Dumble allus sleep outside in 'ee orchard, Granmurr? Him'n doant go t' bed in 'ee durmitory."

"Oh he'm a-stayen out thurr every noight fer long seasons naow, Burrem, waitin' on heaglyburds an' falkies t' come back. S'pose someday they will, hurr."

Together they entered the Abbey, leaving the door open, as it always is to welcome any traveler to Redwall.